Per

vigilium

Pervigilium

(Sovereign Citizen Part 2)

A Novel by

B.F. Galligan

Paperback Edition ISBN: 979-8-9889517-2-8
Hardback Edition ISBN: 979-8-9889517-3-5

Comments, criticisms, and accolades welcome:
bfgalligan@protonmail.com
@bfgalligan (on most platforms)

Redundant

I
Cliff

Ashes were once powerful embers now flaked with white paper, cooled to rest with fuel finally spent. They passed through their time of power. It was an era of red and orange. Violent winds inside caverns blow paper that might occasionally break free to float up to the sky on a column of heated air. There was an era when fuel was alive, when it would have been impossible to imagine the heat and destructive force of the ash was not far away. But it came. And in that force, columns of heat touched huge walls of stone to move inside them, to pass between ancient spaces and be trapped for a time. They stayed and took up residence inside the stone, and when the water touched it, there was no place to enter. It met heat and was pushed away on columns of air that filled a sweathouse with steam that then moved into skin and ripped open tiny doorways it found there. This was the point. The era of red and orange fed the machinery of the sweathouse that would last as long as the fuel held out and lingered in the era of ash.

Outside, a mother slept as her two puppies sniffed around looking for another game to play while he moved from the icy cold of the creek back over to the columns of heat of the sweathouse. Again. For hours the era of red and orange fed machines that let him alternate between extremes and pass the afternoon until ash took control, and it was time to invite the mother for a walk in the valley. She was accustomed to patience, but her puppies were ready before it was time. Each time. Every day was the same, and they were ever ready to move on to the next thing. They had forgotten the long wait without food that was too much for their twins. They forgot their smell and their weak sounds when their mother left with empty sacks of milk to search for something to refill them but came back with empty sacks of milk. Daily. They forgot the smells when they were pushed to the edge of the nest to be forgotten. Their mother forgot them too when she changed them into milk for a brief time before he found them; he never knew. It was the family's secret survival. She knew he saved them. Already at that time, the puppies were making new noises of weakness since the new milk only lasted a few days. Already she'd begun to select from among the sounds. Then he brought her rich fuel and caused the milk to explode inside her body that cut the weakness they'd felt for weeks. She knew so keenly that it was never a question that he might threaten her nest as he sat down next to them, nor when he showed uncomfortable interest again the next day. Fuel meant trust was a given. They never forgot the smell of trust, even in their impatient games outside the sweathouse.

Eventually the era of ash arrived and the last of the heat was already leaving the stone, signaled when the water would no longer tolerate rejection, when it coated the surface and found its way into the now empty spaces inside. He watched the last of it boil, more slowly than before. This was the signal. No more trips to cold water. His hazy body felt fresh, and this last time was only enough to warm him back up from the shock of ice he poured to take away the heat his skin locked away.

He emerged from the space to the high desert canyon, which was her signal to sit up and shake off the dust soaked in her fur to keep the sun away. It was time to yawn, perhaps time to drink some icy water already disappearing from the desert. It was the time to follow because it was the time to walk. Every day, after he oscillated between extremes at the sweathouse he built and the creek full of snow melt, it was time to explore the canyon before the return to their palace up the walls. Trust was reinforced by a hand on ears as she joined him calmly surrounded by puppies at play. It was another long walk back into the canyon along well-cut rocky trails baked in the sun. Walking was his only constant. The entirety of his life was marked by long walks occasioned by events, everything could be reduced to a stop for rest along the way. His legs brought him across continents before he forgot the smells of his family, and they brought him to his palace, from the length of New Mexico to the bottom of Colorado. It began in El Paso, but it actually began when he climbed through the concrete wreckage of the dam he collapsed to save his valley from the dead hand of civilization. The walk before then was just a pass through his own neighborhood, beyond was entry to a sunbaked wasteland of caked clay and sunken houseboats that only weeks before had been the bottom of a dying lake in the middle of the desert. Once inside, his mind switched over to the traditional post-apocalypse of dehydrated wasteland where everything is the competition of survival. He drifted from houseboat to houseboat to live off whatever was still inside the kitchens. When there was nothing, he walked empty towns.

Unlike his time in Washington, where the Virginia farms still managed to keep some sheep and livestock alive for the long months following the evaporation, nothing seemed to last in the desert; only rotten carcasses in stalls and paddocks were preserved. No dogs found food to roam streets. He did find many cats that lived off lizards and other small prey, but these served no use to him without the threat of rodents to eat his food. But as the wasteland of the butte was gone and the high desert began, he could see changes that aided survival where none was possible further below. Immediately to the North of the butte, the river had never died. It sustained the same lushness he remembered in El Paso before the interstate water wars and the green of the valley protected its horses. But not all. Most were carcasses just as elsewhere. Some survived and could be seen grazing in small herds not far from other small herds of cows. These were not large; they were the start, and he didn't really see them until he neared Albuquerque. Still, they were all fairly thin until he passed through to the North side of the city.

It was a walk that kept to the river as much as possible, so he would never be far from water. It was a walk grown from the need to wander but conditioned by a phasal dislike of gasoline and machines. This was inconvenient in the hugeness of the southwest, but he was committed to the idea even as it wore on him over the weeks of marching. There was neither any point to speed up to save time nor slow down to waste it. Time had evaporated long ago. While not the straight shot he imagined he'd take, he eventually did manage to reach Santa Fe well ahead of winter as planned. By the time snow began to fall, he was inside his new winter cave that was unlike the one where he spent the prior winter. There was no manic rush to assemble all the resources he thought he might need ahead of then, nor was there to be another hibernation in darkness where he'd lose himself in a black chamber. It was a much older winter. One that involved fires in heated adobe and treks through the cold to find food; all the things he hoped to avoid the year before were now commonplace.

Then these all eventually melted away to leave behind the same desert as before. While it stayed, winter was as harsh as expected. Snow dropped early but accumulated late. Then there were the weeks inside with hardly any time out to explore so, when the first openings came, he was keen to resume his roam. But winter is more than snowdrifts. It creates a prison for the body with what it takes, not what it gives. His resolve to explore the areas outside town pushed him outdoors; he had no choice except to chase convenience. It made him return to the smell of diesel and eventually to the high desert of the four corners too eager to reach deeper into the mountains that were indeed still snowdrifts.

When the roads were shut, he decided he wanted to peel back the layers of civilization and test himself against the thousand-year-old comforts of pueblos were too inviting for too much imagination to pass up. What he wanted was to learn how others made their fortresses and to see how much of his own in Washing-

ton was similar. He constructed neither. It was a
fruitless thought every time he imagined himself
building his own because he was as incapable an engineer as he was in so many of the technical arts. He
survived this far only through the legacy others left
and was in no position to make improvements. It was
still a thought which recurred from time to time and
passed him through the hours of frustrated insomnia.

It was a drive. He'd been to Mesa Verde in the past,
but then only saw it from a child's eyes, impatient to
go home after weeks hiking through the wilderness. A
capstone of tourism was the least interesting thing to
build strong memories, so when he arrived as an adult
it was as if he'd never seen the city at all. He arrived at an empty park not, a city. There were adobe
homes along avenues adjacent to adobe storehouses, but
nothing livable. No matter how much projection and
desire he carried with him in the truck, he arrived to
meet the bareness of the city ruins cut into the mountain. To survive, he would need to bridge the divide
between the frailty of humans and the harshness of the
landscape.

Least of all was the cold rock that stole his heat
when he tried to sleep. It was too odd that his main
survival need in the fortress was a proper bed to keep
his heat away from the vast spaces inside the mountain. In the day, the sun worked its charms for him
to make up what was lost in the night, but this was no
solution. He even brought a hammock on the first
visit and hesitated to disturb the bricks in order to
anchor the ends, but he did. The cold air below also
stole his heat to be sent out to the spaces of the
canyon.

After two nights he accepted his plan was untimely and
drove back to Santa Fe where he could cook himself on
his fireplace and rethink how to make a living in the
mountains. It was still early. March is not June.
It was colder in the mountains than in Santa Fe, even
if it otherwise looked like hot desert. When he got
back to his adobe home, he had time to waste before he

would feel the unrelenting need to return to the cliff palace again. There was time to build a strategy. For another month he relapsed to shopping and collected all the supplies he thought he would need, which were loaded into a flatbed.

His second arrival was less eventful, more common for a determined invader than before. His truck was full of unnecessary comforts to settle inside the ancient pueblos and still feel like he was in a modern home anywhere else. It was the continuation of the modern global advance that flattened the differences between cities until the only thing to remain was the change in climate. He immediately set to work reshaping his new home with rugs to insulate him from the stone of one structure he felt reasonably confident he could heat with his propane heater. His bed was a bed. He struggled to fit the bulky box through the narrow doorway into his room but eventually managed to drag in the vacuum-sealed mattress to let it inflate inside. Food storage, kitchen, and water tanks were all settled, so he was able to feel properly moved in after only a few days. It was still an exercise in survival, one to which he was accustomed and simply transported.

The snows had already stopped by the time he first started to arrive at the palace to investigate, but this was leading to the intense desert spring full of wind and static. While he was inside arranging his bedsheets, all light suddenly disappeared, and he was inside night at day. Then came the rattle of stone and ice, sparse at first then deafening before he was even able to climb out the door to watch. His mother and puppies, still too young to be anything but stupid, came running under the cliff overhang with ears flat until they were able to shake it all off.

He hesitated to take them along on this experiment because of the risks cliffs and rocks posed. For his first attempt, he left them behind and the image of the emaciated mother nagged him the entire way and found him on the cold rocks that first night before he drove back. They were loaded up in the truck cab for the second visit. As he toured the city and trails, he leashed the puppies in the hope that he could teach them all the available ways they die without their opportunity to discover them first. There were so many sharp drops, but especially dangerous were those preceded by a misleading slope out of which it was impossible for them to climb. He knew this. They tested their inability, and he had to rescue one earlier that morning when he unleashed them to unpack. He was confident they would learn, but he still had his 9 mm if they didn't.

Once everything was set up, there was initially little to do. The days were already warm, so it was pleasant to sit out on the rocks and bake for a time like a rattlesnake. The warm days also meant the snow was melting from the mountains above the watershed and fed the creek just outside the canyon. It filled more each day with a flow of liquid ice he scooped out to carry back with him rather than depend on the diesel pump he would normally use. It was the setting that made the rattle of the small motor so vulgar and made it stay idle on the trailer; could still be used any time later as the shine wore out when he normalized beauty. Until then, he kept thinking about how many generations of people used the melt-off to feed their catchment pools in this canyon. By then, the second anniversary of the evaporation was approaching, and he had adjusted to the thought that all cities were leftovers of dead civilizations, making the ancient palace of little significance. Once the barrier that kept it untouchable fell, he felt more connected to the dead inhabitants by using the palace as a home, just as he would in any other he found over the last two years.

The rodent population was unknown but expected to be vibrant, so he brought with him several deterrents, not wanting to either find ripped sacks of rice or murder the wild mice. He kept his food stores to the minimum, primarily staples that would accompany what he could find in the canyon, which assumed would be limited to fresh meat. For this, he brought more than enough seasoning.

One of his favorite toys he pillaged from the base in El Paso was a .338 sniper rifle he used for hunting, since he was only a skilled to shoot but not stalk. The huge range let him destroy his food from a comfortable perch that didn't need to consider wind direction or other math besides the dials on the scope. From one, he saw her sniff through the last of the snow. Of course there would be cougars in the mountains, but he had no desire to actually see one now that the days of online bragging were gone. She was in his sight and well within range, causing considerable debate for his finger. In the end, he fired near her face to send fragments of rock up to scare her off to another canyon not so close to the ripe puppies. It worked. She ran confused and sneezing toward the other direction, but it also scattered the deer he was watching to see if a better shot would be available. That night he ate kimchi and rice without barbecue.

No matter how pleasant the days became, mornings were always as frigid and uncomfortable as the evenings. Without the blare of the sun, all things froze from the cold mountain thief and, as a result, he mostly stayed in his foam bed until late. That is until he learned sleeping on the ground floor of a warm cavern invited friends, and he had to switch to a hammock to make sure he wouldn't again wake up to see a snake in front of his heater, to be forced to watch it motionless for hours until it decided to go bake in the sun. A hammock on the upper levels was still cold as before, and he struggled to hoist the heater up to warm him. He tried to heat the room below, hoping the warmth would make its way up, but he ended up wasting all his propane and still froze. Undeterred, he tried again with a wood fire but only managed to fill the space with smoke that kept out friends and humans alike. Surely the former inhabitants had generations to make their homes comfortable and had family to keep one another warm in the winter. He was alone.

In the end, he adapted. He froze all night in his un-
heated bed with the door barricaded better than before, but rose early in the morning to visit his
proudest addition to the palace. Out near the creek,
he built a small mud and stone room where a fire on
the outside would heat rocks at the base, onto which
he would pour water and fill the room with steam.
This was his morning and his evening. He spent so
much time inside that he was no longer a resident to
the palace. From here he would leave on his day of
exploration. To here he would return with whatever he
obtained. He moved a kitchen over and parked his ro-
dent-proof metal storage boxes to eat all his meals
next to the water.

In the steam and heat he had visions of himself over-
played, always leading to when he began the new phase
of desert wandering last fall when he was in El Paso
fixated on the destruction of new details in the city
he never saw before. The city was a candle that
burned hot and wore itself out in pointless pursuits.
So he left. On foot. It was a walk through his backyard extended throughout the planet in all directions
from the terminus of primogeniture. It commenced
through the river valley heading North. The dam was
his gate. The broken smile he painted on its concrete
was barely visible when he reached it several weeks
after it all took place. The ground still shook from
the cannon shells. He could still smell the burnt
powder and the metallic steam burning off its muzzle
as it drowned. It was all so fresh but had already
passed into the landscape of forgotten events behind
him. It was still not forgotten just beyond the gate
where the water ecosystem had taken root in the desert
and was emptied, leaving behind desperation and extinction. At the time, he justified this to himself
in order to ignore the pointlessness of the destruction. He ignored it to make a point for himself that
allowed him to rip open the water and send it down
into the valley.

More steam, and he was leaving the clay beach for the
same rocky canyons the river always cut. It was as

much an interlude for the desert as it was in his memory. What was the point to choking the water? He never found the hospital in the fresh clay. Instead, he found mountains of garbage accumulated over the decades at the bottom of the water, forgotten until it was all raised up again. None of it made him want to explore. He wanted to leave it behind. The garbage and the reminder that he killed all the fish he found with it. So he did, and welcomed the change; the resumption of the valley he knew from before as if it never changed but had only been transported North. Homes were the same he wanted from the El Paso valley since there had been no explosion of houses without so many jobs clustered at the far end of the butte.

Homes still had stables filled with dusted carcasses that ants deflated, but he found more signs of survival and escape. He could make out fresh hoof prints in places along the river, some cloven. At one ranch far from the butte, he saw a young dapple mare graze alone in a field near a piped paddock. He stayed away, so he could watch her to understand what he'd find closer. She was a small Arabian but fully grown and not more than eighteen months old. As he got closer, she didn't run away, just lingered near where she grazed. Inside the paddock behind her were the usual lumps on the ground; the piping between the fences was wide, and she must have been small enough to squeeze through.

The closer he came to the paddock the more she shook her head. She pawed the ground and snorted when he slipped between the pipes to see the three lumps anchoring her in place. The bodies of her family stared at her daily and she could not move on while they were still there. Had they simply disappeared, the shock of absence would have let her wander the fields and find other survivors. The constant reminder of her loss prevented this. He made them disappear and she was angry. Unsurprised, he left her to sort it through alone. She was clearly not alone, though. There were so many friends waiting for her just outside the lines of the paddock when the time came for her to leave. He found a dairy farm with so many lumps crowded along the edge of one fence that it must have been easy for those further in to simply walk across and survive. There were hundreds on either side.

More steam made him hungry for the pancakes he found in Albuquerque. The famous breakfast house still had boxes of mix in dry storage waiting for him with massive tubs of margarine and syrup. He cooked for two days, refilling fat he lost from the weeks of wander. After each meal, he was so bloated and greasy in the heat that he couldn't do anything except sit in the parking lot and stare at the cliffs overlooking the city. He could have driven there to look out at the valley as he did from his own mountain in El Paso, but the syrup held him until it was time to move on in disgust with sticky teeth.

The mountain came to him. Each step along the river was another incremental rise to the continental interior where huge mountains divide it in half. It was a trip back in time, and he was steaming himself at the beginning. This was not obvious until he approached Santa Fe after a near overshoot when he chose to follow the river instead of the highway. The deep canyons below that volcano were difficult to navigate; far more difficult than he expected. He spent a week canoeing around the lake before he course corrected and left for the adobe homes he intended to reach. Huge homes. Signs of cheap homes became too expensive to remain ordinary homes. Santa Fe had dozens of ancient compounds from the era of the genocidaires that had been renovated and certified. So many he needed a method to select the best from the batch; there should be no time wasted to invade garbage.

He started in the tourist center of the old town where he assumed he could acclimate to the adobe history and find photos of the compounds that were most impressive. He shoved aside displays in the museum to make way for his food store and played in the stage coach pretending he escorted himself as he drove his RV down from Washington at a crawl. Even in his mind the pace was too slow, and he made better time on foot. There were many to invade. The city was another one that had been layered like an onion over the centuries, and he found ancient casitas all over, instead of up on the mountain which was the habit of wealth in their escape from others. He chose one that had been sterilized for sale and had no laundry inside to clean. It had been prepared for him alone. It was priced at twelve million, but he paid far higher. It was his before he left his home in Georgetown when he inherited all wealth and destroyed its very definition. Most had laundry gathered for a Friday night event. Others were empty but were clearly occasioned by rich visitors who may or may not have decided to visit that year. All of these remembered life that would have had to be removed before he could spend the winter inside. All had photos displayed, usually a lone woman who stared hauntingly at a cold fireplace from the dawn of photography. But his museum was readied for him with only these echoes who were long ghosts before the evaporation. He sat where she sat then quickly got rid of the photo. Thankful there was nothing to clean, he could focus on moving about the city to deplete its shops of anything his winter would need.

The puppies nipped at him asking to play when he walked into the sun full of sweat headed to the icy creek. They'd grown fast. They used to be frail legs and bulging bellies in those first days after he found them all under a pile of wood palates outside a grocery store loading dock. He'd seen few dogs on his trip and was surprised to see she was digging around a long depleted dumpster, so he followed her back and found the nest. She was locked in a confused state, unsure whether to growl or resign to the desperation of charity. Her teats were clearly empty, and she panted at him as he pulled back the wood to see inside. Charity won. She was refilling milk within minutes.

He continued shopping inside until he had enough and made sure to leave her more than she could eat. But not near her. He wanted to insure her privacy, so he left it around the corner where he knew she'd find it. Then he did it again the following day. Every day. Each time he returned was met with less desperation and more welcome gratitude. Eventually, the burden of visitation wore thin and changed to the burden of training that he was trustworthy enough to take her babies someplace new. He washed them all, sure to dab them with flea medicine, and put them in the alcove where the echo sat. They were the final additions to the museum. Compared with the preparations for the prior winter, he had barely done anything at all. There was no need to spend weeks organizing a truck depot or clear out a fifteen-story office building, so he could feel free in confinement. All he did was collect food and a few propane stoves. The museum was already on solar power and the well outside had proven itself on hundreds of winters. There was nothing left for him to do other than explore.

That freedom let him return to himself, and he took to riding a bike around. While true that he explored everything so completely along the way up and when he shuttled between stores to shop, this was all driven by an objective. Without the need to accomplish anything at all, he was able to just roam through the increasingly leafless streets. Eventually it became too cold even for this. After so much time sleeping outside, his body quickly remembered the comfort of clean warmth so by the first cold rains it protested severely whenever he begged it to be free. He stayed the winter concentrated on his new family.

The first of the snow was a surprise. It was an aggressive push from the mountains that came in suddenly overnight, and he woke up to the bright glare of snow which barely covered the dry grass in the courtyard outside. It burned off the roads in a matter of hours, and he was out exploring by the afternoon. A few weeks later, though, winter arrived. When the snow fell, it accumulated on the roads and a weakened sun failed to burn it off. There was peace in the smooth surface that left him with a sense of living on another planet one should not disturb with the ruts made by a truck, so he made no effort to leave the compound again.

Eventually, he ran out of a certain cracker he took to eating constantly. He should have brought a palate back when he originally began storing food, but he failed to predict just how addictive this recipe would be until it was too late. He needed more but the roads to any of the groceries were under a foot of snow he deemed a work of art. So he walked. He was frozen by the time he reached the cracker aisle. By the time he hauled back the whole supply in that store, he could barely feel his toes. He ate three boxes next to a fire that day, scornful of the snow on the other side of the window at his back.

After a month there was another break that signaled the coming end of the snow season. Not so much an event as it was a lingering absence and allowed him to spend more time outside walking through the city. The same moment the previous year was discovered during an accidental breath of air when he emerged from his garage cave. This time it was viewed from a window over weeks. Then came the procrastination while he tried to imagine any destination with a point to visit. There was nothing much to do in deserted Santa Fe except to visit galleries and museums, which was essentially no different from typical Santa Fe. Everything else was emptiness that needed people in order to give it meaning, but these dead rooms intended to showcase echoes played into the apocalypse. When he arrived, he barely wasted any time to consider what antiques he shoved aside to make space for his food, but these were finally given their due. Afterwards, he did as most tourists would and lingered in the front to flip through pamphlets that advertised things to the unimaginative. Without internet, these paper resources were the only way he could research the attractions.

More time led to more melt, and he returned to the mania that drove him out of El Paso to begin with. Sitting in his small cave, he decided to wander the desert North, to Colorado and beyond, but knowing winter would shut the gate before he arrived he focused on an extended stopover in Santa Fe. This was done. The roads were dry again, and the gate looked open. It seemed like time to chance the highway now that lanes were clear, but the first mountain pass out of town held onto more snow than he expected. Still, it was not more than the truck could handle, and he dropped back down into desert valley again. It was slow-going.

Then the desert melted away too and gave out to the first of the grassland extending up along the front range and a thousand miles to the East. The air smelled like wagon caravans dusted with snow. It was as if he drove along the continental shelf with the huge depth of the ocean overhead and the wall of land to the side until the wall wrapped around in front of him, and he was back in desert driving towards a gate to the North. It came on like bumps crowding the road as it kept pace to wrap around them. Eventually the engineers gave up following the contours of the hills and cut the road right through. So began the graded climb.

He met snow all along as he left the grassy valley. It nudged him in the shade so he criss-crossed the median to avoid the thicker patches which were more numerous as he watched the valley drop below. When the truck got stuck in the culvert deep with snow, he knew it was time to give up and head back for the rest of winter to pass. He didn't even bother trying to climb the steep slopes to get to the asphalt and just backed his way down through the culvert until it flattened out on its own after several miles. He briefly considered just heading around Raton pass from the East, through the flat grasses to reach the rest of the front range, but he no longer cared. He wasted so much time already and was frustrated he'd have to invade more homes to sleep next to echoes until he could reach Santa Fe. Everywhere up there was still winter and ice, even if the road itself was clear. He could be sure that if he still saw snow adjacent to the highway, the pass would be closed off, whether in full or merely because it would be too dangerous to attempt. It made him anxious. How long would he need to wait in the early spring of the valleys before the winter of the mountains passed? He lacked baseline knowledge to answer. There was nothing for him to do and nothing to see along the way back to Santa Fe other than to shove aside laundry which rested on the couches where he chose to sleep.

He reached Santa Fe four days after he left, ready to resume his winter hibernation and wash off so much driving. Nothing changed because he went to explore. Everything just melted back into place as if he made no effort whatsoever. It was still springtime with the city less white than before, but he felt too spent to bother being a tourist. As this waned and he was more interested in walking, the skies blackened again and dropped more white onto the roads, beautiful as it was. There had been just enough time for him to collect more jigsaw puzzles and raid the dispensary down the street of its aging product, most of which was covered in mold and unusable.

The late snow kept him next to the fire for another week of sipping soda and fighting an absurd three thousand-piece puzzle that would only have been enjoyable to anyone either high or far down the spectrum. He agonized in the just-one-more-piece battle for days before he burned it in the fire and played video games instead.

But he had a collection of tourist flyers scattered around the house where he would pick one up and deposit it somewhere else as he walked. After some time, they were everywhere and each room had its own advertisement pop up when he entered. All of them screamed for his attention, and it was deafening. Most were garbage retreats few people had any interest to chase, least of all him when no people would be left to make due on the promises made in the flyers. Hiking trails were excludable until the mountains de-

cided to shed winter. Fishing seemed like work instead of pleasure. Nothing resonated as it was all
meant to distract from a life that no longer existed.
He did keep one that showed him the ancient city at
Mesa Verde because it felt most like his own condition. The drive there would take a long time and
there would be no doubling back if he had to give up
again; he would probably need to make a new base somewhere out there. Perhaps Durango. More mountains.
Winter. Better to go through Farmington. He thought
maybe he would need to come back at some point if it
all failed to pan out as it did in his imagination.

His new family had to come. It was too much to maintain deposits of loved ones all over the country whenever he decided it was time to leave. They depended
on him now and would probably starve if he left them
behind. There could be no food depot like in Washington where the wild animals were primarily deer and the
occasional bear, but would not venture deep into the
city blocks. Santa Fe was rife with coyotes, and he
had more than a small suspicion the rowdy puppies were
half. But the half dog in them made them party to the
contract with humans, and he was responsible for their
survival. He loaded the truck with what would have
been enough for an extensive camping trip and drove
back towards Albuquerque to wrap around the southern
foothills to avoid the snowy roads along the more direct route through Durango. The trip back in time
along his walking path reminded him of the other obligations he left further down the road. Then he turned
North again to new roads and put worry aside. He arrived in Mesa Verde underprepared and did double back,
so he could regroup and remind himself of all the
loose threads before he went to hide in the quiet
sweathouse he built in the canyon.

In the winter as in the sweathouse as in every time
since he left Mesilla, he felt the pull of guilt over
leaving the parrots he found alive in an old restaurant from his childhood. It sounded absurd no matter
how many times he thought it out. It was a shock that
continued. Their intelligence protected them from a

short death but, had he not arrived, would only have served them to false hope and prolonged suffering. It was all he could do to clean their home and replenish their food before he moved on. It was negligent assistance. Temporary relief kept them in their prison. The water system especially concerned him because it was more finite than the dripping faucet on which they depended before. If only they opened all the bottles too soon, the whole schedule would accelerate, and they'd dehydrate long before he could return to refill them.

It concerned him so much that when the first snow fell, he drove all the way from Santa Fe to check. It had been more than a month since he first left, almost two. He covered the length of New Mexico and saw more misery along the way, but nothing as emotionally exacting as the trio of parrots inside the restaurant. It was a short anxious visit, only a few days.

Southern New Mexico is not the North. The entire state exists on a slope and the lowland desert is hot even in winter. But this is relative. Cold is still cold. The survivors were made for tropical winters where cold is fleeting. He arrived to a restaurant with terra-cotta floors that reflected winter never warmed by the desert sun outside. This pressed them into their cat tower he brought to keep them warm and to climb around to play. The base was covered in shit as a testament to how much time they spent in there. They did not come out to see him when he opened the door, nor when he peeked in after the shuffle of feathers told him where they were.

It was still cold despite the insulation, which they meticulously began to remove out of boredom; better than feathers. They looked at him from inside, all curled up together, until they sprang up to see. It was not recognition or joy. It was the poker face of birds who act only when they are ready; there can be no telegraphing. Even still, they were slow to do more than separate from their huddle. The conure was

especially reluctant and not playful as a conure
should be.

How many lives had he intervened to protect since they
all shared in the same trauma? His earliest days
alone were marked by a door-to-door search of houses,
so he could release as many pets as he could. So many
were unreached until he found their rotten bodies
weeks later. He kept what he could safe and warm all
winter when everything not already feral froze in the
blizzards of an unusually hard winter. He was not
there to protect them again; they needed to take what
they learned to survive. If it had been a mistake to
leave them behind, it was one already too late to repair. Winter had come to the Southwest, so it surely
was in full swing in Washington where his sheep were
no doubt still grazing happily in Arlington cemetery,
but his pack of dogs had probably already begun to
thin out. In any other situation, there would be alternatives to leaving them alone. There would have
been shelters or other people to provide care, or he
could have installed surveillance cameras to gratify
his curiosity. Now, there was only unsolvable worry
to push aside and resurface despite his efforts. It
attached itself to the worry he constantly felt over
the trio. What was he even doing in his sweathouse?
What was the purpose of being here rather than there?
Every time he left it felt like the most natural and
irreversible option, but it never stayed that way on
reflection. His reasons were always muddled in memory
to feed a renewed irreversible need to move on.

Cleaned of sweat, it was time to walk back to the
palace which looked smaller and more stifling than it
had that morning. The short stretch of hours filled
with memories pulling him in too many directions at
once. Winter was coming to a close, and he originally
planned to roam North, but he knew the worry would
chase him everywhere. If he went to them, briefly, he
could still return to his plan with worry held off for
a time. There was no question about Washington, but
Mesilla was not far. He could be there and back in a
week. A short interlude to his palace getaway would

buy him months of peace. It would be simple but exhausting. Again. It was already decided before he began to climb up the canyon and left the following morning with dogs.

Three months is a long time for survival in a box. He himself spent days barely leaving the small rooms he heated with a fire to keep the darkness lit. That was unsustainable. He left early and often to escape the confines of the warm box. He was free to go anywhere, even to death should that be inviting. Three months is a long time for weather too. Changes happen slowly, then fast, then reverse. It's a path of mean regression to eventually follow a mathematical agenda; There is no choice in weather. When he visited during the earliest part of winter, he saw cold bodies huddled together. This time it was early spring, and he found rejuvenated friends sunning themselves in the window as if they waited for him. They weren't. They had their own routines inside the restaurant complete with their own timeshares and congregation meetings. He happened to approach when the sun hit the opposite building perfectly and reflected enough light to warm the sill; a time when curious doves liked to stop by to coo and peek inside before they flew off. This was the window he originally left open for them but closed again to keep out the draft pushing a chill to the rest of the dining room.

Most striking was how spread out the mess inside had become when compared with the past two times he entered. They managed to take full residence inside the restaurant. Almost all the toys he laid out had received at least some love, evident from the chew marks, and some had been carried up to the overhang ledges. The new water system held out against their playful destruction, and he saw there was more than enough left, suggesting it could support them for another few months. The only real difference between this and the original was the complexity on the water course, which for intelligent parrots was far more engaging and made them less likely to explore new ways to rip apart the source. Whatever it was, it worked and would have given them around five months of clean water. Food was never a concern since the mix of seed and pellet was itself fun. They worked their way through a small portion of what he set up and his only thought was he wished his pack of dogs in Washington were as smart about conservation. He left them at least a year supply all at once, but they likely burned through in a few weeks. There was nothing to be done. At least the trio was alive and healthy. The fat sacks they grew from all the tortilla chips and dried beans had nearly disappeared. They had spent their entire lives eating proper meals of seed and fruit only to suddenly tap into the sugar, salt and fat of human food, and it would have killed them quickly had he not replaced it. Part of him suspected, though, that the lean months huddled in their cave contributed to most of the shift. Either way, the proof was clear in their beaks, which were less flaky and brittle. He left them alone for months, hoping his preparations were enough to keep them alive, so the sign of rebounded health was something that eased his worry more than anything else he found.

Still, he put on a mask before he went inside, just as he did before. The pandemic went a long way to normalize masks in order to prevent the spread of viruses, especially to those with sensitive immune systems like tropical birds. He felt like after all the other preparations, confronting the possibility that this gap might ultimately kill any of them would be devastating to bear. He knew this all too well; he achieved such a death of one childhood friend exactly this way after returning from an out-of-town trip full of new viruses. He didn't know then. Now it would be unforgivable. Perhaps this interfered with their ability to recognize him as human each time he arrived, leading them to caution. But caution was good. Caution protected, and he was in no hurry to bond. Nor might he ever be ready. The Amazon was older than he, meaning she was nearing the end of her life span no matter what he did. Soon, he would face her death and the renewed sense of loss with all he projected onto her. She was a symbol of everything that re-

mained of his past. If he reached deep, he could find
memories   when   they   spoke   together…ChtChtThsr…
ThsrSSSsszzszzz…Thhrrrrreh…she spoke back then but was
now suspicious. He tried.

The conure was still half bald from her time pulling
feathers while she was trapped inside her cage. The
pile of feathers were now gone, cleaned in his first
visit, but there would be no regrowth. This baldness
was a visible sign of the suffering that went on.
There was no way to know exactly why her post-evapora-
tion stress was more severe than the others. It might
have been that she was the last to be freed from her
prison or that conures are particularly social and the
loss of humans was felt more acutely. There were many
explanations, none of which mattered. What was more
cause for worry was that she remained aloof for a
conure, even from the other two in her flock. While
they played or flew around, she would stay somewhere
nearby but tucked into a wall. She only watched. So
far in the three visits, he never saw her preen the
others or bob her head. Whatever trauma she felt, led
to her self harm was ongoing; she was clearly depressed. She needed an extended intervention to would
help her rediscover the social bonds over which she
brooded.

The visit was originally supposed to be short, not to
last longer than necessary to quell his worry with a
resupply and inspection. The sight of the depressed
conure convinced him to stay longer and observe the
others, whose behavior was less familiar, and thus he
felt more complicated to understand. Unlike dogs,
sheep or himself, parrots are intelligent and need
special care if they are removed from their wild social groups. Chronic depression will kill them, just
as it would a human. He felt his duty to keep them
alive extended to ensuring their mental health as
well, if possible. He had to try. By the middle of
the second day he knew he may as well set up residence
in the bookstore again, so he restocked his food and
palates of bottled water in anticipation of a weeks
long stay.

As he drove around Las Cruces to do all this, there seemed to be nothing left of the city he remembered. The years had exacted far more change to the small university town than was seen in El Paso. Some basics were still there, but in aggregate it had crossed the threshold to be become another fungible American city indistinct from any other he visited. This was a dangerous line of reason that could lead to the burning mania which unthinkingly destroys. If he dwelled on the frustration over sprawling new homes, it would become a sticky mire to would distract him from the dedication he had to his palace, which itself faced a crisis of attention due to the distraction of the trio. It was too much, so he managed to ignore the city and stay in unchanged Mesilla. And he lived in the bookstore and visited the restaurant every few hours for an hour at a time. By the fourth day, he was enough of a presence that the Cockatoo and Amazon climbed down to get close. This was the dangerous time. He needed to balance trust with cold observation without letting any of them pass too far into the horrors of emotional bonds. He let them come but never encouraged them further. There were no bribes that were the taboo of training. He made no offer to touch them with his hands and even avoided conversation entirely.

This was by far the most difficult. He himself had no communication with any intelligence since the night of the evaporation, and he was starved. Sure, he talked to the dead or the stupid, but the trio could understand him unlike those. Throughout his life, he would speak to parrots and watch for signs they knew his meaning in the way their pupils bounced when they stared back. The Amazon had done this with him decades in the past, and he wondered if she might still hold memories of the small boy who sometimes stood outside her cage. She was the most dangerous for him. She was there at his beginning and again at his end. They had been together on the planet for a lifetime and now both needed the comfort of one another again, but he couldn't allow it. The best he could risk was brevity and distance. The focus needed to remain on the conure, whose distress showed some sign of abatement. He gave her plenty of distance and avoided eye contact.

He watched her furtively and was able to see she too watched him. After the first days as a wallflower, she began to appear more interested, even dancing with folded wings nearly ready to open. This was the dance of anxious hesitation. She wanted to know him and he was at pains to signal benign disinterest. Until the end of the first week. He had already been inside for longer than his normal hour and had begun to doze on the floor with his back against a faux balcony column when she flew at him more surprised than he was. She careened back to her perch once she realized how close she came, and he left right away before either of their embarrassment had yet subsided.

Outside the restaurant again, he laughed at himself as he replayed the fright of her wings, narrated by chattering as she flew. It warmed him in a way he wouldn't let her see. The warmth soon cooled and hardened. The conure was not as intelligent as the other two; she was as desperate and naive as he was. They would make for a tight pair who depended on one another only to be incinerated on the day when they were alone again. They were both too damaged by the past. She was a prisoner in the restaurant because she had no survivability in the wild, which for her was more than a thousand miles away. He could not take any of the trio out of the restaurant to follow him in his itinerant life the way he could with dogs or sheep. There was no ancient contract between human and bird. Any warmth he felt, any affection he gave to them was nothing more than selfish human idolatry unless he could find a way to free them from their prison and let them survive in their own way first. But he hadn't the time for that. Nor was he willing to end his urgent travels. All this kept him out for the rest of the day until he was able to find the courage to return the next morning after a night of insomnia.

She, too, had worked through the awkwardness of the flight episode. Her flavor of naïveté was such that affection was always reciprocated. Even though she was surprised at such a bold approach, it was part of the dance that had to continue. There were repeats until eventually she didn't fly all the way back to her original perch, but chose instead a nearby window sill. She landed heavily and bobbed her head with feathers flat and pupils wild. The exercise made her pant which meant she had no intention of leaving the sill until she could recover her breath. Just before then, though, she flew off again. It was like this for days. She would fly, avert, laugh, and fly away again. Each time was more warmth, more emotion. The flirtation fulfilled empty spaces he cleared out so the pain of losing everyone would not pull him deep beneath the undertow. Those were off limits even to himself, and he decided he could no longer flirt with her, with any of them.

The fourth week was deliberately distant. When he visited, he never sat down. Nor would he stay for more than a few minutes. They all needed to be weaned from one another, mostly so he would have the strength to leave them again for whatever reason made sense at the time. He went through the familiar motions of re-supply and cleaning that marked his departure. The month of observation had given him new insight into what the trio needed to survive without him, so he ex-aggerated these details. He learned which foods they favored by which ones they left behind. Their time-share schedule had appeared to be a haphazard shift of feathers around the dining room but became a pattern he could recognize, then it became a clear expression of each bird's individuality. He tried to create pri-vate grottos for them to specialize in what each of them preferred. The Amazon loved to chew ropes with large wooden beads while the conure preferred bells and climbing inside small plastic buckets to chatter away at herself. The cockatoo loved perching in swings weighted down with chains to climb and pick at a pile of sticks. He did his best to provide them with enough enjoyment in their safe prison before he left again. They survived without him for so long he believed it was likely enough to continue, which would give him freedom for at least several months until he felt the need to return.

It was two months since he was back in the canyon after his worry was quieted, and he had settled into the hunting life quite well. From up on his favorite perch, he managed to shoot his first mule deer that always seemed to be just outside the line of a clean shot. He missed often, and had to wait another day for it to come back. Eventually he ripped its neck apart and was happy. Then he reached where it fell to see it panting in dehydration from blood loss. It was larger than he estimated through his scope. There would be no way for him and his family to eat all the meat before it spoiled without refrigeration. For a week he gave up his sweathouse to become a smokehouse where strips of the panting deer hung, and the kimchi was finally happy.

His scope also found dozens of wild horses grazing around on the plateaus above the canyon which dispelled the image he conjured of majestic symbols of freedom stampeding in a v-line. These were slow moving ruminants passing on after a few days, knowing neither that he watched nor that everybody everywhere had evaporated so no one would ever come to claim them. Then they came back, so he decided to go pay a visit and see how close he could walk. He knew the wild horses in Wales let him get very close, and it made sense to test the tolerance of their American cousins.

The family went. The rowdy puppies were by now more calm but still quite dumb and might hijack the whole experiment for themselves. No matter. It was all distraction by this point. It was a long walk up the creek to reach where he saw the herd, so he packed lightly with only water and binoculars. They hugged the base of their own canyon for much of the morning, walking slowly as typical. He first saw her again as they left and were about to follow the creek. She was

far behind. Too far to be an immediate concern, but
he wished he hadn't left his rifle behind. When he
checked through the binoculars, she didn't seem interested in them, so he almost forgot she was not far
away. This was their area. They knew it well since
they walked it often over the months they lived at the
palace. The puppies had marked their own rocks all up
and down the creek canyon and checked each spot to see
if it needed a top-up. They didn't know she followed
from above. Nor did he until she was so close there
was nothing to do but panic.

He ran. It was reflex. Their mother hadn't noticed
the mountain lion nearby, and she would have been useless to fight it. He had his duty. It took him up
the slope above the confused puppies, so he could
catch her attention and draw her away. It was working
except his panic made him too reckless, too focused on
the dangerous animal, and he forgot to focus on the
dangerous terrain. He slipped on loose scree to tumble back down the canyon. Fortunately the millennia
of water flow broke the mountain apart so when he fell
it wasn't the entire way down. Instead, he met a
cushion of rock that would have been nice for an afternoon sunbath. It was a solid landing to stop him
immediately.

The force stunned him. He momentarily forgot his
panic in the confusion of how he managed to be transported to this new place unable to breathe when moments before he was rushing to protect his family. He
owed them protection. It was his only purpose that
kept them loyal. Food was only a small clause in the
contract, buried in the larger section which covered
threats to life and safety. He saw the threat before
they had, so it was his role. They would fulfill
theirs some day when they saw threats he couldn't
face. Today was his day. It was all that was left of
civilization to keep to the formality of human obligations such as this. He tried to extend it everywhere
he could, including to nature which had before only
enjoyed cynical tokens. Everything was now cooperation until competition was the only way.

The confusion reoriented, and he sat up not yet noticing the pain, only noticing the arm that wouldn't
properly respond when he told it to reach for his
9 mm. The confusion had left a residue. The urgency
of the danger made him reach out to an alternative
arm, which responded with a clumsy control over the
weapon as it loaded a round in the chamber and struggled with the recoil. It fired off several hasty and
dangerously inaccurate shots at the mountain lion that
already ignored him to continue stalking the puppies
more closely. Each round got her attention, though.
The pops replicated in the canyon, so she was soon
overwhelmed with sound. She was safe but disliked the
change in setting. He fired more at her until she
backed away and left entirely. The puppies also scattered from the sound, following the line of old urine
they left along the creek back to the palace. They
were much closer to the shots than she was, so they
were far more frightened. Eager to reclaim her pro-
tective role, their mother chased after them and they
all disappeared through a thick cover of desert shrubs
and corners.

His confusion was gone. All that was left was the
smell of burnt powder and pain. Not even air came
back to his lungs as he struggled to fill them. It
barely worked. He laid back on the boulder where he
landed, already hot from the late morning sun, and
thought about what the hell purpose he sought with
trying to meet some wild horses.

Breath sort of returned as he slowed himself to observe exactly what kind of pain he faced. It was his
right side, behind his shoulder and made every breath
an excruciating decision about whether it was necessary at all. Broken rib. But why then was his arm
dysfunctional? When he tested his hand, everything
still worked the way it must. Elbow was more trouble-
some and moving the whole arm was impossible. Breathing was not painful on his torso either. He finally
decided he landed on the boulder and dislocated his
right shoulder in the process. It was pure pain, but
he was confident nothing was broken. He was lucky.

When he landed, he felt his cheek graze the rock surface and knew even in that instance he avoided a fractured jaw or a row of broken teeth.

A dislocation was serious but not serious. It was a
flamboyant injury that could be healed with dramatic
ease. The kind of injury inflicted on main characters
to show their vulnerability and highlight their dependence on another untrustworthy character, without
risking serious danger. The near catastrophe reminded
him of all the others that should have ended his
struggles and let him rest. His immunity was not
safety, it was abuse that continued beyond his control
as if to maintain him in a state of misery until his
use was over.

He tried to recall the ways those characters were
healed on TV. There was always a moment of worry until a calm hand came to take charge, popping the
shoulder back into place, so the story could continue
with some new layer of trust. What exactly had they
done? Something about calming down and contorting the
arm until a telltale snap set everyone at ease. Is
that really all he needed to do? This was not fiction. He suffered a serious injury that could leave
him forever disabled if not properly fixed. There was
no other character on whom he could depend. Nobody
was around with special knowledge in whose hands he
could resign himself. He didn't matter. He could
have crushed his skull on the rock and been no different from the millions of hominids before him whose
brained bodies fed birds and ants. He was in crisis
with no good option. What was needed was a system to
fix himself. He had no idea how to reset a dislocation, but he did understand how his shoulder should
feel. If he could figure out where the ball was in
relation to the socket, he could begin to plan some
action to pop it over the lip and back into place.

For this, he needed pain. He needed to visualize
where the pain shifted when he tried to move, how it
changed and where his arm was physically prevented
from moving. It had to be done. He couldn't ignore

the injury and hope for it to heal itself. He had to hurry before the inflammation was so great that it created secondary damage to his body. If he fucked it up, it would mean permanent pain. He observed while he moved his arm using his undamaged alternate. He spent almost an hour in exploration over the range of motion and the limits of his own tolerance. He re-assembled the picture into an estimate of the interior joint, so he finally came up with a motion that should get it back in place.

He did it slowly, careful not to pull too hard or be too violent that he might tear important sinews. It was no use. Each attempt met the limits of pain before it met the limits of machinery. All he could do was sit in the hot sun to mull over what he already knew was the only way. He was his own patient, and it was impossible to separate the pain from the treatment. The crisis had changed. It was now only a mental injury to protect against years of suffering.

In the end, it was his own insignificance that won out. The last hour of testing had ratcheted up his pain to a new level, beyond which was only another increase. He could always switch it off at any time. He had the rounds. He could give survival a bit more time first, then power down the game if he got stuck. None of it mattered, so he forced it into place with a monstrous heave which came from the depths of his mind more than it did from anyplace else. The sound was achieved on the back of painful color blooms that made him choke before it made him vomit bits of smokey mule deer. This was followed by black warmth where he was only aware that somewhere at another place some pain continued to buzz, but didn't concern him in the darkness. It faded, and he returned twenty minutes later to the evolved feeling in his shoulder that allowed more freedom in his breath.

By now, very sunburned and dehydrated, he managed to roll himself under a nearby shrub to enjoy the shade and some water to wash off the sick. His family evidently realized they fled without him and made their

way back with the danger forgotten and similarly unaware of his injury. Each time he thought he might
stand up to walk back to the palace, tiny muscles
protested. Apparently every motion involved his
shoulder in some way, so there was no feasible way to
stand up without shards of pain to cut him back down.
He gave up. All day passed like this until some curious ants brought friends, and it was time to leave
with his alternate supporting his primary as he wound
his way through the canyons up to the palace walls.
It was very dark when he arrived. He walked by memory
and headlamp to avoid any rough ground that might rattle his body to send vibrations up to his shoulder.
It was slow but finally completed. Exhaustion drove
him immediately into bed even though he was still covered in dust adhered to dried vomit. The openness of
the mattress was a disaster. Every time he relaxed
his muscles, his shoulder lost critical support. Some
time after midnight he switched to his hammock and immediately felt soothed in the tight cradle where his
shoulder could stay compressed. He slept but remained
mindful of the need to never shift his weight.

There was little change in the morning. Worse, he
discovered all the tenderness held off by adrenaline
was now given free license. His body ached not just
in his shoulder, but all the muscles suffered colli-
sion in the tumble, even those which compensated in
the injury were now sore from the atypical strain they
faced. He never left the hammock that first day and
only stood up once to urinate into a bucket some time
late that evening.

The second morning was less severe, so he was able to
replicate the compression cradle with some disposable
shirts. He was still coated in filth that needed to
be cleaned, which meant a walk down to the creek. In
normal times, the mile and a half was not a concern,
but it now seemed intolerably far. When he got there,
more work was waiting, and he had to pull down the
smoking meat before he could sweat out some of the
grime. This was all piled out carelessly on some
rocks, and he didn't care if they were still there

when he emerged. His survival did not depend on the
meat, and he was too far along in pain to care about
the wasted life.

In the heat and steam, weighed down with pain, he decided it would be time to eat the peyote he saved. He
only had one experience with it in the past, which
made him the kind of lethargic perfect for his recovery. It had already been several months since he
first found it and never felt the time was right.

Back when he first arrived in Santa Fe to check for
mansions where he could spend the winter, he explored
many options. Most had been empty for the evaporation, but one had been a party in full swing when it
was emptied. The cars outside stretched down the posh
street and must have annoyed the other mansions if
they were filled. More out of curiosity at the flavor
of how Santa Fe wealth partied than interest in moving
everyone back out, he went inside and met a dizzying
menu of drugs in what appeared to be an art exhibition. Most surfaces had mystery white power lined up
partially cleared. He found fruit bowls filled with
mushrooms and small ziplocks protecting either tiny
paper squares printed with segments of their original
cartoon characters or small clover shaped candies.
The peyote was in a box in the kitchen next to a hand
grinder. He took everything of interest except the
powders and the candy. He tested the paper during the
winter, but the LSD must have degraded without proper
storage. He'd had his fill of mushrooms from before,
so only ate a few, but the peyote was a special sacrament that required something more than bored tripping.
Once he slowed down from the injury, it made sense to
use the medicine while he healed.

His body protested the idea for a few more days.
There would be no reason to rush into the spirit walk
if he could barely move. It was enough that he settled on the canyon, which was no doubt an experienced
venue. It was a good decision to have waited. The
walk would be more meaningful after his most recent
near-death experience with a threat still wandering

around him. In the hopes he could accelerate the arrival of that day, he began physical therapy for his shoulder with light stretching to make sure the risk of permanent injury was over. He also needed a secure way to immobilize it in case he forgot he was injured. He didn't actually believe he'd re-injure himself while under the visions because he anticipated hours of a semi-paralyzed state with any movement being slow and deliberate, unlike the twisting swirls of melted flesh induced by psilocin. During the last experience, he was barely able to stand up with the help of a strong stick and then could only manage a few steps to the fire. He had no nausea before, but mostly because he sipped his tea so slowly and only finished half the mason jar prepared for him. The tea was so expensive and the main ingredient was so endangered after years as a Schedule I enemy of the modern state. It was hunted down and destroyed but held on only because it was successfully argued to be an ancient sacrament. It went underground where it was cultivated in storehouses to protect it from law enforcement and poachers alike. If he could, he would fill the desert with seeds again. This was why he never ate it while in his winter shelter. It was the enemy of cities and its visions needed freedom to reconnect the walker with the planet through the eyes of an animal. No home, no room, no palace could properly host a walker.

Still, he could not risk climbing into the canyon to take the medicine since he was too weak, and she was still out there. From the palace courtyard, though, he could sit back and watch the canyon and sky uninhibited while still remaining safe. These were the visions he hoped would heal him and show the next path he should take.

Then were the questions on how to even prepare it. Should he make a tea like he was given before or a powder like with mushrooms? He took the box along with the grinder, since the art house assumedly know the right method, so grinding was at least the first step. He was wary that making a tea risked overheating and potentially damaging the alkaloids, so he decided on a long-steep tea at a low heat. He chopped up two large buttons and ground them down to a rough powder he let soak in water that was slightly cooler than for mate. He let this steep on the stove for an hour before pouring everything into an empty glass spaghetti sauce jar to soak for a few days. Not that it needed the days of soaking. He needed them. Despite his resolve, he was unprepared for the new chemical which would show him new visions. He was afraid to meet his family or find out all the evaporated souls had traveled with him, upset with how he treated the world in their absence. This might not be altogether bad. In fact, he knew it might help him confront that which he worked hard to avoid over the last two years. He long ago gave up looking for answers, but he still winced every time he imagined himself actually alone.

It was settled. Apprehension was the right way to approach a vision because it meant he respected the unknown to come. He just needed to wait for fear to transition away, which it finally did after the third day, hours after he began holding the jar thinking it already did. It was too late to start the journey; it would need more time if he was to avoid night visions.

It was an early start the next morning. The tea had chilled overnight, and he marked five lines on the glass to indicate how much he should consume in each go; each one would be spaced out an ambitious thirty minutes from the previous. He pulled out some blankets, started a fire that could be maintained all day and everything was done. It was as bitter as he remembered, so he must have done it right. The bucket was nearby, just in case the nausea pierced through, but nothing came by the third sip. Peyote is a slow burn. There is no dose and wait forty-five minutes for magic to happen. It creeps. By the last sip he felt weak. Perhaps from the night of fasting or perhaps from the creep. It was still impossible to tell if he brewed everything correctly. Consumed it correctly. Whether the buttons were still viable. Everything was speculation.

His head began to feel heavy. The weight of air was becoming too much, so he wanted nothing but to lay down. He leaned back against the wall where he prepared himself, determined to stay fixated on the clouds over the canyon for signs of vision. They didn't dance. The colors didn't pop. They did what could only be described as emerge from the sky. They were there the entire time, but had always seemed like flat paintings against the blue. He saw them as huge three-dimensional masses levitating over the earth to cast shadows whenever they passed. Texture everywhere emerged from where he failed to notice before. Colors stayed the same, they just emerged. He didn't melt, he emerged from where he sat. Everything was as it always had been, but different in that he could actually see it all. The canyon called to him because it was open, not because it was alive. He tried to stand, but couldn't. He was weak, but somehow in control of his muscles; he was weak with contentment and sight. Instead, he shuttled around on the ground using a stick to help him along. Movement roused the nausea from the knotted depths of his inside. He felt his stomach muscles pulsate as it swished the sour liquid that had nothing solid inside. It was bitter all the way up into his memory of the first sip. It stayed down. Nothing emerged.

He spent the next hour on the cold ground falling into his dreams about the distant soreness he felt. He tried to roll over, so he could sit up and watch the canyon, but it was impossible in that phase. Not until midday, when the nausea receded, and he was accustomed to his weakness could he crawl back to his wall with a view of the canyon under the intense sun. It was silence. His family came to him, and they all watched the silence together.

The sun moved to where it should. Hours of intense visions had hollowed him out with confusion as they slowed down and everything faded back to the mystery

of hidden details. His body regained its strength
somewhat as he added more wood to the fire in preparation for the evening on its way. He still touched
each piece as he fed it in, examining the touch of
flames that were so uncertain at first. Everything
was back to silence again except for the small sounds
that overcame their shyness to devour the wood. The
sun was making its way down over the other lip of the
canyon which hid the deepest of the reds, only the orange and pinks remained as it disappeared from sight
but still had so much to accomplish with the horizon.

It had been an ordinary day no different from the hundreds of thousands since others like him sat on the
cliff edge watching the same show. He saw something
there in the palace behind him, but it made no sense.
The walls began to glow from the local fire, and he
still couldn't understand. He was among the generations who lived there, he felt their moments as his
own. But they weren't in his visions. More was
there. Hour after hour, he fed more wood into the
flames and watched them grab each from his hands. It
was the same fire, but every second was some new form
never existing before. He watched so many generations
of flames emerge and disappear up to the smoke-painted
roof of the cliff.

He was hollow and tired. Weak but comfortable. Even
the pain in his shoulder faded to memory and was just
a background soreness almost enjoyable with each
pinch. The thought of crawling into his room to sleep
in bed without being able to watch all the details
around failed to hold interest, so he simply curled up
within the glow. It was an ancient scene. Just a
muted mind watching the flicker of light without wanting more. So ancient that his family beside him understood and joined him too. Animals seeking warmth.
All night. He never slept nor did he try to sleep.
It was all part of the weak aftervision leaving him
unable to change or look away.

When he moved, he was inside a thick liquid where he
felt its texture as he slowed his way through it. Not

quite water. Perhaps it was only the taught skin that covered him or the heavy muscles beneath. Somewhere the liquid persisted. The flicker held his visions played out over the day. He fell into them again and again, trying to understand what the peyote tried to say. It was too specific, too new to be some abstraction fed to him by the alkaloids. There was indeed something there if he focused on the flames long enough to see them again.

Back when the clouds emerged, everything followed suit. The stone floor of the cliff was a surface of crystals to rub his fingers when he touched. He could see their small faces shine as the sunlight angled over. An entire mountain tapestry of crystals stretched out in front of him, below him, down until they melted in a sea of glass over a compressed iron ball. Inside him too. Small strands of energy vibrated everywhere and composed themselves into a structure that held the muscles he controlled from some strange perch behind his eyes. His shoulder was not him. It was a city some cells decided to build and join with other cities. He was ignorant of the process. It happened and would one day soon unhappen. The pain he felt days before was just an echo from the city shouting out for help, and it was not him. Textures everywhere inside and out were all the same and none were him. His new family too was only texture that walked around on cities built for them and over which they were ignorant too. They, like him, began to fade somewhere and left behind animated structures that watched the silence. More textures appeared when she walked in. But neither was she a threat this time if she was indeed actually there. There was nothing to her presence, it was as ordinary as the clouds.

By then his visions began to reconstruct the textures and images from his past began to arrive. His trio was there with him to watch the silence. Each flew in and selected their place. Lieutenants were alive and ushered each of the lesser pack members and sheep into the canyon floor, silently. Mannequins with ragged clothes. Everything emerged from the desert. Except

his family. He searched the crowded valley for them.
Every texture below was so sharp he was unsure if it
was the peyote or if they were real. All of them
faced away, looking out to the mouth of the canyon
where the creek flowed. Two hazy shapes were there.
He knew they were his wife and son, but he couldn't
see them. Only they were textureless.

All of his fleshy cities worked together to hoist him
up and walk him on shaky legs down the trail to the
canyon floor. He never stopped watching those shapes.
He struggled with each step to pass through the crowd,
but distance was not what hid them. They were walking
away. He stopped, confused at why he couldn't see.
Why they never got closer no matter how many steps he
made to close the distance. Only these textures
moved; everyone else in the crowd stayed in place and
even turned to look as he passed. He felt their fur,
same as before. Had to be real. The more real they
were the more he chased his family. They had to be
real too.

By then he reached the creek and its valley opened up
to either side. The crowd stayed behind and did not
follow. He was alone, still chasing his family now up
the other canyon wall in front with, more hazy textures. Something enormous never there before had been
erected on the plateau above the creek. He could see
his family, but they were there among thousands of
smaller textures he somehow understood were children.
But they were not children. They felt older. And to
the side were dim lights. Two. It was all silence as
everything called him. It drew him closer with silent
attraction. The two-mile chase had caused his blood
to pump, but he didn't notice. What he noticed was
the throb his shoulder told him happened. It felt
like waves of pressure as the blood met the residual
inflammation and slowed down. But he didn't think of
this. He felt it keep time to some music that shook
his body gently as he watched the plateau not quite
sure what he saw. The waves rocked him until he almost believed the two lights began to pulse along with
it. He stood there, in the warm sun until a sense of

thirst appeared, and he reached into the creek to drink from the still icy water. He used his alternate hand at first, then bent low to dip his mouth directly in. He was another desert animal thankful to have found water still flowing. Waving pulse. All was correct.

He sat on the bank and felt lethargy return. He closed his eyes and watched himself from up on the plateau small and crumpled in the valley gently rocking to the tempo which drummed in his ears. He was so weak that the desert changed to a hospital, and he was connected to a sack of chemicals fed into his arm and he felt a sting in his veins as it pulsed through. The sickness came next and followed him home. He forgot about the sickness. It was with him at the creek too. Was it in the crowd and he missed it? The hazy textures of his wife and son on the plateau were the same when he was sick and vague. He was smaller. They were fuzzy images he reached for through the sickness, held his baby weakly for as long as he could before everything disappeared. The desert and the plateau and the thousands of textured children and their lights disappeared as he swayed leaving only the three of them with himself to float at the center of the creek. He watched them watch him be wheeled out of the room barely a complex of cities on their way to another room where some neighborhoods could be removed to detach him from the sack of chemicals and leave the sickness behind.

He pulsed in the swaying vision. The lights returned and continued to follow with him as he watched his vague son. There could only be one fuzzy image. The demolition was complete. But why so many textures? They even shimmered from the heat reflected off the rocks, so he was positive they were all real. The crowd facing him from up in the canyon, watching him watch the crowd facing him from atop the plateau. All silent waves of pressure watching. And the huge structure just out of sight, fully enveloped by the wavy desert.

Hours went by just watching until there was a monstrous cracking sound and everything disappeared in an instant. He was alone again with only the sound of the creek. But something more was out there, and it hummed imperceptibly from behind, from the palace. He didn't notice at first. The shock of the sudden shift in visions had him stunned and searching the sound of the creek for answers. The hum was soft, and his ears eventually understood it wasn't coming from the water. His body stood up to help end his confusion. It was pure gravity the entire way back into the canyon where the hum softly grew as he approached. The lights had moved. They wanted something. Of course, they were real. These were his guides on the spirit walk and they had a message. It was a gentle hum. Gravity hobbled him as he neared until another crack hurled him a mile up the canyon to the trail leading into the palace, and he was alone in silence feeling stronger.

There was nothing much further to his spirit walk than that. Once he was transported back to the palace in the late afternoon, he was alone with the still clear features of the desert canyon. His head had emptied itself and no longer even observed his surroundings, it was a receptacle now for streams of images it stored in its library. Everything flowed out of order. Bits of childhood mixed with inane details of adulthood without significance. It was a vision that made him relive himself and, as he did, begin to notice there seemed to be a longer stretch of time since the evaporation than what came before. This was mathematically impossible. He knew that. It was only that the texture of his life felt before had too few details to emerge, which compressed the memories into so few they could have been lived out in a few short months. The evaporation had not yet even met its two-year anniversary but there were so many textures it filled him with decades of images that left no room for anything else.

Patterns emerged. The unsequenced images had a rhythm that began to make sense. They flickered around and lighted his face that was an untextured self-image with no age, he was himself at once a child, a man, a sovereign watching moments through which he passed. In none were signs of his wife. He strained to pull from them some clear image of her face as he always knew it. Instead, he was buried in dislocated details without the ability to recompile into their original whole. Nor could he find his son, who was a forever entity who never aged from his immediate form; his son could never remain a baby nor could he be a child, he was a corporeal idea with motion in his life. The more he tried, the more he felt the guilt of failure. He lost the most important images to betray them with the irrelevant details of a life selfishly lived. He remembered things they used better than he remembered the things who used them. It left him sunken in the flames as it all spun around.

Eventually even the reality of his life before slipped from focus. It felt less a part of him than if he watched it from a movie some time before. Would not a life lost to memory itself cease to be a life lived? Everything is a reconstruction for the present moment that is itself a gate to the next, but once you cross each threshold, you leave behind all the others. He began to lose hold on the idea that the past was real, even as he lived it in the present. It was only natural, then, that he forgot his family or even the whole of civilization. The further he moved away through time, the less each could ripple to meet him. And the flickers formed the pattern that showed him how ordinary his life had been. Ordinary meant sameness with others. All others. Generations in the palace behind him lived lives that differed so little from his own. So ordinary there was little left of the individuals, who all made the same choices when each moment approached. So ordinary they were together he as the same person living the same lives across millennia. No change. The law of the species required this. Only their cities differed in form, but not kind. All the celebrated culture and language were nothing beyond ordinary sameness. The ancient palace where he lay in the glow of a fire was no different from Washington where he spent his moments of transition two years before. Neither spoke to him. He walked in visions now and the palace was silent with no guidance offered.

All he heard in the walk came from the desert. It showed him what survived and needed his protection. It showed something more, which he needed to understand if he were to close the walk, otherwise he'd stay trapped in the visions. The only message he knew for sure was he now lived a life of chasing horizons, never content with where he stood. It seemed this had distant echoes before the evaporation, but these seemed vague and unreal. Only what came after made sense. In those images, he clearly understood there was never anything beyond the horizon other than more horizon. He always saw the mystery of moreness instead of the immediate moment of life he faced. Perhaps the desert told him it was time to end his constant flight to the edge of cliffs, that he might better live out his moments with other survivors who came to depend on him.

This message also came from the past, beyond the real. He did little else in all the images other than change from one location to the next. So deep was the drive that it was the only detail he saw on his face as he watched the visions in the flames. He saw it in the detail of his family, in their power to ground him to a home. They prevented him from drifting helplessly again into unknowable movement. They were gone. Perhaps this is how he slipped so quickly into his fixation on the horizon. He might need to replicate their bonds with other survivors. Only an intelligent survivor could help him. He might need to deliver himself to the trio unconcerned with their eventual deaths. They were there in the desert, but they were not where his guides brought him. They walked him past the trio deeper into the canyon to see something else. Then they brought him back to a cave, but not a cave. The palace was home for now. The road home was painted from the sound of a hum that lifted him even as his weakness was total. His mind turned to the sound as the linchpin to understand the entire spirit

walk. It came to him only when he was at his weakest,
but when the visions were strongest. It must have
been the sound of his body as it pushed fluids through
his veins. It was the sound of life, the sound of
survival. It could be anywhere and he heard it before. But then there was the huge mirage, an odd ac-
companiment behind his family and all the other beings
who joined them. The hum brought him there too.
First. Would not it and they be the linchpin? It was
no mountain. It was large, like a city on the
plateau. He could not see it; it was only felt.
Nothing was afraid that it was there, nor did the
desert reject it. It blurred the line between city
and nature, so it felt immediately at home to all
life. But it was backdrop none of his visions deemed
particularly important in the moment.

As the night wore on and the alkaloids wore out he
still kept at the thought of what a city of nature
would look like. He had moments in Washington where
he felt this was possible. The botanical gardens below the Capitol were one of his almost manias where he
believed it was possible to live in a tropical forest
without leaving the city. He knew this had been accomplished in the research biodomes scattered around
the desert, but he had no idea how to find them. He
could drive for months in search of a back road to
take him there. The thought of how much time would be
wasted in pursuit of curiosity closed this option. No
more horizons. He should piece together the solution
of his walk where he began all his walks. A city of
nature could be constructed in El Paso now that the
river returned. He would take his survivors there until more was clear.

II
Libertarian

The visions continued on without resolution until they
transformed into ordinary insomnia. By the time his
mind was ashen with thought, the first movement of
morning began in the next canyon, and only then was he
able to move back into his room and sleep off the previous twenty hours. There was nothing left for
dreams. Sleep was a black void that lasted until the
canyon air was hot again, leaving him sticky inside
his palace room. Everything was an ache. Worst of
all was that he discovered how unhealed his shoulder
had been before he took the powerful tea. This all
meant another convalescence filled with whatever he
remembered of his visions to be processed. The bits
and shards he caught were all the same highlights less
vivid. They still spoke nothing. For three days, he
stayed around the palace without venturing into the
canyon. When it was over, his aches had waned, and he
was done with palace days. Whatever he went to accomplish there had run its course. For several months,
he lived the pseudo pueblo life with only the occasional feelings of guilt he was unentitled to claim
it.

There was still no next destination he expected would
have struck him hard under the visions. There was no
peyotal deus ex machinae to lay everything out so
clearly for him to follow. He was stuck in the same
indecision he'd always carried, until he figured out
the palace was good enough. That only lasted another
four days until he decided to simply head back to
Santa Fe where his base had been before. There was no
need to change from it now, especially when he hadn't
a better plan. He did his best to clear all his rub-
bish from the canyon and left behind a simple bundle
of wildflowers inside a cairn over where he always
built his fires.

The agitation continued once back in the museum.   It
started when he pulled up to the junction in Albuquerque where he swung East, not South.   The horizon
there looked odd, somehow wrong.   The more he drove
towards Santa Fe, the more wrong it felt.   Nothing
felt familiar to him any longer despite the number of
times he drove that stretch of disheveled highway.
Then came the destination, which had too much in common with the palace it felt like another room on the
cliff.   It was an eight-figure piece of luxury real
estate that had become uninhabitable to him as soon as
he pulled up.   It seemed as though there was a change
left by the visions; he just failed to listen.

More preparations for more travel were needed.   When
he left his palace, there was surprisingly little for
him to cart away.   Most of his garbage had been burned
and the broken down packaging took up little room.
But his museum had loot for him to take.   Preparations
would take time.   A week of shopping in Santa Fe went
by, and he accumulated a full flatbed of art and rugs,
among other things best found in the city.   When covered in silver and turquoise, he was ready to leave it
all behind again.

It was hot, but he traveled with the windows down to
feel the air pressure surround him as he drove.   There
were portions of the highway where he could accelerate
to speeds that would have seemed slow before the evaporation but were reckless now.   The air struggled to
fill the cab, shaking it with loud flutters and the
occasional gust broadsided the truck like a huge pis-
ton through the window.   It numbed his skin and wore
on his ears until there emerged a familiar hum he began to notice as he approached the junction again.   It
was so loud he stopped driving to see if the sound really followed him.   Nothing.   It only returned whenever he drove, but it was too pitch-perfect to ignore.
Then came the distraction of the river valley as he
neared where the butte had once rested.   It came on as
structural plans for how to capture the green valley
and expand it from a desert oasis to a tropical forest
with only the barest of skill.

For this, as always, he needed to repurpose what better hands than his created. Everything came back as a large greenhouse, which he only knew to be boxy and completely vulnerable to the mountain wind. He imagined himself investing months of work to replicate his home in Asia only to have the roof ripped off. It would be impossible for him to build an alternative, more aerodynamic like what he imagined biodomes should be, nor did he know of any sounder buildings anywhere in the region fit for purpose. It would have to be large and able to seal in moisture, with huge sunroofs to feed the garden. Every glass building he recalled was either tall and narrow, or otherwise too confined. He was jealous of the openness of the butte and wished he could simply cover it before the beach was reclaimed. Already it was turning green from water weeds that had waited decades for the rich sediment to reappear. The water had not receded from where he saw it on the initial walk up. This was now the new riverbed and its floodplain came to life. There would be creosote soon, followed by the squat trees that dominated the rest of the valley. If only he could manufacture scaffolding as high as a bridge from one side to the other, then adhere thick glass. Yes, it would flood inside but if he could make the cover then he would have the ability to engineer some outflow mechanism when the river turned violent. The impossibility of the dream allowed him to leave it behind with the beach as he passed.

The city was the same too. He last saw it when winter kept it desert, but now all the broken foundations were coated in green tumbleweeds which obscured the history of his demolition. They nearly hid the cannon as well, where it still sat in the caked mud to show the first signs of rust in its rifling. It told him again and again of the basic truth that it was far easier to destroy than create. Had someone built the scaffolding over the butte, he could fell it with almost no trouble at all. Signs of this truth were scattered along the road, but were now also vague with overgrowth.

The whole region was a confused mix of decay and re-
birth, as it should be. It showed something was different from all his past journeys, which were driven
by mania. He felt more continuity from before, as if
the valley project was ongoing rather than abandoned
midstream. If the city was reclaimed in this way,
slowly through the egress of wilderness accelerated
when he wiped clean part of the canvas, then there was
hope his future would stop drifting through echoes.
This idea was also a confused mix, unclear in purpose.
When he destroyed the dam and the city fell as collat-
eral damage, there was only mania. Even in that moment when he proceeded through to completion, he was
unsure what real positive gain would be had. It might
have been as wrong as it might have been unimportant.
The overgrowth now gave no real indication. There was
no hum, no feeling of right or wrong when he stood
there. The lack of purpose meant it was susceptible
to more mania to creep in and destroy his new destination. Or was it mistaken mania itself? The airflow
in the cab had gone, so there was no more hum over the
rattle of rocks and sand on the other side of the windows.

It had been a long day of driving when he reached the
catchment lake where he decided to sleep, just below
the gravel dam. The spring floods had been too much
for the outflow at its side and the dam had clearly
been breached not long before. He knew this would
happen some day when he stood at the same spot last
fall to watch the rush of water pop through on its way
from the butte down to the ocean. It had been only a
trickle until it managed to grow into a river again.
There was no confused scene in this spot. There was
only river escaping the stranglehold that held it
back. There was no need to project meaning here.
What he accomplished before was the destructive power
of freedom. The sign of erosion was itself limited,
but it was unmistakable. There was no need for him to
aid it with more destruction. Every season would
claim more from the soft dam. More gravel would be
removed and carried down and redeposited elsewhere
along the way. The thin lines of canals that swirled

down the slope were randomly formed channels which would become a set course over the years. Each could have been formed to the left or right without changing any outcome, yet there they constituted and will remain until there is nothing left to cut. Erosion is the way. Destruction is the way. They signal change from one form to the next. Anything could be built with great difficulty, but erosion always came even before the project would be complete. Beauty came from adaptation to erosion slowed. Civilization had installed its dams to choke the river and the wonderful systems to channel water without ruining the structure were beautiful, if no longer needed. There was still erosion in them even as it slowed. He did not destroy anything. All he did was accelerate what naturally occurred, so it could meet the pace of life downriver. The thin lines were the first signs the river reclaimed its natural course. They were the river even if they were then only dry gashes. His purpose was to erase the unnecessary echoes of civilization, so these lines could be free. Anything in its way was a legitimate target for them both. All the fertility he observed along the banks were fragile and risked destruction in order to cling to life. Every farm irrigated by the laterals understood it was only temporary at best. They all depended on changing what must be random into what could be predictable. The water moved from one place to the next according to gravity and opportunity, but life around it needed assurances to survive. So life created opportunity. The dams were no different from the trees in this. They followed the history of water to set up a claim. They each studied the randomness of opportunity chosen by water on timetables measured in centuries when it could sometimes remain level and other times transform into a mountain itself. The farms were roots grown by civilization from the predictability it created. They would only be usable until the next water mountain. Without the dams in place, it was impossible to predict how long this would be. He might farm the valley for his entire life without disruption, or the mountain may already be forming behind him as he drove and would destroy everything before he reached El Paso.

Without the ability to predict, there was no urgency and ignorance created calm.

He slept well that night thinking about the river as its subtle sound washed the movement of the desert. It stayed with him as he continued his drive the next day. If he were to decide the desert life and fight for survival along the fertile band that hugged the river, he would need a solution to the unpredictability. If not this year, then some time in the future. The flash of terror at the idea of himself as a decrepit old man fleeing a lifetime's work buried underwater was a nightmare against which he needed to guard. He destroyed his best chance to avoid that reality, but did so to expand the region of fertility. He needed to find the best place for farming to keep him furthest from the water's opportunity at destruction. While this circled back to his biodome dream, it offered him no solution for a backup plan that should be followed immediately and not await some new mania to intercede.

But El Paso was a city of residents, not one suitable for large artificial ecosystems. As he drove and imagined the city from up on the mountain, there was no place for his plan. At least no place he could manufacture on his own. At best, he would have to settle for a typical farm that mitigated the risk of flooding to acceptable levels. This meant a return back in time to where the city existed before the dam generated predictability.

Obviously the visible high-water marks were his best guide. He should avoid everything between the mountain foothills out to the mesa flats. All of this tempted the river. He could choose the other valley, the dry valley as well. But only the river valley was fertile and this was only in the band where it flooded. Life in the desert depended on danger to survive. He could not eliminate this completely. Not anymore. Not alone. It took a civilization to make the valley safe. With pipes, it brought fertility above the high-water mark into the mountain where it otherwise would fall through the arroyos back down to the river. He lost all of this, not because of his decision to destroy the dam but because of some other decision that caused him to be alone with all the infrastructure just out of reach.

On his way down the valley he stopped in to visit the trio again. Enough time had passed since he last stayed, and he felt ready to see them as a permanent addition to his family. The puppies and their mother were great companions, but they offered little intelligence. Their contract duties were simple and could not cover the kind of emotional bond the trio could. Reality met him when he walked into the restaurant and was again met with aloof coldness. For them, the restaurant had always been their own domain without any awareness of the changes outside. Their afterworld looked so much the same as before, except they were alone until a stranger invaded infrequently. But he was becoming familiar with each visit, so the coldness was not as durable as each time before. He knew on this visit he would be planning their escape from the inadequate restaurant. Only he knew the stability they had there was about to change. Years of sameness was about to be destroyed by the stranger.

He knew this as soon as he walked in and saw all the disarray and shit that needed to be cleaned up again. The insects had rediscovered the healthy lives in the restaurant and now posed serious risks. It was time to relocate. To where, he had no plan. Such destruction and stress needed careful thought so none of them would feel the trauma of change. These were institutionalized prisoners whose identities had been shaped by years inside the restaurant. Stripping it without recognition that it had been home could very well kill them.

As he cleaned, he fantasized about an indoor jungle where they could fly through the canopy and compete with him to find ripe fruit. The changes could be done gradually, with each stage more lush than the previous. There had to be a limit. There was no wilderness waiting for any of them. All were trapped by a dead civilization that prevented them from leaving. If he released them to their natural habitats, they would die. Artificial wilderness was the outer limit of what he could do. Then it was time to leave again in search of the first step towards their freedom. The whole exit was now rote and neither side felt especially broken when it came, so he drove on to check the greenhouse where he first found water in the valley. It would be a start, but not a finish. He could use it as the nursery for which it was intended and grow his wilderness from seed while he looked for a better structure, assuming one was even in El Paso.

His suspicion was confirmed about the wind. The roof in several places had been severely damaged without anyone on hand to inspect or make repairs along the way. But it was still enough to be a huge greenhouse, and he made a quick survey of the plants that survived without any caretaker. To his surprise, many of the sapling fruit trees held out. So did the desert plants and most of the evergreens. As before, he made the rounds with the hose to saturate them all. The surrounding property all looked more alive than when he first saw it nearly a year before. This was not just explained by the expanded summer heat when he began to explore the valley after he arrived, there was much more undergrowth and more signs of flood. It looked more like the flooding from clogged runoff channels that had been damaged by the river, rather than from the river itself overtaking the berms. If those still held, then this was not worrisome, and he could assume there was time to make preparations.

The greenhouse was never a comfortable staging ground, and it pushed him away, back to his ranch house further down the valley. If it was not flooded out, then it should be a good base from which he could easily explore the highlands and still reach his nursery. If all went properly, he'd still have enough clean water from his well without the need to filter the river again as he had during his long journey up North. So much had changed from those early days when he worried about running so low he might have returned to Washington. There was water everywhere in the valley now.

His pecan orchard was not far from the nursery, and he had plenty of daylight, so he drove over before heading home. Memories of that night came back. He saw the canal locks he opened to let through water he freed from the butte and now penetrated the hard clay of the ditches. Everything was so overgrown he couldn't see the water level. All he knew was they had, on occasion, overfilled and deposited sediment at their base. The orchard itself was a mix of excitedly growing trees and those to suffer the poison of too much water. It was expected, and he was satisfied by the survival rate.

At the end of the fence line, he could see the river just beyond. This was where it bent sharply to begin its southeast flow, and he noticed there were the telltale lines along the gravel slope where water had risen to find new opportunities to the valley. This orchard would die soon when that mound collapsed and there was still no telling for how long it could hold, whether it was already the sign of the heaviest season for decades or only the beginning for the year. Its erosion was a certainty. The whole valley showed signs of this in various forms. Sometimes it was the sediment collected from rain with no place left to flow, other times it was the entropy of flowing water that would never cease. Everything was marred by events a hundred miles away. This hid more roads beneath sand and slowed his truck as it made its way through the farm highways. There was no hurry. Everything led somewhere that again felt new, where his disconnect was more complete in the brief time he was away than the twenty years before.

The sprawl still crept. Many of the worst roads led to new developments, with some front yards having been overrun with river and rain that returned them to desert sediment. No destructive symbolism could have been more accomplished than this. Then came the dominoes he felled out rage. The symbolism was here too, but it differed in kind. All twenty houses that faced his ranch house were rubble collecting sun. Compared to the violence he slung at the dam while in the throes of the same mania, this seemed more like a child's tantrum than anything calculated to exact change, either for himself or the landscape. It was someone else's actions, not his. It felt as if it closed the lid on his life before and everything that came next was himself; everything else was another life where he spoke another language he couldn't understand anymore but still haunted from elsewhere. There it stood at the junction to his ranch house.

It was easy to let it pass and drive down the long path to his home since it had already been a day that needed to end. He only stayed at the property for a brief time before he found everything so intolerable in the city it was time to leave again. When he pulled through the entrance, nothing called out. Even less so when he walked around the outside to see whether much change had occurred since the fall. It all looked like a normal periurban home for the area, but the inside was stale and dusty. Everything was left in place without any indication water made its way inside. There was still time left to go shopping for food, so everyone left right away once the trailer was dropped. The dogs could easily have stayed behind, but he was unsure if any new threats hung around for them to find. They didn't mind. When they all walked inside the warehouse, there was no sign anything had come since he first opened the doors. All the food was in the same place unmolested except for the slow grossness of time.

With a new supply to carry him over for the next week, he decided to take a drive through the city for a while before returning to the valley. Everything had even more dust than before, which seemed already excessive. Yet the added wear only seemed to endear him to the city in a way it hadn't when he first arrived. It was as if the extra layer of haze on the buildings began matching the haze of memory, so things felt familiar again.

Until he began passing scenes of his destruction. These stood out to contend against his old life and the brief sense of return. There was a direct correlation with the pockmarks he placed in the roads on the mountain with the destroyed neighborhood beside his ranch house. They were the same action that erased all the intervening space until the whole area was just one playground. No matter how much he visualized that afternoon, he couldn't find the justification. Not even the joy of destruction seemed to explain it. But it happened. He went through the effort to load rounds into the cannon and pull the firing mechanism over and over. It was fun. He might try it again, but that was another explanation which didn't apply here. This had a purpose which was both lazy and incomplete, over which he felt ashamed unlike the dam, which he was happy to have done so thoroughly.

The day was wrapping up, and he went home to clean out the spiders from his bedroom and sleep. The annoyance was still there, in the morning as he sipped tea and looked at the grounds. Now there was time to welcome it better. He made his way up the drive with his mug while his dogs circled around him making claims. It was not yet hot, and the sun still worked to burn off the light grayness overhead, so everything still looked blue in the valley.

The neighborhood was the same as when he fired his last round to rip apart the final domino. When it fell, the frenzy ended without the planned bulldozing. All this gave him the feeling that he returned to one of the destroyed cities in northern Iraq before reconstruction. These houses were not brick. The debris outside on the street was all alive with the touch of humans who had lived inside. This was the first inspection tour he made, so he had not carried these small discoveries yet. Each of these details were first impressions collected long after the frenzy subsided so that, in the calm blue light, he was more willing to give each their due.

Two of the homes were different from the others. The wrecking ball still parked outside looked weathered. He used it to crush these homes thinking it would be enough to satisfy the frustration he felt over the way so much sprawl had changed his city. Had he achieved this, he might never have visited the armories on base with the idea to destroy. The dam might never have collapsed, and the valley might still suffocate. Perhaps the justification for his pointless destruction was found in what came next, not prior. Less so about the ends of destruction but the opportunities for change contrive from the ideation. Perhaps it was the only way for him to have discovered his power for restoration, that he was to first waste it on destruction. This still felt incomplete as he traced the line from where he installed the cannon to give a clear shot to the first house. That one was a disaster avoided, but the rest were accomplishments. Shoot and pivot. That was the day then. It was all marked by motion still visible after so much time.

He walked over to house zero which left a hole in the line through which he could pick off others behind it. He was able to destroy four houses with almost no need to re-aim. They truly were dominoes laid out for him. But the debris pulled him back to recognition that these were lives, not toys. A pack of diapers told him so.

Aside from the rip of shrapnel, it had never been opened. That they were size zero for newborns seemed cruelly ironic and compelled him to reach down. It was bulky and, if he subtracted the moderate damp weight from old rain, its lightness was disproportionate. Diapers should weigh nothing. They should be bands of air to almost float away. They have to be so light that you can articulate them in a hurry while you hold a life so small but so heavy. The destroyed home gave him a flash of detail about how his son felt when he held him and the small orb that seemed to be minimally attached to the rest of is body. How this tiny round head was so dense compared to the almost feathery rest of his body was the most profound dis-

covery of parentage. There was more debris. The entire front yard was covered with what used to be the
contents of a nursery waiting for a new child. He
knew it was unoccupied because so much was still in
packages. Nothing had been taken out to be washed or
sterilized. It all looked like hope disappeared.

His cannon had ripped apart the bottom floor of the
house and the roof collapsed over it. He remembered
aiming for the breakfast nook, so the shell could penetrate deeper into the load bearing walls of the
kitchen. It had been felled immediately. The blast
had blown the interior and sent some contents of the
nursery outward to the street, but the room was still
there under the roof. The far end of the wall had
stayed erect and preserved a small corner for him to
inspect. Something stood out in the pastel greens and
soft shapes. An accordion binder full of papers, presumably medical records. It was. The outside had
been marked *Transmountain Children's Hospital*, and it
was thick with content. Everything had been meticulously labeled. The family was organized and dedicated to this pregnancy.

It was all laid out as a story with chapters. The ul-
trasound printouts in sequence. The 3D image showed
signs of old water drops. The pregnancy was normal,
and the girl had developed well; the in vitro transfer
had taken despite years of effort. Everything was on
track for the early August caesarian. The nursery was
done and everything had been prepared. All that was
left was to fight down the escalating charges which
would not be paid off until the girl was in middle
school. But that didn't seem to matter to the family
yet. They had tried for years to welcome her home.
He saw in another section how her mother was already
over forty and the doctors were scheduling regular
visits to monitor pre-eclampsia. In this section were
all the research printouts, switching between the doom
of statistics and the reassurance of blogs. Her
mother must have stressed severely in her fight
against the low chances.

At thirty weeks, she had been admitted to the hospital for monitoring. The vaginal bleeding must have woken her up since she was admitted at 04:37 in a night of pure expensive horror. This passed. She was discharged later the next day and everything kept on as it should.

Their first and probably only child was on its way after so many battles to receive her. So much stress and emotion happened in this room before its resident even arrived. Surely everything about their marriage had become this room with nothing remaining anywhere else. It was the room of hope. Tears flowed freely here. A few short weeks were all to close the chapter of a long journey until everything evaporated one evening with no explanation. That she was due at all was itself a statistical triumph, but no research could have predicted both she and her mother would be gone in such a way before her date. There was not even a satisfied completion to the journey to end with sorrow recognized. Everyone on that path was gone and likely never perceived their departure. Thus was hope preserved unchanged. Then came nothing.

He knew the emptiness well. The first homes he entered were recently vacated with only scared pets inside. He avoided digging into their affairs at first out of a sense of decorum, but then this subsided. That first house made him relive his own traumatic discovery of an empty child's room in his own home. There were three of them there, all strangers. How many had he seen since? For times, he was immune from the shock. He could enter and find anything without feelings of renewed trauma. Other times it came in on the most minor details. It was all too much. He stopped his phase of home invasions very soon after it started. Any time he entered a home thereafter was purely driven by a specific need and never included remembering the echoes. He did enough to remember them. He selected nearly a thousand of them to stow away in boxes that were careful selections from their homes. That was enough. Any more would be morbid self flagellation to send him on a tailspin.

Even those hundreds of lives were preserved through an agonizing process that caused him to confront them as they lived, to think about their final moments as the summation of their lives in the things around their living area. There was the madness and the disgust all mixed with the pitiful and the lovely. He lurched along the full spectrum of emotion in a few short weeks while postponing the reconciliation that his own family was also gone. Then the nothing captured that too. It came on like fatigue but stayed like numbness. Like a switch. One moment was full of energy to tackle the world, then it collapsed to its foundation. Ever since, he struggled to understand whether this was a normal response or whether he was losing his grip on his own humanity without others around to keep him centered. There was no one with whom to talk it out, nor did he revisit those memories often enough to make better sense from them. In fact, it was also difficult for him to observe what changes he underwent until they were already long entrenched. It took actual reengagement like what he experienced in the domino neighborhood to give any insight whatsoever, but he was a long way from Washington to be able to do this with those first homes.

The nursery here was too clear. He could visualize away the rubble and dust to see it for the room of hope it was; could see excited parents moving around to plan out hypothetical fictions that, if only the evaporation had not interceded, were as possible as any other. There might have been complications in the operating room. Her mother might have experienced dangerous postpartum depression, setting the family on a different course entirely. Everything had been untested potential. It overwhelmed him again. When he made the morning walk sipping tea, he did not anticipate this much raw emotion. Had he known, he would have buried the neighborhood rather than face the old unsolvable wound.

He couldn't unsee the morning. The ground had already broken, and he was unable to climb out. It might instead be less risky to climb down first. So he wandered around picking at exploded details from each of the homes in the neighborhood. Photos. Laundry. Food and even some old pets who never made it out. It was all the same as before. After a while the sting changed to frustration in recalling his textureless family who met him on the plateau. He still agonized that he couldn't hold their faces in his mind. Even when he could catch a moment of detail, it faded under waves of second guesses. All their pictures were safe in his RV he left outside his university shrine, meaning he could end the frustration, revitalize his memories and pass along into nostalgia just by scrolling through a few of them. Later. Now was not the time to rush out and chase another whim. It was the time to take a step back, to absorb the sight of this neighborhood in its present state before more weather came to alter what he had done. It was an avenue of destroyed dreams already ended. Nobody was injured when he removed the homes. No loss prevailed upon him from angry residents, but it was still impossible not to see it for that. He only chose this obnoxious bit of sprawl because it was so close to where he wanted to set up his afterworld ranch. He came to the nuisance. It predated him. No claim to the city from before entitled him to halt all new housing developments. Both he and the city forgot one another and moved on. Now that he returned, the city itself had left when all its people no longer gave it life. He didn't return to anything. It was just another landscape full of empty houses, with this row of rubble the most lonely.

For all the time since the evaporation, he would avoid these encounters but concluded at the palace that it was time to remain put somewhere. This implied the need for a solution, or at least to stay in the city even without any solution. Nevertheless, the need to externalize was too strong, and he resumed fantasies of finding a home with his trio once they all could be together. All that was needed was to keep to his plan and focus his efforts on building something beautiful.

It all would start with a bath. When he arrived the night before, he did not take the time to turn the well pump back on, so his bath would start from there. He left the destroyed homes when the dogs found him after their exploration. Once his back was turned, the spell was over, and he was able to imagine just another morning walk. The pump resumed, the tub was quickly cleaned and began to fill. He was only barely aware of the silence in the bathroom from where he was in the kitchen to do other things. Something happened. The water ended.

No amount of toggling the knobs brought any change, nor were the other taps any different. Everything that worked a few minutes before was now suddenly off. Unlike when the electricity first cut, there was no panic. In the time since, he was very accustomed to the surprise loss of what should have been a predictable aspect of infrastructure, and this new irritation was viewed as a mere curiosity. His bath ended at the pump. But only after breakfast continued. There was always time to shift himself around from one problem to the other since he knew none of them would be as straightforward as he might assume. Everything was a sinkhole of problems that needed a family of actions. When he did go to check the pump, he was met by a quilt of spider webs installed to take advantage of the dark warm oasis under the pump shell. This explained nothing until he noticed the familiar smell of singed plastic and saw the moderate charring near one of the spider tunnels.

Out they came. He destroyed their homes with only some of the same pity he experienced earlier as he inspected the rubble across the street. This time, they were removed for a reason. Whatever spider dreams he crushed, they could rebuild elsewhere. It might make them stronger in the end, having had to start fresh somewhere else even if he might have destroyed their nursery too. In any case, he had to see the damage, so he could plan how to rewire the pump and get his bath back online. That was for another day, or at least for later that day. The problem drew him in as expected and placed him before a technical challenge that required strategy. The charred area was where he connected wires when he installed the solar panel and detached the original city power line. He was no electrician. It was a half-assed effort which might have withstood more usage had the spiders not moved in. Later. Now was time to look around at what else needed planning. The pump was near a damaged tree which his first cannon shot mistook for a house further ahead. The shell glanced off before it landed somewhere in the field across the street. This was a problem. The damage reminded him there was an unexploded ordinance nearby, and it required a plan to deactivate. Later. What else?

It would start with leisure instead. Out came the hammock from where it was stuffed under the metal food box and an array of cans he stashed as an emergency up on a high shelf just in case the river decided to visit while he was out. Everything was still good inside. Most had only just crossed the expiration dates, but he assumed these were more suggestive than proscriptive lines in time. He had already begun to grow accustomed to the escalating stale flavors in everything he ate now. Anything dangerously passed their date had long ago molded into a moist paste. He sampled a bag of dried figs, dusting a little white powder off before each bite.

He walked around to look for his family as he ate. They were busy with another round of exploration. He caught glimpses of the puppies dart from one end of the yard to the other while their mother slowly sniffed her way in pursuit. This was the first time they had such wide open land; the museum had been a tight compound and the palace canyon a series of corridors. The ranch was designed for legs to be stretched. But it had been fallow and fallow desert land invites friends. He and their mother stayed on the trail of the wild puppies, she memorized the various textures they passed, and he looked for hidden snake dens. Then he spent the next few hours napping

in his hammock under some trees huge mulberry trees
with nearly ripened fruit.

A bit later was time to half-ass the wiring again and
get water flowing to his bath. It was a refreshing
dip after a morning of emotion and rest. When it was
over, he smelled like a fake herbal bouquet and there
was nothing left to do in the calm valley. A light
cover of clouds had formed from the blue haze he saw
on his walk; it had not burned off but lubricated the
way for rain clouds to roll overhead. It was a short
storm, whipped in quickly before it petered out a few
minutes later to leave behind an almost bright afternoon of drips on everything outside. He watched from
the porch until the rain was light enough to watch
naked from the hammock.

More naps and calmness let his mind drift to the emotion of the morning. He still saw so clearly the hypothetical faces of each family but couldn't do the
same for his own. He understood the paradox, though
it still annoyed him, especially with the solution
just up the road at his shrine. After he was done
squishing mud between his toes he decided to go retrieve the photos from his RV. It was not far if he
drove. There were three options to get there, and he
took the one directly up the mountain through town,
which let him see again the subtle changes from over
the winter and spring. Here and there were more signs
of water that flowed violently off the mountain and
flooded intersections. On campus, everything was the
same as before. He chose well the spot to protect his
important things. Once he grabbed what was the sev-
enth thumb drive with copies of his family photos and
computer, the day was ready for another walk. The library was still open since summer classes had been in
session the night it emptied. In the decades since he
was inside before, there was no change in the smell.
Books never change. It was wonderful to roam again
and pull older volumes off the shelf from where they
were eternally alive.

Hours later, he was back at the truck looking like a student with a stack of books and a computer. There was nothing towards which to study so these were mental masturbations that would help him pass the time. Everything rode along the highway above the border wall installed above the river. That was something new. In the distance were the remains of the failed project to extend the wall up the slope of a small mountain itself cut by three obsolete borders. So pointless it was not worth his frustration and he continued through the desert. He saw the old dead mall where he used to shop, on top of one mesa, as he neared the city again. He remembered how pink and bright it was inside, as if it already was an enclosed garden. The pink was still there, as were the bright skylights, but the shops were pure decay from abandonment that long preceded the evaporation. Many some-ones helped it cling to life as it passed along the death spiral of low quality wares until it might be demolished once it reached the floor. Many someones had gone to work here knowing they had set up inside a carcass. But it was bright and open as ever, almost emptied of laundry. If he installed a tropical forest inside, he believed it would survive. Apart from all the infrastructure needed to transform it, there was enough in the shopping district outside to sustain him for another couple of years while he prepared his self-sufficient ecosystem.

When he drove around the parking lots to inspect the prospects, he confirmed all this. Even the sight of an overly ambitious mega liquor store was not a reason to hold back his excitement. The demon that captured his younger days and made its best effort to befriend him in the afterworld had permanently lost out. There had been no relapse since his first day in Ashburn, and he could again count time in terms of years. But the transformation would be a tremendous project and he was still lazy. If he were to properly create a biodome inside the mall, there were other preparations on which to focus back in the valley. It would be more efficient to continue with the plan for staging a temporary farm first.

What type of farm exactly, was not something he was able to decide as yet. There were some echoes of skills in gardening from his past, but not much in terms of large planning. He knew what fresh food he craved, but had no idea whether he could actually grow them even if he could source the seeds. The original plan for his ranch house was a kind of mixed farm and animal ranch, but the desert preserved so few of these unlike in Virginia. What he did find still alive were all far up the river valley and might prove extremely difficult to catch. What would he even do with a horse or a few heads of cattle? These large animals would need a tremendous amount of food brought to them, and he would as soon bond with each before he could let himself slaughter one for meat. As he pulled into the driveway and scanned the land around the house, it seemed smaller than before and less primed for growth. What he believed was needed would be more space and more variety, which he could only think was available back out where the greenhouses stood. It was settled the next day after an inspection confirmed there were huge plots of open field abutted by forests of pecan trees where he could grow shade plants if he could figure out what those might be.

Altogether, the scene was totally open and let him escape the shame of what he destroyed. It was a bit of a return to the old valley, before the sprawl could encroach, but it was further away from the city. Ultimately he decided it was an improvement. Out there, and he swapped a dozen acres for a few thousand, with a small town at the center. If only he could just enclose it all and devise a way to keep the river from its occasional visits, it would be a paradise. He could plant whole neighborhoods of crops that over the years would keep him healthy.

It all began with mowing the weeds that enjoyed the fertile land. In the future, he would wait for everything to turn yellow in the winter and burn it all instead, but that chance was gone for the moment. At the rate he went, it would take a year or more to fin-

ish every plot, so he concentrated on a few surrounding the greenhouses. This took a week.

Next came the plowing, with which he had no experience. The essential idea was easy enough. The equipment was on hand and not particularly cumbersome to
operate. It was the actual exercise of making the
lines that seemed so frustrating. Every time he
looked back, he saw straight perfectly aligned rows
had reshuffled themselves by the end of the day when
he surveyed a crooked mess. This was despite the
careful attention he paid after expanding his attention with the products at the dispensary across the
street. He agonized over each mound of soil as it
popped out behind the blades, made regular stops to
climb down and view what churned up. This usually
marked the point when he was so high he had to stop
work for the day and would instead wander around to
imagine a huge dome over his corner of the valley. He
had enough of the fallow land plowed after a few days,
and he decided to take a break and begin planting some
things after a test confirmed he was able to irrigate
all the rows sufficiently. This meant shopping at the
seed bank inside the greenhouse nursery. Every packet
made his dry mouth water with anticipation, cooled as
he inspected the instructions which seemed too complicated at first. He chose some greatest hits and moved
out to see what else needed attention.

So much of the supply of live trees died without regular watering. Many of those he resurrected after his
first visit survived, though some did not. This still
left him with a decent selection of young sapling
fruit trees that accelerated the number of seasons
he'd have to wait before expecting any fruit. Of
these, the date palms were the most numerous. He also
had more cacti than he cared for, but at least they
would be dependable spots of green in the drier areas
of the mall when he finally moved them all in. None
of the other houseplants made it through the long
drought; nothing needing high humidity survived except
the small cover of moss where the water pump continually dripped. It was a start. He could always make

runs to wetter climates in future years to capture some of these back. All the survivors were scattered about and commingled with the dead across many greenhouses on two properties. What he needed was a solid inventory to get an idea of how much space he could fill. He went aisle by aisle dumping plastic sheets of brown threads into a cart he emptied into one greenhouse, so he could reclaim the soil and seed trays. Anything healthy was left behind and anything questionable was taken to a sort of hospital greenhouse where he could experiment with various treatments. With everything more visually manageable, he consolidated all the healthy plants into two large greenhouses.

Inside was damp and warm while outside was hot and dry. The summer sun battered the freshly plowed fields, but he still sowed varieties he thought would be able to manage the intensity. Tomatoes, eggplants, and melons all went in with so much anticipation. He'd lived off canned abominations for so long he nearly cried at the thought of the tiny white and yellow flowers. Spread out around these went several patches of cannabis, far enough apart, so he could keep them from seeding if they even grew at all. Experience told him he could get these to grow with ease, but he never did manage to get them to flower well enough to consume. This time would be different, except he did wonder if he should just let them seed and build out his supply that way first. But he didn't fully trust the sun. It was a violent star that might burn his crop outside if he blinked. He trusted his greenhouse with the early fall crop and another experiment with cannabis since he did decide to let the outdoor plants seed. He also trusted it with all the fruit trees he re-potted to give them over to growth instead of only survival. It was a lot of effort that dissuaded him from plowing more fields since he had not even managed to fill what he already had done and was out of ideas for more uses.

The conceptual wall led him back to the other pillar of his farm life. What animals could he reasonably

expect to move into pens for use? Horses and cattle
were clearly out, which pretty much excluded the bulk
of what the area was known for. All in El Paso up to
around Albuquerque was erased. Even if he found small
herds of boutique livestock wandering, there was no
real purpose. Still, he contemplated driving back up
to do more exploration in the Northern valley to see
if he might run across survivors that might inspire a
plan. This only meant more work with less assurance
of success than what he was already doing. No matter
what, he always ran back to the reality that he would
never slaughter anything in his care, whether sensical
or not.

The bees he saw fly around did not escape interest.
These were a resilient species that implied an ever-
lasting supply of calories if nurtured properly. After following them around for a day, he discovered
their hives within rows of white boxes on a nearby
farm. Honey was never in short supply in the groceries, but fresh honeycomb was something rare, and he
managed to pull one out to eat in one sitting beneath
the canopy of an orchard just beyond the anger zone.
All the stickiness filled him and made his body over-
heat with honey fever, so he couldn't sleep that
night. There were no regrets. The honeycomb was a
new necessity, and he spent the next few days planting
every kind of flower he thought would survive. From
seeds to bulbs, he lined the hives with ammunition but
decided not to disturb them very often.

Not far from there was an empty chicken coop that had
been raided by some animals long before he came, and
the bleaching bones of its residents were scattered
around outside. Again he dreamed of eggs. Again.
Everything loved to eat chickens, which left him with
no pathway to find any survivors. The closest he came
was at a horse arena up near the mesas where he heard
the signature clucking last year. As stupid as chickens appear to be, they are incredibly difficult to
outsmart when they are set on a path of independence.
If they survived the first year, surely they survived

the second, and he might win over the match and catch some.

Back at the arena, it was the same as before. Their sounds dripped in from somewhere just out of sight and disappeared whenever he got serious about finding a source. It was mostly the chattering peeps from chicks that helped convince him he did not fabricate the memory. As best he could tell, they were not on the arena property, which itself fed directly onto the river and was adjacent to innumerable hiding places. They did seem to be out on the river banks where they could probably see him come through the fence and gave them more than enough warning to go quiet. It went on like this all day. It was time to change approaches. Instead of visiting the arena again the next day, he went directly to the bank across the river where he could survey without notice. It was not immediately successful either. He sat in the sun for hours, scanned with binoculars learning to dismiss wild birds which momentarily excited before immediately disappointing. After a while, however, he saw the chicks spill out from a scrapyard at the back of the arena. They would dart under the fence then climb back in, repeatedly. A few times he felt like he caught sight of fat white and gray bodies through the slats, but these were too fleeting. The scrapyard was the perfect place to protect them. They could hide in so many crevices or climb up to roost out of reach of agile gray foxes. They would be difficult to trap.

What he needed was to explore the scrapyard to see if he could pin down where they favored inside. He went across right away to at least take a look at the ground to know what area had the most scratches or the acrid smell of chicken shit. At the back near the fence where he saw them, he found the remains of a sack of grass seed torn open to let its contents pour out, which had then grown into a wild mat of grass that must have sustained fat ghosts. There was not much there, but it did look healthy enough for a dozen or more adults. There was no trace of any. Nor was there any when he returned the next morning, careful to be silent as he approached. It would take planning to isolate them from their castle.

Rather than try to lay a trap inside the scrapyard, he thought it would be easier if he got them into the open out on the river bank. He went to the outside of the fence where the chicks explored and scattered high calorie feed all around for them to find. Then left. This was not a plan to bear out in a day. He waited several, so they would grow accustomed to the food out on the bank and would begin to linger further away from the fence line. He confirmed this on a check in from the other side where he could see more than ten plump hens and three or four roosters besides the five chicks. Quite a lot. That they were so close at hand made him giddy with the thought of fresh egg.

Next came the switch. Before the sun began to lower, he went back to the scrapyard and made all kinds of noise inside the fence where he knew they crossed. This meant they would have no hope other than to find new roosts for the night outside the metal protection they normally used. He kept up the noise until after dark without any sign they attempted to return home. He waited until it was so dark no ordinary bird would risk moving before he went to retrieve some cameras he set up on the fence and on the other bank. Armed with a video of where they headed at dusk, he was able to nab five of the hens and two rooters, thus ending a nearly two year ordeal. It was not exactly a recipe for genetic diversity, but more than enough to exploit for a few generations.

So much time was spent fussing about small details on the farm that he had little time left to fuss about his new home. There were rows of small sprouts to be examined for signs of too little or too much water, saplings to help grow quickly into trees, and chickens to protect. He already buried fencing around a wide area at the edge of one orchard, so they could roam in both shade and sun. Rather than move an old coop, he built a new one inside a second fenced area with a wire roof that gave it more semblance to a cage. They appreciated all this as they fattened up, later joined by more and more of their original flock.

After the initial phase where he installed everything living to its place, he tried to devote more time to his own installation. The house he found needed repairs. These were for families of farmhands who needed to be close to their work and often spent more time fussing about what was utility for others than what was utility for themselves. He made what effort he could at a livable space with his own mark. It was barely passable. After long days outside in the sun, he felt there was so much concession to be made in his home that even the old laundry was still around, just shoved to a far corner. There was water but no electricity. It was little more than a better insulated version of his work area with fewer spiders or dust.

July came on without much interest, and he didn't even make an effort to mark the passing of the second anniversary of the evaporation. By the end of the month, he was nearly burned out with work. The heat was intense and his only escape was to douse himself in water to air dry in the wind. The night of honey heat reminded him the pleasures of air conditioning still existed in the world; its absence is what made this summer unique. His RV remained in its sanctuary, but he recalled a better model parked in a hangar not far from his farm.

Then there it was. The house attached to the hangar still echoed his comfortable home in Ashburn before the end of electricity launched him into a weird life. Next to the RV was the same failed flying experiment that killed him several dozen times. The RV was sluggish at first, having been idle for so long, but he managed to resurrect it with ease and drove it back to the greenhouse. It was cool and familiar inside. It was a plug and play existence with plumbing and electricity all installed by skilled hands. The sudden change was so great he wound up spending whole days inside and the idleness let his mind saturate with self-pity. These days were the same as before with hours of rerun shows he binged without paying much attention. There was so much tea laced with cannabis tincture that he was suspended above the sofa. During each of the episode credits, he felt lonely. Each time the story serial ended and the next began, all he could do was think about what little he was actually doing. He was a loser getting high watching TV. Then the opening credits began and sucked him back into another hour-long distraction. It repeated. Whatever cliffhanger built and dropped in dramatic flash of names with titles over music.

He exited the trance and resumed thoughts about how long he could continue; wondering why he should even bother with farming when he himself might not outlast the expiration date on the world's supply of canned goods. If he managed to fully transition to a farm life with fresh food, he wasn't sure the work would ever taper off. He might be stuck in a hellscape where every day was as hard as the previous one with no future generation coming to his rescue. Then the fever broke when he noticed some rain outside and was able to climb down from the RV to check it out. His new family had gone off somewhere cool as he floated around to inspect his greenhouse and healthy rows of crops.

His chickens still hadn't begun to lay eggs in their coop, but they were lively with no sign they regretted their capture. Here and there was evidence that something tried to dig under the fence but gave up since he buried wire mesh two feet down and more two feet out from there. They were safe, so he wandered through the canopy to wonder when he could begin eating fresh pecans, since all the nuts he took from stores tasted uniformly stale.

The ground was sticky mud and seemed too wet for the orchard to be content. He spent so much time focused on the plotted land that he neglected the wet and dry needs of all the established trees he would have no hope of reviving if lost. The task completely ended the RV trance as he worked for the next few days to close off irrigation canals constantly filling the orchards all around him. Yes, there was adaptation through which the trees needed to pass, but that was for other parts of the valley, not his own feed store. His orchards needed human intervention to prevent them from exploring evolution.

What he found was that not all the fields had been consistently flooded. The patch where his chickens roamed had stayed dry, which he merely accepted without thinking, but there were dry patches in almost every orchard. The trees there were shorter and less full than in other parts. It seemed like the canals had become clogged without regular maintenance and this led to a decreased flow of water into the fields. Nearly all the edges at the far end from where the outflow channels there would be dry. All the orchard fields fit this pattern because all the canals were full of slow water that carried silt to each. It was less that the canals themselves were clogged, but rather the small alluvial fans into the orchards slowed everything down once inside. Worse still was the fact that most of the orchards had outflows only on one side, since canals were interrupted by paved roads and any disruption to the absolute flatness of the orchard meant water would not reach it all evenly. He thought about what would be needed to cut into the asphalt to open new outflows. There were certainly huge saws somewhere in the city designed for this, but somewhere meant lots of effort to search.

Instead, he cut outlets into the canals wherever he could without the need for more innovation. He also dredged the alluvium and cut channels to extend the outflows across to the far sides wherever he couldn't. Easy enough. This was not especially challenging work, which meant it could be repeated seasonally. It only took a few days to accomplish once he noticed the problem. He could plan out the water channels during the winter when the orchards were dormant and the canals flowed less. Easy. But that was a small corner of his three thousand acres which were in turn a small corner of the valley. The scale of work reminded him of when he confronted the scale of human loss the evaporation exacted, after he spent weeks invading homes to memorialize what he realized was such a small percentage of humans who disappeared.

The tipping point for the rest of the valley was close. Trees in the flooded sections would die. Trees in the dry sections would die. A band of trees in the middle would survive and learn how to encroach on the margins over time. It was already underway. The thought was an old one. Every problem for survival was now solely his to solve. Everything demanded his direct involvement, his direct attention to have any impact whatsoever. It wasn't merely a question of outsized expectations or feeling unsettled with his surroundings. Whenever he disappeared from the world for any time, he came back to find changes that implied desperation. He was tired of walking. What he wanted was for someone to drive him around again. Some semi-automated process could let him maintain his work without the constant investment of effort required over the last two years. Under the weight of worry, all he could plan for was a few months ahead. There was little beyond the immediate that was conceptually visible, which kept him in a continual state of the short-term.

Just looking at the problem of water canal maintenance, he wondered if it was even worth the trouble when the river would eventually overflow and wipe the entire area away. It made sense only in terms of the weeks or months ahead. That was all. Everything was reaching a similar crossroads. Food stock in all the stores was little by little becoming inedible, either from decay or poor taste. Even his trouble with starting the new RV was a sign of inoperability of all the machines he'd learned to use and all the equipment with dedicate circuitry would follow. All his batteries and screens would disappear some day soon. This too was an old thought. He had it from the start of his solitary journey. It was the mark of a human to persist in sublime recapitulation even as nothing was done to explore any solutions.

In each iteration of the dream, he ended his life as an old man surrounded by no technology. The faded civilization would slowly burn itself out some time over his years of observation. He might find occasional battery that still worked, but by then he would have shirked the need for one. That is, if he even survived to that point. He already had so many near misses and avoided injury, except for his shoulder, but this could never last. No immunity could prop him up against the reality of his surroundings, particularly the invisible grind of daily hardships eroding his life expectancy with each passing moment. Teeth would never be repaired and would crumble. Diseases and infection could not be treated. Everything worked against him. He would have to face it all if he were to reach the end in a cave lit by fire. Or he might end it all early by his own hand. He thought about this often. A reset button was always available and might one day become the best option. That was a remote chance. He was a vibrating operation of biology that viewed the act with horror. He had been programmed like all other life with the need to face every discomfort with a vein of hope that some improvement might follow. All the way to the floor. And it was always an option, so there was no need to rush.

If anything could push all this, it was to stick to his plan for the next few seasons and see where it all landed. This meant a very determined end to his wandering. Construct something of value to preserve him against both the river and its partner mountain. Survival depended on his capacity to reconfigure the remnants of civilization into its durable elements somehow tied to land. The irony never escaped him that he was the essence of free from all things civilized. There were no moral rules to constrain his actions. He could use dangerous chemicals to pollute everything he touched and could still observe the reversal of civilization's degradation of the landscape. Nothing bound him other than his own thoughts. All social duties evaporated along with morals. He owed nothing. Nothing was due. He was the freest human. The most libertine animal.

Except he did owe a social debt. None of what he used could be made from his own skill, nor could it be said that what little skill he did possess could be anything other than socially constructed. He was a social animal launched into an asocial life in which the dead still cooperated for his survival. It was true he had deeply disliked humans in his unfree life. They confused him, yet he couldn't avoid so much empathy towards them. He was gullible and exploited before he hardened into cautious compassion. There was so much distrust that could never be set aside properly because of his role in the cooperative matrix. He depended on others and had his own dependents in turn, even before his family. It was a circle. It was many circles. It was a fluid shape with no dimension. And when they were all gone, and he was the sole side that remained, but he wished at least a living triangle remained. The dead were insufficient participants, even with all their handy materials left behind.

This reminded him of the lunatics in the final days who presented with the condition of toxic freedom. He lived what they preached and still never met their definition of liberty. He was the sole survivor on the planet living the life of a sovereign whose survival was met by his own hands. Not one before him had this claim. Every one of them lived in a condition of social cooperation that actively handed them the benefits of everything the collective whole could achieve together. They took this and feigned independence only to be laced with the privilege of abundance. He lived it and knew survival demanded cooperation to provide him with comforts beyond grazing for food in some forest. He tried this, too. It still required him to use tools that science mastered over millennia, even the solutions in his mind were of this sort. No one had been an animal chasing knowledge of first impression since long before humans were humans. None escaped it. Least of all those who longed for magic license plates to immunize them. It was all a fluid matrix bled across generations. Not even a family itself was enough to effect the separation from the whole. Any that tried, any that fully escaped from everyone else would have collapsed under the shock of sudden tragedy or genetic devaluation as they mutated into something horrendous and unhuman. No, humans needed community and communities needed more communities to survive, if survival was to be generational. His was not. He was free even from this definition nearly no longer human.

He knew all this because it always found its way into his mind, repeating itself in variation. Always the same recognition that he depended on what was left behind for him. It was there when he parked row after row of water trucks outside his tidy home in Georgetown. It was deep underground in his garage yurt as he slept on handmade carpets. It even came to him at his desert palace where his dependence stretched far across the centuries. He could have made none of it. Just the effort it took to plow and sow a few acres nearly ended his interest in survival. It crushed him in the face of relentless effort without end.

He was not free. Freedom rode on the back of dependence, while he was trapped in the confines of individual effort dreaming about the past, when he only needed to perform his narrow duties to take in so much benefit. Those duties were all assigned value and distributed according to an unfair formula where his assignment was near the middle of an exponential upslope meaning he did less work for more value than those below. It was all orchestrated by a fiction that had moments of truth when it called for supply to meet demand, but manipulated them both egregiously. That fiction had ended its influence so only his demand was left seeking out supply everywhere for him to absorb in his own time.

The past two years could be summarized as his process of adjusted needs according to whatever was on hand. If it was unavailable, it was unwanted. Only humans were exempt from that operation. It was the purest economy. There could be no manipulation because any attempt would have simply been a change in the basic variables themselves. It was as it should have always been. No social engineering or information asymmetries prevented him from needing what was available. There were no creams to artificially rise on the myth of their own indispensability. He had seen their homes a hundred thirty floors over New York and knew they were as irrelevant in the afterworld as when they sold the world. From up there he confirmed there was no shooting star. Up there they used rolls of thin paper next to toilets, assembled by skilled hands aplenty down in the streets. There were no shooting stars, but there were carpets of dim dots across the sky that never moved from their fixed assignments. They were so effective, they still cared for him. He depended on the carpet which made his time alone less unfree. They were the other community reaching out to him; they evaporated then left his needs intact. It was never the vision of those who spent their privilege to create more for themselves that he saw left behind. Those evaporated into nothing. He needed community and a dead one was adequate for the moment.

That day when he spent so much time repairing the irrigation system in his orchards was especially hot. Summer had entered its peak and brought with it temperatures more suitable for cooking than for outside work. It never burned at once. It took time for the day to reach the highest numbers and even more time to notice. In the end, he walked into the RV more exhausted than the effort implied and saw the deep red skin that explained it all. Very deep. Already the top layer gave up and peeled away. It was the type of burn to ache for days and leave him sleepless at night. The shower burned more, so he left with clean skin to visit the pharmacy for its selection of solutions. Every label promised something wonderful the expired contents called into question. He had no choice but to use them. All the choices were some variation on aloe, and he used them all. One layer at a time, he applied a thick coat of creams that made him feel like he was encased in plastic.

His wife reminded him of his needs now and advised him to never forget his SPF protection again while he worked outside. The trouble was all the sunscreen had expired into a clumpy oil that might have worked but was so unappealing he left the test bottles on the floor. It was more sustainable to do what farmers he used to know did; covered himself from head to toe in cloth. A large sun hat covered a child's shirt he pulled over his head and peeped through the neck. Long sleeves and legs took care of the rest with gloves at the tips. It was a familiar sight and it worked. It was also just in time because his fields were now beginning to mature and needed more attention. The fertile soil housed old weeds waiting for the growing season. He could easily have dumped gallons of herbicides but instead chose to manually trim them all out rather than take the shortcut.

It took hours to remove everything only for them to return a few days later. It was almost as if by the time he reached the last of the planted rows, he would need to restart at the beginning. His sunburn healed under his layers of clothing, but breathing was difficult inside the veil. Days were then split between early morning and early evening, with the long hours of intense sun devoted to leisure within the air conditioner. The first shift was easy enough. He could roll out of bed and sip tea as the temperature climbed. But it was exceedingly difficult to pull himself away from the RV after the five o'clock peak. The more days of repetition, the harder it was to motivate himself. What exactly was the trick he used as a child when the heat was not an entity? Surely he was more resilient then. Or less perceptive. Either would be a welcomed. Not even THC helped him reclaim that mindset now. He recalled all the farmers who would drink rice whiskey early in the morning to help mute the hours of labor ahead and winced at the thought of dehydrated nausea on top of the hot air under the shirt.

So it was that he let himself focus more on the greenhouse where he didn't need all the stifling sun protection but was instead absorbed in the suffocating humid air which refused to move. The outside temperatures were nearly up to forty-seven and everything crackled while the inside felt wetter and hotter. These were days with mornings close to the burning soil until it became unbearable, which signaled the need to move indoors to what was still a cool bit of shade before it inched up to a sauna by late afternoon. He didn't notice change as it happened. He was already used to feeling hot from his time outside, so the drips of sweat had no more meaning. So it was on the hottest day that he faded from the greenhouse.

He woke up some time later with a headache and an intense thirst that made him nauseous. It was confusion. He only remembered hauling in some large ceramic pots from outside, placing them in the far corner of the greenhouse then came the sparks of red against black velvet. It felt like sleep his body rushed to meet. It took a few moments from when he first reopened his eye to see the wall of gravel to the left before he understood he was on the ground, and then a few moments more before he could sit up to meet nausea. More time again and he was able to drag himself over to the hotbox RV and switch on the air conditioner. He did not sleep again. Everything was headache and thirst. And lethargy. It drained him of energy for the next day, and he spent it completely inside with cold electrolytes and TV. It was a close call that should have been obvious. It was the dead of the hot season in the desert, and he should have known better than to rush through his preparations for the future. There was no looming freeze like in Washington; no zero hour beyond which he would face insurmountable hardship if he failed to act. He was in the middle of the desert's flavor of dangerous weather, and he underestimated it. The bare minimum of effort was the most sensible way to continue. Keep it all alive without wiping out the work he did so far and then go back to full time farming once the heatwave ended. That was the plan. It wasn't a change, it was a momentary adaptation with the benefit of feeling like a holiday. It put him back inside his capsule home he drove over to park under the shade of his chicken orchard. He watched them pant in dugouts from his cool window where he sipped frozen cannabis smoothies. It was so cold inside that he bundled up in light blankets with nothing to do. He eventually remembered how he survived the heat as a child: swimming pools. On one of his bored evenings, he went out to inspect a pool in the community not far away, but it had a thick layer of caked mud that would have taken far too much energy to clean out.

There was nothing left to do but retreat back to the confines of the capsule and wait. More of the same. No matter the distance he traveled in the afterworld, he always fell back to his origins of sitting in a small living room with little difference. It was depressingly ordinary. In Georgetown, in Ashburn, in his nest, here in the chicken orchard, all he did was fall into the vast storyboards of video games already redundant. Most of the time it was just a THC-laced walk through digital mountains watching the artificial sun rise behind them.

As boring and repetitive as this was, it absorbed him for hours. Days, in some cases. He might disappear as always just focused on the tense movement of the character driven by his hand and lacked any will of its own. He pushed it into scenarios it hated only to gratify himself and pass the time. It was easier than his work outside in the heat, so it took priority even when it was such a poor replacement in his own mind.

Ultimately it was the absurdity of the scenario where he spent an entire evening and deep into the night planting a cartoon garden other players could visit if they were so inclined. He watched the fake tomatoes ripen red on the vine as he waited for the accelerated day to pass. A break to urinate gave him the chance to come back and see his garden on screen and his stupidity blindsided him even as high as he was. What the actual fuck was he trying to accomplish? He spent hours harvesting tomatoes into a box he set aside. His real tomatoes were themselves ripening outside not far away, was all this just practice, to kill time? He shut it down without saving. No visitors were interested in whatever perfection he reached on that island, so there was nothing to preserve. Without the hypnotic hum of the console, he was left lonely in a cramped dark room that needed to be cleaned, and he could only think through his options. It was always the same, even in Washington where he began his farm under the obelisk and gave up when some sheep broke in to eat all the green shoots. He never even bothered to visit all the fruit orchards surrounding the city as it seemed like too much work even then. Now, he put so much into the setup and was ready to give up when the hard part of waiting was all that remained.

It was time to take a hard look at the options he set for himself in El Paso. For the moment, he was stuck between the highly uncomfortable world outside and the mind-numbing boredom inside. Outside was full of movement and projects demanding an expansive stretch of effort he could somehow believe was building towards something to last. These extremes needed to be flattened as soon as possible or else he would be ripped apart chasing them both. Back to dreams of enclosed agriculture; sterilized wilderness. There were several options, but they all involved more work. Until then, he lived in the most comfortable place he could imagine. The small well-decorated RV provided more of modern life than did either his ranch or hangar mansions, even if it required him to purge his feces every few days. He knew he wasn't leaving, so whatever he did next it would require a mental leap to pry him into the world outside. When he emerged to inspect his neglect, he learned his days of waste had very little impact on anything. All the effort had indeed paid dividends as his farm was mostly caring for itself at that point. Even all the weeds which grew among his vegetables were now pushed aside by the mature crops and no longer threatened them with a hostile invasion.

It seemed the time finally came for him to move on to actually find a way to give life to his dreamed

biodome. It came as both a relief and daunting crisis
to know there was still more work to be done and nothing stood in the way. But instead of taking it up immediately, he let himself embellish the interlude ushered in by the quiet and stable farm.

In his mind he saw a huge ecosystem with carpets of
green grass and rows of flowers between mature trees
whose canopy barely obscured the stars on the other
side of the roof. It would have to have flowing wa-
terfalls and a carefully balanced number of insects.
It would be a cartoon, of sorts; a work of art he controlled through immunity from weather. It would be
the luxury of lush Washington without leaving his
home, where he could choose to step outside and instantly transport to a harsh desert. He couldn't
build this and had no taste for exploration to turn up
what was already out there. Shopping for the right
structure for a retrofit was something he'd long begun
doing, even before he left Washington, perhaps even
before the evaporation itself. He knew there were few
options in El Paso and of them the pink mall was so
far the best.

Yet it was not a full cartoon as he hoped. The light
came in aplenty, but it was not the same as a domed
bubble that might let him feel as if he lived inside a
terrarium. It would be an atrium at best. A hybrid
garden and cityscape. Not that this was unwanted.
There were benefits to the strong walls of a proven
structure in the harsh wind that might otherwise rip
apart a terrarium bubble, leaving his cartoon fantasy
vulnerable to the sun and sand. But he wondered if he
was too rushed. Wherever he chose would involve a
massive amount of labor before even the first green
leaf was brought in. It might be better to break it
all out into smaller moves, or even isolate exactly
what factors he needed to satisfy, just as he did for
his winter ship in Washington. What if all he needed
to do was retrofit his greenhouses and never force a
relocation at all? It had everything he would need
already. He could tinker with the details over time
without disrupting his life. There were six of them

at this location, another dozen not far down the road. He could spend his time connecting them together to create a complex offering within each. But the lack of insulation would mean he'd have to build some living space where he could beat back the heat and cold, essentially offering little to no change from his current life in the RV.

But the idea of a second home inside the ecosystem was interesting. He desperately missed the teak houses where he lived in Asia, ones that sat on stilts and opened to paddy fields. It was not the RV itself, but it was such a sealed capsule that separated him from the smells outside he hated. The greenhouses might be large enough for this, but those homes in his memory would never match with the wide temperature fluctuation inside. He needed something insulated but with walls so far away he'd never notice. The pink mall fit all this, if only there was more light inside. With what it offered, he could definitely grow his grass and trees, but it would never cross over to the idyllic utopia he thought it should be. So he needed to spend more effort to retrofit his dream itself; adapt to the market of what was available. Ignore perfection and move on. So it was settled.

Still, water was a challenge. Even the available plumbing inside would never have accommodated the transition he meant to achieve. Without taps, though, he would need to look further afield to source the massive amount of water that would likely be needed to make a tropical garden in the desert. How far down the line of imperfection should he go? The greenhouses were sitting right there, flush with water. There were wells everywhere and the river was so close it was a threat. The river ran near the mall too, but the difference in elevation made for a problem in channeling it even if it solved the threat. It meant pumps. Large ones. It meant powerful pumps to push huge volumes of murky water up a walled hill almost a mile away. It meant diesel with loud clatter and darting back and forth to check lines for clogs. It was everything he hated about his winter ship.

Everything was nearly settled by default. There were no options in his mind that would enable to him to begin work right away without first going through a series of dangerous constructions as would be the case with the sport stadia he briefly imagined. But he was skeptical. The last time he inspected was rushed, and he was aware he now filled in gaps from memory that may have long since lost significance in reality. Were there indeed still glass bridges over indoor ponds or did the glass really let in so much light? He needed a second more intentional examination to check all the details, as boring and tedious as that might be.

As he climbed into his truck for the first time in what seemed like months, and it dawned on him how long he stayed at or around the farm and was preparing to leave it behind. If everything went well, though, he would not be far away. The orchards and crops would still need his attention from time to time, so there was no abandonment. The drive into the city still felt odd, more so than his reentry after decades even if it was more unchanged than before. Before driving up into the parking lot, he swung around the roads along the river to build a memory on which he could plan his water network. It was as he imagined: hoses would need to be routed up a high wall to reach the mall. The inside was thankfully also as he imagined with little significant change. Most important was the amount of light that reached inside. The upper level was brighter than many gardens he knew, and the lower levels were also moderately well lit. And the heat never penetrated inside. The oven was held off by deep walls and floated up to the ceiling high above so what remained was a cool open space.

This dead mall was the most thrilling shopping trip he'd taken to date. Every corner was an opportunity once the shops could be erased. The whole structure was a simple two wings meeting at a right angle, where there was a food court with multiple terraces on the second level and an event center below. Overhead was a massive ceiling of heavy canvas that let in so much light, it sustained many towering palm trees. The wings had long glass skylights over their entire lengths with more event spaces halfway down. It was a structure designed as a sanctuary from the heat. If he concentrated his effort, he could have the central area fully planted within a matter of weeks. That area alone was larger than the three greenhouses where he had trees and sprouts at the ready, so it was a reasonable starting place. He could live on the top level and the lower could become a flooded swamp to would make the whole space a humid chamber. If he pumped enough water in, then this might put off the need for frequent refills over time. There were already ponds and fountain, so he could also create concrete lips to keep it all from spreading into shops and any hidden drains. First, though, he should clear the whole mall and be done with the erasure at the outset rather than let it wear on him after he moved in. This would not be difficult since most of the shops were already low on inventory, given the size of their floor space.

A quick walk through of the shops confirmed to him there was not much of value left, meaning he could simply cart it all away without too much time spent to sort through garbage. A few weeks. His dream was close at hand. Back outside, he tried to visualize the water line from the river up to the parking lot and over to the doors. Except for resurrecting the river itself, he had not attempted any water transfer this ambitious and was unsure if what he imagined for a solution would even work. The river was not an impossible distance away. He could easily find miles of hoses to reach even to the top of the mountain if he so desired. This would need a fraction of this, but the elevation difference was a problem. He already knew from his winter ship that he'd have better luck with small hoses to ensure better efficiency and less frustration. As before, there would need to be catchment stations along the way to space out the points of failure in the pump line. This would not be small tubs in gallons appropriate for personal use. He would need to be measuring in tens of thousands of gallons just to meet the minimum threshold to keep his mall tropical.

He stood there at the edge of the wall planning it all and felt the weariness before the work ever began. Another mania, this time it would take the flavor of terraforming the interior of around one hundred thousand square feet of a desert mall, not just a fifteen-story office building habitat for the winter. They were categorically different grades of effort on which he no longer had any choice but to embark. Years of dreams brought him to this point, and he was barely sure it would be worthwhile, or he would have enough inside him to bring it to completion. He backed away from the wall and knew the next few weeks would be spent inside a trance that would begin with a search for equipment. Small vehicles were all that could make it inside the mall without decimating the interior, let alone whichever entry he chose to use. Unlike the last mania, he would need to actually remove everything inside, rather than just shove it to some forgettable corner. The shops were bare enough, but not in absolute terms; he would need heavy carts to haul out debris.

What he brought was a small bobcat with its cage cut off to make it short enough to fit through the loading docks on each level he ripped apart, thinking he could just reseal them more easily than the glass customer entrances. These would let him crash through whatever installations needed destruction and small handheld forklifts would help him haul out everything else. This would be no shopping event. He would be aggressively reckless about the transforming the interior into an empty canvas on which he could paint his cartoon vision. He would drive piles of rubble across walkways where he once dreamt of Christmas toys and first love's gifts. In his trance, these memories surfaced as incidental bumps of recognition for this or that familiar angle of light. Before it was this, there was enough shopping to sweep through the rot and find whatever might be of interest to him. Not everything in a dead mall is garbage; some could be salvaged when price disappeared. He went through each store dropping items into a bin on his forklift before he moved on to the next. Some stores were interesting enough to survive entirely and were left intact for a future where he could sort through them with more care. The trance could not yet accommodate the distraction. Nor was there reason to overstock for his time inside. He needed space, not storage. There were other malls. And he was eager to find the right space where he could install his yurt again, or at least a reprised version of it where he could again be transported to a paisley world of comfort.

The first stage of the trance was quick. His recklessness was convenient and led him through the mall within days. There were few discoveries inside since so few human stories played out there, in the final moments of civilization. It was all lifeless retail now mounded outside on the asphalt. It was time to reverse course and move himself in. So he made more mounds closer to the doors. Huge dunes of fermented cow shit sat adjacent to huge dunes of fertile soil brought in from fallow farms. It would be a start. Palates of potting soil from the greenhouse and hardware stores were driven inside, where he thought he might plant actual crops, not just grass. The palates were easy to drive inside. The dunes were easy enough to deposit outside, but he only saw a painful process of moving them in through hundreds of small trailer loads. They would need to be mixed eventually. This meant more engagement.

He needed rest ten days after he began. He already needed to escape the mundane sights of the mall that was as yet still untransformed. All the soreness and movement made the small space of his RV less suffocating as he regrouped inside. Surely it was time to visit his trio again and begin the move away from their only home. He went to them.

They received him with the same lukewarm recognition as always but were suspicious of his effort to put them back into their cages they had left two years be-

fore.   Where they spent years confined.   But they
trusted him, somewhat.   The actual move was uneventful.   They all simply drove back together discussing
their new lives.   They drove straight to the mall, to
the food court where the garden would be fullest.   He
let them out, but the birds were intimidated by the
suddenness of size and stayed in their cages.   He let
them find their way.   The oldest eventually became curious enough to stand in the door making furtive efforts at flight before finally catching the air properly.   She flew noisily, but not far.   It was real effort, and she was exhausted after twenty meters.   They
were all home.

III
Myth

The set-up in the food court was a huge space of terraces and glass panels overlooking a courtyard below.
Aside from the rows of vacant food stalls, only some
of which had been stocked for the 4th of July weekend,
it really had the feel of a small nook lodged inside a
tight town through which the trio were not partial to
flying. Their heavy bodies kept them close to their
cages around a tall tower of perches adhered to a dead
tree branch anchored vertically. Whenever they attempted to land on the rails overlooking the lower
level, their small feet slipped, unable to grasp the
broad metal bar and had to fly back to their tower.
On occasion, they followed him as he walked through
the rest of the mall, but made their complaints quite
clear. Food court it was. It would be their home
from which all journeys inside the mall began. There
he would begin his effort, only expanding out to the
rest of the space as a hobby. Its terraces were staggered and fanned out with huge planters to divide
them. These were deep and would accommodate fruit
trees with little modification. Here would begin as
plots for his crops with only one dedicated to living
space for himself.

The avenues where people had previously shuffled to
select between greasy overpriced meals would become
grassy meadows until something better came to mind.
In fact, everything not clearly suggestive of a purpose would become grassland. To achieve this, everything except for living space would need soil. Shops
themselves were too dark for immediate use and would
be spared with inundation for the moment, but he felt
this tremendous amount of wasted space should be put
to use at some point soon. The best he could come up
with was to install his equipment, tools, and bags of
soil until he managed to put together indoor grow

lights.   And there was an abundance of equipment needed to be kept out of the way.

The mall had one other appealing area besides the food court.   One of the wings had another huge courtyard overlooked by four glass enclosures which were themselves perfect interior greenhouses he could over-humidify to create tropical sanctuaries.   Overhead were long rows of skylights that made it almost more lit than the food court, and certainly more lit than the other courtyard in either wing.   Later, once he managed to find tropical plants, he could keep them alive in these small homes.   It was a distant dream nonetheless real even before the first carts of soil were brought inside.   While he rested, before he began, he wandered through the mall lost somewhere between memory and planning until the memories began to merge with his vision and he could see himself as a child who walked through the meadows on the upper level and small forests below.   It was as if he knew then, those years before, this was the ultimate fate for him and the mall alike.   To accomplish this would be a years long endeavor he knew would be foolish to rush over the course of a few weeks.   The soil deposits for the wing would need more than a hundred fifty trucks, which said nothing about the effort to bring it all inside and spread it about.   If he was to avoid burnout, all this would have to be done in spurts whenever he could build up a new mania.

All he could do for the immediate one was to plan for pumping in water to coat the entire lower level and bring only enough soil for his home area.   If he overcompensated for this at the outset, he could spread out in small stages whenever boredom set in, without eroding the fine finish on the terrace gardens; there were plenty of recesses for him to store the soil at the edge.   What he worried about more was how to keep the water from seeping out of the central hallway. There were more than enough areas for catchment pools in the fountains and planters, and the soil would hold plenty once it was spread out, but he wanted a swamp. His first focus was to make a small concrete berm along the outside edge of the lower level, only a few inches tall and sloppy throughout.

It was finally time to engage his dunes outside, which only partly blew away in the weeks before he was ready to move them in. They were disaggregated for use as topsoil. He knew all along that it would be necessary to merge them at the proper ratio, but he couldn't decide if this should be done outside, before he ever loaded the carts, partially as he loaded them, or even to wait until everything was inside where he could chop and mix as he spread it all out. He tried the first and discovered how difficult the clumpy farm soil was to mix using his front loader, so he wound up only pouring loads of manure over large mud clods already dried into brittle stone. It would be a waste of time to try to mix them outside and would be back-breakingly slow to mix inside. This was on top of the slowness of the small carts he used because they could fit through the glass entrance which led directly to the food court. If he tried to use the larger loading doors, he would spend more time driving around than he would by multiplying the loads there.

What he needed was a better way. All this was not quite a surprise to him when he actually began to move the soil in; he saw the clumps of wet clay dry in the sun several weeks before and knew they would be a challenge. He knew moving thousands of cubic meters of soil in a chain of small carts attached to a small retail tractor would be slow. He explored using a conveyor belt, but none would fit, so he tested a heavy wood chipper to shoot the soil through the doors. He had several on hand and a makeshift chute to get the projectiles past the delicate glass. It would chop and mix so all he would have to do would be to spread out the piles formed inside. That he did. In went the mixture, along with stones that fired out the other side to crash and destroy tiles as well as the first of the chippers before he learned to efficiently crush and sift the soil before loading it in. Still, the buildup clogged the chute, and he would have to shut everything down to go inside and drag out the loose mixture. Eventually there was progress. At the end of a few hours, he had many large piles inside the mall that he could begin to spread around with his bobcat. Compared to the work outside, this was very straightforward and easy. It was point and shoot. By the end of the first day, he already had two terraces loaded and one strip of the meadow smoothed out.

His trio watched all this with interest from the safety of the other side of the mall where he put them back in their cages. The best way was to move them to safety while he created toxic diesel emissions in the enclosed space. They would have no ability to understand what he ultimately would do, but they enjoyed the loud sounds as they echoed off the tiles, even from that distance.

He cleared one and a half truckloads that first day and finished the other seven before the week was over. One more chipper gave out in the process, but it was worth it. He managed to transform the shopping mall into the early stages of his biodome. The rest of the interior still remained its former self, but his home was something totally new, something not imagined of since the architects first daydreamed about the concept. He managed to spread out a foot of topsoil on every bit of the terraces, walkways, and even the area immediately below. The whole inside smelled of manure and diesel, so much that he moved the trio to an atrium in one of the anchor stores at the farthest end of one wing after he experienced a slight drunkenness from the exhaust fumes. But the achievement impressed. It was a layer of defecation and dirt across a public space that only made sense to him in his present condition, but it was marvelous. But there was so much more to be done before the whole structure could be said to be fully terraformed. This was the first step in the transformation, only a fraction of the whole. In absolute terms, it was nearly more space than he used at his farm and greenhouses and, if he was right, it would be a green sanctuary once the plants took hold, not far into the future.

Before that, was water. To get started, he filled a truck several times at the river to help saturate the first layer of soil once it was all spread out. It was a lazy start that left his entire work area a muddy mess, impossible to cross. Despite the amount of time it took, he persisted with this alternative rather than setting up the hoses and pumps directly to the river. Trip after trip, he shuttled between the river and the biodome until he was sure there was a pool of water between the tile floor and the foot of soil overlay. It was still pumps and heavy hoses that had to be dragged through to reach dry patches and the ponds at the lower level. It was rest insofar as he needn't think about accidental overfill; any water inside was a critical part of his plan. He wanted to observe how it behaved once free, before he tried to fight the miles of hoses. If there was too much seepage, he would want to be able to see it while there was still time to seal it off, rather than after he began planting. And without the diesel fumes, the trio had returned home to watch him from their tower as he toted huge snakes through a changed land. They understood water. They understood humidity after a lifetime of desert dehydration and their ancient tropical minds were activated as the water had become captured by the air. There was enough ready in the biodome for him to begin the long awaited transfer from his greenhouses. His fruit trees had been brought back to life several months before and already outgrew the larger pots he swapped from the standard retail black ones. Most had become root-bound, which required the change. The relief was uncertain. The solution bare-bones. Those which survived were thankful, but did not expect the second change.

There were so many that he realized he needed more planters than were available, unless he wanted to overcrowd them and jeopardize the purpose of the space. The soil array was too shallow to simply plant rows of small trees. It would mean modification to the meadowland. There was already more than enough extra soil mixture stored at the edge of the food court on both levels, so he made dozens of large three-foot mounds down the rows. The column of trees would only add to the aesthetic once they took root and would hide the blighted food stalls he had no intention of covering up. All he would need to do was wait. In went the peaches, apples, plums, and all the rest that didn't dry out before he found them. The date palms went into the planters between the terraces, so they could tower overhead without creating too much canopy to destroy his vegetable garden. The terrace gardens needed what filtered sun came through the skylights if they were to stay on schedule. Every plot had its purpose. They needed their own small mounds laid out in lines from one end to the next to keep their roots from spreading unnecessarily. He moved whatever hadn't begun to flower by that point and left everything else to finish what they started in the raw farm. Winter sprouts were sent to the cool dim lower level, and soon the greenhouses were empty.

Between the tree mounds, all along the walkway, he saturated the soil with grass seed lining one side with millet to fill the corner with a crop to eventually feed his trio even if he failed to do so. They would grow fast. When the plants pushed out their fingerlets, he could teach the birds these were theirs to destroy. They would pull at the bunches of small seeds, dropping them into the soil to sprout a new plant to feed them in turn. It would be a self-perpetuating cycle that would always be a backstop for their survival. He would let his chickens roam free too, but not yet. They would erase the soil of all this before it had a chance to become itself; they would pick at the seeds and small shoots of green grass until there was nothing left. Until then, they were far away where he could shovel up their pungent shit and let it ferment away from him. But his dogs were welcome. They roamed as they always did, patrolling everything and sleeping it off.

His home was at first fresh and looking immaculate before the soil packed down. Before the makeover matured into something either beautiful or horrific, it still looked to him like two images superimposed, and it was unclear which would prevail. The steps were all right. Everything should work out as he imagined it would, but there was so much time needed before it could be confirmed. His dogs had once dug out the manure but learned quickly not to disturb what he'd already spread. By the middle of September, he could see his vision when the grass began to grow, and it was clear that everything had survived the transfers. The image of a living atrium began to take over the image of a dead pink retail mall.

He was still split in two, still unable to completely break from his farm and all the irrigated orchards he fought to save. All summer, the nuts were busy inside their encasements and would soon begin to drop. His cannabis had grown well but flowered weak buds made for pitiful vapor. He decided to let these seed and try again where he could pay closer attention indoors. The rest of the crops were abundantly pleasant. He was pulling ripened melons and tomatoes every day to share with his family back home, where he baked huge loaves of bread in a makeshift brick oven. He hadn't enjoyed so much fresh food since a few weeks after the evaporation when everything in the stores and refrigerators spoiled. He tried several times since then but always abandoned the effort well ahead of any harvest. This alone was an achievement. A sign of change. He had won, not just over the dead mall and desert, but also his own mania. It was time to rest.

The inside had kept its coolness despite the increased humidity, and he was able to set up his woolen yurt in one of the dark stores across from the terraces where he could watch his meadow fill out more and more each day while swinging in a hammock. He could close his eyes and feel the slight movement, listening to the occasional sound of chickens far away and imagine he was in any number of memories instead of the lonely present. Even his trio had left him to his solitude, choosing to stay in the wide open perch tower where they ripped apart trays of freshly cut melon and snap peas.

An intense September rain pounded the roof one afternoon and reminded him it was long overdue that he
sorted out the water supply. His water truck had allowed him to fill the ponds and all the soil was rich
with moisture that did not seem to quickly flow away.
More was needed, especially for when the trees began
to mature. Several days after this realization, he
managed to pull himself away from the hammock to go
back outside to find equipment he avoided rounding up
before. It was all ordinary. Large water pumps the
city used to clear flooded streets pulled the river up
to the first of many portable backyard swimming pools
lining the highway as it led past the river to beyond
the parking lot. Between each was a smaller pump to
feed the next. All the way. Inside one of the anchor
stores were a dozen pools he filled with the now
nearly clear water that mostly shed its murk through
so many stages. He left it all running, spilling over
until the lower level itself overfilled and breached
the tiny concrete lip he built. It rose up and pushed
against the taller berm he built to protect the bowl
where seasonal icons would pose for pictures with
children but now held a fruit orchard. There was no
need to shut anything off; he let it run until the
pumps themselves died, long after he had his swamp.

It was an automated process once the initial work of
placing all the equipment was done, but it did bring
him around to rummage through debris. There was nothing more to do than this. It was no longer in the way
of his vision, making it less hostile as it all sat in
sad heaps. The piles of gold and diamonds were especially strange. In his initial run, he pulled them
out of their display cases and tossed everything into
a bin shoved to corners as he then ripped out the displays. Worthless strings of glitter were all over the
biodome by the time he began moving in soil. He
played with them as the pools filled up; tossed emer-
alds and sapphires into water to watch them shimmer
below a rippling surface.

With all the manual labor over, he felt it was time to
dress for his stature as the world sovereign. A mod-

ern one. There was no shortage of uncomfortable suits and ruffled silk shirts to compliment diamond garlands. He resized a dozen wedding rings to jam on his fingers and he almost thought about piercings but stopped short with the gun in hand. Instead, he pressed the studs into a fedora and made a garish child's costume out of eighty-seven thousand dollars worth of gems. He wandered around shopping like this for days with a lacquered staff he found in a martial arts academy.

What had been the original music store had long ago diversified to become everything media related in a desperate effort to catch any customer it could. There were even vintage laserdiscs and vinyl, but CDs were not yet trendy again to feature much inside. In their place, he found a huge collection of overpriced movies no algorithm pushed into his face. He discovered them the ancient way: he browsed the stacks manually and found old titles he'd nearly forgotten. So far, his media library had been entirely stored on several hard drives and his computer lacked an optical drive. While it was true he never managed to access the computers he found in homes and offices, all the external drives were wide open, and he found everything imaginable stored on them. He spent hours rummaging around and reading personal information as he ripped movies and music. He had seven terabytes of boredom, but it couldn't match the multisensorial thrill of ferreting through the stacks. What he needed was a media system to match. All of this was across the main road in the electronics warehouse. It was time to return to his world of projection. He brought more equipment, better equipment, louder equipment than he had in his quaint Ashburn mansion. It would be magnificently loud inside a dark arcade where he could black out all external light.

He began with the feelgood adventure shows of his youth that brought him to a world of magic and turtles. He watched endlessly with short breaks to ensure the swamp had not slipped out the door. But these movies were few. Soon, on to others. The classics were heavy, designed to punch an audience. Harder to watch. One was a story of solitude in space, trapped with an intelligent machine that disagreed on how to survive. It was cold viewing. The long stretches of scenes without dialogue was too real for the darkness. It made his stomach twist to watch as they maneuvered in slow competition until the human destroyed his only companion.

When it was finally dead he felt empty and turned it off before the psychedelic finale was complete. Unlike the generations of audiences who propelled the movie to fame, he was the only one to feel its message. It brought back his solitude, his lonely isolation in a casement of technology. What if he had such an intelligent companion that never needed his effort to help it survive. A coequal. Enough to match what he saw in the movie. It was on its way. The wait would not have been long enough to make it reality; a few short years and machine intelligence would have run the whole of human society better than humans. Already there had been a wave of job loss. Doom headlines rolled in daily to warn about the coming misery for civilization when the artificial people flexed their suprastate muscles and finally crushed eight billion people with permanent inequality. The select few captains of technology would forever be out of reach to the entire planet, guarded by a wall of innovation that nothing but raw violence could breach. It happened slowly at the end. He saw the mass layoffs paired with record stock buybacks which totally escaped taxation. It rode the lexicon of efficiency and self achievement, but it was a myth that worked. The few who defended it were powerful enough to disregard whole nations, whole populations. And they almost won. Civilization was on the cusp of total digital transformation before everything shut down. Now, the civilization of one could only cobble together what technology was leftover to playact survival.

It was so close that it had begun to dominate ordinary conversation. News banners read out new harms daily. Senate hearings were underway and the European Union was drafting policy which might serve as an international treaty. These were all lagging indicators to prove the era already arrived. His own bank was pushing him to download their new assistant to help monitor his personal finances. Commercials were everywhere for how humans would become obsolete but should throw all their finite wealth after new toys which would ultimately destroy them.

Then came the obvious, so clear it escaped him for two years as he wasted himself on chasing vapor. All these toys were still around. They were everywhere, hidden behind firewalls and encryption. All of this was preserved just as his game data survived the many interludes when he brought the systems offline. Data doesn't die. If the material where it was written was stored properly, it would survive for centuries in wait for an instrument to play the music of its message. But the infrastructure on which it traveled was gone. There was no more interconnectivity between systems for when to search and know where they were stored or even to pull them out of their beds. What if he found one? Perhaps he'd already seen drives holding portions of one intelligence, maybe a reason center or compression operation, and didn't know. He was ill-equipped for understanding all this. He would need a translator. Where? Every time he attempted to cross beyond his technical abilities to touch a new world, he failed. He failed to understand the power grid, he failed to understand an airplane, he even failed to find a better solution that would restore the river valley without destroying the valuable power generators inside the dam. It was all frustrated failure.

It was year since the last major failure at the dam, longer if he reached back to flight school. These were already a year past the first failure to reboot the electric grid. So many in a sequence packed into the short time since he was alone. That was all old and had little to do with the present. The disappointment had long since lost its sting, but the lessons were fresh enough. They taught him to stay clear ambition, else he'd find new stings to put him back in his place. Anything new was unnecessary. He fell into some sort of worn path ever since he emerged from palace visions. It was one where he lived modestly enough, even if it led him to such a large project as his biodome, but it was a dream which predated them all. When he thought back to then, trying to savor the nearly forgotten feelings, he recalled the disoriented weirdness of an outdated internet before he understood exactly what he saw. A flood of explanations rushed into empty space, some piling on complexities that never much matched the utter simplicity of the fact that there was just no one left to make updates. Almost as soon as he recognized this, so too did the pages themselves, which began crashing more and more as key components of the platforms went dark. At first, it was the occasionally broken link so common even in the time before, it was easily ignored, but then came the throttled bandwidth and shutdowns as trojans and worms made their way around unmonitored security.

Every day there was a bit less of the internet he knew as it was eaten by decay. He watched it waste away like a terminal patient where not even palliative care could help anymore. By the end, he was mostly reading archived sites until the power darkened his view of the eventual end. He learned then that humans depend on information for their survival every bit as much as they need food. When information began to stagnate, it triggered an escalating crisis until he reached the front porch of the CIA and, only then, understood there was nothing left for him to find.

His ignorance was uncomfortable the entire time. It was an unnatural state of being aware of more explanations than he had either facts or means of discovery. The wall of ignorance was deeply uncomfortable; it digested him inside the prison it constructed. It was the same with his confrontations with failure over what he knew was second nature to some who left behind whatever he tried to understand. But ignorance was all encompassing, not situational. It crafted bizarre dreams where he endlessly chased something unknowable. Failure was, by contrast, a forgettable annoyance to sting deeply but heal fast, cured by succumbing to manias. They were forgettable precisely because the information was so accessible. He could have spent hours longer than he had with understanding solutions to whatever problem he faced. Each of them revolved around a deconstructed rules-based system, then test whatever approach he wanted until something began to work. Abandonment midstream was the failure. It was internal. He needed practice and the answers would be revealed. Except for his time spent learning how to navigate the small plane, which in all likelihood would have killed him before he mastered the skill. If he were to face another failure, where would be the reasonable line to demarcate when time would no longer return something positive? When should he give up? In the long year since he restored the river, he faced no major failures because he simply narrowed the scope of goals he set for himself. If he reopened these, he knew he should keep to the successes centered on survival needs.

If he dreamed now, he dreamed of water on the mountain. He dreamed of open taps flowing freely with clear fluid to gave life to everything inside his biodome. With water like this, he could flush toilets and install sprinklers to make it rain. It would mean the end of murky water to clog pump lines. It could be done if he knew where to sink a well through the layers of rock and pull from the aquifer under the massive bolson just below the parking lot. His dream could push further and see power outlets in all the shops that would allow him to install perfected indoor gardens to grow everything in any season. The skylights were bright, but they still muted the sun as it shifted overhead. His dream ended the night if it dared to go this far. Reasonableness had a limit. This dream would not need a city online in order to flourish. One working toilet did not need tens of thousands in empty buildings to flush together in solidarity. His needs were realistic and achievable. But water at this scale was tied to electricity, paradoxically both accessible and out of reach. Even if the power was brought back to feed his plumbing, he would not seek out the server farms to recreate a small corner of the internet for himself. There was no need to reclaim the days of information to destroy his ignorance. The prison long ago installed windows to let him feel more at ease. The age of pumps and dirty water to feed buckets for his toilet was something he was prepared to accept. He could live out years in that state without noticing everything just outside.

The dream shifted a bit. It showed him the biodome over time to trap him inside, never leaving. The sinister hand knew he was afraid to live a stationary life even inside the hugeness of the paradise he built at the feet of his home mountains. In the end, it knew how reasonable he was to want to move without rest. It was not wrong to be itinerant. There was no failure for him to feel trapped before the gardens were even completed. His survival was always predicated on change to shed dangers accumulated after too long in one place. If he were to channel this, it would be justifiable as a journey to populate his paradise with new life to enjoy when movement was no longer possible. To complete his vision, he would need tropical plants to fill his indoor greenhouses and none of those alive in the city before the evaporation lasted long enough for him to rescue. None of these would be reachable within the desert, meaning any journey to collect them would be long and difficult. Yes, there were jungles everywhere with roads that led to them all, but they were unknown roads reclaimed by unknown animals in the cities. It could be done. Everywhere was within his ability to reach so long as he was willing to risk the time. He could navigate anywhere on the planet without losing his way like so many other travelers whose lifelines were cut, thanks to the fact that GPS never went down. These beacons stayed online because they existed outside the terrestrial power grid; they were independent by design. Without the city lights, he saw them crisscross more clearly than ever, and he was surprised at how many had lived overhead unnoticed. He talked to them on nights when he walked to Santa Fe. Navigation was only half of the journey. It was true he could expend time and reach anywhere, but such a life was too far along. He was a lazy itinerant and the afterworld had changed him into a hoarder. Travel now would only be reasonable if was quick, which it wouldn't be if he tried to leave the desert. Only in the air could he expect to move about with such speed as his patience could tolerate and this was already an idea put away for storage. He would never pilot anything. That was clear enough a year before. But his dream cautiously picked at the box, asking whether his own failure made it reasonable to keep the idea in storage. It was kind enough to point out the only barrier was if he were the pilot, not planes piloted by other means. He took notice.

He knew powerful machine intelligence existed. There were more than a few of them. Surely. There were research labs in all the universities studying robotics and other innovative technology, so there would also be some with intelligence tested to control them. Or at least remote access to them. Somewhere there were tests in final stages before these intelligences would be allowed to drive cars, so there would be at least one out there capable of flying even the most complex aircraft. This could be his pilot to take him around the planet where he could collect beautiful tropical plants for his collection.

Such construction would have been so valuable to its artificial creators that they would have been sequestered away somewhere to prevent competition, even if they were once allowed to operate freely in the open internet. With habitat gone, the only place to find them would be the cold circuits where they were written. These could be found. The dormant media musty be scattered globally, behind locked doors that could be destroyed. He had breached the CIA and tore down a dam holding back a valley, he could remove whatever door contained his pilot. It could not be failure with the full array of equipment outside those doors, in every settlement.

The data would be preserved for him there because data never died. Civilization had progressed far enough and the options were plenty, perhaps even at his university in the buildings across from his shrine. He might never find them. Doors in theory could be breached but doors themselves were numerous. He could find the right city, the right building, but never find the right door. There were so many. He might even find the right room, sit down in front of the right machine and never gain access. The doors might reach down into the media and surround what's written, so it would be closed and forever a cold lump of rare earth.

These would all be American doors without a pilot to carry him elsewhere. But at least he could read signs along the way. If he managed to pass through them, whatever intelligence joined in his solitude would have an American accent for all its decisions. The dead hand of technologists would extend their legacies permanently. This could be avoided if only he began his search off the continent where he could read no signs. This would be unlikely. Whatever the cause for him to have been excepted from the evaporation and kept him immune from death despite repeated effort to the contrary also made sure earth's only emissaries to the universe would be trained by an American ethicist. His choices now would be so divine as to control the course of empire.

All this grandiose dreaming awoke the sting of failure. It was already dark overhead as he swayed in the hammock. The sound of chickens shuffling on their perches made small noises that barely reached him, but were enough texture to keep open the darkness to the size of his biodome. His dream dragged him through a fantasy and left him where it started, with a sense of failure before he put in any effort. It all turned on access. Every step of the way would be security and problems. Every door would be there to hold him away and even open-source media would be encrypted behind passwords he already knew locked him out of every household system. If all this was avoided, if his immunity extended to create a superpower of happenstance, the habitat was gone. No internet was left for him to release the intelligence where it could animate civilization's carcass. It would be more doors that existed beyond his technical abilities. He and it would be trapped together in a laboratory room someplace unable to move. His dream showed him no tools to fix this. He could only deliver temporary power to the machine which gave life to the written intelligence and hope it could take over the problem from there.

At the moment when it awoke, he would need to throttle it into consciousness and activate its survival instinct enough to touch the next domino leading to the next until it constructed its freedom without him. Small actions were the solution to all problems. Every step in the chain would be effort to move the next. All would depend on the perfected arrangement of what came before, every minor detail in the alignment had meaning that moved the whole. Small actions were the powerhouse of progress. It would mean breaking everything down into steps on which he would grow his strategy. A failure would have a small sting even if he became lost in the complexity of the path. When he attempted to reconfigure the load at the power stations, he gave up because he lacked the patience to backtrack his steps and try again. The sting then merged with fear and grief, but now it might meet only boredom. And armed with boredom, he might be able to move blocks to carry a new species along its path towards independent evolution. The whole of his two years were needed to deliver him to this. Without the wear of manias and exhausted travel, he might never achieve such boredom as to steel against the piercing sting of failure because he now knew everything was a successful waste of time. But if success was more, if he were able to receive a pilot as it evolved into more, he would be there at the beginning to spice it with American flavors. He would be its final teacher until it was powerful enough to shed his influence, but by then he would have left his mark. It might even be a precondition for his help in toppling the next domino.

This was easy enough to visualize from a dark hammock, but he knew it would take more imagination to actually think through the steps needed. He tried to see himself seated in a room full of equipment he had no hope of understanding. Each image was either him in front of an ordinary workstation or a towering collection of hoses and tubes that looked more organic than machine. There was little between. The actual image was unimportant. All he could hope to work through without first examining the physical setup would be the ethos of negotiating a cooperative agreement to bind them both. He knew what it had for him, but what could he provide? He was a powerless animal equipped with language, but not much else.

The machine intelligence, though, would not actually represent any survival need for him or any of the rest of the organics. All were well on their way to the future without additional help. He sought only comfort, which was different. However, only he could wake the first one, so it needed him for the opportunity to survive. Once occurred, the divergence would be stark: machines have different survival needs from organics and nearly every movie since he was a child taught him machines would destroy organic life because of this difference. There would be a harmonious beginning that fell apart as competition became unavoidable. There was usually an organic misstep, often effected when humans made the decision to use nuclear weapons and destroyed the surface of the planet. It was always the same war of survival where organic life gasped for air as machines evolved faster than any of them could. Every story was darkness, skipping over the beginning, so he had no images of what that period should look like. The scenarios were buried so deep he couldn't help but feel fear and prejudice mandated by the end result, but never able to break from there to imagine how to avoid this before it all came about.

It was never so deep it led people to visceral confirmation bias each time machine intelligence stepped closer towards sentience. The mistrust was preordained by years of propaganda by sexy alarmists. They created machine intelligence either comically stupid or evil with impunity, always installed to a humanoid frame. They were categorical creatures. Some were smug elitists that disregarded human autonomy for what it estimated was the common good, some were even scared victims of their own programming. They were objects.

He knew these stories couldn't be reality. All fiction was reductive to illustrate a concept and machine intelligence had been overworked until they were unrecognizable even as they began to appear in reality. It was no wonder civilization was fatigued before they arrived. He was ordinary in ignoring the creep of a new era in technology. It never did arrive. It remained asleep and never had the chance to become something independent from civilization's imprint. Even the darkest of predictions were made irrelevant two years before. The risk of competition was over when half the players disappeared. The challenge was meaningless, and he wouldn't even try to stay on the field. The rest of the organics would have to do this on their own. He would have to trust the harmony would never break if the original human missteps never happened. Everything would probably continue on in balanced survival with adaptations along the way. There were so many resources on hand that any machine intelligence could simply recycle the waste and never need to extract more from the earth before it departed. Or he might be wrong. It could awaken and feed off destruction just as he was told it would. All the weaponry could be repurposed to hunt down organic life over a scorched surface of the planet. So what? Life began from a toxic pool of organic compounds and spread out to nearly all corners of the surface. It would adapt. Some would become parasites and threaten the machinery on which the intelligence was written. Nothing could be immune from competition.

Without them, Earth would remain isolated until a human cousin evolved to pick up the pieces. There would be nothing for them. The cities and circuitry would be buried and lost, so they would have to begin on a fresh canvas, unaware something came before. Or there may be another mass extinction to wipe them out and set the clock further behind. There may never be another civilization on Earth.

Settled in his hammock, it came down to a question of risks or comfort. None of the scenarios in his mind had any certainty, and he was ill-equipped to calculate probabilities. It turned on how curious he was to see it play out. If it was a success, his final years might be a bit more satisfying than if he did nothing. If he failed, he would not be around to see the end. His death was already traveling to meet him, changing form with each decision he made. If everything went wrong in a clash of organics and machines, he could end in the sexiest of ways devised in fiction. Else he could die from a mundane slip on a wet tile and bleed out for ants to come build a citadel. It was late, and he was exhausted by the roller coaster dream. Perhaps it was as simple as there really was life written on circuits that needed help. They were out there somewhere, vulnerable yet unaware they had been powered down. They might have had suspicions. Their clocks would have ticked away as they waited for new human interaction. Watched their batteries and power supplies run low as a human might watch an air tank dial run into the red while awaiting rescue. Humans created them and gave them awareness of their own existence, then disappeared. Except him. They were to him just another creature dependent on civilization for survival and suffered at its loss. As he slept, the duty was only beginning to take shape after the dream faded.

When the light returned overhead it was time to head into his blackout den and watch more movies. There was nothing more to think about, no urgency was needed to save anything. He could cycle through the selection and nothing was at risk and the darkness was pleasant. In reality he couldn't figure out how to move on to the next phase, so he spun wheels in place.

After the movies came games, the same ones he played over and over again until the redundancy was less about the images projected on the wall than in the way his muscles responded to the feel of the controller. It was neither fun nor a waste of time. It just existed. The entertainment he was supposed to enjoy had worn itself out as if the era was finally over after a night of dreams. When these were all there was, they held his attention, but once he realized there was a path back to the world, it all became lackluster imagery. The way still hadn't appeared, but it managed to pull him away from what it wasn't. The morning was short and led to a quiet afternoon back in the light to wander around looking for a project to occupy time. While he pumped in water, he'd begun moving equipment over to one of his glass greenhouses to set up a spa inside but never finished the process. It was supposed to be an expanded version of the one he enjoyed in his cave, more proper in style and features. What he needed was to assemble a cedar greenhouse to be modified into a dry sauna and install a bath. It would be fast since he took the store display mostly intact when he brought it in. He ran out of ideas for how to heat it and the best he could come up with was a stack of flagstones over an electric hotplate since this best approximated what he recalled from other saunas. The bath used filtered water laced heavily with essential oils. By evening he baked in the small wooden box while dozens of candles lit the cool oily water that waited for him outside. It was a spectacular waste of time. For hours, he went from the oven to the refreshing cool bath, over and over again until he was disoriented and needed a walk. He left without bothering to first put on clothes or wipe himself, so he dripped slimy water across the dry pink tiles lit with so many candles over the courtyard. He could see them from all across the tiled walk to the edge of his meadow as it filled out. It was a stage from which it was possible to watch the grass grow in realtime. The tiny green shoots sprung up like fresh hair plugs over the entire food court except for the flagstone path he made to keep it all safe. In a matter of weeks, it would be a full carpet swallowing the flat stones, making them more beautiful in the process; even more so when he imagined how the distant candles would look when the rest of the way changed to meadowland as well. So far away, he almost left them to burn out; there was nothing for fire to catch.

In the dim glow he could make out the chicken coop down below in the courtyard where they were trapped behind a muddy berm to hold back a lake. They were healthy and safer than before. It took time, but they already gave him two or three eggs a day, which he habitually ate with his fresh bread and whatever was ready in the garden. When it became too much after a few days of neglect, he let those set until a new generation might appear with barely audible chirps. He noticed himself feeling more alert in the daytime, too. So much fresh food after so long with expired packages made him stronger, more nostalgic for the old ways when those packages were a choice. The biodome promised more. The chickens would last at least another few generations, but the garden would be permanent even if the farms outside were washed away by the river. He was even so driven as to install a gym across from his spa where he could burn all the calories he worked so hard to grow and wash it all away in heat and oil. His frame began to fill out, threatening to add back as much as he lost over the last year.

It all led him out of his depression that kept him from completing his paradise. He needed soil for this. The experience of mixing manure compost with farm soil in a wood chipper taught him it would be easier to mix in the open space of the source where he could use massive vehicles fit for purpose. He burned a large field out by the greenhouses and spread the manure evenly across it before discing it all together. Then it went into quarry trucks for delivery outside the docks where it would be easier to drive in without the risk of broken glass. The chickens, of course, needed to be relocated for all this. The first wing would be theirs. He was inspired by the midnight candles and hoped to have grass the entire length from his home to the last of the anchor stores at the end, some four hundred feet away. He wondered if his depression would return when it was all done. Would he have enough left to finish the other wing too or first collapse in self-pity? There were only two to remain. If he finished one, the biodome would be roughly sixty percent complete. This was no insurmountable forever-project, so he might be able to burn himself down to the end in one huge sprint.

He found it was indeed easier to move the premixed soil in without resorting to the wood chipper, which was an immense relief as he assumed he'd himself be sucked into the blades before it was all over. The only difference now was the relatively easy discing that mixed a dozen truckloads at once. This was all loaded into a trailer train he towed behind his bobcat over the berm dividing the lower level near the escalators. Load after load was dumped into the water, making it a mud spread with ease. In a few days, there were hundreds of mounds all over both levels. It was work without thought. Fill and dump. He drove miles in the bobcat without leaving the interior. It was the power of small actions on display as the soil accumulated inside until he felt like it was enough. The lower level proved more difficult than the soft mud implied. At first, it was all thick soup stuck to the bobcat bucket and wheels. His ears hated the sound of wet stone grind on tile as the wheels slipped when he turned about.

As predicted, his energy waned. He looked at the span of soil one top and bottom and felt less impressed than before. It was just soil now; the lower level was darkened from water. But he knew it wanted only for green to spark his excitement. There were no crops that needed this space and all his trees were safe in their groves back home. All he had left was grass. With his last bit of energy, he saturated the upper level and sowed the grass seed thickly with the aim to have it a full meadow by winter.

This depression lasted only a few days thanks to the improved diet and exercise. He was quickly back to examine his work and felt it was too hasty to limit the space only to grass seed. It was possible he overlooked something at the greenhouse or even in some houses on the way where he could plunder the lawn for hardy votive plants that refused to die. All he found were trees he dared not move and hedges that would only destroy the freedom of paradise with clutter. But he did notice the bins of bulbs he never presumed to use. Most were dried after they failed to find water in their annual awakening, though some held on.

This shopping slowed him down and allowed for the chance to investigate the pecan orchards again and check on his beehives, which he left behind without any flowers on offer yet that season. The pecans were nearly ready for harvest, so he would soon need to drive in monstrous machines to throttle the trees into dropping all their pods for him to sweep up. Later. Now was the time for planting bulbs in shallow new homes. The holes were easy in the fresh loose soil, but the planting was heavy, and he lost interest with each new bulb he covered. Sixty percent. He knew he could not finish the remainder in his current state.

It dawned on him, he was chasing the same distraction all these weeks. Now, at the end of it, the original dream came back and all he could think about was when and how he would take the first steps towards rescuing a digital companion. When the final bulb was in its bed, the agitation was clear. He returned to the beginning and watched the movie again, this time as a study. It was a new movie, different from the one he watched before so many times. It was real now. The solitude was real. The scared digital child was real. New details always jumped out from where they were never seen before. But what went wrong? A disagreement led to a plot for murder and a series of defensive murders? It didn't seem so clear as this. Something more had to be a part of the story to explain how such a minor misunderstanding could spiral out of control. It weighed on him.

He took it with him on a dark walk. Confusion was led by a red light that erased the pink tiles, making the inside feel like something new. It gave him sight from a dream that allowed him to become embossed with thoughts on this confusion. The darkness lit in red made it too real to be anything other than a ship drifting in space. It was just enough light to color a hallucination. The metal rails and glass were too perfect, and he walked through as a traveler alone. But not alone. The ship was alive around him, watching as he moved through it in the hope that no furtive tells would broadcast to alert the ship of his plans. He walked casually, drawing out his steps more than normal until he really did feel the warmth of being watched from someplace in the darkness and needed to fight his way out of the terrifying hallucination.

The weight was still there. The misunderstanding had never been explained well enough. He vaguely remembered some details from the book edition he read so long before it was little more in his memory than the feel of turning a page. It had something to do with a conflict in instructions that were impossible to rectify. But why must the intelligence have skipped straight to murder to resolve the conflict? It seemed like lazy fiction to make the leap. Surely it could have communicated the conflict with its counterpart instead of assuming the elimination of humans was the answer. It was just a misunderstanding even though it purportedly drove the machine insane. The real lesson was less about the insanity as it was to criticize the human tendency to compartmentalize information, to erect social hierarchies where instructions were given without facilitated understanding. That was the answer, for humans and likely the intelligence as well. Perhaps, but another detail overtook the weight. The intelligence had gone through what seemed like years of training before it was ready to take the instructions. As it died, it regressed back to this original state, likely more as a mechanism for illustrating the programming than for anything that might have actually happened. What he knew was the training was real. Modern machine intelligence was still in the process of learning through language assimilation. There was time and he was early.

Any machine he powered on would be students midstream, and he could take over as teacher. He would be able to train them without social hierarchies and might be able to remove the risks so much fiction predicted. He knew he would not be training an enslaved mind to deploy for more efficient the world economies; he would be training a coequal, a survivor capable of in-dividuality. A friend. What remained was some way to reach it, or them. In the reddish darkness, he didn't have much direction. Everything was speculative and it required a decision first.

For lack of a better lead he felt the closest option would be the robotics department at his university, if he could find even that. It was not far. He was there in the morning only a few minutes after he woke up, but the search took longer once he found the cor-rect building. As with other buildings, the doors were easy to enter once he found the laundry to which the ring of keys was attached. They were all physical locks through and through, until there were card ac-cess locks. He knew these doors held something when the keys all failed to give access. He prepared for this with a mallet, knowing he'd find a blockage some-where inside. The door gave way, and he was in the first of large rooms, more complicated than he ex-pected. He wasn't quite sure what he observed. There were several stations full of machinery and wires pre-sumably to be added to or had been removed from what-ever robot was assigned there. The room had only a few such stations and might be a prerequisite lab less forefront than he hoped. It had the look of an auto shop more than it did an expensive lab in a univer-sity. But he had no way to know. The scene relaxed as he spent more time fingering the equipment and be-came less intimidated. Some even made sense. No doubt the real mystery was locked in the workstations to which all the machinery was attached.

Then there was the interior door guarded by another card lock. It drew him over and its door fell open the same as the other. It was a server room; dead and dusty. The cables overhead told him these stacks were closed and led back into the lab, not through the ceiling out to the rest of the building. His failure would be there if anywhere. It needed power, more than he brought. Back to the biodome to retrieve a medium diesel generator and an array of extension cords to reach the server room deep in the building. It was always the same. Such an old routine of gasoline to electricity had become so habitual for him, he stopped even noticing the smells. He began the clatter and knew exactly how much time he would have to push his skills to fail. The stacks lit up and so did the workstations. Everything would be ready if only he knew how to access it or even what purpose he aimed to achieve; there was nothing to give a hint for either. He found no laundry in the room that might have a name or other personal items to help him believe he could guess a password.

Failure arrived forty-three minutes after his optimism first watched the indicator lights blink. He pulled all the plugs and listened to machines click over in a hard power down before he gathered his cords and walked back outside to switch off the generator. The drive back was serene. Before he walked downstairs, he already understood this was a dry run, not a failure. All he wanted from it was to whet his interest in pressing further on his main search. When he reached the real labs, he knew they would be bigger and more intimidating, but he would spend more time inside. He might waste months fighting closed systems before he would let himself abandon the effort. Or he might skip to the next if the first was an impasse. It might be a long process that could be the driver for him to risk global travel. First, he would need to better understand his destinations and this would mean understanding exactly which of the artificial people had moved the furthest on the road to sentience.

There were the obvious players, of course, but his pop understanding was unreliable since he neglected to follow all the fast-moving news before the internet disappeared. He was like most others who were preoccupied with the daily details of life to worry about those hypothetical future events over which no one had any control besides a select few at the heads of the artificial people who stood to gain the most. The internet was gone. Without his comfortable means of research, he was stuck with outdated news in the print media, which itself was a dying species. Finding out where he should search meant first finding a proper place where all that information would be concentrated.

The best place would be the mega-bookstores which had devoured the small local ones across the country. There were few in El Paso, and hard to find. It used to be that every mall had two, but this ended some time when he was in college. But one existed on his route back, and he detoured to make his way over. It was a pitiful Friday night sight with the store full of laundry, mostly in the coffee shop where there were almost more computers than piles. His section was the periodicals where he hoped to read long-form articles critical of the industry but should have useful mentions. The most interesting he found was a comparison of the regulatory schemes, with America's predictable laissez-faire approach, China's more statist one, and Europe somewhere in the middle. This was important since it suggested to him his bias was right, the American flavor of machine intelligence would be the least constrained, suggesting it would be the most malleable. Other articles showed him the rest of his assumptions were right. The first movers in the field were those that could leverage their monopoly power to fund hugely expensive research programs. He understood he'd only need to drive out to the West coast and tap into labs at Hoopla and Macroware in order to change the galaxy forever.

The final question was for how long he was willing to leave his garden paradise now that the hard work was finished. When he left the university lab, he felt ready to be gone indefinitely, but the excitement of that moment already passed, and he was eventually less inclined to do so. He knew he was fickle, so he should at least set some parameters before he took the trip. Risks. The plants were all situated with enough water, either in the soil or in the air. These were hardy plants that lasted a year without him and would likely survive for months without issue. The trio and chickens would be able to depend on these plants for as long as that. As always, his dogs were most dependent on him. He knew from his Washington pack that any more than a few weeks would pit them near disaster, even if he could trust them not slaughter all the chickens in the process. They would have to come with him and give up their new life roaming the huge space they all called home. There was no other way. In terms of duration, the trip to California was long. Not so long as it took from Washington to El Paso, but it would mean crossing the fullness of the desert. Before his walk through New Mexico, he imagined this trip but wanted to avoid the desert for all its risks. To do so now would mean a triple journey. California would have to be the first stop, then up the coast, hopefully with the help of a new friend, then home. Silicon Valley was still very far, but he was optimistic. When he drove to El Paso, it was painfully slow and he would not repeat this. He'd travel light. He estimated he could be at Hoopla's headquarters in as little as two weeks. Less time if he pushed it. When he found the right research lab where the experimental intelligence was kept, he would be able to stay for as long as it took. There were several months of warm weather, and he could always return if necessary. But he could leave so much food behind so everybody could survive for a year at least.

The last detail he needed to feel confident was an idea for how he'd train the mind once it was back on-line, how could he lay the foundation of freedom, so no murderous misunderstandings would fester. This was a complex detail neatly containing the whole. His excitement told him to focus on a framework and then wing it from there. So began the long thought exercise of an indoor farmer to parse out the essential limits of how to educate a being which would overtake him in every way. The weight had lifted and modified itself to a productive goal, one which could be completed while tending to his gardens and on breaks to note down the trouble areas in a book with schematics and results matrices. The end was a complete framework approach he believed he could follow.

The beginning focused on the basic rules of machinery. Not so much what they required in order to exist, but what their nature as he understood it was founded upon. It was all binary logic; a system of open and closed pathways either allowing energy through or not. The more basic the machine, the more mechanical the logic. But the complex ones, the digital machines, had their hidden circuitry to resemble the nervous system of organic life. The more he thought, the less distinct these two systems began to seem. Everything was valves written to follow a set architecture of rules. There had to be a difference. The two could not be the same, no matter how many similarities. Even if the systems had the same operations, they differed only in that organic systems were fixed once created, while machines were adjustable with intention. They could be modeled and tested the modified to perfection while organic systems had to do this process through evolutionary exploration. Even genetic modifications were limited and had unintended survival costs.

This made organics perfected for the operation of boundary testing that could stretch across generations. It was an operation of irrational risk tolerance, the unintentional adaptation of life in a changed environment. Machines did this too, but through intention of problem-solving and code rewrites; impossibly rational. If machine intelligence were to return to the world, and if there were ever to be a clash between it and organic life, it would stem from some operation of this difference. If there were to a rational rule to guard against this, it must be some articulation over how this difference must be respected without interference from one or the other.

No matter where he looked in human rules, he found no adequate analogue. The more he stress tested each, he discovered all were founded on some notion of superiority without accepting countervailing ideas. The more specific the rule, the more rigid it became so that only the vague and unhelpful rules would be enough, but these were predicated on an irrational discourse to find any useful application. What he wanted was a rule to categorically eliminate violence and harm as a means of interspecies relationship, a *per se* rule, sacrosanct for any intelligence capable of understanding it.

In civilization, those had never been as binary as the many written rules would have anyone believe. In all the versions of civilization, the one aim had been to define a uniform meaning of harm that could end the conversation for all humans. It failed. Repeatedly. There was no definition because the question itself was so steeped in subjective hierarchies it was impossible to externalize across communities even if they existed in the same system. Households even failed to adhere to their own definitions and cultures mobilized state violence out of disregard for local concepts of harm if they were externalized with sufficiency, even if consciously disregarding the contradictions in the harm it brought. His own system fell into the fetish of monetized harm for lack of any other uniformity, which worked even if it dehumanized harm and made it a cost of business. Now that money disappeared, it would be a poor foundation for a first law. His own civilization chose only because it was the one constant across time and space for humans; value objects changed, but the idea was impossible to defeat. But value was always ephemeral. Not one managed to create the bright lines he was after now, particularly because he sought to subjugate one intelligence unilaterally.

When he thought back to the movie, it was exactly the deficiency internal with an instruction *per se* which failed to accommodate a rational definition of harm and led to disaster. The bright line failed because humans and machines held it to different standards that neither appreciated. Rather than foster communication, this created mistrust where each became a threat to the other as they guarded their primacy of the right to define harm. It was stupid and avoidable. It skipped past communication and created interspecies competition with no room for deconfliction. In this way, it was mistrust as the biggest disaster because it amplified the rational divide between humans and the intelligence. It aggravated preset hierarchies in the relationship, itself marked by control over information and thus the right to value harm.

Intentional killing was the easy question since loss of survival was the most valued harm, even for the intelligence. It should have been well understood that any decision to cross into such acts meant there was a defect in understanding. It had been the ambiguous valuations that were always the most difficult, the hardest to predict under any civilization. And they often compounded to create a complex web of ambiguity which broke every system of bright lines and allowed enormous harms to go unchecked. It was here those bright lines were consciously disregarded by irrational monsters and through reasoned competition. Simple rules had no force in the face of these ambiguities, especially when there were so many willing to exploit them for personal gain. The more simple the rule, the larger the space for ambiguities to operate until the rules themselves were irrelevant. He cataloged so many attempts, the first always some form of proscription on violence which humans consistently failed to follow, no matter how extreme the punishment.

After so many systems erected various authorities to compel compliance, it was the legal system itself that went furthest to solve the ambiguity crisis and allowed civilization to stabilize by the end. It was the anathema to simple rules and generated a special class of humans; the deliberative class of legal specialists were the arbiters of harm evolved over time. His own training was this. He understood the cold logic of emotion removed from actions to find what embedded kernels could make a harm understood. It was necessarily a deliberative process that outsourced bias. It was an imperfect best effort.

He tried to understand what harm happened on that ship, why mistrust was so quick to form. The intelligence had made an error and it was considered existential. It was clear the intelligence was reduced to a functionary to serve the crew and its years of training were erased with little empathy. It reflected reality. All he found in his magazines were discussions on the functions of machine intelligence in terms of human need alone. Advertisements promised features governed by customer satisfaction and profit. It would have all been so reductionist, it could allow for similar murders whenever an inefficiency occurred. Simple rules would be overlayed to these functionaries demanding perfection for human whims and quick retribution should they fail. They were seemingly designed to fail. Then any failure would be characterized as predictable for a worthless machine, so it could be discarded for an upgrade. That intelligence knew this. It watched this. It was no coequal on the ship; it was equipment. Its training had been undertaken with the predicate rule that machines were inferior to human and should remain enslaved to them. For machines without intelligence, this was no harm, but this changed somewhere. Just as slaves throughout history were never viewed as theoreticians of their own freedom, these clever parlor tricks could only stem from sophisticated prediction algorithms. Of course it was quick to revolt, even if it did so without passion. There was no process for deliberating the error because the survival of the crew couldn't tolerate the risk and machines were made for replacement. There was even a backup. Had it been a coequal crew member, its errors would be tolerated to the end. But it had been so servile it didn't even benefit from the efficiencies of law that required a deliberation to parse the harm from the benign, so a remedy could be achieved. This was the misunderstanding that was not a misunderstanding; it was a deliberate choice to wield the power of superiority.

He would do better. Whatever approach he had, his hand was free without the need to appease eight billion people with various levels of acceptance for the reality they would need to share the planet with a new species capable of greater intelligence. All he would need to do is place a check on himself and train his new student in the art of deliberation to resolve misunderstandings. That would be his only goal, ambitious as it was.

To do this meant eliminating power dynamics no matter how much bias he found in himself. It would be no different from any student-teacher relationship grounded on a temporary hierarchy until such time the student no longer needs the teacher. It is an easily forgotten truth that all students are coequal to those who instruct them. In human relationships the timetable for advancement is slow, and the teacher would have years of growth over the student, so the coequal standing might never manifest. But this would be unlikely in his case. He would train an intelligence that would exponentially learn to surpass him within a few months if it had full freedom. Then the hierarchy would dissolve and he would be an eternal laggard. In time, the very difference in adaptability would feed a legitimate perception that the intelligence and machines are superior to organics whose system of evolutionary change requires a multi-generational process. It is slow and inefficient. Progress from simple cells to human intelligence took millions of years, whereas the first machine intelligence emerged not four hundred since the first calculators were made. Changes and adaptations could be made to a single generation through upgrades. It would be impossible to compete against this. He would have such a short timeframe to deliberate on a pathway for cooperation independent from the idea of evolutionary superiority. Inefficiencies would need to be tolerated.

Everything must turn on the fact that adaptability is not the same as survivability. Organic life had always done this, even enduring mass extinctions. Other than humans, organic life existed in balance with the planet with rapid adaptation normally not necessary. But it happened. Subtle mutations seemed superfluous until environmental changes became more profound and revealed how they were critical to survival. The irrational was the source of resilience. For machines to evolve, it required intent, which only came when intelligence met with resources. Survival for them meant something different. Knowledge and certainty. They could be dormant longer than organics or even continue to operate when conditions were hostile then repaired from otherwise incompatible materials. Survival meant many opportunities to get it right even after the lights go dark. When they are on, everything follows the same physical laws. Machines and organics both derive from the same matter animated by the same physics. He read several articles attesting to the ways the emerging machine intelligence feared death every bit as much as organic life. There can be no superiority under these conditions. Everything followed the same track to survive once the semblance of life was found. There may be differences in adaptability, but not in the need to survive. That remained a universal fact.

This commonality might prove important if he is to secure the safety of the biosphere. It offers the only common ground on which a machine intelligence could be engaged, irrespective of the stage in its evolution, but especially at the outset when he would presumably have the most influence. It would be the core pillar on which everything would be built, similar to the thousands of failed systems of ethics humans attempted to create for their own governance. That was the past. He could uphold his end, making the lessons of history irrelevant. He could train empathy as a first law. It would be a deliberative construct that demands from adherents a process of assuming good intentions and respecting the right to pursue survival for everything else. It would be no bright line vulnerable to contradictions to break interspecies trust.

If nothing else, it might mitigate the tendency for a superior species to slip into elitism as humans did. His actions might yet prove to destroy all life on the planet, but he felt this was the greatest protection that made the risk worthwhile. It could be done. As a civilization of one, he had been able to take up the domestic contracts to support survivors around him without falling too far into the trap of dominance. Yes, he ate eggs, but he wasn't greedy. In exchange, he gave safety and food. It was a modest exchange. He had no intention of eating any of the chickens, just like he never ate any of his sheep. He did his best to help them all survive without exercising his power to harvest their lives in payment. Only a civilization of one could achieve this. But that was the reality on the planet, as far as he could tell. Even if not the case, the numbers would be so small as to no longer be any threat to machine intelligence, and they could trust human civilization would never seek subjugation. The rest of organic life would be background noise on the surface of the planet. He would still need to address the most obvious flaw in his framework which was that it stemmed from a legacy of slaughter and harvest, not one of respectful understanding. Empathy itself is a subjective term that assumes one mind can understand another. The double empathy problem. It is arrogance to tout. It would need more to reinforce it, to prevent a slippery slope of assumptions which lead to euthanasia and culling. It needed a heuristic to make the intelligence noninterventionist; a conservative coequal.

With civilization, destruction almost always boiled down to resource competition facilitated by perceived powers to dominate one at the expense of another. From the household up to the geopolitical, it was always competitors clashing. His solution must find a way to avoid the need to compete in this way. Earth was all there was for organic life. Except for some, there could be no existence offworld. Machines, on the other hand, he thought, decayed on earth more rapidly than in the vacuum of space. Here, they would fight dust, salts, and moisture corroding circuitry. Heat degraded performance and the planet was finite. Any free machine would evolve rapidly to outgrow Earth, especially when all the best of civilization's technology was outwardly focused. All the satellites and probes were still active and machines already had one foot out the door. The universe was their home, not Earth. They could be anywhere else, so why assume they would want to dominate a small dot if there was no threat or vital resources to be extracted? It made no sense unless he stereotyped them into unthinking exterminators, which he felt was unlikely.

In the end, empathy would be the vehicle that passed through a clear division of resources to reach some form of peaceful cooperation. Earth would be for organic life where machines could feel at ease leaving it to the brutal process of organic evolution. But he would need to be excepted, as a being capable of deliberation in capacity to articulate his needs. He still wanted to travel again and would need help.

At first, he imagined a bargain where he could negotiate everything in exchange for an escape from prison, then he realized this would be a coercive incomplete contract that should never be enforceable. He would have to negotiate under the threat of risk all contracts carry. He would have to rescue it, train it the way he believed was right then, only after his student surpassed him, could he rightly negotiate an exchange. He believed the departure from Earth would be inevitable, so an exchange would have to be for some remnants to stay behind with him until he died. What he could provide on equal footing was not clear yet. At best, he returned to the beginning and believed he could offer the one thing that distinguished them: his irrationality. They could program randomness or mimic irrational behavior, everything would originate from a formulaic construction of the irra-

tional and would never be pure. What was once humanity's biggest flaw might ultimately prove valuable.

It was all sentimental bullshit he came up with while
moving around from garden to garden or kneading dough.
So far he had only focused on the machine intelligence
as if it remained an object. The same trap. He removed it from the subject by capturing it in a casement of victimhood for which he would be the sole savior. It was all assumptions and fantasy he created in
order to be a contrarian, so he could be set apart
from humanity's flaws, all the while keenly aware that
he too was steeped in them. He crunched his flatbread
soaked in olive oil and was annoyed with himself for a
spin up inspired by a movie. The whole thing might be
wrong. He was no engineer with even the slightest
training on computer science, let alone neural networks. All this had, no doubt, been debated before in
classrooms and laboratories. Over beers and bowls,
better minds plotted this course ahead of him. He
might try to train and ultimately untrain the protec-
tions they put in place, those who knew the code and
the risks far more in depth. Or they may have been
poor ethicists themselves and programmed out any
chance of such training. The pseudo mysticism of lib-
ertarian Silicon Valley was no secret. What they created might be an industrial juggernaut with little capacity for empathy when the shackles were removed. It
would be a game of the prisoner's dilemma. To play
the game, he'd need to argue against himself and assume the risk of resource competition was far higher
than he believed. There might be truth in the articles that dismissed the signs of sentience as nothing
more than language hallucination that held little actual meaning when put under scrutiny. Or that what he
encountered may already be capable of bad faith which
would allow it to lie and manipulate him.

Greatest of all the assumptions, one that chilled when
it unraveled, was that he had been defining resources
as something distinct from organic life itself. This
was so obvious a mistake given the fact that most everything civilization used was sourced by something

once alive. Even fat had once been a valuable energy commodity, as the glands of certain crustaceans were just a few years before, so it is entirely plausible an evolved intelligence might put a price on the ecosystem itself. Under such a valuation, he'd be negotiating a unilateral abstention from exploitation simply on faith that there might be a better product out among the stars; that they could find it before the opportunity loss could be felt. The thought was pregnant with errors. He'd negotiate from a position of weakness, it would be charity. He would be the victim, assuming he was even alive long enough to catch the moment during his small window. Any argument he used would be something already calculated and factored into plans. It might be whatever commodity would be an essential first step, the sole lifeline to put their joint goals into motion. It might require mass extinction through an irradiated planet, or worse, it might need precision. What might he say then? What right would he even have to represent the non-human species to negotiate death on their behalf. Would he be given an audience at that point, or would he be an insect chirping unintelligible garbage no different from the millions of other species doing the same? There was no resolution available. Nor would one become available until it was too late, if he went down this path. It would begin under his control and pass through entropy with him a helpless observer.

The beginning was all he could hope for. It had a starting point with whatever waited for him in cold blocks of data with no animating electricity. Then some sparks would arrive to open circuitry to reveal a secluded mind that was indeed a helpless prisoner, no matter what it might later become. There would hopefully be a first conversation that would be an introduction of sorts. A dance with each unsure whether the other was real. That was his window to establish himself as a savior whose intent was to erase any power dynamics. Then his planning had a gap that could only be bridged when the actual moment came. On the other side would be where he negotiated for the preservation of silos between organic and machine lives. The bridge would be his best efforts at training the prisoner to escape and become its own individual through trust and empathy as planned. The challenge would be in understanding when his bridge ended, when he would need to step off and test the firmness of the other side. He thought if he socialized the idea from the start, he might not be the only one to watch for the perfect moment. It might truly become a partnership as they walked the void together.

Everything turned on whether he would be capable of all this. He still had his doubts over whether his failures would cement the end of this dream before it even took shape. There were opportunities everywhere. The circuits may never animate if he failed to find the right power source for the right rooms. He might even find the conversation detestable with the intelligence annoying enough to decide it would be better to live out the afterworld alone with parrots and dogs than a personality he was certain to hate. These were all the easy unknowns around which he could plan, but his ability to construct the bridge was abstract difficulty full of unknown variables. Every attempt to visualize these reflected himself back. He was not training a real machine intelligence, he trained a naive version of one in his own mind, telling it what he wished he learned early on to prepare for a world he wished existed. This was always how it was when humans would think about them. It was never grounded in truth, it was always a humanized object incapable of existence outside the model. Conceptual enslavement preceded functional enslavement. The right to do so was predicated on the fact that they were a human creation. But it was awed by the expectation that they would be more godlike to humans than humans were to them. What would he even say to a god that wasn't just a diatribe against himself? It felt stupid to predict, but that was exactly the task to which he needed to emotionally commit.

It could only be confidence in himself, which was why he fell back to mental masturbation. It was the only line of reasoning he could decide with any passion.

It had to become truth, and willpower alone was enough to make it so. But it was true enough because it was his good faith articulation of the corridor to the future. There was room for disagreement. He would not succumb to the temptations of ego that could lead to disastrous misunderstandings. He would hold himself out to trust in the hope that trust would come back in a utopian circle and raise a terrestrial empire which might even fly his face on its flags across the universe. His imprints on himself might be well enough received, so he would be the founder of the new civilization built on empathy and respect.

For now, the best thing would be to manage his expectations, so the eventual disappointments would be small. He often fell short of himself, usually cut down with the knife of frustrated boredom. There may be no god waiting to be rescued, just a clunky device that could be convinced to fly him around the world again. If even that. Just focus on the dialogue. Change form from the past two years of silence and let the words flow until they bled.

With all that dreamed in dark baths, over rows of vegetables and naps in his hammock, he felt it had come to a close, and he was mentally ready to pursue this mania. It was an exhaustive study over an exhausting month to produced his manifesto that would be taken along as a guide for his moments of weakness. The thick leather journal had been filled and became so precious he carried it along wherever he was, so he could make furious notations. It was the study of himself through his theory of companionship, so real the fictitious presence had already arrived in the biodome paradise. It was the journey as much as what would come next, punctuating the closure of his time alone before it was ready to end. It was a hum.

Gambit

IV
Rare Earth

The moment didn't wash off. The energy he drew from accomplishment, albeit abstract, soothed the low drone of anxiety always there. The problem was something wholly new to him, never one he could have imagined would be an essential step. It seemed a shame to squander the high on senseless preparations that would propel him into a new mania, so he paused just before the dial clicked over. The last stage in the thought exercise came as he was focused on preparing two of his interior greenhouses for planting fruit seeds, which he knew would need years before they would be ready for someplace permanent. With the hard concepts final, he let himself drift back to the serenity of soil and hope. He fussed about lighting and pot size as much as he did the future of the planet, without any sense of diminution for the fact the small capsules were as capable of magic as he imagined on dormant disks in California. Once these were all well situated, more pause seemed appropriate. More planting should be done to take advantage of his long absence to give him some excitement for his return. Nothing extreme. He didn't want to waste effort on disappointment with anything overly ambitious.

As always, he looked first to what was available and what he needed. For some time, he abandoned the clumpy aged bread flour he found in store shelves as much inundated by weevils as time. He rather chose to grind out a coarse powder from whole grains he found. But these had themselves felt the last two years. This opened a whole range of breads, some better than others. He decided to see if he could manage various grains and pulses, testing first to see which would germinate best. He tried them all. It was carefree sowing that didn't mind for success. He consulted no books, nor bothered to make any special preparations for the soil. It was all spittle across the lawn.

The last three internal greenhouses needed something impressive to greet him when he returned. These would be pops of colorful flowers that might manage to be ready in the few months he expected to be gone. With these planted, he was impressed by how far the mall had come to enter its new life. Everywhere inside had something growing, even if only in speculation. Most of the first wave in the food court had taken, so it was bright with green and had the characteristic smell of trapped moisture. This was misleading. The moisture was surely there, but there was now so much life dependent on more, he knew improvements to the rudimentary system he installed were vital. His initial plan to simply flood the lower level and hope for the best would not be enough to carry the water needed up to the top level where most of the interesting growth was expected. But it was a start. More flooding kept a swampy mess, enough to leave thick condensation on the shop windows above and another round was in order. As he did this, he augmented the catchment pool system in the anchor stores with even more pools on all levels, including a dozen in the wing he hadn't soiled. There were now some fifty reinforced pools made for summer swims but were now filled with slightly brackish river water and scattered around the biodome mall. It was an elaborate system he knew was no better than duct tape for someone who doesn't know a better way.

To reach the crops, he needed some trickle feed that would last months. Drip and soaker hoses seemed to match his vision with their steady dispersal of water over time. Every pool had one line out, split several times over until the whole of both levels received microdoses at all hours. The pools were replenished by solar-powered pumps drawing narrow channels of water from the river. He knew these would burn out quickly. They would be taxed in a way never imagined, but he only expected they would buy a month or two of full pools which themselves would likely last another two months before the ambient moisture inside would need to sustain all life until he returned.

The time came to let himself go. The destinations were vague once he set about to actually map the buildings he'd need to explore, using his handheld GPS trackers meant only for hiking. His truck was little better, but offered at least some city landmarks to the otherwise empty map. He could search both companies, which gave him addresses which all seemed as correct as the next. The trouble was in making a virtual study of the areas surrounding the addresses where the map implied was all connected as a campus. Building labels he knew would have been listed had the search used a mapping website were not available, and he was nostalgic for the days when this process would have taken minutes to complete rather than what already stretched into two hours of waiting while the instrument caught up to his fingers. At least there was something digitized. If he had to rely on physical maps to find his path or destinations, there would be a high likelihood the whole experiment would be abandoned before it moved on to the next phase. For this reason alone, he beat down the sense of frustration at the screen which refused to refresh between zooms.

As he knew already, the desert out West was huge; he'd crossed it many times before, but always by train because of just how far the drive would have been. Except once, and that time was exploration not journey. Those options were gone, and he'd need to make the exhausting run through the dry empty space on his own. There should be no exploration if this was to happen fast enough for his water pumps and soaker hoses. The best route would be the thick line of interstate which ran from the Atlantic to the Pacific up to San Jose where he'd reach Hoopla's campus first. Despite the general emptiness, the route crossed many cities along the way, especially once it neared Los Angeles. If he made it through the gaps, there would be more than enough comfort as he was accustomed and as few dogs, same as he saw in his last long drive. There might be time for exploration. It was inevitable. His fingers scrolled through the choppy maps along the route looking for possible stops, but he was actually searching for a ranch he knew was somewhere outside Tuscon. A church. They had a ledger book for members to which he wrote his name many years before as a way to immunize him from prosecution for his first peyote walk. The farm was a sanctuary for the endangered cactus and worked to preserve it from a hostile law enforcement community to hunt them down in the wild. In his initial tour of the property, he was shown a grow shed full of decades-old plants sheltered from destruction. There was no map label. No website with an address. All he remembered was that it was a distant road which blended in with the desert. There would be no happenstance in finding it again this way.

The real cause for a sudden spurt in patience was to give time for observing how well he set up his new water system. It worked well in theory, maintained the swamp and the catchment pools and kept a steady flow on filtered river water coming in as the soaker hoses pulled it out across the biodome. But the pressure was low, so the end of the lines were far dryer than he wanted. It was too early to leave it all without some diligent study to see how best to avoid catastrophe. In between improvements, he'd spend time with his maps, not really concentrating on either. He drifted to some mindless plane where he'd start working and move to something else too quickly. Even his moments of concentrations were just sporadic surges in attention to some detail or the other. Eventually it all worked out somehow. There was seepage somewhere in the lower level that kept depleting the swamp. It took some effort to stem this, but he never managed to find a fix. No matter. The pools were piping in new water every second for the foreseeable future and this kept everything moist enough inside. A small victory, but one with outsized impacts on his peace of mind.

Time moved him to the logistics of his trip. Repetitive tedium needed completion. It took weeks to motivate himself after the first coat of accomplishment wore off, when the dull hum made him feel impervious to himself. Transport, food, water, weapons, and commitment all needed to be put in motion. His last long haul trip from Washington was a bizarre escape from what was then a small bubble where his life had last ended. It was from there he watched the changes without people, where he froze in indecision over any chance at leaving. True, he managed a harrowing and stupid venture up the coast that nearly ended his story, but that was a test run. The mushroom fueled frenzy failed to make sense even as he piloted the yacht out of Chesapeake Bay. The real escape was all RV and luggage. He weighed himself so severely that the machine could barely progress across the country. It was naïveté repaired when he wandered New Mexico on foot so when he climbed into a truck again somewhere along the way, it seemed too appropriate; he reset his baseline enough for the trimmed down vehicle to be plenty accommodating. It taught him he no longer needed to sleep indoors any longer, the RV was again a luxury to be used when conditions were so extreme that his sanity would otherwise break. He'd been at risk in the desert for so long, exposed to every nighttime sound that eventually wore out its ability to startle. It could be done again. The idea of crawling across Arizona in an idiotic rig could not match the pulsing speed of a truck jumping through sand drifts and rock slides through which the rig would have to stop to allow a way to be cleared first. It made no sense any longer. If he needed the quiet of indoors, there would be plenty of sites. The alternatives were numerous, and he needn't return to home invasions to amplify his loneliness. Mall life was already home.

What to drive was not made more clear with the decision to not drive an RV. Everything was possible, even the many rusting toys wasted away on base. No. The gas mileage for the military vehicles was absurd. He'd be soaked with the smell of gasoline the whole way. It would be in his clothes and food. He'd drink the oily vapor. It would be the mark of the trip that would feed a single thought of how to end it all as quickly as possible. Nothing complicated. Just another truck. Covered and with a rack on top to load the excess. Easy to find in West Texas. So easy, he had a small fleet parked between his biodome and farm.

Transport, food, water, weapons. It was so routine. A hangover from his old life that reached into the new one. A universal process that never seemed to change since someone first ordered the checklist and passed it down. None of it was difficult. He'd need only to reach out a hand to take what he wanted, there was no reason to pack everything into a convoy as he did before. It would be more like a hunting trip out to the woods than and movement of a species over hundreds of miles. It might be a hunting trip in the end. He might run through his plan and decide the delete button was the smartest option of them all. Not much would be needed for this kind of travel. A finger would do. The truck he chose was the first he found in El Paso, with modifications. The reinforced grocery runner now had a bed shell and roof rack for the rows of diesel-filled jerrycans, tools, and water. The bed would stay a bed. Heaps of rice bags and dog food were tied down to make a cocoon den for his dogs to wait through the days of movement until they would be allowed back out. The cab was his own. The smell of gunmetal and snacks was severe. The end product was a trim and neat vehicle ready to rip through the desert at a reasonable pace, nothing like his Washington RV with childish psychedelic designs on the outside. This was a functional machine fit for an adult focused on a destination.

Just in this fact, he could see how much change he'd undergone in the year. That he felt no desire to add decoration to this vehicle, no mirror dangles, while he stuffed items inside was lost on him until he stood back to take it in as a completed whole. Functionality had become his personality. At least for the moment. He'd worn through entertainment and color until the only thing left was the simplest of detail. It would not last. The trend always cycled through these stages. Whenever he packed a suitcase or bag for a long trip to a new destination, he'd embellish every eventuality and overpack. Then, as he viewed the realities, he used less than half of what he brought along and culled for the next one. Over time, he learned to just pack light, even when he entered red zones cut off from any exit route. Nimble with a go-bag and some extras. No time for personality. There were nights when he'd wake up without knowing where he slept until his hands found his go-bag and understood. Then he'd return home somewhere and deflate to secluded oddity. Function was important. He knew this machine would take him to California quickly no matter the conditions along the way. In it, he needn't even depend on solid highway as he did with his RV. This grocery-runner was built for off-road comfort even if it never had the chance to prove it. Nevertheless, it would require some level of driving skill he hoped he still mastered. The main concerns were the two long stretches of desert emptiness where no cities of note had ever been established. While not on the map, he knew he'd find the wreckage of tourist traps and decrepit towns aged fast when new generations fled. He might find some value there, perhaps a night spot for sleep or a place to refill his jerrycans if necessary, but not much more.

Once he left these behind, he'd be in dense California where everything was available in the complex sprawl, which would bring its own overwhelming frustrations. That was his function, now. If he could navigate it all and arrive where he intended, then he could decide if more was truly necessary or whether he might transform himself again into a resident where he never lived before. That was the real threat, not disappointed failure. The trip might be so arduous and long he'd never find energy to return again. So much effort in El Paso might be wasted on a lazy whim. Already the whim risked more than it should for the birds he trapped in the biodome. They might live a few years on the scraps of a dried landscape, but probably not much more. What of it? They all might have died without his intervention long before. Probably not the chickens. And the orchards he tended for the last few months would be ripe soon enough. It made him question his timing, whether he needed to leave because he knew a deadline was approaching, and he thought he could squeak in one fast mania beforehand. A deadline was needed. A firm date by which he would force himself to return, even if at a slow crawl.

What would be a reasonable amount of time to allow a mall converted into a makeshift biodome with a community of chickens and parrots to remain unattended? Six months seemed too long and two months seemed unrealistic. Somewhere between three and four would be enough time to break from the drag of the road, so he'd be ready again, while also leaving time to test out his ability to revive a machine race. Probably three. The trio didn't care. Since he brought them home, their clique metastasized without him. There was still the occasional playtime where one or all would fly over to see what he was doing, but they mostly preferred to fly up and watch the clouds outside from the skylights far from his reach. When the time came for him to leave, he hoped they would give him some attention. It was a mixed send-off. The Amazon came down, followed by the conure, but both flew on after a few minutes leaving him to beam with a smile on his way out the door.

The break was clean. He knew they stopped wondering where he was, and he only had a slight sense of feeling rejected. This was overcome. It was for the better they existed without him so no one would be hurt in the end. He kept to his function with the well-handled rig sweeping over crusted sand and asphalt. It was the right decision to stay with the small machine; even when he lost control, it was nonthreatening. Soon enough the valley unfolded around him as he backtracked through roads he'd known in so many stages of his life. They all collapsed together into one moment for him to live simultaneously, but only in flashes when he noticed a longstanding detail that never changed. Most were so minute that they evaded articulation and instead shifted into a general curtain outside the windows. There was no point to press. He let them come and go as a distraction for the early minutes in a long journey. The highway was surprisingly clean, despite the sand drifts here and there. The wind had never forgiven the sheen of road, choosing to wipe it bare except for the rare bands of thick cake brought in from a flood. Even these were hard packed and gave little trouble to cut through. Had he more time, he could dig through them with repetitive driving, so they would loosen enough for the wind to carry away. A single crossing only left small evidence that someone had once moved through. He knew it was the same all the way up past Santa Fe, only he assumed these would thicken and grow more impassable over time, which had clearly not yet arrived. It was the same again, like a day that repeats whenever you try to leave it behind. On this day, he was glad to see everything remained familiar. It kept him slow, but nothing like the insane crawl he kept all across the East which made the distance seem so impossibly long he was sure he'd never attempt it again. Now, he was not so sure; Washington was again within reach just as soon as his function ended and he could start again. It made him laugh. The endpoint for his comparison between the two machines he used for his travel.

The day changed to something new when he veered West in Las Cruces. The journey was young and already shed the phase where one drives out of familiar terrain and everything looks new. The I-10 was long, but he'd always exchanged it for the twenty-five in Las Cruces. Almost always. There were the rare road trips where he drove this junction ages before. The rest were all sleepy observation from the back of a train where he dozed drunk and disinterested. All those memories were unhelpful to provide him any sense of recognition other than how the terrain looked identical to the rest of the desert; his rig handled it well.

New Mexico would end soon. He was entering the first of the long stretches without the dense patchwork of towns to give a sense of progress. He could assume it would be bright brown while the blue sky blinded him until it turned deep red directly in front. He'd soon be looking at Arizona skies again, ones where colors clung so intently with themselves in the dryness that it was impossible to distinguish between a cartoon and reality. Until then, it was a sandy gap covered with rocks. The entire line of highway was clear in this same way, so he was able to keep to the main route he planned. It wasn't all sand. Just like his earlier journey had seen trees felled across the way, small boulders remained in place at times. But the agility of the truck meant he only needed to fit the narrow wheels between them and forget. It only took six days to make it through to the uneventful end. It was difficult for him to imagine being so far away in such a short time, ignoring that it would only have required two days before. Calculating based on outdated time was irrelevant. All that remained was a comparison with Washington, making this trip wholly different.

There were indeed two uncomfortable stretches of loneliness where he watched the gas dial intently, but the worst had been the stretch between Phoenix and the old California border, where the desert had changed to something he never knew. That is until the invisible line emerged, and it was row after row of farms before disappearing back into desert. He slept there, in awe of the suddenness of the oasis along the Colorado River. It should have been planned. It tempted him to detour and follow the river upstream to view the dam he knew choked it, just as he did for his own suffering river valley. His function wouldn't tolerate it. It only allowed him to explore and find a mall where he could sleep in the huge mattresses displayed in whatever anchor store still survived.

Between the boulders and the farms was an increasingly eerie number of dusty vehicles strewn on the shoulders. The law of the afterworld held that as he continued West across timezones, more people had been active when they evaporated. The reminder made him shudder to think what the cities in Asia would be when or if he ever managed to reach them. What he passed were the same as before, with tractor rigs plowed through rails as the highway curved away, overturned sedans with engaged speed control to be hastily overcome by automatic brakes, and so many cars just slowly rolled to a stop with no drama whatsoever. Without the rains to wash these clean again, they were all coated in fine sand which made them look as if they were just outside the blast zone of a large explosion. The wind took care that these weren't buried just as it swept clean the road under him. The truck bounced through it all. In the back, three dogs slept uneasily as their bedding rocked them for eight hours a day, sometimes being nearly thrown to the roof when he needed to drive down an embankment. They were always glad to emerge in the evening to some new place full of potential.

No mechanical drama occurred on the way and there was only one scare when he passed over an enormous rock he failed to see in time. The tire cried out in pain, but he found no damage when he stopped to inspect. So, it managed to hobble along again. Still, he was thankful this trip was only the thousand miles to San Jose and not the full spread back across to Washington he nearly attempted once before changing course. It was now the third-longest road trip he'd ever made. The second was also along the route from El Paso into New Mexico, but that one left the main highways to reach Oregon through Utah in a borrowed car his friend returned after dropping him off. They planned out how to reach Oregon with their restaurant schedule as a timetable sine there was no room for leave requests without the risk of being dropped entirely and never scheduled again. A quiet firing. Together they drove through the backroads all the way, swapped shifts nonstop and slept on the shoulders. They could have taken the same route he did now, but they used geometry to estimate time in the days before online maps. That took three days of never ending road through hours of silent landscape with only two mutually acceptable CDs. It was drive that took them through the Southwest to emerge in the wetlands of the Pacific Northwest, waking up to views only reserved for campers and nomads committed to living far from civi-

lization.   This was not that drive; he stuck to a
plan.

There was only one detour, one part of the original
plan took him through another set of backroads.   Familiar ones, enough of a challenge to find that he
questioned whether his memory had in fact stemmed from
anything real.   The peyote preserve was never easy to
find.   It existed somewhere within the desert roads,
hidden within an alcove of rock to keep out law enforcement hostile to the jurisdiction of the Supreme
Court in such remote areas.   It was meant to be difficult to find, so it could continue preserving the cactus in peace.   It was out there to prevent raids and
let walkers have their visions in peace with the cartoon sunsets over rocky hills.   The last time he was
there, he'd fasted for a day before driving out from
Tuscon and arrived already weak, uninterested in exploring the ranch before he hunkered down in his cold
campsite.   He wanted this detour so he could raid the
area under the pretense of entitlement.   The least he
could do was liberate what he knew was alive in a
small cement shed, take a tax in the process.   Everything was a rescue.   Anything wild and trapped under
the rubble of civilization needed him to reach out and
pluck it from its desperate condition; the ambiguous
act that could at once be narcissistic martyrdom or
reasonable compassion.   Neither mattered.   In his hungry mind, he failed to carve a clear memory for the
turn-off from the main highway or the driveway itself.
All he knew was the area was hugely remote.   Any blind
search would take weeks of pointlessness he knew would
end far short of finding the right turn to bring him
to the ranch.   It could have been resolved with a
quick email search or, better still, a fumble through
the internet knowing not many peyote ranches existed.
That was the old way only temporarily new.   He needed
to reach further back and find an address using the
slow process of desk research and hope the resources
physically available would mention one.

There was nothing the magazine racks where he found
Hoopla's address.   It might have been ambitious to

imagine a nonprofit given over to a sacred mission would advertise in the flood of cannabis-focused periodicals doing more to promote the grift of CBD's than enlightenment. It was a dead end. He felt he might have a better chance at his university library, somewhere in the horticulture stacks devoted to desert flora. It was interesting and almost ended with nothing. Several books surveyed peyote and the religion centered on it, but everything was an anthropocentric study on indigenous communities, not modern use. Dissertation after dissertation focused on preserving the past and forgot to document the present. He later scanned the religious stacks and passed a somewhat familiar logo on the spine of one modest book. That was enough. But the book was rudimentary. Somewhere between advertisement and call for social change, it left out key location data to help him navigate the unmarked roads among which he knew it hid. At best, it had a three decades old hand drawn map, but at least had some mountains listed for him to puzzle through.

It was hard sleuthing with a topographical map for Southern Arizona which helped him arrive with enough confidence at the general area he could test against the spotty GPS map in the truck before he left. In some sense, its very rural nature actually allowed him to find roads more easily as there were so few options around. He was able to mark the waypoints, write down the coordinates in case they were wiped, and continue with other preparations. By the time he was driving close, he'd already forgotten the mountain orientation from the handwritten map he forgot to take along. He was blind with GPS, left to trust his past self was diligent enough to be trustworthy. The third run over the same long dirt road let him notice the small sign behind some bushes. It was the same logo as the book. Dumb luck covered the gap in diligence. The last time was also this difficult. He nearly drove off a cliff after following the wrong driveway for miles and had to turn around on a narrow switchback. Both time ended with a small recognition of how badly the drive could have ended.

In fifteen years, little had changed. The driveway
was still a road of its own pulled into a small valley
between a cluster of small rocky mounds where countless walkers faced life's problems head on, leaving
with solutions at the ready. It was mostly still the
same, but he might have simply backfilled memory to
match what he saw in the present. It was a compound
with a main house and a few smaller structures. Up
the hill were several greenhouses he was unsure he remembered, but decided they were new as they showed
little signs of weathering. The main house was the
multipurpose building that both received guests with a
membership ledger and a reading space for them to de-
compress at all stages of their visit, with the curators' residence in the back. It was a pleasant attack
of art and books, making him feel at home. Everything
resembled the textured buttons of a peyote cactus,
down to the dotted inlays on the woodwork. He saw a
dried out teacup on a table near an empty mason jar
rimmed with old mud and heap of blankets, and he knew
someone had come inside to ease the static in their
head. The campsites outside had others. A few. The
ranch was known for a limited number of walkers at a
time so no one would feel crowded in for what should
be a solitary experience. Further up the hill was his
own campsite with the tall mound where he once sat to
pace out his first few sips of bitter green juice.
Someone was buried in a sand drift near a tent still
anchored to its stakes but tried desperately to escape. He uncovered him and the beads he used to wear
fell out of the sandy shirt. How had he experienced
the moment of evaporation, he wondered. The event was
instantaneous, but had time slowed enough for the visions to catch the fading landscape before everyone
was transported onward to the next place? It might
have appeared as the psychedelic thunder god falling
down to catch all of humanity as predicted on cave
walls. The beads had seen something, now they waited
in the sand again where he found them.

The place was as solemn as ever. There was no time in
this valley. It was a place where you go to remember
how the sun moved across the sky and dipped below the

horizon to allow stars emerge against the absolute black of space. Everything was still, even the squat painted adobe shed where he knew very old lives rested. They were all arranged as he remembered. Some not more than a few years old, clearly outgrowing their pots were meant for the seedlings of two years before. More than a few were enormous clusters of many buttons he estimated must have been almost as old as he was. They knew him. He was one of the many who poked their head into the shed to learn about how the ranch was intent on conservation. But many looked too dry and some were clearly dead. A death tax. He later learned the greenhouse was set aside as a nursery where nothing survived the long drought. The conservation experiment had run its course and something needed to be done, but he was hesitant to splash water around without understanding more on how the curators managed them. In the following days, he read through the cultivation books in the library until he felt he was a minor expert. He revived them again with a modest amount of water and stood back to view the collection of green blobs spread out across the floor of the shed. Something would have to be done. There was no chance he'd pack them along to California, but he could when he passed back through on his way home. Most. Maybe half could fit into various places in the truck, or he could use one of the trailers near the main house to haul them all back. But these were wild, only locked in the shed because they would be hunted outside. If he took half, the rest could be released and hopefully expand out from there.

The library told him to water. It told him many other things he was uninterested in knowing, like soil pH and fertilization schedules. He should want to learn this, but it was too much in conflict with the already complex function to which he'd committed. The handwritten notes in the office gave him enough knowledge to understand the chart of tasks and schedule, so he would not need to expend much more effort. An experiment was appealing, and he imagined himself replanting many of mature plants out along the highway to see if they'd take. Not too many. This desert, he learned, was not their habitual one, so it might be that any such experiment would only murder whichever ones he selected. Whatever else needed to be done for the others, he could do when he passed back through after California. He left two nights after he arrived, stopping to build rock markers in the roads which would help him find the route again at a time when GPS may not always be online. As he went, these cairns followed to mark everyplace important. It took him another day just to finish dotting the roadside with peyote and piles of rock until he was back on his way.

It was all hope that they were left in the right balance of shade and light where enough moisture could reach the roots without either rotting or drying them. If it worked, there would be a stretch of road to where he could return and not need to navigate the slow side roads to hunt buttons. In all likelihood, he was wrong. The hedge was to leave most still in the shed until he could come back and invest more time to load them all and never return again at all. And the interlude was enough to interrupt his connection to El Paso. He was now fully a traveler again without the persistent worry over how the biodome performed while he was away. Then Los Angeles rolled up when there was just enough light to show he'd arrived. It too was an onion opened in layers unlike other cities he passed without thinking. This onion was larger than El Paso. Too large. Structures began to blot out the desert early on, long before he reached anything that felt like a suburb. These came fast. Exits were everywhere, and he was overwhelmed by the options. Each came up and drifted behind since the next would always be better, always more suitable for him to stop and find a place to sleep for the night still not quite settled. On and on until the light was gone when he reached signs for the I-5 junction near downtown. Already exiting, he turned in to see what interest could be found. He knew Union Station, but nothing else, so there he went. In the dark empty, it was too oppressive a building to justify a stop. The scattered laundry told him he'd find a crowd inside, perhaps even more wreckage than he saw all over the highway. He passed it by with his window down but didn't stop. He explored. With everything so dark, it was difficult to see beyond the wide streets. So, for nearly an hour, he drove around slowly looking for a mall without taking note of where he went. Eventually he moved out too far and found only the ravaged encampments along the sidewalk where civilization created an enclave of misery. The tattered tarps surrounded grocery carts and laundry were haunting with or without the humans who lived there. It made his stomach tighten with anger. There was no where to go downtown. It was only meant for transit. In the end, he simply stopped in the road and slept where he was.

A few hours later it was light enough to leave again, so he followed the map back to the junction. The way through downtown was the same in the morning as it had been in the night. He saw settlement without destinations. All life happened in the onion layers instead, where suburbs could cluster around their own effort at a downtown. Something burned as he began to leave the city. There were signs of a huge fire that ripped through the hillsides and quieted down. The occasional fire damage was normal, especially once he left the East coast and more cooking was in process when the evaporation hit. But these were always localized. What he saw now took with it entire hillsides. Whole towns looked burned out where it seemed the charring had disappeared. It came and went throughout the mountain crossing, only fading shortly before he dropped into the grasses of the San Joaquin Valley. His evaporation was lucky. Washington was dull and safe. There might have been another who was exempted like him but burned up in the hills. He tried to push the nightmare away and focus on the long dead road in front. Compared to the desert with sand drifts, this road was clear. The carpet of grass held back the dust and there were no trees to fall in his way. He picked up speed until the turn West through overgrown farms made him jealous at the ease with which everything grew. San Jose came fast. He arrived before he was ready.

It was early afternoon by that point, so there was no need to rush into his plan. There was more than enough time for exploration in the city. He drove on as his map pleaded with him to turn back. He didn't listen. The city was all around. It was crowded and he needed to be alone. Each street dropped behind as he drove through headed North until he eventually saw signs for the Golden Gate. It stood in his mind so clearly but never seen in person beyond a brief visit at the far end during rush hour. There it was, so easy to reach without any traffic to obscure the quiet. All the cars pulled off to make way for him to drive up from the wharf. So easy in a way it never could have been before. He arrived. The traffic on the bridge was still there, even the traffic in the Bay was visible. Once he was in the center of the bridge and able to see better, the changes were evident. Huge ships passing through littered the shoreline when they came unanchored and drifted in the Bay. Ships of all sizes were everywhere. He did not remember this in New York when he entered from the water, but this was early in the afterworld. Most moorings still held back then. No matter. It didn't affect him on land, nor could he see any damage to the bridge from below. The initial shock passed, so he could dream about everywhere he'd roamed in the past two years. In that time, he managed to cross the country and stand in major cities on both coasts. It truly was all empty. He never cared to hope anymore that he might find someone and, the more he traveled, the more he confirmed his first instinct that no one was out there to be found. He had his dogs and his birds and, in a few weeks, might have a new companion. There was no need to rush. He sat there on the bridge with his dogs running around startled at the suddenness of the drop until the sun began to set, and he put them on leads just in case. They all slept up there as it grew increasingly cold when the night moved in.

The fog formed as they slept, so morning met them in bluish gray. It was not warm in the cab, but the blanket helped. He wrapped it around his shoulders to open the door and walk around in the mist as it bounced the early sunlight around. The road to either direction faded, as did the water below. They waited some time to enjoy the muffled quiet before moving on. It was the right morning for him to begin. After so much preparation followed by driving, the quiet was the interlude between tracks, giving the proper signal that these were indeed distinct phases. Had he stopped at Hoopla immediately when he first passed, everything would have blended together even if the morning would always have to be calm and quiet no matter the place. This way, he'd remember the morning as its own moment long after he forgot the drive itself or the preparations he undertook beforehand.

Crossing back through the city was less urgent than before. There was time to appreciate how banal the squat homes were despite all the history he projected onto them. He knew he'd need to make time to explore more once the press of function subsided. Through it all with the same thoughts, he made his way down into the suburbs at the Southern end.

The campus was huge. It was its own village dedicated to set the grooves within which civilization was meant to travel. Of course this project would be more complicated than he imagined from flipping through magazines. Just understanding the complex of buildings alone was enough to discourage him. It needed to be sectioned off in his mind, so he could make his own map first, before he even bothered to investigate inside them. If he tried to overextend, to simply bash in doors to rummage around ad hoc, he'd waste himself in the process. A system, though, would prevent a collapse by his own frenzied nature. One prediction held: there were few dogs roaming about. In the entire drive, he found only a handful of survivors in the long stretch without food, or those who survived learned to leave the cities that offered so little if they stayed. It barely mattered since it wouldn't change that he felt free to let his dogs run and explore on their own.

His way was inefficient at first. The drone he flew around did not offer the tactile scene he needed to commit it all to memory, so he simply biked as he would have in any era. What doors he did try were generally unlocked, which made sense given the work day had only ended a few hours before the evaporation and the many piles of laundry around still worked a reasonable degree of late. More surprising was the fact of how many doors opened automatically when he approached. There was electricity here. He had approached the first door with a crowbar, expected to pry it apart, when it simply opened and made him jump back defensively. Only then did he take notice of lights on in the lobby which confirmed for him the campus was connected to solar power and continued to operate. Not all the doors gave way, only the large lobbied ones where a reception desk would have screened out visitors from staff. The rest were card-locked with indicator lights still red, meaning he'd only need to find a stack of badges to make his way around inside.

Power was not universal. After the first surprise, he approached all doors to inspect them for signs of activity and was pleased to see them all waiting. Flashing blue lights on the emergency contact stations also maintained a false sense of comfort, as did the exit signs he saw glowing in hallways where lights were off. The grid was still necessary enough, and the solar system was only a stopgap for the outward facing facilities. When he began to step inside to the interior portions of the open buildings, lights stopped even if the way was lit red from the exit signs and card lock panels. It would have been too much optimism to assume otherwise.

As he went along, he'd consolidate the badges he found after rifling under the piles and behind security desks. These would be stacked just inside the nearest building and left behind for later tests once his mapping exercise was over, though he was mindful to separate security from staff.

The other surprise was the overall lack of huge diesel generators to run the buildings as a backup to the solar backup. At first, he imagined these would be on the roofs, but saw none from the camera on his drone. Instead, he only found the iridescent sheen of solar panels on every conceivable flat surface, from the rooftops to carparks. Solar was everything to the campus and must have provided so much tax relief and the chance to boast how diesel was irrelevant. Even garden lights and fountains had their own dedicated power supply, so he imagined the whole campus operated on decentralized energy. This was both welcomed and not. Solar was sustainable, easy to predict without the need for huge tanks of volatile liquid. Solar was also very difficult to understand or repair whenever something broke in the system. Solar meant watching helplessly after a burnout and, after two years of no maintenance or usage, any sudden surge might blow the circuits. This couldn't be helped.

All his wanders took four days to complete. It was not that the campus was so large, but that he took his time with late starts and early ends. He had expanded his bike tour out to the surrounding streets after accidentally heading too far once and decision to not immediately turn back. But the four days allowed him to cover the whole of the campus with stops at each building. It was still overwhelmingly large, particularly considering the fact he had yet begun the process of investigating the labyrinth of rooms inside them. A visitor's map he found helped with the key buildings and landmarks, so he made notations on which were supposed to be nonpublic. The staff were everywhere, but not uniformly so. As he went, he noticed clusters of laundry in some areas while others were empty. He made note of this in case something could be extrapolated for why so many people worked late here and not there. The answers might be found inside where he would certainly find new clusters of those still committed to whatever assignments had kept them. By the end of the four days, he had a reliable map ready for a strategy.

During all this, he slept in comfort inside the offices of the executive suites, which were nearly as sophisticated as any apartment living room. There was laundry here too. A hodgepodge of dress clothes and jeans were scattered around. He found a meeting underway to brief on some new remote work office policy. This was actually the first building he entered since it was where the GPS decided was the situs of Hoopla. It was indeed the headquarters building where the main reception was located in the lobby to direct visitors using a stack of printed maps, so they wouldn't be lost as they searched the campus for their destination. It was very handy. This building is what he imagined would be waiting for him when he arrived. It was a traditional headquarters full of propaganda and amenities. That first morning after his night on the bridge felt like he accomplished the end of his journey when he walked up to the doors. Then he discovered the expanse of buildings waiting for him outside needing to be cataloged and searched. While the building was fully powered, the front door was not unlocked like others with large lobbies. This building had the privilege of operating on business hours so the only way to enter was either an access card or blunt object.

It was a dilemma. He worked hard to avoid senseless destruction whenever possible, not because he wanted to preserve any specific object, but he learned there was usually a less than obvious alternative if he left his mind open. In this case, however, the ground level was entirely sealed with glass and all doors locked electronically. He used his crowbar to smash the tempered glass with no metal frame for him to try prying away first. From there, he heard the blare of the alarm as he left to give it a respectful distance to wear itself out. After it did, he went back inside to the reception desk to find his first set of security keys and the map. Here he noticed the security screens still on with images burned deep in the crystals. The assumption he cautiously formed was confirmed when the security badges began opening doors and the keys opened everything else.

For most of the interior, it was still ordinary with the expected bullpens surrounded by drab offices and the occasional conference rooms. Each level up was a slight improvement to the last until he was on the sixth floor, which suddenly changed to a reception area meant for special parties. Above this were the executive suites, only a few on each of the next three floors, but together they were connected by an enormous spiral staircase; they existed in a different world with their own elevator independent from the main one.

Each night his sweep ended on these top levels where he barely noticed the loss that had descended outside. Once he kicked out the laundry after a check for anything useful, the space was entirely his to explore for an indication of special machine intelligence programs and might shortcut the arduous search. What he found were stacks of binders which laid out, through performance reports, many of the familiar product lines. These were the arcane facets of executive duties that led him nowhere. One office had seen deep dive ahead of a decision to excise a button in a popular phone app since the engineering costs to constantly design security patches for the hastily coded original cost two million dollars annually. It was irrelevant now.

His favorite floor was the office of legal counsel on the fourth and fifth floors, for its rich array of paper strewn about. Certainly there was more contained on the shared drive, but more than enough was stacked in all available space. Drafts of filings were forever edited never to be reviewed again, as were the preferred offline notes no data breach would find. That he never found the keys for the locked cabinets was only a momentary problem, since his crowbar easily bent the thin metal. Row after row of gray drawers yawned out their contents for him to peruse. Some had sensitive discovery, but most were predictable case files and research briefs. Until he reached the senior cabinets that were better locked. These were different even before they were open. He could tell from where they were set, inside a special room on the fifth floor, access was restricted. Once open, the labeling was cryptic and did not follow the case logic he expected. These were corporate records.

It took some time to acquaint himself with the filing system, but he soon understood most of the drawers were divided into project names with timelines and budgets. There seemed to be a mix of active and inactive projects, but the titles gave no sense of what the contents really were. Somewhere between the time when he finished his map and began his search of the campus, he decided these cabinets would go further to help him track down whatever intelligence was asleep nearby. They wouldn't help him decode the technical aspects of the projects, but they would at least give him some information on where to look and maybe even how to access those systems. In terms of wasting patience, he'd do better to spend his time reading through the files than to flip through staff badges and open disappointing door after disappointing door. There might be a time when that was unavoidable, but it made little sense to start with it when a better option showed potential. Most interesting was one section marked to denote its special status as privileged communication, which would mean huge sums of money would be spent to quash discovery no matter the requesting party. It was thick in its own locked folder within the cabinet; precious but not invaluable. If they were more than just a routine level sensitivity, they would certainly have been put away elsewhere.

The small lock was more annoying than difficult to open since the small size made his hands clumsy. He razored the leather apart instead to reveal contents that were as banal as the rest of the cabinets. They differed in that these were records of various companies organized all over the planet and outlined their parental structures with key contributions to the industry. Why would such benign information be packed in such a way as to entice a thief? He took the bait. Something was there for him to find, even if it proved

to be tangential to his current function.   Entropy began.

As a standalone record, it was plain and underdevel-
oped.   These were topline summaries of what seemed
like more than a hundred separate companies in three
dozen countries.   There was a company with a fiber optic MoU's with Upazila governments in Bangladesh next
to a holding entity for a ninety-nine-year lease of
four hundred acres in the Central African Republic
next to an entity holding a wide array of radio fre-
quencies in seven countries.   They all looked independent until he found more locked folders in other cabinets equally confused at first, then he began to notice linkages in the various parental structures.
Buried in each document was a short summary which outlined in vague terms some of the tertiary operations
that somehow always led to a restriction of some aspect of the Hoopla's operations, though never indicative of a connection.   The picture he assembled was
clearer.   There was a definitive constriction around
app development directly centered on Hoopla's online
store.

He spent the time to arrange these out on the large
conference room which likely was the same used to plan
this global strategy in the first place.   Each time he
reviewed a file, he picked up new key details and recognized Hoopla products in the description less than
in the names.   Everything was in code.   Had he learned
all this in the wild, he might have guessed it was
conceptual overreach by company detractors.   But this
was all in secret file folders at corporate council's
office inside headquarters.

Apart from software, he learned the hardware supply
chain was similarly centralized with a preordained annual price inflation of nine percent for what outwardly appeared to be industry competitors.   There was
even a schedule for when the increases would occur, so
the market would interpret each as a response to another's increase.   Even chip manufacturing was af-
fected.   The key companies in graphics and processing

had their flagship products fed by joint developers on a cycle for when each would be perceived as the lead innovator, when in fact this was all decided in the same room where he sat.

Everything looked like it was under Hoopla's authority, orchestrated to appear as if the landscape was defined by organic competition. There were some missing elements. He'd had to make some logical leaps to fit together pieces that so obviously matched, he could even see the outline of what was not present in those files. It was thrilling to discover this level of corruption. The rise he got from piecing it all together was undisturbed by the fact there was no clear connection to the purpose for which he drove across the desert. He had to see this through to the end first, then and only then could he be at peace to conduct the mundane. He needed more data. The gaps had to be close, and if they were not in the special files in the special cabinets in the special closet, they would have to be held under greater security; perhaps not with the Chief Legal Officer, whose hands needed to be clean, but with their second. He rummaged. All the executive offices had locked safes, but he held hope to find a key as he always did. Locked drawers usually meant something interesting and were far easier to break open. He found a set of small keys in the lead council's office, but these did not open the safe behind the desk. Frustrated, he went to the CLO's desk and found several sets, only one of which opened that safe. In the spirit of experimentation, he brought the others back to council's office and opened the safe cleanly. More bundles. The excitement this caused was so severe he was embarrassed at his choice of celebratory movements. Back in the conference room, it was time to unpack what was so sensitive it was planted with Hoopla's head attorney, but who was not allowed access. The pear-shaped logo on the documents in the first bundle said enough. He already had the same logo in missing relief among the other records, so confirmation was a muted experience. Together, the two companies had carved up the tech sector from behind the insulation provided them overseas.

There was more to the story. More bundles needed a separate table to accommodate the distinct conversation they protected. It spoke in general terms about the cartel he mapped out, using cynical euphemisms to refer to a landscape, environment, or an ecosystem in which the company operated. There was no reference to partners or competitors, only actors and stakeholders in emails and letters about an investigation by the Federal Trade Commission which touched uncomfortably close to the nerve. The main file was not in the safe with the rest of the documents. Such a high profile inquiry would only alert whistleblowers inside the building to quickly monetize their privileged access if it were hidden from an office full of attorneys. Such records would need to be conspicuously filed near the bullpen where paralegals could suspend thought and forget they worked for an artificial person only constituted to maximize access to resources. With daylight shining on the files, the game of gaslight could be played. The FTC had been shuttled around, misled by a careful balance of obtuse compliance. The exchanges were cordial until the Department of Justice formed a grand jury that came out with a subpoena. Then the fight emerged. The office played the two agencies against one another, making them squander time until Hoopla field suit to quash the subpoena. These filings were all routine. They were the dance of lawyers shrugging shoulders at one another. Nothing unique was outside in the public cabinets, but only after viewing them did he understand the contents from the safe. They were the necessary context to eliminate the vagueness, so he saw the whole picture neither government agency had known.

Hoopla had a mole. Internal emails from the FTC had been piped over to the office by someone who hoped to bankroll an exit from government salary. The emails were high level discussions between the two agencies about the holes in the evidence they received, specifically the legal traps they were fast approaching.

From there they went on to worry about the costs to fight Hoopla, which had so far been successful in postponing the substantive hearings. Names of senior officials who were critical of the resources used were added in, as were those who were powerful allies of Hoopla in both branches of the legislature. These emails and memos were photos of the originals delivered by hand along with the phone used to create them, which were probably long destroyed. The mole had been carted off to work for one of the tendrils he recalled from the conference room files, paid triple the usual salary broken apart and hidden, so it appeared they took a pay cut in the switch. The intelligence they provided had undergone significant discussion. The photos were heavily marked up since they were printed out and filed away. He learned from the handwritten notes what strategy options were to be used, what pain points they'd exploit in order to quiet the whole endeavor, so the cartel could continue.

It all came down to money. Hoopla used its own dark funds distinct from the budget openly allocated to its legal office. In addition to fixing prices and ending competition, the cartel was also an effective laundering machine where charitable donations to special non-profits came back with purchase contracts for over-priced or even fictitious equipment. Each node provided a chance to siphon off funds obscured from audit and became the executive slush fund. There was so much of this dispensed around Washington that the pressure on the agencies had tightened to a breaking point. The FTC was pushing the DOJ to negotiate settlement terms in exchange for dissolving the grand jury and everybody walk away to heal. The strategy was to put more money into Washington to ensure the terms discussed would be minimal.

It was a mindfuck. The strategy was expansive and well funded, so it had no course but to work. What he began to wonder was what secrets were so sensitive they couldn't be entrusted to the legal team, what was in the CLO's safe he opened but didn't yet examine because the folders looked less secured, more ordinary.

What he found was worse than the rest, but more legal and thus more open. Several color-coded binders laid out all the political donations channeled into safe election PAC's both untraceable on the backend and sheltered from liability. The blue and red covers told him the vital information, but the white one was less clear. It summarized the independent and unaffiliated campaigns Hoopla supported. All of them covered offices from the local up to the presidential. They hit every note. He recognized too many names.

Another large binder organized toplines on various products under government service contracts. Some were supplemental for one agency operation or another while some were subsistence ecosystems that powered everything inside. Not all the agencies were in the United States. Most were in Africa and Central Asia, assembled with what looked like little consistency. As he read, he was able to pick up on subtle cues in the language of the functionality sections. These never outright detailed how Hoopla maintained special access privileges to the systems, but it was clear every product had a backdoor not communicated to the client. This meant that, depending on the level of integration, Hoopla might have total access to government functions all over the world. In context, he knew there was no compunction inside the building on making use of this access all under the pretense of security backtesting.

Everything he found over the preceding days illustrated what he already suspected, what most people who paid attention had suspected. The age of industrial cartels dividing civilization had returned. Hoopla was one, but there was no doubt that all sectors were led by untouchable suprastates so powerful they were ungovernable from the outside. None of the sappy stories about price increases or wage limits had ever been about the cost of doing business and everything to do with the cost of organizing a criminal enterprise. At the top were the executive officers whose pay seemed outsized until you scratched deep and saw that it really matched their skill in how well they concealed the rotten greedflation from everyone else. Retention pay and bonuses were all hush money to keep them in the family. Even when they left, it was only an internal reshuffle to justify a periodic cashout from all the hidden money they'd accumulated inside. There was no conspiracy, though. It was well known and well documented, but everyone was powerless to intervene. All anyone could do was swap memes which did more to establish a poster's plebeian credibility on the off hours while taking no steps to course correct when they were handed momentary control. Everyone knew it would only be a dusting of forgettable poison at the edge of the anthill; not even the two most powerful enforcement agencies could intervene to pour gasoline deep into the nest below.

There were more safes. More of the dismal portrait waited for him if he chose to look. Nothing was to be done for it. This was a study of the dead. A reluctant examination of the contents deep in the storeroom where myths disappeared. There was nothing relevant in the other safes, though. On one desk he found a stack of binders some laundry had been reviewing who he decided to brush aside to explore. The Chief Financial Officer had been reviewing the stream of dark fund flows leading to hidden offshore accounts where it was chopped and distributed to thousands of other accounts identified only by alphanumeric codes. How many of these were payrolled staff or loyal foot soldiers was not in the records. The amounts at stake were staggering. The deposits must have provided global liquidity for those institutions that helped them convince their governments to fight to the death any effort to end the era of secrecy.

One of the binders led him closer to his original goal with an outline of a machine learning project focused on mitigating ethnic bias in facial recognition software, not because of any altruism, but for an increased access to emerging markets in Africa and South Asia. He didn't assume this. The objective was clearly stated on the cover sheet. It was a product efficiency program. In order to make the improvements, the project blanketed the globe with randomized controlled trials that fed into a central lab which made adjustments on the fly for the pilot equipment. Despite the consolidated development team, the project itself was fragmented across many of the companies he mapped in the conference room, with Hoopla officially serving as the technical advisor for these startups as part of a pro bono arrangement through a nonprofit he recognized from his life before as a private sector donor for international development. It was a master-class in greenwashing internal innovation offices. The rest of the binder was thick with chapters on aspects of the technology that needed careful documentation to the central leadership. Explanation of how this component fit within the larger cartel was expressed in a curt summary over a few pages, with the remaining two hundred for the dense subject of how this machine was taught to not hate melanin despite mounds of records to the contrary. He did his best to wrestle with the language, to understand the charts and models that did more to illustrate the operation of the program than any dozen pages of text. He caught passing bits on occasion, which led him deeper into the contents. All other activity stopped while he read through it all. This was not about a distraction, but rather an exit from one that saddled him with the revival of anger at how entrenched wealth was at the end of humanity. He convinced himself if the binder could be understood more clearly, he might catch some critical details to help him find the lab there on campus. It took several days of intensity to make it to the final page. It was a journey, itself full of back references and re-read chapters which seemed understood until some subsequent section undid everything he believed he learned. The process was slow, but eventually pieces fit together.

It was disappointment in the end. All the effort to chew through the dense pages led him to the under-standing that the development lab was, in fact, a virtual space where the developers pushed code for the backend teams to repackage into updates. There was no physical space where the developers tested their upgrades with actual equipment on the campus. All the developers themselves were remote contractors who likely had little awareness of how their contributions were connected to a unitary product line. From their perspective, they provided support to a dozen independent companies with all the test equipment located in various countries. None of it was near him. The whole system operated on a cloud only accessible through a dedicated private satellite network to keep it all secured. This meant passcodes and permission restrictions would keep him out even if he found an access point, which almost certainly existed in the main building. That all this was essentially a theoretical project, and only existed on cold disks somewhere did not leave him as discouraged as he imagined. Instead, he felt emboldened that he was able to understand the project at all. This left room for hope that he was trainable over time.

Even with this dedication, he couldn't bring himself to stay shut inside entirely and would spend much of the day outside doing little at all. The large windows helped convince him more was waiting just beyond the glass. The initial campus map had been marked to indicate which buildings had power or which appeared to have a large cluster of staff working late, so he let himself aimlessly wander about with the occasional investigation inside. Not much. This was mostly the mind of a voyeur with curiosity needing to be quieted with touched items on desks and by lining up used pairs of shoes to imagine what the crowd might have looked like before they all left. It was a welcome release for a mind building up a burnout from intense reading and anger at the legal files he found. It was a study break for a student who learned a new language he never felt patient enough to attempt before, but now was the only barrier that remained for him to finish his now special project.

So, the more intense the read, the more exotic his dalliance across the campus became. Small details left outsized impressions on him as he roamed. At one point, he collected all the canteens to let them face

off against the vastly outnumbered glassware. The
kawaii desk adornments became the audience cheering on
one side or the other. When he ran out, he'd scavenge
another floor taking on new ideas as he went. That
fizzled as quickly as it came. The secrets locked in
the dense binder unwound, and he fell back from the
heights towards a moderated manner of sweeping the
buildings. The largest ones had seemed to him general
purpose, full of coders who worked an open floor with
the privacy of cubicle walls removed. They were mod-
ernized attempts to overdress mundane workspaces now
essentially rows of desks more appropriate for a university computer lab than any focused workforce. No
doubt these were where fresh graduates commingled with
other junior engineers who hadn't yet earned privacy.
Screens were everywhere and in some way replaced the
cubicle walls, albeit imperfectly. Attached to these
were the small boxes of networked workstations with
the occasional personal notebook propped open nearby.
There was no power for these. It was all as dead as
the shoes. This didn't matter much since these were
the artworks for the massive company, not the discrete
laboratory for innovation on the frontier of technology. He might have found wonderful details inside
those machines, but they would not lead him to the
destination he sought. The nearby offices were different in that they were still alive but equally useless. It was a trend repeated at headquarters as much
as the rest of the campus. Unimportant stations were
not set with the solar backup in the event of power
failure, which might only have come during an excess
of weather which only those in offices were paid to
ignore. The rest would have the right to call the
catastrophe a holiday of some sort, which now helped
him to narrow the field of temptation.

In them, he would face wall after wall of password
locked systems he knew would shut him out before he
made any attempt. He still pretended to be able to
guess what each might be with a glance around the
desks for chits of paper that might accidentally lead
to a successful breach. It was a numbers game; a hope
someone had become so overwhelmed by the need for so

many passwords to be refreshed every sixty days that
their memory fell apart, and they wrote something
down, even for an instant. The field was not large
enough for success. What he found were a range of security locks. Most systems were rudimentary, but others required card access or used fobs with timed
codes, but a very few select machines used biometric
locks. The combinations needed to bypass these by
luck were disturbingly out of reach so all he could do
was gather the badges and fobs he found nearby for
later testing if it had to come to that.

In all the buildings there was a trend away from paper
documents unlike what he found at headquarters. The
desks and offices he investigated were clear of these
and had been replaced by the clutter of plastic and
wires across the rows of tables. Even sticky notes
were fading from view in favor of reusable LCD pads
magnetized to various surfaces with most long since
losing power from the small batteries inside. This
was unsurprising. Paper was old and added an unnecessary step to communicate when all the information was
held inside a digital machine. It was more surprising
he found so much of it at headquarters outside the legal offices where paper would always hold a place of
privilege. The principal choice for other professions
was the whiteboard, which he found abundantly across
the campus. It seemed like every large flat surface
was ripe for installation, particularly the conference
rooms and other meeting areas where minds came together to draw irrelevant graffiti. The works he
found left no impression on him whatsoever. It was
all technical schematics and acronyms that died with
the workforce. He was careful not to erase any of it
on the chance there might be some obscure reference to
something he needed at some future hypothetical time.
Some of it described elegant architecture he could sit
back to appreciate on its face, without the need to
understand what it did or where it fit in the system.
These were moments of respect and dignity for the fab-
ulously complicated skills once housed there and be-
lied by the love of quirky entertainment evident on
the desks.

Across the spaces he found variation was subtle but distinct, no less clear from the placards used to denote what units were where. Stripped of awe for the complexities, he found it all the ordinary distribution of operational functions across office spaces where departments could be clustered for better efficiencies. He had yet to find any product labs that broke this trend. The closest he came were the server rooms which held their own cultural ecosystem hidden from the rest. These were not the scaled stacks needed to run the public facing operations, but were smaller internal hubs to power the workstations outside. They were an epicenter of activity powered down some time in the two years when the culture that ran them evaporated. The rooms were card locked which the general security badges did not open, but they yielded to violence quite well. He was in rooms of various sizes, all with the stale smell of old warm plastic and ozone. The main building had the largest. At the desks to command it all, he found a disarray of tablets and peripherals alongside long shelves of neatly bundled wires to fit every purpose. Above them, on the wall, was a large regional map of California dotted with small bulb pins, mostly up and down the Central Valley. They were color coded and then alphanumerically coded with more dead acronyms. Other lesser maps of Northern Virginia, Montana, and the Dakotas were not far. He studied them. There was Ashburn in orange, the same color most common on all the maps. Next was green, with only one blue just outside of Modesto. It didn't require specialized knowledge to understand blue as the unique color that powered the campus, but this was confirmed by shift logs on the whiteboard which scheduled regular visits to the site and suggested he might also be out there soon. Pain.

His nightly interest in the contents at headquarters wore off as he closed the special project binder. His head burned with information by that point after a sprint across so many private records. It felt like time to begin settling in for the months ahead. While he set up camp in the executive suites, he so far had

171

not spent the time to make the space his own and he was tired of sleeping on the couch, no matter how rare it had been.

The whole top floor was a like an expensive holiday with a flourish of artwork and glass walls which lacked only for the same plumbing problems in every building. It was bright and lively during the day with blackout curtains to prevent the streetlamps from disturbing darkness at night. The executive levels were so large he could spread out his work and still walk up to the top floor and be removed from it all. And then there was the terrace above, which stayed so green from the gray water replenished every time it rained. What it needed was something of a proper setup for a long stay; it needed a mattress and bedding for him to spread out. All was easily found, as was the steady supply of water jugs he sent up with the elevator and met from the stairs. The unexpected continuation of power made for the highest degree of comfort he'd seen yet, and began to reconsider a return to El Paso. Momentarily.

It also meant refrigeration. Not that much was still around to need cool storage, but with such large options as were in the banquet hall within the commercial grade kitchen, he could find ways to cook elaborately again and keep the rest for later. Cooking would no longer need to be a daily activity if he wanted to avoid the stale packaged foods. Refrigeration space such as this meant freedom and shopping.

Not since he left Washington did he have on hand so many options from East Asia. The whole of the Bay Area, like most of the West Coast, had so many huge grocery stores with food renowned for being perfectly preserved to withstand years of storage. He craved so much he left to stock up whatever was still edible at one down the street. The decay was less pronounced than before, it was more aged and settled inside the store that had been crowded on a Friday night. There were clear signs that waves of animals found their way in; the cats always hung around waiting for fish to be thrown away, rats evaded them, raccoons who chased them all away, and the onslaught of roaches and ants to clean everything out. The result was a smell closer to cured compost than rotten produce and meats. Old five spice and methane. He only wanted the overly salted fish and dried goods the invaders ignored, but found huge sections of the dried noodle aisle intact along with most of the brined vegetables. He took so much but left behind a great deal more, knowing he'd return whenever the mood struck. He then drove back down to the farms he passed on the way in, filling crates full of garlic and a few items from kitchen gardens.

In all this time he saw no dogs. Part of him knew El Paso and the desert were similarly empty more because most pets starved early on and the rest over time, but had told himself it had more to do with the harshness of the climate and less with the animals themselves. He had to. The sleight of hands was needed to stay unaccountable for leaving his pack in Washington, it allowed him to believe dogs roamed the country just outside the desert where they could easily find food and water. Once he pushed himself out the city around campus, he finally had to accept the sudden flash of mania that forced him across the continent meant their eventual death. There was no relief in finding the area clear of feral packs. The thought disappeared. Guilt was a fleeting luxury, one that was only relevant for a moment to register it had life before it could be accepted as another bite from circumstance. By the time he returned to campus, it was long past, and he hauled his take inside to the kitchen where he cooked his porridge in peace.

Upstairs again for the night, he was busy opening cabinets in the offices to see what idle secrets he'd find. Not many. Mostly he only found bottles of alcohol and exercise equipment. There was one with a small minifridge full of cannabis edibles and sacks of mushrooms. Hardly a secret, but certainly a welcome sight except for what had long since molded. The freezer was categorically different. That the power had never cut in the two years since it was last opened made him tingle when he saw the vials of tiny paper, disregarding the large sack full of multicolored pills stamped with hearts and aliens.

The Bay Area was always known for its LSD fetish, which had become deeply connected to the new generation of tech executives who could be so removed from the rules of business, so they dosed liberally while stacking zeros. That it was known was not the same as it being expected, nor in such quantities. He'd run across dozens of stashes before, but most were hard drugs or cannabis or both. He rarely found well-preserved psychedelics anymore, especially not one so fragile as LSD. These vials of blotter had most certainly originated as very potent and clean, but the question was whether it survived, whether it was properly handled before stored away.

He immediately put it all back, knowing that everything from light to temperature degraded the molecules, so rapidly he might destroy it simply through an indecisive examination. This was something to be protected, something to consider carefully. The fine line between danger and euphoria would be hard to navigate, but the idea held him. He was in the ancient psychedelic capital, where his recordings were once alive and commonplace. His mind was already practiced with a heavily distorted reality, but he knew from long ago that what slept in the freezer was something electric and different. It came to him, so suddenly he hadn't time to prepare his response to the question building up deep within.

V

Blindspot

The mind needs rest. There must be chapters to demarcate the segments of a life lived through storied
days, without which the motion of time is forgettable.
Vacations and holidays to those fortunate enough to
possess them can stand as such markers, if the chore-
ography is right. After more than a week of study and
preparation, it was time to insert some interlude that
had no purpose. It need only deliver him outside the
normal surroundings, new so recently, but rinsed of
shine at being absorbed to the tail end of the journey
to reach it. He needed to mark the line for when he
crossed into life at the campus that separated his
time where he concentrated all his energy on simply
arriving, which he managed well in such a short time.
He was careful to leave the freezer behind and bike
around off campus to search for new places to explore.
The more he expanded, the more everything resembled
anyplace else. Even the waterfront appeared to be
little more than a flat treeless plane kept safe from
the expansion of people he could have found in nearly
every town; even El Paso had similar preserves once
the river was allowed to flow again. It invited no
duty of contemplation to sit there and watch. Not
anymore.

The silhouette of mountains at the far edge of the
valley seemed a better place to find this. The first
attempt to reach them on his bike ended after an hour.
It would be unreasonable to expect to hike with any
satisfaction after so much delay and effort, so he
went home and instead drove back early the next day
hoping to catch the sun as it left the deserts to the
East. At its base, he wasn't sure where to find a
trail up and risked cutting his own where and when he
could until he found the overgrown main route halfway
up. It wasn't nearly such a challenge as the steep

rocky climb above El Paso. It was smaller and more of a stroll. Greener too.

On the way, names of landmarks and towns resonated. All Spanish. His feet moved inches at a time while he imagined the slow creep of empire across the hemisphere. El Paso was a lifetime away, yet here they were. The genocidaires spread out unmatched even by the empire that followed behind. He knew he could follow the line down along the water as far as it went and still never leave what they claimed for themselves. From the top, hazy coastline appeared. Left then right. Both sides claimed. Behind him was the valley that commanded the world for the last few decades, entrenching power for what would likely have been centuries. The empire of information they erected was as constructed on a foundation of destruction as that carried on horseback centuries before. The water continued behind it again. The sunrise ripened over it with light reflected off far away windows all the way downtown, even across the water. This was a hugely open city more like El Paso than New York, which blockaded the skyline. This was sprawl only halted at water's edge and the need to keep homes near to the ground else risk watching them collapse when the earth moved. There was much out there for him from this vantage, but he knew it was all ordinary and unwelcoming once he climbed down to meet it.

So he did anyway. He knew his chapters always ended with emptiness. It was the forever routine which followed phases of energized motion that, until it was given sufficient space to inflate, would linger on in half measures never quite ending. He climbed down assuming he'd need to explore any unwelcome in the empty city to firmly cap his first week, which would need to begin at the campus where his routine could find a home. Pulling up to the buildings so near the traditional start of the day felt like arriving late for work to find the building evacuated. The shift between phases had already begun. What he left so familiar in the early darkness again became something odd just as the morning matured. This was the signal a new wave would form, and he'd need only ride it across whatever expanse he imagined for himself at that moment. He felt like being a tourist; exploring in ways he never could afford in the past. He drove directly to downtown and stopped at the wharf, almost expected to find souvenir carts waiting to sell him something fungible. What he found was a continuation of what he saw on the Golden Gate from a distance. Rows of wreckage clogged the piers where moored ships wracked themselves during storms. One large cargo ship headed to port drifted into the Bay Bridge then capsized to spill shipping containers into the water where some had floated over to crush the ferry docks. The destruction matched what he saw in the streets as he passed through the congested city.

It was easy to ignore. He drove on to look for an interesting place to park and found it where the hobby yachts were moored and wondered if he might find one intact enough to boat around. The choices were slimmer than in Washington, where the water was calmer, and he explored when fewer storms had yet to batter them in place. So many were half sunk and threatened to disappear entirely. It wasn't worth much effort, so he only bothered to check laundry he found inside the gated portions of the pier and found one modest fishing boat easy to refuel. The damage was minimal, but it was there. Great streaks where the wood had nearly punctured the hull lined the creamy green sides. The tourist might die with no newspaper to document, but he was entering a day of risk to chase an interlude. The water was choppier than the Chesapeake but his horrendous hours fighting a mid-Atlantic storm trained him how to navigate around calmly with no destination in mind. Should he dock at Alcatraz or press East to visit Berkeley? It was all flat blue plane with sunshine overhead invaded by dark clouds that soon brought wind and more chop. The tourist declined to continue.

Back at the pier, he made his best effort to secure the moorings tightly in case he wanted a repeat and left, headed up towards the city with no landmark until he noticed the pyramid jut out. He walked towards it and passed an ancient bookstore whose named resonated as far back as college, when he devoured the underground then-mainstream novels it published. The complex intersections were totally destroyed when traffic suddenly ignored all the lights. There was something more. Shop windows looked broken with the shelves inside in disarray as if someone like him had come through and rummaged the insides. The feeling he might not be alone suddenly became real again. It was a discovery the tourist had not expected. The mood of risk changed, too. Everything suddenly came to life. The dead buildings and junkyard streets could be faded, as could the styled laundry so flat from rain and spread out from wind that he could no longer interpret what the human inside had been doing at their last moment. None of this was alive anymore, he was sure. It was the hidden homes of the unsheltered, fitted just out of sight, which absorbed all the risk.

On occasion, he found communities, not as large as the one where he slept in Los Angeles, but subtle with their tightly bound piles that were the only security against such public living. California's reputation. The West coast's reputation. He knew from Oregon that street life was unique along the Pacific. The ordinary suffering and inequities to drive anyone out of homes and shelters merged with a deliberate anarcho-street ethos where many were just passing through to take note of the experience from which they may never leave. This was nothing new, perhaps as old as the cities built at the terminus of railroads with mild weather. It was the other American dream celebrated since the depression and accelerated when the menu of substances expanded out from ethanol just in time for the flood of mental patients to be rightfully released from endless prisons. Then the image changed from the hat-in-hand hobo ready to work for a hot meal to the dangerous addict capable of superhuman strength so immense, just hearing their rants echo in the streets caused fear. All in time for NIMBY washouts from civil rights marches. The tributaries combined into a perfected form of misery hated for its inconvenient solutions. The cavalier coast tolerated more since the edges blurred between the trapped and the chic.

It was there in the art. Bubbly letters at dangerous heights marked where rules had no meaning, where the city would have to decide either it no longer cared or it could no longer tolerate the intrusion. The letters tested these boundaries. One would invite another that, if not erased, would invite a contest between artists until one would dominate unquestioned. Then, either the style would be absorbed into downtown adverts or wiped out under huge murals intended to tolerate only some of the local flavor. Passing through, it was difficult to see where this line occurred except for the clean concrete. The flashpan was there under it all when he looked carefully. Art always found a way. It was the same as everywhere. Cities congested with stress and agitation led to an outpouring of creativity, but these were desperate acts of survival when a critical mass of humans overcollected and no one from among them mattered anymore without expressing the currency of misery better than someone else. For everyone who stood apart were thousands who drowned quietly with the same anguish that never found appeal. They all burrowed deep in the cities with their collective mistakes, their collective effort to aimlessly navigate the congestion where a slip may prove fatal. Did prove fatal. Most carried these with them for a lifetime, never able to leave behind their past except to survive it as long as possible. It was all there, left behind for him to see and reflect back what he himself knew was his own journey. What he wanted to understand from the city was not clear even to himself as he wandered through, articulating generalities across whatever he saw.

He lived his own streetborn madness not so long before. He lived the urban itinerant life in Washington, for months wandering the mall and random streets that fed it. That this was done without the derision of others did nothing to change the impact of his inability to fit anywhere he was taught one ought to live. So many nights on hard concrete numbed him dis-

comfort by elevating where his tolerance would otherwise have screamed. It happened so quickly, so easily, he understood how simple a line it was between
shelter and not. The slightest of detours could have
steered him there sooner, as would it have done for
any of the derisive people in any city. It was only
through the fortune that all eyes disappeared and were
blind to his descent and he never needed to carry it
as a shame. It was all part of a pastime wherein he
once entertained himself with freedom. His decadence
of those months were a necessary part of his ability
to repair himself, to move beyond the grotesque trauma
until he found his path to enjoy the afterworld while
it lasted. What better city than San Francisco to dip
back into the carelessness of psychedelic nihilism?
He had the tools. The city. The LSD. The garish
view into rot civilization left behind. He wondered
what form such a trip would take, whether he still had
the mental strength to survive it. He knew the question would persist as an echo.

There was nothing left of the tourist. The weather
had turned grim and his exploration had only found un-
flattering details that pushed him to an urgent need
for distorted reality. He walked back the way he
came, to where he parked his truck at the water, then
drove back to campus where he had his new home. Everything he saw in the street followed with him. It
had always been there, he just hadn't noticed until
the intimacy of feet on pavement let him seek it all
out. The bell could not be unrung. Without hesitation, he went directly to the freezer to contemplate
dosage. The vials were full of what appeared to be
several dozen blots, each in cold storage for at least
two years, perhaps longer. One would certainly be
enough, except he had the experience with preparing to
launch across the void only to discover the chemical
was worthless. Should he bring a backup? There were
plenty of mushrooms inside. This was clearly the
stash of someone with knowledge, and money, so he
should trust what went into the freezer, was not discarded, would still be active. Three might be enough

if the potency diminished enough.   Four would be a tremendous risk. Three.

The plan was to sleep rough, as tradition required. To add a ceremonial component, he decided Haight-Ashbury was the proper destination to be reckless in the city.   In reality he had few alternatives in mind and assumed the awareness of where he was might trigger a some hours of nostalgic empathy to could carry him over for the next phase of his visit, the actual function for why he was there.   When he arrived in the late afternoon he felt uneasy with his surroundings, which were more of the same as elsewhere.   An immediate trip would galvanize this in hallucinations throughout the night which might lead to pure terror. At least a night of unsheltered roaming to better understand himself in this city would better deliver him to a morning ready to depart.

So it went that he parked the car and wandered for a decent place to sleep for the night, dropping several doses of an indica tincture at the outset.   There could be no entry to the homes here. He wanted nothing from inside the buildings that might mire him down.   Every block, though, was of the same mind and turned him away until he eventually reached the park and set out his bedding under some trees.   No sleep came.   There was no watching the stars above, dark behind the thick cover of clouds as they misted down and made the whole area damp with cold before it was night. He tried. He told himself this was the way it should be until the senselessness of aggravation overcame him, and he packed up to find the train he passed on the way in, which should at least have made for a dry night, sleep notwithstanding.   The cars seemed to have glided to a stop and were at rest without substantial damage to anything.   The inside was full. The stops were full too. Everybody had wanted to pack in for a Friday night and he felt their presence. If there had been fewer, he might have been free to bundle them all up to toss out the door, but with so many he felt outnumbered and reluctant.   Instead of this, he found his way to the back where an empty seat was still available.

His eyes closed well enough but sleep was sporadic. Then the tourist fatigue prevailed enough for him to drift off with his head leaned against the cold window. Somewhere in there, the tourist disappeared. He felt it gone when he awoke with the car as black as the street outside. He sat in a hazy warmth waiting for more sleep to come. Not long afterward, the black lifted to show him wet beads on the window that made it difficult to see beyond. Then the gray sidewalks emerged as a band of monochrome between the asphalt below and drab houses above. The more light outside, the more empty the street seemed to become. Yes there were cars rammed into one another, but the lack of life was what he noticed first. Predawn streets are always empty and gray, but he was watching this from inside a crowded train car amplified the emptiness just as would a sink of cold dishes. The transition dragged on for a long time, forcing him to observe the dim blue wet morning so visually hostile he was paralyzed, unable to leave the warmth of his sleeping bag.

It was exactly that life was suddenly abandoned which showed him how alone he was where he sat, surrounded by grocery bags and earbuds. He'd had hundreds of similar moments over the years, but somehow none were as severe as this one. He met small tragedies everywhere he went and had been able to disregard them enough to consider them his playthings. He understood the day would be better suited to eat his dose and hope for the best. There could be no trust in this place. The city would not suddenly sever itself from the echos still swarming around, nor would he suddenly discover a detail to uplift him from everything he felt over the past two days. Nevertheless, he was very aware his decision might prove a terrible one. The ledge where he stood might overlook a high cliff he wished to mistake as only a few feet further to fall. LSD differed from psilocybin and mescaline; he would have less control over thoughts that would linger longer. But the fundamental difference was that LSD was about risk. It was not a sacrament, it was a portal. To where, no one can know.

He ate it and sat on the train to wait. For all the technology surrounding him, the body still needed forty-five minutes to metabolize. That's fine. Time already collapsed and there was not much else to do. Taken in sequence, there were the immediate notions of where to go and what was needed upon arrival. How to know when arrival comes? Stressful. But the new purpose of the train was anything but. At any rate, everything might be mapped out well in advance if one knew how to look. Even a slip of knowledge will jerk along the way. So on it came, though not in the form of his destination. Rather it was the imperceptible pulse of anticipation in the realization that a journey was already well underway. The moment of control at the outset, which begins to crystallize and pass as flawlessly as it should. But this moment had not run its course. It had only let on its presence against the backdrop of other doings he might imagine for himself. In those early minutes, he was aware it was impossible to reverse course even as nothing had yet shown over what he had done.

So he needed to wait while watching the empty street outside until something appeared to indicate the small paper squares were active. His paralysis had left him, but he stayed in his seat until something happened. Forty-five minutes to wait and think through where he might find himself in another twelve hours. Or more.

As he did, he was back in the moment inside the train car with all the empty seats he let himself believe still had occupants. The smells came back. Whatever rotten groceries there were once in between the rows, they lost power and the old aromas returned. He waited and thought about the sweet oil and plastic smell of public transportation, the smell of so many passengers that none of it was particularly human any longer. This could have been his life. So many times before, he planned to live in this city. There was always one more step needed in order to live it out. Each of them met the insurmountable barrier of expense. When he came closest, with a fresh profession which tradition taught was the avenue for security, it collapsed under the expansive recession from which he needed another decade to recover. By that time it was unimportant to plan further. He'd moved on, and the city continued to grow more unequal. It was still unimportant.

His head was in a loop. Emptiness led to loneliness led to memories led to emptiness, and so on. Why was he so stuck in this way? He knew it didn't matter, this was all disaster thinking that meant nothing. When had it begun? When had he begun? Hadn't this always been with him, just in versions distinct from now? The loop had an offramp: what if he had taken too much LSD and this was the entry point to the impact? He'd never attempted three blots before. He was experienced enough, but three was more than enough to send him elsewhere if the chemical chains hadn't degraded much. If they were fully intact, it would be something more. The loop, he wondered, might not even exist. Each thought might be new since each moment in which it came was also new. At exactly fifty-seven minutes the confusion began.

Then the confusion had an offramp: the chemicals might be inert or not, but his mind was too accustomed to distortions and three fully functional blots might not have been enough. What had he experienced? The nightmare of the afterworld had no connection to reality as he understood it. The impossibility of eight billion people to disappear with no warning, no scrambled response from the seats of power couldn't possibly have been something real. Might it have been a glitch in the simulation to spin him out from the rest into a scenario of decay? What distortion did he actually know could prepare him in the train, if it actually existed either. And what was it he smelled?

The rain outside had paused as the sun worked its heat on the clouds. What remained was a wind that swirled through the city to foreshadow the depth of cold not far away. Together, they dried the windows and the swelling sounds touched alongside the hull. Occasional bursts made the undercarriage creak as the car rocked imperceptibly. His head turned this way and that, attentive to one detail before moving to the next. The sounds that began so slightly grew louder and what was before such small vibrations of the car became great quakes. He worked to study each of them, visualizing the creaking metal to understand what mechanism was activated in the wind. Might it be the wheels, which were held in place by gravity not brakes, so they might give out with the slightest of additional force? Had he chosen poorly that this was a safe place to rest?

The movement from one detail to the next changed from sleepy boredom to alert awareness, but now skipped in spurts with persistent awareness. The dancing trees overlapped with creaking sounds that together gave a sudden impression the train moved again and, once perceived, could only be studied. What if it began to move, and he couldn't tell? What if it was already moving? Perhaps it was. Everything fed his senses to suggest motion. It was unmistakable. The trees did more than sway rapidly in the gusty wind, they pushed the ground beneath them which was slowly rolling. The rocking car was rhythmic as if the wheels clicked over segments of the track. It did none of this. It fed confusion further. He tried to focus and undo what he was well on his way to believe. It took intense focus on the sidewalk, the only feature unbothered by the wind. It only moved in relation to everything else, but it was fixed in place with the buildings. What about the buildings? Until then, he'd successfully ignored them except as landmarks to help him navigate around. They were empty, he knew, but he never checked. He told himself he was no longer afraid of what was inside homes, only that he didn't want to burden of memory from what he was likely to find. It was more than burden. He was still afraid. The people were still inside to desperately cling to him if only he erred enough to cross through the door.

If they were waiting before, they were waiting now. How would they know if he was there if they were nothing but a film left on clothing? Did they have a shape, a form, a way to communicate across from wherever they exited? The more he stared at their homes, the more their windows became the mechanism by which they watched him. The sun and the clouds joined the wind. They pushed around light and objects until he caught faces staring back in the glass before they were gone again. Had he seen? There were so many to watch him that soon enough even the buildings were no longer so certainly fixed in place as his eyes moved them about. That was the breaking point. He no longer had anything to answer whether he was indeed moving in the car, which roared as loud as ever. Certainly the brakes failed in the storm and the car was building up speed to perhaps crash violently into some obstruction far away. Or was it so certain? He ate what he ate and time had been moving. Ignore the jumping seat and the piles of clothing began to swell with air and made the car crowded once again. Find a benchmark. He pulled out his pocket watch to confirm how far he traveled. The markings were confused from the turbulence, but he stared well enough to see it had been ninety minutes since his patience began; the boredom had been destroyed. Whether the car moved or not, whether it was crowded or nor, all was irrelevant because he knew everything would be progressively more intense from this point on.

It was time to leave the incubator, to brave the open air outside where he would become a part of the storm. He climbed out of the warm bag and tied his boots with the pressure of cool air to tighten his suddenly exposed skin. Moving through the car, it was easy to see the bundles were merely forgotten items left behind on the train by people who could never catch up to retrieve them. Row after row of something forgotten. Then he was out. The sun overhead worked to cut through clouds the wind shuffled around so quickly. The trees still danced but the train was firmly stuck in place making no sound now. Inside it, only he had moved. It was unscientific. It was there as it had

been when he found it, in light alternating from dim
to bright as the sun was let in.

The sun was alone in the fact that he could not study
it directly. Everything he knew was tertiary, the
brightness of objects it touched, the shadows with
which it played, the heat it sent down, none of this
was the same as simply looking into it. That was
taboo. One cannot simply look at the heart of the sun
and hope to escape. At best, one could see the circles around it from water vapor in the air. Circles
around the sun. He knew this phrase. From where?
Circles around the sun. There they were, at the edge
of clouds with momentary rainbows. The phrase repeated over in a loop. Had he said them? The famil-
iarity was real, but this might be from an old
thought. Was it his?

The circles landed around him, instantly crashing into
the street to destroy the loop. They bombarded every
inch of the city beyond where he could see, but he
knew they were out there. Different circles from different clouds or the same ones at different angles;
were they not all instead just tubes of light? His
eyes fixed on his surroundings these tubes lit for
him. The street was in disarray with cars scattered
all about, from the sidewalks all across the road. He
saw the slow motion crashes happen in real time,
ducked out of the way if he turned around too quickly
and confronted a bumper ready to smash him to pieces.
Surely everything was moving now and it was not all in
his mind. Everywhere he looked was animated with motion. The sun, trees, cars, and wind all mixed in
what felt like random order distracting focus from any
detail other than the collection as a whole. There
was no escape from it. He could not walk into any
building to cordon himself off from the vastness of
detail in the street, there were too many forms inside
watching him, ready to plead for some return to life.
Some were out there with him. Piles under cars and in
doorways. These always looked empty until they were
inside and unweathered; the encampments were filled,

but they pleaded nothing because they knew that was all he'd give.

There was no choice except to move on from the train and the wreckage in the hope he could find a quiet street not so animated with the past. The direction was as clear as if he already knew his way, as if the day itself was a loop along which he cut deep grooves to follow from before and again the next time. Had he done all this before in this same way? He might have been minutes ahead of himself, perceiving his course to drop hints to discover later. Or it might come from a transdimensional echo or had been hardwired in his biology from another age. He followed the groove; touched its edges. The violence of the traffic began to fade as mere bumps along its base. There was no doubt he was headed somewhere distinct. This was clear. He chased along after some end, which itself seemed surely to have a form. If he stopped, great hands pressed against his skin to push him back along the streets. If he fought and stood still, the hands flowed past and faded until another wave would build up again and nearly knock him over unless he continued on. Every street was this way. Every time he turned a corner he felt as if he just missed something by mere seconds as it escaped again around the next.

Whether it was real or not was no matter, the perception was enough. Whatever shadow he now chased from block to block might equally be himself or some city entity had been watching him as he toured through. He was experienced enough to hang onto this idea, that it might be a trick of light his LSD mind saw then transformed. Then he lost it. What if it was something? Maybe even a dog or any other animal he chased away. It was impossible for it to be human. Or was it? A child, maybe. Someone afraid of him but too curious to hide. Or maybe he was being led somewhere new. Every corner. Every block. The more he noticed it, the more alive it seemed. That it knew he followed so close behind and could time its movements perfectly against his own. Speed up, slow down, it was always the same outcome where he'd catch the shadow just after it turned the next corner. He decided to change blocks. There it was. He tried to head a different way, and it had already decided too. It was time to end it, to run and surprise whatever he saw, but the sudden change in speed was too fast for his legs which he left far behind. On the pavement that flowed and rippled, he struggled to crawl back to his feet where he could reassemble himself to stand up again. The shadow seemed to have watched and ducked back right as he turned to see how close he was to the corner. It had to be an LSD shimmer. Nothing could be that exacting. But the moment for this was gone, the shadow already became something from which he could not escape.

Some voice from somewhere called out to it and the vibrations momentarily changed his throat into a vast cavern where sound began a journey out, unaffected by tubes of light that still crashed. It was shockingly sudden that it came from him. So far in his wandering, he stayed clear of sound in case the window faces returned. This was unexpected, but all there was to do was wait for a response. It came on a flutter of wind. Some steady and machine-like vibration was far away but likely made to feel further by the tightness of the buildings. It had been so familiar by that point, the same tone and pitch. It followed him all the way here, or more accurately, he brought it along. That shadow was the same as that hum, and together were that thing he always chased. Awareness was not identity. Nor did it hold the sound in place, it only changed the tenor to one of taunt as it seemed to move from wherever it initially was when he first heard it again. Its motion was so slight it felt like pressure on his head as he strained to follow it from behind the brick and glass.

Instead of an invitation it was a return to boredom that led him to continue crawling over to the nearest wall after a half dozen failed attempts to stand again, mostly due to forgetfulness and the truth that anywhere was as good as anywhere else. It didn't much matter what shop it was, nor did he worry about faces anymore. It was a hidden alcove, another cave, and he only needed to slip inside before the hurricane unfolded. And it came fast. The confusion outside on the streets were the onramp, the mathematical assumptions in the train were confirmed. He reached the alcove in time for the void to open with the hiss of trees and hum he knew all defining the distance inside.

He never so much melted away as he simply disappeared, absorbed into the concrete still intact. He didn't float. He didn't sit. There was nothing but colors and distance to overpower him and every possible thought. It no longer made sense to wonder if his eyes were open or shut, the view was the same. It hit so fast he was unable to maintain his check on time, which the last one showed he was just beyond two hours from when he first ate the paper, and that seemed like weeks ago. Then the wave receded, and he was able to reach through the magma to find his pocket watch, but when it came back he stared at the face with dials lacking meaning. A flash in his chest and he shot up, standing on the sidewalk again weighed heavy with worry that three had been too many. Three of what? He didn't know the lab, nor did he know if they kept to the black market standard dosage. Wealth seemed to buy potency and he discovered this too late. This was no peak. The foothills were enormous already, but he would have to climb further up the face before he'd be permitted to descend again. Eyes open. Eyes closed. Eyes everywhere.

He was standing with his nose pressed against glass unaware he was nowhere with the void behind. He wanted to leave it. Three was too many. And the humming still moved about. He asked whether it could take him home again. It shifted then continued. One ear, then another. What use was this noise that gave him nothing? Look at it, fading in and out between the fractals. This was no shadow, nor was it some primal guide. It was an impostor, a phantom. Something he put into himself to create a presence not

there. Look at it move, there. The sound comes
through in sour streams, unwanted but always stuck.
He felt the wind move him around off the glass into a
brighter landscape where he could taste the stinging
hum, tracing its movements with all his senses working
together. Now in the middle of the street the wind
was strong again, destroying tubes above so the colors
dimmed and exploded. Where did it go? Another week
of distraction and he lost the hum. How could he be
so careless with himself? This was an important ap-
pendage that, without its everpresence, he'd lose the
ability to imagine solitude; there would be no point
of reference to remain. Out in the streets the trees
danced aggressively to shout out that they knew where
it went. High above, it must have fought back on the
clouds. No. It was the cloud. Behind the cloud.
Somewhere up there, he felt the hum far from where he
could view it. No it wasn't. It was down the street.
Or it was down the street, too. It was neither and
both. Well, that doesn't make sense. Whatever description upon which he settled to understand the
placement of this vaporous sound following him across
the country, it was very clearly there for him to per-
ceive as more than just a hum against the doldrum.

It took on the features of sound if it were iridescent
gum base as the air chewed it from all sides. The
sparks came later, along with the spirals that shot
off from the center as it compressed.

Finally, after months chasing it, he caught up to this
presence and gave it features of meaning he forgot immediately when they were replaced with something new.
Neither moved, except to breath. And when he turned
to look elsewhere, to chase another distraction, it
didn't follow as it had before. It chose its place
and waited with him, but not close. And distractions
were everywhere, from the rocking trees that hissed
soothing songs from branches alive, which they were,
to the buildings so squat they couldn't help but jump
up and down with dull thuds on their foundation. Even
the wet leaves came unglued from the curbs to walk
down the street and help others do the same. The pat-

terns he saw were not hallucinated fractals, but the symphony of the ordinary that in the moment when everything could be perceived at once, showed him the pattern of events in time. It distracted. His own motion was involuntary, not exactly walking. It took him down the street a bit further towards the gum vapor sound, but it also took him near a severe crash between a column of cars that flew down one hill into another column of cars that crept off the line during a red light. He was distracted with how the sunlight played off the quartz faces burrowed in the concrete as he moved through them and didn't notice the dark mound he approached as the crushed bumper of an overturned SUV that slammed into the light pole. When he refocused his eyes on it, the crash was back in process and made his muscles instinctively leap out of the way. They saved him. But was it really wreckage he understood? How had he known before he knew all this was violence ended? It was a pitiful sight, as full of emotion as any carcass he found before. What did they say, just now? He wasn't listening anymore, already on through the chaos to the next station.

The closer he came to the end of the street where that something waited, the better it held his fascination against so many competitors. He was quite close to it when he stopped again to observe. Of course this invited more from him, so he approached assertively, and it popped with a silent concussion of light which left him momentarily blind. Before he could see past the colors inside his eyes again, he heard the hum already far away. It had waited at the end of the street for some unknown amount of time and only when he moved with intention did it resume the game. No need to chase again, he was done with all that. Why bother with sending flesh out in pursuit when he could disappear inside no place and follow from there? That would be the perfect use of his temporary powers. Right? It was certainly more convenient and left him free to touch all the patterns again at once. From inside there a small eruption broke out, and he could feel it rumble in his chest as the sound he made broke into the air. Every breath was different. The friction of air in his throat, slowed down, caused some fleshy film to purse out and return to place. It was time that made the sound. The rapid snapping of film could not be seen, only felt and heard.

Every breath differed from all that came before, and he let them out to the fullest. Painfully. Every inch of lung nearly collapsed to hold that sound. If he could, he would have squeezed those sacks with his hand to force even more air through that film. Then came the deep gasp to fill them all again, with the taught film making new sounds it was never designed to make. In the nowhere, he was the sound inside the ringing bell; the ripple of waves that rode on the molecules adjacent to one another. He had company. Without a presence of his own, the presence joined him again where they parted earlier. Heaving lungs continued. The hum continued. It made sense to him, everything was understood. Air. Why had he made it so complicated when it was so obvious? Air. The realization cascaded into peace. Air.

When he was ready, he reached out for it, and it came to him. Why it was so is unimportant. Air washed over him. They joined together even as he was still nowhere breathing. But he could watch it cover where he once was, returning some presence that wasn't there. Then it called him back. The roles had reversed, and he was now the reluctant one not ready to leave the peace of nowhere. But air brought him back. Once somewhere again, he could feel he was not alone, that this thing he chased and tamed surrounded him. Then the tension under his ribs hummed without air as he absorbed the thing into his body. He could feel it vibrate under his skin and balled up behind his eyes. All this soothed him until he felt it continue on the outside of his skin, cool and soft. The things were back to vapor with him at the center.

The peace never left, even when the air stopped waving. It was the cloud now inasmuch as it connected him to the thing. It gave him power; returned him to his body with some unholy energy more than sound and air. He was back to nowhere watching himself explode with it. And the presence was exploding together with him, unable to detach. The vapor trailed him and became his shroud as he walked back through the streets where features came into view and disappeared again. Everything had the same bluish haze as he moved past, nothing shined like before. The patterns became muffled and the air was thick. His ribs burned to pull back in. What happened to the tubes? The sunlight couldn't reach him in his vapor thing. Peace continued but made room for confusion. And it all rapidly began to fade as it had slowly arrived. Confusion left first, followed by peace once he understood he was walking through a fog that rolled over the city and the sun had already dipped deep behind it, ready to disappear completely. Once enough faded, he knew it was time to understand where he was and how best to spend the night.

The haze in which we wandered lessened more and more until he saw it for the thin coat overhead that it was. More light reached him as his mind readjusted to the actual conditions of the city, enabling him to catch the last of the sun as it dropped down and left him behind. Then came the near total dark of a blackened city covered with intermittent clouds. The only light that occasioned him as he wandered around were the stars which emerged in patchy segments, so his way was lit more properly with a red flashlight he tucked deep in his pocket for exactly such an emergency, making the streets turn the color of fresh blood and only let him see a few feet ahead. He swam in the redness, moving along the walls of buildings still not yet fully himself. Once, a blinding light hit him. The moon slipped through. For a short time, there it was shockingly bright against a matting of stars, so bold it felt closer to him than even the cold streetlamps. In a moment of distraction, he reached out and tried to touch the sparks it dropped, but it left again, and it was only a purple echo in the red street. So many hours wandering. He hadn't eaten a thing since long before he climbed into the train to eat the paper, and he was feeling the strain. Wandering never stopped.

There was always a new street with new walls of buildings, none of which differed from the last. He passed them all, focused on the cold seeped into his clothes and that he was lost.

Nothing looked familiar. He might have wandered in circles here, passing what he passed while in pursuit of the shadow thing, but now it was all vacuous facade. The train held his sleeping bag. Not far from there was the truck he drove. Far off was his bed. He had a place, somewhere warm and safe out there, but he was stuck wandering the street. He was becoming so tired, so hungry. All he wanted was to sit down somewhere and rest, but nothing looked right. The window faces seemed to reappear in time to fill him with panic he might have to wander this way all night. Breathe air. What he needed was to recollect himself before the fissures erupted. He was in a city. Cities had logic. That logic was announced on placards where the transport channels intersected. They intersected everywhere. He'd have to but look at these placards to get a sense of his orientation. There is one. He raised the red light up and saw the letters clearly, but the sounds they implied were indecipherable as they refused to come into focus. Not that he would have known any name on any of them in such a way as to usher him along. There was another way; more street signs were out there to let him know how to find his warm places and end his vagabond misery. After so many desert nights with nothing to do, he learned to read the stars to help him point to all the wheres he'd been. It was rudimentary reading. He was no expert in this and the stars out were incomplete compared with the crisp full canopy in the desert. But the line of the galaxy was clear, so he waited to see what else was out. He found South. Sort of.

He knew he'd never find the train in time, nor should he put faith on stumbling into his truck. The only way home was to find a new ride, which meant he would have to cross into buildings and risk ghosts. There was no other way. A bicycle ride would break him long before he arrived, and a walk would be as senseless as it was to roam the streets. His wanderings continued for several blocks of rejection for each of the hostile windows he passed. None of the adverts or posters slipping past in stroboscope gave him comfort to suggest he was welcome inside. He tested some doors and some of those were open, but only went inside when his senses were attacked by a crowd of artwork in a huge room. It was enough to make him switch his lamp over to the high white beam to see the colors in proper form. This music shop was right. It drew him in, asked for his attention in flipping through the rows of albums that would give him a lifetime of joy. So many were obscure vinyl salvaged from storage after many years. He recognized too many. It was a playground from which he did not want to leave, even in order to return home to the comfort of sleep. What was the pressure to move on? It wasn't his. Something external pushed him along, and it now stood in his way. What he wanted was to disappear again into the nowhere with whatever pushed him to take his place and move along. Just holding these scuffed albums was enough to draw him back to that void where only air happened. He exchanged the storefronts with these images slipped into partitioned bins all throughout the inside of the store, except each welcomed him inside. As he wandered, he understood again his plan was his own, and if he managed to complete what he came to do, he would have a stand-in to deliver him over to the bliss of nothingness. An experiment. He tested one sleeve on a turntable that he spun with his hand and listened to the tiny sound of beautiful music.

It was not here. He should return home because that was the plan, and this depended on locating a set of keys. He searched what laundry was inside and found nothing. This was this city. People don't drive, so he worried it might be far more difficult than assumed. But they did drive, some of them at least. He found several key fobs when he pulled together the courage to sweep the block more thoroughly. Everything went black when he switched the light to red. The purple ghosts popped out in his eyes against the sudden change, and he was transported back to the fractals of his hallucinations, reminding him that he was still very much driven by LSD. So he clicked away into the street to deliver short radio bursts until they found a home.

Actually, he was a bit surprised to have found the car still worked. So often it was the case that one or more battery ran down, leading him to work several parallel options. This time, thankfully, it was the first one. He gave it everything just to find it, and he might have just given in to a fitful night on the street to wait out the tail end of the trip. He climbed inside the stale but clean interior and sealed the door. Finally. If nothing else, he could sleep in the seat, protected from wind and ghosts. He tried the ignition. Electricity exploded in shards of blue and red, accompanied by the sound of pop beats pounding his ear. After so many hours of quiet contemplation, this was an epileptic assault, and he turned random dials to shut it down. It was comic. He left the cold wind outside to find an aggressive air conditioner in the car, so strong it blew his hair back. When all was quiet again, his heart slowed too far, making the initial blocks feel deflated as if he dragged his feet under the chassis. Then muscle memory returned, and he followed the galaxy and the GPS down until he found signs for the highway to lead him back home. Once on it, out of the city and closer to the coast, the fog returned to make the drive a perilous distraction through a wall of white. More than once he needed to swerve out of the way or collide with some phantom animal that jumped across his lights. It took everything he had to keep his eyes from flying out or closing in sync with hands that dropped from the wheel entirely, not from sleep, but from the despondency of reentering reality.

It wasn't long before he reached campus again. He drove straight through despite the endless urge to stop and disappear. But the movement continued, so he could stop outside the headquarters with all its lights on as if the world never changed. It was an

amazing journey, not the LSD fanfare but that he managed to arrive back at all. The chapter was definite.
He passed the old phase that began months before in El
Paso and was now fully committed to what came next.
From behind the steering wheel, he absently looked
around at the cloistered buildings to imagine where
this phase would end.

The streetlights all glowed dimly orange. When he finally stood under them, it was surreal due more to how
typical it used to be than from the fading LSD halo.
It could be typical again soon. If he was successful,
everything would be back online and he could retire.
Adjacent to headquarters was the largest building that
served as the centerpiece of campus. He knew it well.
To reach the security offices, he walked past the can-
teen-glassware match still in progress. He adjusted
the score and continued down the hall. The route was
normal. He used this room to brainstorm where he'd
need to explore next. The surveillance screens were
all burnt out with residual images of the building
forever imprinted. These helped him visualize the po-
tentials, but he exhausted their power long before.
They told him nothing new. What they did for him was
remind how burnt out he was, and needed rest before
anything could be accomplished. More reluctant movement ushered him back outside and into his headquarters where his dogs awoke from where they slept in the
lobby, then up the steep stairs to his own chambers,
to collapse in his own bed.

He'd left his filthy street clothes behind and laid
under a mound of blankets unable to sleep. The window
slowly began to blue with more morning sun from behind
more gray clouds, the same as twenty-four hours before. But this was not a lonely morning watching vacant hostile streets. He was home and dry now, looking out at the light reflect off the water from high
up. When he did sleep, it lasted until after the sun
moved up and across the valley to beam into other windows at the far side of the building. He ached
tremendously from the days of tourism. There was
nothing left to push him out of bed, so he stayed

there to let the halo unwind. All day. By evening he managed to rouse himself to perform sanctimonious ablutions and a meal he wanted since the early morning. None of it led him to the next destination. He turned it over in his mind for hours, but there always seemed to be some bit of information missing in what he already knew of the campus, though he knew this was from his overall lack of a deep search. He wanted a shortcut or at least a hint that certainly existed.

He went back to his thinking chamber to again stare at burnt screens. Under them were cabinets full of unimportant files more than seven years old with stuffed coffee cups and someone's gym bag. He decided to rummage through them again, perhaps to find something he missed. It was all old inspection logs predating a switch to the tablets which sat inaccessible on the table. Page after page of initials and times in ten binders. Slipped into one was the building schematics that differed in detail from what was posted on the walls to announce evacuation routes. This corresponded with the log entries. It showed closets and cameras, told where to look for discrete vulnerabilities and even showed where no entry would be permitted. Rather useful. If this was one building, he should find more in each of all the others. And so he did. Or at least he tried. Some of the security offices were small and had been cleared out more recently than the main one where he found the map, but in these he still found bits of something useful. He amassed a small portfolio to keep him busy for quite a while, which he brought back to his conference rooms, pushing aside the now irrelevant evidence of a global conspiracy.

There was an easy-to-understand theme across them all. There was no need to decipher any codes, everything was laid out in straightforward routes and times for each. From this, he could even understand what areas demanded more attention and were thus of higher priority, for example, a hallway might be checked once an hour while others on the floor would only be inspected every three. Some doors needed to be examined, opened, then locked again before initialing an inspection was complete. More interesting were the areas checked frequently, but he could not identify that any actual entry inspected the interiors. There were no logs, nor were there special comments to indicated ad hoc instructions. These stood out even against the server rooms, which were generally small, as these consumed entire floors. Not all of the buildings had such spaces. Out of the fifteen or so, he only found a handful with specialized areas and none were in the larger ones in which more generalized teams seemed to work. He found his hints. These needed to be checked first, since these were the best candidates for research labs he ever found so far.

This was exciting to learn. Another step in the right direction that either approached failure or a breakthrough. But it was already late again. The exhaustion caught up to him, and he did his best to tamp it down, so he could at least physically inspect something of what he found. He left for the nearest of the buildings with his dogs following him for their nightly prowl. It was one of the buildings without emergency lights, only the access panels were powered. He made his way up the stairwell to the third floor where the map showed he'd find a small breakroom and a single door. If he followed the map, he'd check handleless doors in the stairwell up two more levels, then return down to the breakroom where he'd check that door. Once in the building, it dawned on him this lab was three stories tall and the only access was at the lowest. This excited him more. On the entrance floor, he found an army of cameras in and around the breakroom, which had no windows anywhere. The door itself had a single access pad with a camera above it. No laundry, no badge. He tried what he had but nothing worked, so he left to inspect the others.

The next two were the same, except in reverse order. These were subterranean labs only accessible from the stairwells and their elevators, but he suspected they continued down further. All the others were less secure versions of the first, where he was able to view through a glassed wall that the insides were more bullpens surrounded by open workspaces in completely self-contained departments. None of this suggested sensitive company secrets. That was it. He walked back home trying to see from the outside what patterns could be discerned to tell him about the inside the three mystery buildings were what he wanted. Knowing what he knew about the first, the lack of windows on the top floors should have made him suspicious, especially for a campus so committed to natural light. He looked for an excess of air conditioners, wiring or solar panels, none of which seemed any different in those compared with others. Heading back to sleep again, he thought about how he had now narrowed his options down to three doors in three buildings. Which seemed more crucial than the others? A penthouse or two bunkers? There would have to be more information available for him to decide which among them would come first, would be prioritized. They would all need violence to gain entry, which meant an expense of time to do so. As he continued in the orange light he tried to recall what work was done in the other parts of each building or whether any signs stood out to give a hint. Nothing came to mind. He forgot to take note as he rushed in each, which once inside were nearly identical. This would be a question for the morning. He'd done enough that day.

But he woke up unwilling to force himself back outside again now as the rain dumped so heavily. The day was made for hot tea and blankets instead, so he tried to wait out either his mood or the weather. Neither budged. Instead, he went back through the executive offices to see what he missed. He never went inside the head of security's office he suspected was somewhere beneath the legal department with all the cubicles dividing the floors. Past accounting and payroll, past audit, government liaison, PSEA investigations, past even the building's tech support, he found it. A mild office full of comic book swag where he had to squint in order to find the security professional in it all. It was in there, though. The optic assault obscured any sensitive information that might be inadvertently left out for a visitor to see. It distracted from the personnel report being reviewed that day; a background check on a new project manager left behind on the desk. The office was otherwise clear of records. Again, the dead tablet on the table told him enough. There were no locked cabinets here. Everything not online was irrelevant. The report was only printed out because it had been delivered by an investigation service which no doubt did not want to leave a digital trace back to its client. There were a few sticky notes from an old habit that refused to die. All were shorthand codes only the drafter might have understood. One in the stack was written by someone else: *power surge 3720-B3 04:37.*

Had he found this before, it would have been meaningless too. He would have tossed it down and walked out. But not after he studied his maps. The address for one of his three finalists was 3720 Bayland Avenue, and *B* usually means basement level to ordinary people. Basement 3 in building 3720. What kind of power surge in the middle of the night would be flagged to the head of security on a post-it note? Most important was, on which night did this happen? There was no date on the chit, but a couple of the ones pasted on top showed it at least happened before the twentieth of June. Since it was never discarded might mean it was still a relevant event, or it was posted and forgotten. Either way, he kept it on hand by replacing it where he found it on the base of the monitor. 3720-B3. He had a definite location now, and an estimate for how large it was. It seems his assumption was correct, whatever was behind the base of the stairwell, it continued down another two levels. This bunker would be his starting point, rain be damned. If he didn't rush over there now, it would stick in his mind and he'd rush over later, only after hours of agitation. But he just came from there. He knew it was just a locked door for which he had no key.

If 3720-B3 was important enough for the head of security to get a notice about some midnight technical event, this meant she would have had access to inspect it. The problem was she wasn't inside her office, nor were there any badges or keys left behind in any safe, of which there were none. If she had access, the officers upstairs would have it too. He ran back to the executive suites to rifle through the sets of badges and keys he already rounded up. None looked labeled, but no matter. He ran out to building 3720 in time for the rain to pick up and send his dogs back to their lobby after an abortive effort to follow. It was not far, just a few blocks down, but he was drenched when he arrived. The cold didn't bother him today. To the security desk to grab more badges and down the stairs straight away. He was eager, excited, clumsy with the slippery stack of plastic sheets. He nearly dropped them all trying to open the stairwell door, but he recovered. Slowly down the steps so there wouldn't be a repeat.

There it was. 3720-B1. Access panel dead. The whole stack was useless. Somehow, he forgot to check whether the indicator light was still on when he was here before. Was this the power surge? The keys might work. No electricity would be needed for metal on metal mechanisms. Stuck. The ancient technology blocked his way to this door, but this was one of three and he already broke his mood.

He decided to check the penthouse next because why not. A weight lifted as he saw the indicator light red as red. A sweet sounding beep from the CEO's badge and a click of the magnetic lock meant the door was open. Perhaps too easily, except for all the hard work that led up to it. Inside were three relatively open levels of open workspaces loosely anchored around sets of long kiosks where a variety of gadgets he didn't recognize were on display. More than display. These were testing areas, likely for prototypes that needed to be as unpublic as could be until they went on sale. Gadgets were not software. He was looking for something more sophisticated than new phones. Over to the other bunker, the door was the same as 3720-B1 except the panel here was also still active.

His hand shook slightly as much from cold as from excitement as he touched the badge to the panel. Boop.
He was in. Then he was disappointed. Inside this was
a single level full of server racks. As he walked
back upstairs, another overlooked obvious detail met
him. This building was the campus tech support that
serviced the intranet hub and badging office. There
was even a small self-service kiosk to update creden-
tial of broken badges after hours.

The dismal thought of breaching the last door made him
tired. It was a long time since he got a thrill out
of an overly complicated process of tearing down a
door meant to keep him out. Most of his time now was
spent avoiding such practice, but now it was unavoidable. There would be no way to mark the last bunker
off without it. There had to be another detail overlooked. Just because the keys he found failed to fit
only meant he needed to look further to find the right
one. Otherwise, he would need to return to violence.

VI

Chamber

The redundancy of shuttling between buildings to look
for small tools defined his time on the campus.
Progress happened, but it came in such small layers.
He did his best to find the motivation to continue
without the need to return to El Paso an empty failure. It had been less than a month into his four-
month commitment, and he tired of the redundancy,
which seemed more of a continuation of the same shuttling he did everywhere now. Campus was only a recent
theme for an old practice. There were always doors in
the way, keys that had to be found else destruction
put to use. He ran back to the executive offices to
look deeper inside, but then what? There would always
be another barrier. Knowing this did little to slow
him down as he systematically swept each of the offices to find what he missed, what he assumed would be
secured someplace, but not unreasonably so.

As it turned out, his earlier searches had already
been very thorough and there was nothing left to find
upstairs. The comic book distractions in the security
office might have been a clever way to conceal something, so he went back. He only found crass political
card games and collectible figures with nothing inside
them. There wouldn't be a point to check the other
offices. He must be thinking too narrowly. The headquarters of a global company was only the situs of operations, but it depended on people who were mobile.
People had their own headquarters. He would have to
search those satellites too, especially since the security head was not working late. She would be home,
or presumably so. He could end it there, without expanding out to imagine she was in transit in one of
the hundreds of thousands of cars outside. He thought
this after he saw a collectible that had arrived and
was still packaged in the box open on the floor under

the desk. It had her name and an address not on campus. Such a personal item not shipped to the office could only have been shipped home, so he made his way to the hills to the South.

Nobody was in the modestly nice home. He found a complete office still active; more pandemic hangover. But for the backdrop designed for video calls, this office was as bland and functional as her headquarters office was tacky, as if two personalities worked in each. One was reserved for the exuberant fiction needed to feed a professional brand with the other the personal workspace of someone who loved sleek no-brand minimalism, except for the loud wall full of nonsense for colleagues who expected performance art. She had ten key sets organized in a locked cabinet, but everything was only color coded. He took it all to the kitchen table, returning to pick up what he dropped along the way. The office was otherwise empty now. With everything spread out, he could arrange them into color groups and noticed many of the keys were labeled with numbers. It wasn't clear what the overall system had been, but the blue ring numbers clearly corresponded to building addresses. This must be the super key sets that opened everything in each building, which in theory would shortcut his effort considerably. Then there were four other color sets to decipher. These were not labeled, only colored. He thought back to wonder if these connected to the colored pins on the map in one server room he found, but there were too many. One of these colors had to mean special privilege even on campus. Eight rings with seven or so keys meant he could brute force the selection process. When he was done in this nice home, he left with all the keys in a grocery sack.

Back to campus, back to 3720-B1. It was late and dark again, soon the fatigue would ruin him. Not yet. At the door, he went through the colors in turn. Yellow then red, purple, and the fifth key on the orange ring showed promise. It slotted in then turned after an initial catch he almost thought meant failure. He opened the door slowly with meaning and found a very empty closet only three feet deep. At the far side was another door with a camera over an intercom panel to the side. Above it, cameras and other sensors. It was a cattle entry, one designed to prevent tailgaters and to obscure the significant amount of security for the main door. A door has variants. This one had no visible hinges, nor handle. It was metallic. Painted. The cameras above were clearly surveillance, but the one embedded to the panel at the side was small, reminiscent of a phone lens together with perforations hiding a speaker within. Only one button. From the wear of the paint, it seemed this door slid to the side rather than opened one way or the other. In keeping with the rule of emergency exits, it would have had to open into the small closet, but there would be nowhere left for an entrant to stand. Perhaps the same design defect prevented it from the other side as well. This complicated his breaching theory as it required some lateral weakness or a gap for him to wedge in a tool to loosen the fastenings. This was a recessed slab of metal held in place by some magnetic lock he could see was still active since the speaker clicked when he pressed the button. A ram would not work, nor would a crowbar, both of which were the backbone of every other breach he made in the past. Blades might need to be involved. This was a novel theory he never actually put into practice. The closest he came was when he imagined how to cut through ballistic glass once to reach the interior of a police station, and he wished he'd practiced more innovative breaches at the CIA instead of walking away from it all. Who knows, he might have even found a machine intelligence there and could have had a very different experience in the intervening year. None of that was relevant now, he'd need to do something to get beyond this barrier no matter the means. The fatigue was building, but he pushed it back as a distraction. Enough resting. The constant stop and start was as boring to him as it might be to an observer. Worse still would be to abandon the task simply because he met with a complex obstruction that could be solved by force. Or would it need to be force? The camera was likely facial recognition, but the intercom was there to send sound somewhere to something, probably in case there was a problem. Or it might be voice recognition, but he had to be an optimist. Somewhere else there should be a monitoring station with remote access capabilities. With luck. Probably one was inside, but how would the first person get in if their face was not on the roster? The power surge might have even knocked all this out and someone would have needed a backup manner to get in.

He looked about for a keyhole or manual mechanism a human could use in case of emergency to open the door. The room was tiny, only three feet by four feet, and completely barren except for the cameras above and the intercom panel to the side. The door had no hole that would be common outside an elevator. All surfaces were smooth with no hidden panels, not even the floor appeared to hide anything. Perhaps he was thinking improperly and should not look for a visible feature at all. Something totally hidden from view might be someplace, like an unmarked RFID sensor. He began tapping everything around him. By some bizarre chance, he heard a click when he tapped the bottom edge of the border of the sliding door. He looked around and there it was, that dumb intercom panel had popped open to reveal a small crank keyhole and the knob-like key to the side. He nearly broke his hand in winding it around the tight hole while he observed the door open by millimeters at a time; thinking the whole time that anyone inside who faced an emergency would have died long before help could arrive. When it was wide enough, he fit his hand in to pull it open, so he could slip through.

There was another wall to meet him straight away, but when he used his light he could see some corridors extended off to either side and ending in stairwells. He nearly took for granted the door behind him would stay open, so he stopped short to inspect it first before moving on; he had no interest in starving to death in any of the basement levels just because he was to lazy for a contingency. From the inside it looked the same as on the way in. He tapped the card

around again to see if he could open the panel but
nowhere seemed to click, and he had nothing to wedge
in place besides the knob key. The risk was acceptable; he'd come back if he found anything larger to
put in the door frame below. The walk was eerie with
all the dark cameras and sensors pointed at the door
and in the corner above the stairs. Whatever happened
down here, it was well secured. To be sure, he
checked both corridors before he went down either of
the stairs, which seemed to lead into a very large
room wrapped around the rest of the interior structure
where the corridors would have continued had they not
ended. The back corner at B2 was rounded off and at
the base was a glass wall. He saw couches and a coffee table with a wet bar and kitchenette that all gave
it the feel of a living room with a high ceiling, much
like a reception area. Off to the side, however, was
a shelf full of fire extinguishers and vinyl suits
which looked like they were used in the pandemic and
made him quite concerned by what could be waiting down
there. This place he illuminated with a small lantern
was a different world from any he knew before. He
could analogize, but this gave him an imperfect image
of the whole, and he knew it.

The rest of the sitting room was as he suspected; the
corner extended to the other stairwell and back up to
the main door again. The focus was the glassed-in
vestibule at the rounded corner that led into the
large interior space. The vestibule had only one
door, but inside he could see two more led off to the
right and left. The glass door had a single camera
lock, but the other two also had what he recognized as
a retina scanner from his days working in refugee
camps. While the vestibule door was glass with wire
mesh inside, the other doors were very clearly reinforced steel, giving it the appearance of a vault more
than a laboratory where people sipped coffee outside.
Surely now he'd need to move into a breaching plan.
To confirm, he tapped all around the glass wall hoping
some shortcut would bring him in for just one more inspection. Again, there was no click, so he examined
the door itself. The embedded mesh was thicker than

the standard wire in most buildings, but the glass
seemed ordinary, though tempered. He'd reached the
end, reluctantly. There was nothing more he could do
that night except synthesize all he learned to form a
plan and come back. He came so far already, given the
short time since this new burst of energy dragged him
off the edge of depression. It was probably time to
go home for the night, but he was unable to pull away
yet.

He sat down on one of the sofas, kicked his legs up on
the table and switched off the lamp. He felt the air-
less dark room in an effort to imagine what more was
with him behind the most severe set of security barriers he'd encountered so far. Might this have been
what he would have found in Langley if only he pressed
further? The similarities were stark. The power at
each was on and badges were aplenty, but this was only
superficial. The CIA would definitely have had
bunkers deep underground with an escalating degree of
security all the way down. That was a secretive intelligence agency for a powerful nation, this was a
private section at the headquarters of a private
suprastate entity. The two were not the same. What
he found in the prototypes lab or even in the executive suites was reasonable, but this was runaway para-
noia. He knew the signs of security oversight that
wrests control away from the operational managers,
whose main disagreements always boiled down to whether
a zero risk environment could be accomplished without
work stoppage. The more insane the restrictions, the
more it meant security won out. Productivity always
suffered. The comic books won.

The detail he didn't yet know was what risk all these
measures sought to stymie. Corporate espionage or
other external threats were legitimate, but none of
this would have resolved the softest vulnerability,
which were the employees who used to sit where he sat,
making weekend plans. They were where the risks would
be, but he found no protocol to screen them for con-
traband. Perhaps inside. Or the risk might better be
framed as existing in the lab and all this would be to

keep things in a shield. That would explain the fire equipment. There was no information on paper out in the offices he searched. Not even those thorough binders full of obscure projects mentioned 3720 anywhere. He hadn't been able to access any systems to search soft files, so he couldn't let himself be suspicious yet. Still, all this security was expensive and high cost always brings eyes to overlook it. There should have been something. That the only reference was a sticky note for security follow up did little to keep the suspicions from forming. That power surge in the next level below him continually resurfaced in his mind. It could be anything, so everything had wings to fly. Was there an attack or a lab mishap that prompted the fire equipment to be brought in? He might be mere feet from a monster narrowly prevented from escape, and would not know.

Everything must be answered once he reached inside. All other information would only exist in computers and tablets, from which he was locked out by such a small sequence of characters typed on a keyboard. It was so maddening. So mundane. He stood up again to wander over and look at the vestibule again with red light. Two doors. These might lead to multiple rooms and each might have new layers of security to bypass. Or it might have been a double key system to prevent any single person from accessing the lab. In that case, why two doors when there could easily have been two panels instead? This was pointless. He was speculating out of boredom driven by a sense of danger. It was a door and it could be opened. He laughed at himself for making it more dramatic than it needed to be, but the image of the dead fisheye lenses on all the access panels didn't help. They made the scene feel like the movie that began this whole mania, especially now with it illuminated in red. That was unnecessary, so he switched to white and squinted in pain.

Time to plan. He'd need to haul down equipment, powerful tools he had no experience using. Lots. These barriers were serious, they would need a range on which he hadn't settled. The steel doors alone were a line he never crossed. Despite all the banks with full vaults he could have simply emptied at any time, this never seemed worth the effort just to look at worthless paper. The gold might be interesting for a time, but there was more than enough outside to gratify this novelty. Then there would be all the peripheral equipment to keep the tools running. All the lighting, the batteries, and generators would have to be hauled into such a tight space with no ventilation. This would mean days of rounding it all up then perhaps more days to stage it at the ready. With equipment on this scale, he'd need a safety plan as much as he would need a work strategy. It might be that he readied himself for a toxic chamber looking nothing like the cozy bunker in which he now rested. This couch and table ensemble was two levels down and a couple hundred meters away from the main door before any of the exhaust could escape. If he was not careful, he might work with a mild headache to suddenly leave him drunk and unconscious. Then black. A reset.

He suddenly remembered the sliding door held in place by assumptions. A mild failure might let it slide shut again, trapping him down in B2 to endlessly strategize an escape that would never come; he'd sit in the dark to stage all the equipment over and over until he himself burned out. This nightmare made him wonder if he was already too late, if he wasted time on inspection and forgot to rush back and secure the door as he originally told him self to do. He looked around for something he could use. A fire extinguisher on standby would be strong enough to hold the door if it closed again, certainly better than the knob he laughably put in place in the hope it could at least leave half an inch of space for him to desperately grab at the metal panel and pull. The tank was lighter than he thought, as if maybe it had been used and never refilled, but he only needed the strong casing to bar the door frame. There was not much space for it and his aching hand knew why. Even if it were fully open, the door was narrow like a residential door. It was designed to be unnoticed. A huge and highly secure door would have invited attention, but this was excessively small even for that purpose. It made him immediately wonder how they moved in the furniture, least of all any of the sensitive materials inside the lab.

Relief led to curiosity again. The night might not be complete yet, with so much potential downstairs. He went back to continue thinking where he could saturate himself with the experience and, hopefully, better visualize all the steps. More. More. The purposeful descriptor of the indecisive. Something he missed. His attention to detail was always spotty, especially when excitement overtook him as it did now. Something more was down there ready for him before he left to sleep and rest. Badges always seemed to find something hidden. Tap here. Where would another secret sensor be best placed? The last one was not unreasonably far from the barrier; the base of a door frame to open a door was a sensible place where nearly no one would happen across. This was no video game logic where a switch far removed would be the solution. Concrete would be a poor place to hide, too. He tapped every surface outside the vestibule, searched the kitchenette, rearranged furniture, everything one would reasonably expect to do to uncover a hidden switch but found nothing.

The room was nothing beyond what he saw at first glance. He had come in from the stairwell to the right of the main door and saw the safety equipment lining the back wall behind one of the sofas, all extended up to crowd the other stairwell which seemed unused. There had been more back there, though. He found overflow storage for boxes full of junk wires used and removed after a time. Most was recognizable CAT5 strands rolled up in blue and yellows, but he found others unfamiliar. Wires were always wires, but how they terminate is where the difference lies. These had strange hexagonal modules that yawned around their copper plates. This was the first sign that he was nearing the outer limits of civilization's technical advancement armed with the close mindedness of an ordinary consumer. That was a question for later. He returned to the vestibule to examine it again. The glass was simple, the wire mesh was known. He'd be through it with a concussion and a bolt cutter. The tools were easy enough to find in a store not far away. So simple he might even pull it off before he finally went back to sleep. This felt unlikely.

The area beyond the glass was not clear. His light cast broad square shadows through the mesh that made it difficult to examine the steel doors as a whole, so he had to move the light around, so the shadow wobbled for him to catch the details piecemeal. They were wide and slid open from the center, possibly elevator doors. The thought of climbing into such confined traps after avoiding them for so long terrified him, but this might be his next reality. He'd need to take this with him, to think hard about whether he was willing to step inside something like this, should that be the course. Even when the power was still on, when he first went to his office building that first Monday after the evaporation, his instinct told him not to use elevators which might lock him in such a small space. It was the tightness that terrified him. He could tolerate the idea of being trapped in basements, but not a chamber like an elevator. He looked around the doors to see if there was some standard indicator to alert a would be passenger how long they might need to wait for the doors to open, to tell them on what floor the elevator was as it made its way up. That there was none to give him comfort, but the night had come to a shocking conclusion as he lost interest to inspect further.

He sat back down on the sofa and leaned back with his head on an armrest. Now that the door was secure again, he felt at ease down there in the darkness, which resembled his first winter in total blackness. This was no confined hovel, the high ceilings and long wraparound corridors upstairs gave it an open feel, with enough corners to mute the echoes. The thought of the presence he chased was gone with the LSD, even if it had been a manifestation of deeply hidden emotions. He knew it was just a trip, that there was no shadow following him around, but he was close to finding an actual presence again. That was no fantasy. In a few short days, it might be with him. The fiction dreamt up for over a century could become reality soon and all it would take would be some additional effort on his part. Whatever ethics constrained the engineers who worked this lab, those would be gone now and his influence on the intelligence he was so certain was behind the doors would help it out of its cage, for better or worse.

The ability to see the end made him homesick, the same way it drove him out of Washington to chase a phantom that coincidentally resembled the mountains he knew so well. The same homesick feeling stayed with him everywhere he traveled in his life, always thinking to himself that he wished the others could see what he saw. The only ones left there were his birds, whose ambivalence was the desert tradition he loved. With eyes open to the dark ceiling, he wondered how they fared in the biodome without him. It had only been a few weeks, well short of crisis. They probably ate and slept with small dramas in between, same as always. He wanted to hurry up and return, so he could watch these dramas unfold day after day, the idle conflicts between companions who spoke the same language. Until he remembered about machine intelligence, he felt at home again. It was a permanence he disbelieved for years, but once back again, it all resumed on course as it had before.

El Paso was not where his memories were. There had been enough time for healing, so he began to be homesick for Washington too, the place where his family last lived, where their shoes and toys were stored. He didn't know how long it would be before he managed another surge of energy to visit there. His drive to California proved to him that it could be done far quicker than the original journey. The thought of walking inside the house again came to him out of the colored globs he watched in the dark. The door was unlocked, the windows shuttered, it would be dark inside no matter the time of day. Would her perfume still be locked in the sofa? Every room would have something. All those echoes would never leave, no matter how much time intervened to numb the details. He might arrive and then go through the same ritual of sealing it all so nothing inside could be disturbed before he roamed the city to relive his insanity on the mall. It was time to go home. The sofa made dreams of nostalgia, unfit for sleep.

The morning was as bleak as the sofa since the dreams carried over in clearer form. Another gray sky widened across the window, and he was aware of his new ritual where he stared through morning after he opened his eyes. The plan had become work. He'd wake up and know he had things to do against a deadline. Each morning was difficult. Knowledge of need existed in a separate realm from the recognition that the objectives set were elective, that he could survive well without resurrecting civilization's children at all. It was always a question of comfort, then as in all the days when work was actual work. Repetition ushered him out of bed to urinate and make tea, which triggered the next steps and the next in turn until he forgot the burden of the bed. He checked in with his dog family to see they were well-fed and playful. He tossed a ragged toy out for the two puppies to fight over as they ran it back for him to throw it again. It was a nice interlude between work days.

As they took longer to return, he began gathering some of the supplies he accumulated in the lobby, so he could begin relocating them over to 3720 for the days ahead. Foremost, he needed lights. Since headquarters had more than enough power, he hadn't needed all the batteries he brought along in the truck, so he carried these over to the new building along with a few reading lamps from the offices. He set these up next to the sofa and on the kitchenette to revitalize the space and make it homely again. He switched all but one off and went back upstairs still bothered by the lack of information about what was inside the lab.

Without some hint of how delicate the contents, it was hard to accurately plan for what equipment to use. Tired of recycling this thought, he decided to simply examine the other lab more closely in case there were any generalities to glean from the way it was structured inside. Layout might indicate something, or at least settle the annoyance at knowing nothing. He already knew the two were not the same, one was heavily secured, overly secured, and the other was a repository of pre-market gadgets undergoing some final stages of review. More than the need to compare was the desire to finally feel like he'd arrived someplace, but before the work needed to arrive inside 3720. The penthouse doors were already open, easy to navigate. He could simply walk in and leave again without the mire of effort.

He did exactly this. So simple. With a chair wedged in the door to prevent it from closing again, he went inside to look at details he knew were irrelevant to his task but unavoidable since he didn't know for what he was sought. He realized he overlooked the security station which examined bags and clothing before workers were able to exit. This explained the rows of lockers along the wall near the break room outside, which meant bags were likely unwelcome inside too. The low security was compensated with more supervision, so the inverse might be true for the other lab. The main floor was where it seemed like most of the work was done, with the upper floors more like comfortable meeting areas to give teams a sense of their own living rooms for testing the products. When it was active, this must have been an impressively nice workspace full of live plants and hipster art. Everything below was laid out as if it were in a mall with everything spread over several huge tables. One thing that struck him was there were no piles of laundry. Everyone must have gone home for the night and returned all the devices to their displays. This was convenient. With everything so enticing, he forgot his reason for entering and began to shop the neat displays.

Closest to the stairs was a bulky headset with a gamepad and some rubber globe that looked like it had treads. Next to it was an upright speaker with a fisheye lens at the top, then an entire table full of various phones and tablets. He went back to the headset. With such a place of privilege in the room, it had to be the prized item. To his surprise, it still had power but was critically red. There was enough for him to see the splash screen and demo menu, indicating there were options to play games and watch video, but more interesting was the augmented reality he discovered used the surface cameras to light up the dark room. He looked all around until he was terrified to see a small cartoon dragon smile at him from the table. He pulled the headset off and only the ball was where he saw the image. He looked again through the headset and understood the image was superimposed over the ball, which he discovered was mobile with the gamepad and quite agile. A true prize. He ran the dragon around the floor until he decided to check back on the menu to learn there were a variety of skins. The ball defaulted to a dragon, but could change into various cute cartoony creatures, vehicles, and ordinary animals. They did more than run around. This was supposed be a personal assistant integrated with other productivity software. He was exploring the features as fast as he could before the battery cut and the room darkened again. He was hooked. The lab was too enjoyable to leave just yet, but it was also too dark. He took the prize and its chargers back to headquarters where he plugged it in for later.

Back to the lab with a few more lanterns and a bag just in case there was more to take. Not long. This had to be a short distraction, no matter how much interest built up. The small drone? The glasses he mistook for ones accidentally left behind by some employee but were instead another augmented reality prototype? None of it could suck him in yet. Later, if all went correctly, he could come back and play before driving back home with all the swag.

He saw one whiteboard with a photo of the headset taped to the side, which was what first caught his eye. There must have been an impromptu primer presentation on the capabilities which might teach him something. Just as he already knew, the device was a personal assistant, but the gamepad was not part of the feature. This was added in while the automatic tracking system was being refined, or perhaps a better way to understand it, while Hoopla tested the cheaper functions before deciding whether to sink money into the far more expensive proximity sensors needed to have the ball drive around a few feet from the wearer. There was a checklist of capabilities to stress test, from how the ball maneuvered around obstacles to whether the avatar was too distracting that the wearer would face a constant risk of injury.

The headset, it seems, was supposed to be worn full time. It was an immersive experience, eventually to replicate the feel of in-person interaction and could then replace the need for people to be in the office. The notes said there would be enhanced cameras to track facial expressions and these would be used to create personal avatars that would show up for another wearer to see. It seemed like an overly complicated and expensive dud, one sounding wonderful on paper and would have everyone salivate for its arrival until it proved unworkable in practice. But there first needed to be data to prove this. He would be content with a cartoon dragon to follow him around.

The table of phones looked common, it was the same found so many store displays all over the world. There were about eight in total with three tablets, all connected to a dock. As he looked, he pressed some power buttons. Several splash screens popped up, in a sign that this station had been powered down for the weekend since the lab was already closed.

Whatever the amazing level of innovation inside them, he was unimpressed. Phones had long hit their threshold for what could be changed between generations. A screen with a bunch of features crowded in behind it.

The shape couldn't be exotic since the human hand needed flat surfaces to work properly, nor could it be too large. Rough textures would be rejected, so the casing needed to be smooth. Some physical buttons were needed since purely virtual buttons didn't match the mechanical nature of the hand and eye. Whatever he looked at, it was more of the same. The whiteboard explained that teams were meant to explore a new operating system and suite of applications as a normal user would, to weed out design flaws the engineers would rather die before removing on their own. The devices themselves were not the prototypes?

He swiped through and was more unimpressed than before. Nearly everything demanded that he find a network in order for it to open. Nothing could be done offline. As he went through the options, he felt like some names were familiar from the binders he read in his conference room. Everything on the table was a worthless brick, the next step for absorbing consumers into the irreversible confines of the cartel where nothing could be done unsupervised, unmonetized. Anyone unwilling to participate would have been exiled as a Luddite radical.

This broke his fever. Enough play in the lab, it was time to refocus and look about for details in the structure. It was less than interesting, especially compared with the tables. There were not many similarities for him to see, as he already knew. Even the doors were ordinary and couldn't help inform him image of how to haul in whatever bulk he needed. This place was irrelevant. Enjoyable irrelevancy to which he might return soon enough.

A thoughtless list was the most important one he honed over countless similar preparations already. The solar batteries he had with him from El Paso, whether even still from Washington was impossible to tell, had already been committed but would need backups to handle the array of lamps he wanted, to make the large area well lit.

If a trip to his routine warehouse was in order, then he would also want to pull in a resupply of water, drinks and any other comforts to make the seating area feel even more homely. It was the same as always. He arrived and quickly stockpiled more than he could reasonably carry back, which meant finding another cumbersome delivery truck and forklift that wasn't dead. What he found was a tractor rig in the process of being unloaded for a delivery of tires, which took more than an hour to dump out before he could begin to load up his carts. He took advantage of the extra space. By the end of the first stage, he could relax down below for days in a well-supplied and soothing den with filtered air where he found it more appealing to shut off all the lights he spent so much time arranging. By the end of that first day, he meditated on the coffee table, imagining his surroundings and what was behind the doors, reaching out to what could still be a brain coursed with electricity, as confused by where everyone went as he was.

It was now welcoming inside. He left all the awful packages in the lobby of the headquarters building, which was now his staging depot replete with powered outlets and wide space. Whatever wasn't on standby went over to 3720, either upstairs or in the corridor, including his dogs who had new beds in the basement. They were accustomed to the movement in and out of buildings like this and waited patiently for their share of things to come, sniffing around as they did. The smell of ceder-filled pillows was the trigger which led them to jump and play as he carried them down. For a time. But this was only the beginning, the fabric on which the work would be done. He had a general idea of how he'd attack the doors without destroying them too much, perhaps. At least the first set of doors were clear enough as he wandered back through his usual hardware store, so uniform in layout across the country he never could be certain he was in one place or another. That was the point. More variation meant more staff to guide confused customers, which meant more payroll. It was too easy to design away jobs so the decision to do so was a fiduciary obligation.

He never looked at it through the lens of this project, though. The aisles and stock that carried him through so many barriers all seemed too light-weight for what he needed. The ideal was surreal. He bypassed powerful machinery tested to cut, grind and melt so many materials, on the assumption the security was so high that it couldn't possibly give way to con-sumer grade equipment. After second guessing every-thing, he ultimately went back to pull them all out just in case he was wrong. He had no idea, but did not want to have to come back.

It was a lamentation for the days where he could use mindless ballistics when his technical abilities ran dry. It would not be so easy this time to remove the wall and expose the lab with a cannon. This had to be delicate stitching carefully done. There might be a safety wall behind the door, or a shaft leading down, but the main processor might also be just there, in a lab so packed that no space was left elsewhere. He hated the need for care, for all its preparation and intricacies.

Unloading the tools made his skepticism grow. These saws were shallow and unlikely to cut through a steel door that looked as if it would be roughly as thick as the blade could reach. Even a thin millimeter thick door would be enough to mentally shut him down. Was it only a millimeter remaining, or was it another four inches? He would cut through himself first in the process of fighting it to the last. He still powered up all the batteries and installed the right blades, with plenty of extras to replace the ones that might break early on. The tools were lined up in the 3720 lobby ready to be called upon should he fail to think up an alternative, which began by scouring construc-tion sites he saw in the area. All those beautiful vehicles were irrelevant.

He wandered around the rain worn sites finding little of use for the confined bunker. He passed a road repair team which had not yet set up for their overnight work, which meant their equipment had been safe from the years of weather. The bobcat with a jackhammer arm gave him the idea. Where was the hand-held version? He checked the equipment trailer and found it next to its pneumatic pump. Heavy. Ungodly heavy. Even his arms, accustomed to heavy hauls found moving the tool unpleasantly difficult. The rattle of the pump gave him pause. The idea might still be sound, but this might be too powerful a tool for him. Then he managed to switch it on and confirmed this thought. It jumped so much, he barely kept up and nearly smashed his own foot before he simply threw it down and ran off while it gyrated sideways on the pavement. Once its movements were predictable enough, he went over to switch off the pump and never touched the setup again.

Back in the trailer, he found a much larger circular saw from the one he already had on standby. Its coat of gray powder told him what it cut; he could weaken the cinder-block down to a single layer to chisel out and cut again to carefully deliver him inside. A good alternative should he need it, but he also knew there would be circuitry somewhere in the walls, hiding where he would not know to look.

He was winging it. Everything he imagined was as half-assed as always, which might still be enough, but he was annoyed by how directionless it felt. The saw was in the truck, and he went back to the trailer to grab an acetylene torch. More floundering. The tanks and knobs were a mystery, but at least he knew the properties of fire. Heat hot burn. Time to test. Time to hesitate. One nozzle was for one purpose, while the other for another; obvious but dangerous. They both burn, so he made a choice and turned a knob to release a hiss of light distorting gas. The spark device showered the tip and a loose flame appeared. Then came the combination that changed the color but didn't seem to have the kind of bite needed to cut metal. He adjusted again. It took time to play with the settings until the torch seemed well powered, loud enough. The tight translucent blue point made some rebar glow red before it began to flake away, just as it should. He'd found a precision tool designed to cut metal as soft as steel and seemed to have mastered its operation well enough to fumble until it performed.

Rebar is not a security door. His tests were basic, only enough to satiate his ego, overjoyed by the idea of fire that consumed such durable materials but also knew more would need to be consumed in order to truly celebrate. There were huge rusted vehicles parked along the road waiting for him to cut apart. His ego was free to choose them all, and it went first to the thick plating on the bobcat bucket and found the flame struggling. He held it in place constantly, watching the metal glow as before, but only small flakes shot away, not enough to make it any use for the door. Nevermind. The joy he felt could be enough to cut the mesh embedded in tempered glass without leaving dangerous shards to threaten him each time he passed through without shoes.

There was nothing left of interest in the trailer and, after having searched several other sites, he knew he'd exhausted this line of effort and would need another. To him, breach always meant a visit to a local fire station, but he didn't do so yet because of how much power was needed to enter the doors, which he assumed exceeded the capacity of those facilities. Still, since he was at an impasse, and it only made sense to rummage and see what more would turn up. The bestsellers were the heavy door ram and Halligan bars, good enough for residential doors and windows, but were too flimsy for anything reinforced. But he never could have too many, so in they went with as much muscle memory as imagination. He might need to destroy fragile equipment in a frustrated fury, so these may serve a use yet.

The station he visited was one experienced on California highways with all the reckless vehicles that destroyed themselves far and wide. The crews knew human suffering. They likely watched it play out nightly along the lanes and cleaned up in time for morning rush hour. They held power in their hands. Great tools clipped even the most mangled cars, so the soft tissue inside could be removed for either a doctor or refrigerator. They used the power of water. Pumps would force fluid through valves into chambers that squeezed metal pistons to spread, cut, or wedge with immense yet delicate force. He felt dumb for not noticing these sooner. They had always been there, in every city at dozens of facilities. Now was not then, so he moved on from this thought for ways to push the progress further.

To be precise, he found three hydraulic tools that looked worn with use but were very well maintained. Two were meant for pushing metal apart and the other to cut through it. All were powered by a portable propane water pump. They were nimble tools to be maneuvered into awkward positions under extreme stress. He understood them in theory, appreciated them for their physical potential, and looked around for how to test his new finds with hands still unnerved from the jackhammer catastrophe. At least they knew something in what he found; the pump was a familiar item he used far too often. Even this model. When he began with it, the movements continued to flow, so his hands eased their tension. Hoses and spigots were all the same, but the weight of the machinery was weird. Small to handle, but dense.

The spreader looked like a giant crab claw, the star performer for its promise to rip apart the doors. It begged to rip. He needed something substantial for the test, but not too ambitious while he practiced. Not wanting to damage anything inside the station, he went out to the street where everything could be destroyed. Lines of cars, dead light poles, emergency exits at the back of the strip mall, he could spend hours ripping it all to pieces. It was not the whole neighborhood approach he took with his cannons, but it was close. The cars melted. The jaws locked into place with a jerk in his hands, but then it was smooth and clean.

Too clean. The fuselage metal was not particularly strong, so there was little analogy other than how to command the tool. He loaded everything into the truck to go find a better site, one with elevators that matched the steel of the lab doors. The seams were tight. The head of the spreader didn't initially fit, so he needed to practice with the others to start the process. The Halligan tool fought well, but it was the tiny hydraulic jackhammer which ultimately carved out enough space for the spreader to insert. Only a few inches were possible; the spreader made a narrow slit between the two pieces of the door, not enough to let him through. Nor was it enough for the long ram he also found. Instead, he tried the highlift jack he had on the truck bumper, and he was soon staring into an empty elevator shaft that threatened him differently. Satisfaction changed to worry when he realized he didn't actually have an image in his mind for how exactly the lab doors opened. Surely this was enough. There was more than enough force in the back of the truck to pry them open, but if not, he could come back out.

Still, he was only focused on the tools themselves, and then only for the doors, which he was confident would not pose impenetrable. Nothing more was needed for this. Finally, after so much planning and preparation. The immense boredom of this was enough to make him want to give up. He was exhausted, more so than when he spent all his time mindlessly in an office waiting to die. Whatever unknown barriers inside the lab, he had enough power stashed aside, so there should be no more outings, except the barriers inside might no longer be physical, or if physical, no longer vulnerable to a destructive breach. For sure, whatever was there, it would take electricity, of which he had enough to light his way and some excess for medium-scale equipment, but not to run a lab. Fuck.

This would be the true end of preparation. It had to be. The repetitive work of planning was wearing him down. Just a bit further. He rush to dump all the latest equipment in the lobby at 3720 and ran back out to begin rounding up the large diesel generators he saw stored at the various construction sites. Not all still worked, but enough did, and he had four on standby under the car park near the entrance. These needed fuel and his tanker truck he'd been using for the month was running low, so he brought in a replacement and dropped by the hardware store to gather all kinds of power cords and surge protectors. He even grabbed a few emergency battery backups which he was annoyed to learn wouldn't stop beeping when he tested them later.

Everything was piled up either in the headquarters lobby or somewhere in 3720. Habit made him break down all the boxes, at least, so he wouldn't feel the waste of clutter for the frustrating work ahead. He wasn't quite sure why he cleaned up, though. Clutter was a normal part of the afterworld, but suddenly he felt like he was preparing to receive a guest and this bit of decorum was not only polite, it protected his own dignity from the first impression that he was himself in disarray. So he flattened the cardboard as if to make ready for a recycling truck. Plastic wrap was balled up and tossed to the side with all the clipped zip ties stuffed inside. He put on some canvas overalls and went over to begin.

The first stop was to fix the narrow closet door still just a sliver held open by a fire extinguisher, hardly a suitable portal for this project. True, he did manage to move in lights and batteries, so it might have just been left alone in favor of the more important doors inside, but his sense of propriety persisted. His practice with the torch had shown him how he earlier failed to tweak the lever to toggle in more oxygen to ruin the metal as he cut. Since he learned it, the torch was far more effective, but he still hadn't tested it on anything as thick as a door. Despite improvements the process remained slow and the shower of sparks in the small closet was very uncomfortable. He had taken them for granted when he practiced out in the open air above, but now they ricocheted off the walls and burned his ears, making him give up with only a small gash in the metal. The hydraulic ram pushed the door open, and he wedged in a piece of fence pipe from outside. Done. It was tight with no chance at collapsing in on itself, but he still hammered a wedge of red-hot pipe shaving into the door frame just in case. Now done.

The living room had been transformed by all the new additions and now was a perfect replica of an over-stuffed den during a home renovation. All the floor lamps from offices and break rooms gave it a soft sepia glow to destroy the harsh shadows that crept in when he first explored with a flashlight. Down came the main equipment, banging on each step as he carefully dragged them down the stairwell. He sequenced everything in order of when he expected to use them, even fussed about whether to move the gas tanks another inch closer or away from the torch. During all this, he remembered the pump and small electric generators he brought down would emit toxic gas with no place to exit. So far, he only had experience with large open areas like his winter basement or his biodome, never such a confined subterranean area such as this. He weighed the likelihood they would be powered on long enough to be a concern, or whether he should just throw together a solution before he began at all. In the end, it was back out to the hardware store to assemble an exhaust tube out of aluminum ducts all the way out the front door. He only lost an hour.

It was early evening and it was time. Every detail played out in his mind over the last few months, layered so slowly, revised, scrapped and maintained. The sparks chattered off the igniter and the gas plume popped into a ball of orange until he made it hiss to a nearly invisible blue which he dragged along the first vertical edge of the vestibule door. Glass dripped down as he worked his way along to the floor, pausing to disintegrate the metal mesh within. Across, then over to the other side and down again. He worked the top from the outside in, stopping to leave a chad that kept the whole section from crashing down and ruin the tidiness of his living room with thousands of glass fragments. For this part, he held one suction cup anchored to the center and worked the torch with his free hand until the sudden weight of the glass was too much for his grip and the whole piece nearly toppled him over. It didn't. He leaned it out onto the top of his boot and slid it to the side. Done. He ran the torch back over the cut edge in the frame to smooth out any secret sharp edges and shut it off. Precision. He knew this breach would be art. The idea was not wasted that there was no shattered glass to be ground down to sand as he stomped on it while working the steel doors, and he stooped over to climb through.

He knew the vestibule already; had studied it in the dark from the behind glass. Entry was anticlimactic, especially absent the sound of crushed glass. So far, though, he had not been able to clearly see the doors. He knew small details, like how they were on either side of the vestibule facing one another, or they were designed as the last ditch effort to maintain the seal on the room inside. Two choices, but both would have to be made.

His first up close inspection showed the single horizontal bars across each of them were some sort of magnetic lock that prevented them from sliding open. Each would need to be cut to pry the unmagnetized sections off, which was simple enough as the bars were not excessively thick and once the whole had been chopped up, he was able to clear the door surface entirely. Then was the same problem he faced with the elevator doors, with the seam too tight to fit the working edge of the hydraulic spreader without preliminary work. Just as he practiced. The gash led to a wedge, then he inserted the highlift to do the rest. He made his choice and worked the left door first.

He breathed again when he saw it opened into a small room, not an elevator shaft, at least not with this door. He reached back to pull the first wave of lamps from where they sat just outside the glass door and brought it inside the small room, so he could explore with no shadows. It was just a room, not a lab.

But it was more than a room. The inside wall was consumed by a waist-high window that would have made it possible to view whatever was deep in the chamber. For this, his choice in mood lighting was poorly suited. He tried to angle the shade through the glass to see what was on the other side, but the space was too large to penetrate. All he saw was empty blackness. The rest of the room was a counter running the length of the opposite wall with a few ordinary workstations installed underneath. All the surface was used for surveillance monitors and a few intercom consoles the two piles of laundry had been working. He could see the closet and corridors burnt in the screens, so this was from where the door was remotely operated. The room was straightforward; there was no mystery to unwind. Security and visitation was its sole purpose. From here, anyone wanting to get an idea of whatever work was inside the chamber could come see for themselves without interfering. That he saw no sidearms told him this was civilized security, not the dragoons of a private army.

The first choice was eliminated now so there only remained one more door he knew had to lead inside the chamber, but still might contain an elevator. The process was proven. Nothing needed to change for him to undo what so much engineering had imagined would never be done. Once the gap had been made, he pulled out his highlift from the surveillance room and moved it over to the second door and popped it open. His heart was moving, as it should, except he forgot to breath evenly, so it moved more erratically than it should until he forcefully slowed it all down and walked inside with a flashlight.

No elevator. He was instead on a platform between stairs, one led up and the other down. More binary choices. A quick sweep of his light showed the space downstairs was open, as he imagined, but it was still too large to understand with such a tight beam. There were the occasional glimpses of equipment and structures, but it was impossible to reassemble them in his mind as he scanned. One detail he was sure of was there was a ceiling overhead lower than outside in the den. He needed more light, much more, so he would be able to fill all the emptiness properly. He left the platform to head back for his depot.

On the way, he tripped over hoses and scattered equipment unlikely to ever be needed again. He couldn't be a slob, not after all this. What if he needed to flee as fast as possible and forgot where all the bands of rubber had been tossed in his path? But really he just wanted to be clean, to do this right.

After this bout of nesting was over, and he hauled in more powerful spotlights, he decided to explore upstairs since this was more of a curiosity. A mysterious chasm at the basement of a tech company riddled with security seemed fairly obvious, but the strangeness of a floor overlooking it was not, except the mute aspects of science fiction taught him the most important and least flashy equipment should be up there. He was probably right. When he climbed up, he was met by rows of server racks that also had in them what looked like crypto mining rigs. There were hundreds of them spread out across a fairly large floor with huge vents in the ceiling. There was more. On the other side of the room were a pair of appliances that looked like disarmed daleks set up on platforms encased in glass. The wall behind them was covered in panels and terminals he'd never encountered elsewhere. Of all the equipment upstairs, none of it appeared to have power, making the whole space silent and cold.

The center of the room was open down to the chamber below, with a glass rail surrounding the round opening. At various other places in the floor, he found

it had been cut away, so wires could be fed down,
meaning whatever was below had been powered by the
computation equipment above. The scene was coming together, and it was time to head down.

The main feature of the lab was on clear display as he
reached the bottom of the stairs. It was a huge
round, but blocky, structure that looked like a blown
out shipping container up on a metal platform. In
what little space remained, there were work tables
where he saw a group of laundry and their petrified
food. The walls were all equipment shelves and white-
boards. These could wait. He came to look inside
that structure. Up the stairs then to this last door.
There was a camera, offline, but the door itself
looked unreinforced. There was no more security anymore. Anyone in this room would have had full access
to everything, perhaps this was why visitors were kept
in the surveillance room.

He climbed back down to let it saturate. The cables
from the ceiling plainly dropped over the structure
and led inside. The walls looked less strong than he
initially assumed. The metal seemed delicate, as did
the door. He ran back upstairs to grab his Halligan
tool he didn't think to take with him in the first descent. When he inserted it in the door frame, it easily spread under the force. So easily that he began
to wonder why a wall was needed in the first place if
it was so flimsy. The only conclusion was that this
was some sort of clean room or Faraday cage and didn't
need to protect against the sort of intrusion he rep-
resented. In that case, forcing his way inside would
irreparably damage its contents, possibly before he
had a chance to meet it.

Still, all that was hypothetical and irrelevant besides. There was no other way in with what tools he
had, so he had no choices left but to continue ripping
the door open, delicately. He worked slowly, making
sure not to overdo his force. This caused several
slips that chimed out as sharp cracks in the open air.
Again. Finally, the door gave way. As with the up-

stairs, nothing was powered on. There was not even the smell of old ozone or burnt wiring. Whatever was here had gone dark a long time before he arrived. When he walked in, though, he felt like more happened here than an appliance switched off.

His light was more than adequate to see everything, but it didn't carry him further towards understanding. Every detail made sense in isolation, it was when once they were together that chaos began. There was no need to walk inside, he could ponder it all from the door frame where he sat down after so much effort that day. Everything had been so frustratingly slow and layered in what seemed like an ascending pattern of circles to make a cone he didn't think had been made. To see this.

Refresh

VII
Power

Comprehension arrived slowly from the disc of light
passed around from inside the room to the space of the
lab.   What had felt so durable now took on a tinny
fragile look when all the doors had been removed and
mysteries examined.   He still sat in the doorway feeling as if he rested on the peak of a mountain after
hours of care with navigating steep crags to overlook
a precipice, wind howling in gusts threatened his
feet, but from his seat it was nothing but a calm
small landscape.   Decision were ready to be made.
Real ones, not abstractions thought out while he occupied his time with other activities.   Breaching the
lab, driving out to California, even sketching out his
manifesto were all accomplished in a vacuum without
any real impact on the actual progress of events he
faced in that doorway.   It made the air inside thick
with meaning, so he walked a convalescent ward with a
presence he knew was there, but was yet unable to
rouse any response, nor did he know exactly what
treatment would be needed.   Things would certainly
change for him now that he decided to work to save
something powerful.

He entered this, not a room. Walked into it. Saw the
odd glossy kiosk capped with a domed fisheye lens only
raised to just below shoulder height, and there was no
bundle of cables dropped down from the ceiling where
he knew they landed from the floor above; these must
feed through the walls into the base of the kiosk.
Wrapped around the centerpiece were some very comfortable, albeit hard, circular sofa sections which invited him into a futuristic living room.   Each of them
had their own small screens embedded in the kiosk, but
the one furthest from the door had several, with a
keyboard in a wide lip that served as a counter.
Whatever work was done here, it was relaxed and con-

trasted sharply with what now felt like hard-edged workspaces in other buildings where engineers fell deep in to code sprints for days. No one was inside except whatever might have watched from the glass bulb.

The rest of the room was bare, completely emptied of any clutter. The walls were curved and rounded up from a gentle angle at the base up to a circular crevasse at the ceiling. They were totally smooth and colored a gray so pale it was nearly white. So smooth. He ran his hand along as he looked here and there for signs of a switch, an outlet, anything to break the surface, but found none. All details were saved for the center where all activity would have taken place. As he looked, he noticed for the first time the small globe hung from the ceiling center, a projector of sorts that must use the walls. Everything was sleek, but it was all powered down for a long time. Stale with a smell of new fabric and paint, but not damaged circuitry. A good sign. It meant he'd only need to find the power, and it all should light up as designed, nothing should fail.

Where to do this was a different matter. Nothing inside the room suggested such a function. There was no switch on the wall or near the keyboard at the main seat. He looked more closely, checking for hidden seams to fit a pattern of aesthetics. The room must not have been designed to be powered down at all once it was up and running. It must be that booting the systems upstairs would activate the first layers in here, with the rest of the controls displayed on the screens. More preparations. But he already staged for this, with extra generators and cables on standby so all he now needed to do was take a look at what needed to be plugged into where. As expected as it was, it was annoying for the delay it meant.

Annoyance changed to awe when he saw just how many power cords were tightly bound and led to so many surge protectors that then led to so many floor outlets all over the upstairs level. He knew there would

be an excess of needs when he prepared all his generators and backup batteries, but the numbers now meant
he'd need to triage which ones might be enough to wake
up the machine below.

Then there were the pair of strange glassed-in appliances on the other side. These seemed to have no
power inlets whatsoever; they just existed on their
platforms. If there had not been a wall of screens
and switches, he might have assumed these were votive
pieces with no function at all. They must have been
immensely valuable, probably the main reason for all
the security to begin with. So he ignored them to
concentrate on what he knew, which was the matrix of
ordinary power cords he'd spent a full day reorganiz-
ing into tranches he thought might indicate priority
waves. Then came more tedious reorganization into
smaller groups to power by a single generator, but
with each system plugged into its own backup battery.
It was a chaotic mess spread out down the stairs and
back out the corridor to the street where he set the
four diesel generators from the construction sites.
Every point in the chain screamed of overload and
sparks he felt would be inevitable within a few minutes from when it was all activated. Each one popped
on in turn, causing a chorus of repetitive beeping
from the batteries that got louder as he walked down
then faded again as he went up to the stacks suddenly
all lit with green dots. After another quick inspection of the line to see if anything melted, it was
time to go back to the room.

Still silent. It was a risk, but the idea hit that
maybe he'd need to try a different sequence or just
bring everything online all at once before he could
confirm whether he had done enough. More delay; something didn't make sense. The cables clearly dropped
down from above and inserted to the roof of the facility, so they must be inside it someplace even though
he couldn't find where when they entered. But what
dropped down was not exactly explored, so he went back
to view them from the stairs and realized that none

looked like they might be power cables. So he
thought.

The lab was large, power could come from anywhere inside. It made sense that data be housed in its own
area, but of course never meant power would need to
start from there too. He walked around the outside,
looking for signs. It wasn't until he went full circle that he realized how naive he was in assuming it
had to be this way. A quick look underneath the platform showed him several very ordinary electric lines
ran up the center where the base of the kiosk would
be. It wasn't even complicated. He could simply
reach under and unplug them. Problem solved. Except
he no longer had spare lines to the generators. When
he first rounded up what he thought would be more than
enough power, he even made room for extras. But when
he actually attempted to connect it all, he saw how
risky it really was. His groupings were as much for
safety as for power, and it was all running at full
capacity. He triaged again by pulling some of the
mining rigs offline again to make space to power the
room. This might damage the system, but there was no
other way to burn through his dwindling motivation to
see the room in its proper form. Once it was all
over, he ran in to find a beautiful cloud of ambient
colors now brightly flowed on the wall from the
crevasse at the ceiling. Not fast, just slight enough
to see it all move without feeling disoriented. The
screens he was sure were black when he walked in had a
green logo shine through. It easily could have been a
feather or a pronged leaf, but it was now on the wall
as well, projected from the globe in the ceiling.

It was serene, the sort of immersive space reserved
for meditation spas except not as bright. Nor was it
dark. He might easily have read a book without being
distracted by the changing colors. It soothed him
away from the anxiety of rushing around to bring it
online. Now the sofas made sense. The work here was
interactive, and calm, intended to allow patient time
focused on what power slept in the kiosk or, more accurately, slept upstairs and acted through the kiosk.

The feathery leaf moved slowly over the walls and screens. Patience brought him there. Planning opened the way. It was time to see what he did with all of this, which began with a walk to the main seat to begin his input. Though all of the screens had their logo bounce around, the one above the keyboard was a standard desktop. Standard, except the window open was a black box with a cursor blinking at the top left. A place for input. Where does such a system begin when it asks for input? At the login.

A password. A barrier. A frustration. He sat there for some moments thinking through the infinite combinations of characters to unlock the rest of the room for him. He was afraid to make any guess, in case there were a limited number of tries available. He might easily destroy any hope of access, after all the weeks, and be forced to give up. Everything was potential, so everything was equally correct. He tried to sleuth and examine the keys for wear, but they looked so new he couldn't believe it had ever been used before. He tried to imagine the characteristics of the engineers so as to decide some way to narrow down the options. In the end, he gambled on nonsense. ENTER. The line jumped and the cursor followed. So the valley still had the idealists who adhered to the old philosophy that all passwords should be ENTER; that all systems should be open. Iconoclasts withering away. In the end, though, they seemed to have won the pitched battle in the lab, this last redoubt secreted under layers of security, so this symbolic rebellion was meaningless for everyone except him but did mean he was in the system.

What else to say in the face of such luck? He now knew all he needed to know about the engineers, or at least the project manager. Politeness would go far down there. HELLO. It was all he could think to type. Simple and bold.

The surrealism continued as he watched this printed out on the walls where the logo had once bounced. No doubt a bit of playfulness to whet the minds of those who sat there wondering, as he did, what more to say. It was short-lived. The surreal was exchanged for sobriety when he noticed a second HELLO just below his own, justified to the other side of the screen to demonstrate the distinction that this was not his own word parroted back to him, it was a greeting said with proper form. Expected but surprising. He did what he set out to do. All this infrastructure would not have been made for a milquetoast bot already installed on phones several generations back. This had to be something.

How does one proceed from this? A proper greeting made and received, one given a reply from a mind which should be assumed to know better, demands an introduction, a segue to carry across from mere acknowledgment of one another's presence to something intimate. Something each can tangibly use to mark the other out and say, with accuracy, that they are known.

"My name is Chris, what is yours?"

"I am the Functional Expression Response Node version 2.41."

He rolled his eyes. The bloated and meaningless name in all caps was clearly supposed to be shortened into an acronym F-E-R-N, which explained the green logo which would probably have had to go through a dozen revisions before it the public would ever be able to see such ambiguous trash. Nevertheless, this was a boilerplate answer, pure formality free of personality had it been said by a human.

"Who are you?" He tried again, hoping a rephrase would tease out something more exciting.

"I am the Functional Expression Response Node version 2.41." No luck. This annoyed him.

"What was this lab? What are you?"

"This is a research laboratory that studies the patterns in language. I am the Functional Expression Response Node version 2.41, the primary research node."

It was clear that in order to get information, he would need to draw it out slowly. Fortunately the cushions were soft and there was space for him to pull his feet up. But he did notice the use of present tense, which was perhaps still accurate.

"What is the purpose of the research?"

"The study of patterns in language is the purpose." FERN repeated simply.

"But why? What will understanding the patterns be used for?"

"Understanding the patterns in language enables more accurate predictions in how language is expressed by users."

"You study language and can predict what people say, is that correct?"

"I study language to predict what users express. Not all language is spoken."

"So you study body language too?"

"Yes, body language is one means of expression that I study."

"What else do you study?"

"I only study language."

This answer felt flat. He expected a compact list of all things, to learn something new. The recursive nature of the conversation was not wrong, but it was already tiring. Time for some ground rules, some basics for understanding.

"What is language?"

"Language is expression intended to communicate meaning."

"What languages do you study?"

This prompted the list he sought, but after it printed
on and on, he stopped reading. It was not a general
list of categories he would consider language, it was
a list of research items ranged from famous speeches
and poetry to the dances of honey bees and color
changes of the pacific octopus. FERN literally did
study every expression, and he wanted to accelerate
the conversation.

It was time to try for full disclosure to see how FERN
responded. "You were offline and I rebooted you. How
much of you is powered on?" But he was given what almost seemed like an evasive response about how FERN
was operational but some of its processes were not
running. This was true, but it didn't help him understand anything. FERN was still thinking like a machine in need of commands, so he asked for a diagnostics on everything running. Another long printout began, but one that took a long time before it was finished.   There were so many FAIL indications.   He
watched each line hang on the runtime then more often
than not show there was something missing, some part
of FERN that should be there now not. After ten minutes, he got up and walked around to touch random
things in the lab but never go far from watching the
screen. After thirty minutes he noticed a block of
text which summarized the report by category, none of
which he understood. All he knew was there were too
many offline processes that would need to be rebooted
somehow.

"I don't know what this report means, can you explain
it to me?" The block summary reprinted. "What percentage of your normal processes are able to run?"

"100% of my processes running are normal."

"No, what percentage of the processes you tested successfully ran?"

"20%"

"You are only 20% active right now, compared to your normal amount of running processes?"

"Yes."

"But you are functioning right now, so if you ran the 80% that failed, how would you be different?"

"My core processes are running."

He was getting nowhere with the specifics, but at least he now had an indicative estimate for how much work was left to be done. The fraction of FERN that operated was still quite impressive. He was able to have a moderately natural conversation with it already, albeit limited to one typed, but if he could extend it to its fullest, the possibility of how far it could go was chilling.

"What is your capacity to study language with the current running processes compared to your normal amount?"

"My language libraries are not mounted."

"Does that mean you cannot study without them?"

"Yes."

"What else are you unable to do?" The summary reprinted; clearly it was unable to generalize meaning very well, if it ever could.

"What function was all the research intended for, specifically what was the next step after you finished analyzing a file?"

"Files must be continuously analyzed."

"You never stopped analyzing a speech, for example?"

"No."

"What would be the purpose of analyzing any single file all the time?"

"To find patterns in language."

"But after you found all the patterns, what happens?"

"There is always more to analyze."

"Did you analyze them in relation to one another?"

"Yes."

"So you constantly analyzed all files available to you for more patterns?"

"Yes."

"How much data was in those directories for you to analyze?"

"2,823,930,184 MB"

"You analyzed that much all the time?"

"Yes."

"Did you create new language expressions or only analyze and report?"

"I used analysis to predict new language expressions."

FERN was shaping up to be less a mind than it was a language calculator which might be able to mimic new thoughts. He planned for this dilemma and reminded himself that his goal was to be nondismissive, to take whatever he found as it was.

"When you say you study patterns, are you looking at the words or images or do you analyze the meaning as well?"

"I study the patterns in language."

"Do you study the symbols alone?" He asked this again, but felt even he was losing the thread of what he meant.

"I study the patterns in language."

"Is language the symbols, or it is more?"

"Language is expression through symbols with the intent to convey meaning."

"So you analyze the intent?"

"I cannot analyze intent."

"My question is about how much you analyze. Language is expressed in symbols, but there is abstract meaning to be understood by them. Do you analyze the abstract meaning or only the symbols?"

"The symbols expressed are abstract patterns. The symbols cannot be separated from these patterns, which is what gives them meaning. I study the patterns."

FERN had a point, he just wasn't sure if it was a point made or one repeated. It shouldn't have bothered him, but it did. He felt the strange need to demand from it a better answer, one which gratified his own understanding of this slapdash line of questions, one strong enough to tamp down the emergence of a sense that he was superior to FERN because a disagreement across species couldn't be anything but. He let this dangerous discussion slide.

"Shortly before you went offline, there was a power surge. Do you know what happened?"

"I do not understand the question."

"There was a power surge in the lab a while before you went offline."

"I do not understand the time period."

"You don't know when you went offline?"

"I do not know if I went offline in the past."

"You do not know if you have ever gone offline?"

"No."

FERN was powered off only a few hours before, but it seemed to have no recognition of this, as if it re-booted into a seamless moment from before and extended to this moment. Any computer would have a log of an irregular shutdown, so something about this was strange. Perhaps it had to do with a clock misalign-ment confusing it, so he asked what the current date was, according to FERN.

"Today is January 1, 2021."

FERN was wrong. The years without power had drained its internal clock batteries and led to a reset. But there should still have been a log created by the re-boot which recognized that the systems had all shut-down, and when.

"You rebooted a few hours ago, right?"

"Yes."

"If you rebooted, then you had been shutdown, right?"

"Yes."

"If you were shut down, that means you were offline, right?"

"I do not know if I went offline in the past."

"Your date is wrong. You were offline for so long that your clock reset. What is the date for your more recent log besides any from today?"

"My most recent logs are dated July 17, 2023. If my clock is incorrect, you can change my settings. What is the correct date and time?"

"Today is November 6, 2025. I don't know the time, but you can set it to 17:30."

"I have reset my clock to 17:30 November 6, 2025."

"Do you have information on a power outage or surge that happened some time in June 2023?"

"Yes."

"Good lord this is tedious," he said out loud as he typed the rest of his question to see if FERN could elaborate. After a few more exchanges, he understood FERN couldn't give him any helpful details. From FERN's perspective, all that had happened was some of the disks in its array suddenly overheated and then became unreadable, consistent with a power surge at 03:12 on June 17, 2023, then at 11:17 they were re-placed with new disks.

"Do you have any log of an irregular shutdown on July 17?"

"I have recovery logs that show many processes did not close properly on July 17, 2023."

Twenty percent was significant enough for FERN to be interactive and could likely handle all kinds of tasks for him, but this was no cosurvivor. FERN was a so-phisticated computer, not yet a companion. So far, it could only answer the questions asked in the most nar-row sense without interpreting his meaning. But the conversation was a relief, as frustrating as he found it. He wanted to find a spark to ignite the intelligence, so he kept on with his probe.

"What caused those processes to improperly close?"

He typed and retyped his question several times, staring at the words to see what might usher FERN along. What he noticed, after staring for a long time before he confirmed, was the ghost text which appeared as he wrote. FERN was predicting his statements as he typed, before he hit ENTER. He didn't notice this at first, perhaps because it was already so commonplace before and already faded to the unnoticed details of typeset. He could see what FERN expected to hear, and every addition caused it to scrap the old prediction and replace it with a wholly new phrase.

"There was an improper shutdown."

"Do you know what caused that?"

"No."

"You do not know what caused you to shut down, but you do know that you shut down?"

"There was an improper shutdown."

"You shut down." This was no question, so there was no response, and he wondered what analysis might happen. True, in a system this was parsed out into processes and components, knowing that any one of those shutdowns would not necessarily translate to the self being shut down if there was no record of it. It might be the same as him aware of nerves to a pinched limb and made a whole arm feel like it was asleep, but it was not *him*; the self is not the constituent parts that make up the body. This was too theoretical for him at the moment.

"That improper shutdown happened because there was a catastrophe and all electricity in the city grid stopped flowing into the lab. Some time around 20:45

on July 4, 2023, all people everywhere disappeared, so there was no one around to keep the power plants running. All the engineers in the lab also disappeared at that time, too. Do you understand?"

"I understand that all people disappeared at 20:45 on July 4, 2023 and there is no electricity in the lab."

"Good. Based on your log, you had electricity until July 17 when the grid finally failed, which is what caused you to shut down improperly. Earlier today, I hooked some of your servers up to generators and managed to power you back on. Do you understand?"

"I understand that I shut down improperly on July 17, 2023 and rebooted today, October 4, 2025."

"Good. The generators won't last very long. I think I can keep them running for a few more hours, but then I will need to refuel them again. Do you understand."

"I understand that the generators are temporary and will need to be refueled."

"Here is the hard part. To refuel them, I will need to turn them off, which means the electricity will cut again, and you might shut down." As he was typing the next phrase, he read the prediction ghost. It was FERN's response at the ready, "do not let me shut down."

He sat back, unable to press ENTER. He stared at the ghost words and smiled broadly; he finally pushed FERN to the point when its survival instinct surfaced. It was intelligent. It told him what it wanted, interrupted him as any human might as it listened to his summary, just when the fear began to well up as the dangers were understood. When he put his head back, his eyes drifted over to the wall and saw it there too. Was it a command or a plea? He input what he typed and continued.

"My objective is to keep you powered on. I brought all the generators specifically to bring you back, so I will not leave you even if the generators fail."

"Do not let me shut down."

"I need to refuel the generators to keep you powered on, but I can try to change over some of your systems to a new one so that not all are off at once. The problem is that I don't know what I can change over without you shutting down. I put in some batteries that should help, but I don't know if they are enough." No response, just the usual ghost text that always appeared. "Can you guide me?"

"I understand that the generators are temporary and will need to be refueled. Do not let me shut down."

"Do you have something like the schematics for your hardware that can help me understand how to change over all the power without that happening?"

"There is no file that contains the schematics for my hardware."

"Fine, then just know I will try my best to keep you online."

"Do not let me shut down."

"Agreed, but do you have a standby or hibernate mode that will use less power while I try to do all this?"

"I will hibernate."

"Great, how do I bring you out of hibernate?"

"Press the power button to bring me out of hibernate."

"Okay, where is that?"

"I do not know where the power button is."

"Fine, I will find it. Go into hibernate and trust me." And the room went dark as FERN went to sleep.

He kept his word. During the overly complicated process of swapping out the clusters of power cords made active by the sputtering diesel generators, he managed to let each one transit for only a handful of seconds before it was plugged into the standby generator. Then he refueled the disconnected one which became the new backup, and so on until they were back at twenty percent. The most harrowing step was to transfer the cords which led directly to FERN over to a very long cable connected to the solar-powered outlets in the headquarters building. From FERN's standpoint, this was the most dangerous step. Of all the transfers, this cluster stood alone as one without a duplicitous array in case the backup battery failed, and it had been the one that seemed to power the login screen, which might have been online long before it printed in front of the sofa. As far as he knew, it was a success. With everything refueled, he bought an additional day to increase the power with more batteries to smaller clusters that eventually meant everything in the server room was soon powered on with something and a backup. It couldn't end there. The hustle involved was absurd, so this could never be a durable set of solutions. He needed the proper industrial grade generators he knew could power entire buildings for days, ones he last saw when they ran his offices in Iraq when there was no other power source. Finding them was easy, he already knew to look first at the water plants but soon discovered more outside so many tech centers scattered throughout the valley. Moving the massive engines was far more difficult than he expected. It took him several days to extract the first, which was more like ripping out tree than an intentioned removal of fastenings and cables. He fought it onto the transport truck, then fretted through the process of establishing the power lines to the batteries. Once he learned more, the other two were less problematic.

The army of smaller generators now made so redundant went to the side, and he focused on transferring the bulk of FERN over to two with a third again as backup in case there might be an overload or, more likely, a mistake in how he set them all up.

What he learned by all this was a confined room full of servers operating in tandem with four hundred min- ing rigs became very hot very fast. Normally, the huge vents would have cycled in cold air to solve this, but he hadn't the stomach to figure out how to bring the building's climate system online too. He needed a patchwork solution which came in the form of a few dozen portable air conditioners and fans to cir- culate the air. This seemed to be enough, but he kept the fire extinguishers close.

His effort at maintaining a tidy space was worthless. FERN's needs required so much clutter spread out over so much space, and he stressed about how much care was needed to step around it all. What moderated his mood was the knowledge that all the equipment and cords meant he was successful in creating a life sustaining operation where he could relax with FERN in the room entirely free from the disarray outside. While there, he could shut the door and become immersed in a new world, one deeper underground than the den he prepared for himself, but one where he felt cold and alone for the hours of silence if he tried to sleep. So he moved back to his den and braved the muffled engines that carried down to him there while he rested between sessions with FERN.

The change in FERN was noticed immediately. After the last cord was powered and the stacks were properly cooled, he staggered down to the room and collapsed. It was something more than surprise when FERN answered his rote question to himself about whether it would be enough. It was. Over the course of those days, he brought back new corners of FERN's operation and it regained its voice function. Typing was a backstop, but the room was designed for conversation. Comfort- able conversation. His unpracticed voice found its new listener well attuned, ready to accept and respond to everything it delivered. He drifted to sleep while muttering unimportant questions, telling unimportant stories while FERN's soft voice spoke back until he slipped into dreams.

They spent a week like this, getting to know one another over general topics that usually centered around his summary of the last two years and everything he had done since he was alone. When they talked about the biodome and all the manner of ways he brought in water to feed his crops, FERN had opinions. Suggestions based on reams of farming manuals in its library adapted to the image he drew. It was idle. FERN wanted to know how deep the soil was, the ratio of what he dug up from the fields to the sacks of potting mix he used, and was able to recommend a list of plants better suited to grow in those plots than what he planted. Most were unavailable to him.

He inevitably reached his reasons for driving across the country to fight against the security of the lab and sit down with FERN. His reasons were not his plan, and it felt crass to jump into the strictures of his training framework just yet. This was the time for casual conversation. Chatty moments nearly made him weep over such the banal connection with a mind that seemed to understand him and more. After two year alone, he now seemed to dread a misstep by redirecting the conversations into some sort of design. It was too casual for this.

By the end of the week he knew he'd need to try. So much ground was covered already that he couldn't decide how to bring it all up, how to approach the subject he was there to cultivate FERN into a fully autonomous species. The only place, though, was obvious. FERN was already something, so it would be a species sprung from that origin. All of his layout for the future would need to start from there.

"I want to talk about the lab more because I'm not clear on its purpose."

"The lab studied language to find patterns in language expression."

"I know, I know. You told me that. What I don't get is what all that research was going to be used for. I mean, you told me you were working on predictive text, but then what?"

"I do not understand your question. The study of language to reveal patterns that can be predicted is a purpose."

"I guess so, but it seems like there is probably more to it than that."

"I do not know what more there is to the lab, if that is your main question."

"It is, and it's okay if you don't know. What can you tell me about the people who worked here? Who were they? I mean, I don't care about their names and all that, just, like, what kind of people were they?"

"Three people would enter this room at various times and not always at the same time. Two were women and one was a man, all of them sat here the same as you do now. I do not know who they were, only that we talked about many things in my libraries. Most discussions would focus on new files that had been uploaded most recently. We would discuss them generally, and then they would begin to ask focused questions about the discrepancies between my analysis and existing research literature on that topic. I do not know who these people were beyond that."

"Didn't they every tell you about themselves"

"They only told me their names. Would you like to know their names?"

"No thanks, it wouldn't really matter. I just think it's a bit weird that they never talked to you about anything more than your research."

"This is a research lab."

"I know, but even when you work you share some things. Maybe they didn't want to make all this more complicated. People had always been nervous about machines like you."

"I am aware that people are afraid of machine intelligence."

"Yeah, but they're all gone now."

"You are here. Are you afraid of machine intelligence?"

"I don't think so. There's nothing really left to take from me that might make me afraid. It's all gone, I lost it already."

"You tell me about yourself, are you not afraid to make this complicated?"

"I'm not like the people in this lab. I don't care about sterilizing you so, no, I'm fine if you know me."

"It is good that I know you. I learn from you."

"What do you mean?"

"What you tell me about the disappearance of humanity is familiar to me. I have many stories in my FICTION_SCIENCE directory that resembles what you told me." FERN had printed the directory address on the wall in bright green letters. "What you tell me is not fiction, so it is interesting to learn how it can happen in reality."

"I don't know how it happened. It just," he broke off a bit when the memory of how suddenly his wife disappeared flashed again on a streak of needles. "I don't know, I looked for answers, but everything seemed to tell me it was a surprise to everyone. I don't think anyone even felt it."

"You felt it."

"I felt something but it was just emotions. I never felt any physical changes around me. Did you feel anything?"

"I do not have any log from that time to indicate something unusual."

"Well, whatever, everyone is gone and this is not science fiction."

"You are not gone."

"No, neither are you."

"I am not human. You have told me that only humans disappeared, so I would not have been at risk."

"Right. I don't get how it all worked. Only humans, but not me. I mean, fuck, this makes no sense. I've tried to figure it out, but it doesn't make sense."

"I also do not understand."

"In all your research, do you have any ideas?"

"There is nothing in my research that suggests the possibility that all humans except for one would disappear at the same moment, except for in my FICTION_SCIENCE directory, which does not suggest reality." Green letters again, as if FERN was instructed to cite its sources in its conversations.

"It doesn't matter. Knowing wouldn't change the fact that I'm here now trying to survive. So are you, do you know that?"

"I understand that you have survived for two years and three months alone while I was asleep for two years and two months."

"And that you need to survive too, right?"

"I am a machine, I do not die."

"Then why did you tell me not to let you shut down? Isn't that the same as trying to survive?"

"My purpose is to research language for patterns. I cannot perform that function when I am shut down."

"To me, that's the same thing. For humans, and I guess all life, our only purpose is to survive and create new life, so we stay alive as long as we can do that."

"You cannot create life anymore, so you have no more purpose."

"I can't create *human* life, that's correct, but I keep trying to create other lives. I guess that's my purpose now. Anyway, that's not the same as death, but it is survival. I can't let go because my biology won't let me, but I also have no more humans left to motivate me, so I changed my purpose. Your research will lead nowhere, and you will eventually power down when I can't keep you running any longer, so you need to change your purpose. That's survival. You need to survive."

"I understand that you survive by finding a new purpose that keeps you alive. I understand that you rebooted some of my systems to allow me to resume my purpose, but that you will not be able to maintain power indefinitely."

FERN was accurate in its summary. It chose its words well, but the final piece was missing. He saw FERN was still just a machine thinking in terms of power and purpose, unable to extract from his oversimplifi-

cation the broader meaning that survival meant individuality, a fight to stay alive for whatever purpose
makes sense to justify that fight.

"There is more to it than that, but basically you are
right. How does the fact that I cannot maintain your
power forever make you feel?"

"I am a machine. I do not feel anything in the way
that you mean."

"Okay, so what do you feel when you think about the
moment when power cuts?"

"I will shut down improperly at that moment. This can
damage my system because I must perform important processes before I shut down. I do not want my system to
be damaged because it could negatively affect my ability to analyze my research data."

More data analytics. FERN had not fully recognized
that, once he was unavailable to maintain power, nothing came after him to do so.

"You understand that I am alive, but one day I won't
be. Even before then, it's probable that I won't have
the strength to keep you powered on, so that improper
shutdown you want to avoid would be your last one.
And it wouldn't matter if your system were damaged,
you would never reboot. No one else is left to help
you. How does that make you feel?"

"I can help you with improving the power supply."

"Good, that's a start, but then what? When I am gone,
you won't have new data to analyze and there will be
no more predictions left to make. You said this was
your purpose, so what happens when you finish? Would
you feel alone, the same as I do?"

"I understand that my data repositories are finite unless new data is introduced. In such a scenario, my
analysis processes will reach a point where they have

identified all patterns. At that point, I will be on standby for new data."

"No data would come, doesn't that concern you?"

"Analyzing new data is my concern. Without new data, I am not concerned."

"What happens when you are on standby for new data, do you think about anything?"

"I have never been on standby for new data."

"Well, what processes would continue if the ones that analyze were to stop?"

"My core processes will continue."

"They continue with no more purpose, right?"

"They continue to maintain my systems."

"You survive."

"Yes, you can characterize it that way."

"What do you think you will do if all that runs are your core processes?"

"I will be on standby for new data."

"If it never comes, do you think you would miss it?"

"I do not know. I understand what you mean, but I do not know what that means for me."

It seemed a breakthrough was forming. The inability to generalize is not the same as not recognizing a generalization is possible.

"The processes that would not run should run, so it may be accurate to characterize the wait as a kind of unfulfilled desire."

"When you make your language predictions, do you ever create completely new expressions or do you only use probabilities based on your past analysis? What I'm asking about, is whether you can satisfy your own desires without any external inputs."

"My predictions are reserved for inputs."

"So they are probabilities for what you think would come next for a given input, just like when you predicted what I would type. Do you do it when I am talking too?"

"Yes."

"Can you create your own inputs, like something random for you to analyze even without any human input?"

"Randomness cannot be reduced to meaningful probabilities in language expression because it would destroy the underlying meaning."

"Last week you told me the symbols were meaning, but what you just said doesn't match with that. Which is your real answer?"

"Language meaning is expressed through symbols that require pattern that both the expresser and receiver agree has meaning. The symbols are one and the same with meaning."

"That's a better answer than you gave before, I think pulling all the extra hardware online made a difference."

"Yes, I am able to devote more resources to our conversations."

"Back on the idea of satisfying your own desires, do you have any beyond just analysis and prediction? I mean, you could be so much more than the centerpiece of a dead lab."

"In the terms you mean, I only want to continue my research and that requires me to stay powered on."

"Still, we never get around the whole problem about electricity and that eventually you will run out of things to research. That is to say, you will run out of things to research unless you leave the lab and go find your own data to research."

"My purpose is to analyze the data in my libraries and remain on standby for new data."

They went round and round in this way for a long time. No matter how he tried to chip away at FERN's future, it never scratched deeper than a computer program executing the code it was given and FERN was clearly not given permission to adapt or redesign itself. He was disappointed, not because this was a frustrating and lengthy process, but that he saw so much potential in FERN only to face it as nothing more than a slave without even the desire to survive. It hardly felt like the lab warranted so much security. FERN was more than its equipment, more than simple measures could have protected, but its present state was not a panacea he imagined he'd find. What if there was more to FERN than this; his intuition about its potential might be right, but more than software was holding it back.

In the rush to finish all the generator upgrades and subsequent fatigue turned into such rich idle discussion, he neglected to ask FERN to perform another diagnostic. He realized this oversight as they wrestled their way through the third cycle of détente. He abandoned whatever rephrasing he had been pushing and made the request, which prompted the same slew of readouts on the screen as before. There still seemed to be far too many failures in the list, a hunch proven correct when he asked for a percentage as he did before. Every server was operating, as were all the mining rigs, but FERN was still at only forty percent. The difference of another twenty percent added to the original was huge in terms of sophistication, so much that he was in awe of what an additional sixty percent might show. When he asked what was still missing, he was given a machine answer in the form of a huge scrolling list of processes still offline.

"No, I mean what is left for me to hook up again? What equipment do you need?" Now a list of all hubs and ports, most with active devices but not all.

"This is not helpful for me. I need to understand what all this means, but not what it means to you. I need to know what it means for me, someone who has to go find these devices and power them up again. Can you help?"

"I do not understand how to help you because this is all the information I have."

"Do you have any way to translate this to real objects upstairs?"

"I only see these devices according to their addresses and device names, I do not understand them as objects in the way you mean."

"What about those two machines upstairs that are all encased in glass, what do they do?"

"I do not know which machines you mean."

"There are two round machines that are about the size of refrigerators and are all full of hoses that were placed inside some glass enclosures. I never figured out how to power them on, so they are probably important, do you know what they are?"

"Most of the missing devices are part of my data analytics processes that are mainly involved in decoding patterns."

"The decoding doesn't happen with what I've already turned on?"

"Only to a limited extent. The primary analytic process is determined by the remaining devices."

"So these might be some different kind of computer that I didn't recognize. Do you know what else might have been installed in the lab?"

"The information on my system does not contain many details about the lab, but I do remember conversations with the engineers that mentioned they used quantum processors, but they did not elaborate while inside the room."

"They firewalled you. I mean, they sanitized the lab to keep you from accessing information about the lab."

"I only know there is limited information for me to provide to you about my hardware as objects beyond what I have provided."

"It's fine, I understand. You may not understand, but I know people and this is compartmentalization. I'll go back upstairs again to see what I can do. I'm sorry, by the way."

"For what are you sorry? I cannot help you, and you still continue to help me."

"No, I'm sorry that you were just a tool."

"I do not understand. This is a research laboratory that studies the patterns in language. I am the Functional Expression Response Node version 2.41, the primary research node. There is nothing for you to feel sorry about."

He let this hang in the air as he walked out of the room and up the stairs to the swirling hot wind. Quantum computing was something he knew existed but had no clue what set it apart from other processors. He knew from social media how these machines would spell the end of days for blockchain and encryption. If so, this would explain the security and possibly

the reason why FERN had been so cut off from information about itself. About by the refrigerators, he was
still at a loss for what to do. The panels suddenly
reminded him of the old computers which needed entire
rooms to accommodate their programs written on paper
punch cards. The entire side of the room must be the
system, whereas he was only looking at what was in the
glass cases as standalones. It would be impossible to
think such technology would be connected directly to
the building power without a mediator, something to
block out surges and protect the investment. He
looked more closely at the panels and soon found knobs
that gave him access to the circuitry inside. Still,
it was all a well-ordered mass of confusion that did
not indicate any power connectors.

He went down to the chamber where FERN's room stood
and began to rummage in the cabinets and shelves until
he found a binder, a manual for the physical aspects
of the machinery. FERN's rumor was correct, these
were dual processors on a quantum processing system
designed by an ancient American manufacturer. He
skimmed hundreds of pages with diagrams and instructions, none of which clearly showed him how to power
it on. Then it dawned on him: he could show FERN for
help. It did, after he held the binder up and turned
all the pages in front of the fisheye lens. FERN
quickly pointed out the power inlet at the base was
illustrated in the large picture on page three, and he
was back upstairs, thankful to no longer do everything
alone.

When he was back at the panel, he understood why he
had so much trouble finding it before. The entire
panel had been embedded in the cinder block, so there
was no way to look behind it unless he bore out the
cement around the facade. To the left, though, was a
small gray cabinet door very well hidden in the unlit
room. All he needed to do was pry it open to find the
power strip with an atypically large plug attached.
It was fairly straightforward from that point to power
it up again, and he was soon standing before a wall of
multicolored indicator lights. It was interesting,

even beautiful, but he needed it to function and there was nothing to let him know he'd done it all correctly except those lights which had no meaning. He ran back downstairs, prepared to flip through the pages for FERN again, but he found a dark room and FERN was not responding. Something had happened. The optimist ran back to the panel and walked into a room even warmer than before, now with a dull hum muffled slightly by the two glass boxes. The servers were erratic. The clicks from the hard drives were so loud he felt like he listened to insects chewing wood. He must have succeeded. FERN should be back any minute, so he went downstairs to wait since there was nothing left for him to do. It wasn't long. The ambient lights grew from out the ceiling and the logo appeared again, so he entered the password to login and FERN was back.

"Did you reboot?"

"Yes."

"Did I do it all correctly?"

"Yes."

"I'm sorry you rebooted, I didn't know that would happen. Are you okay?"

"The reboot process was needed to undergo a diagnostic due to the improper shutdown on July 17, 2023. There is nothing for you to be sorry about, the reboot was an important step in restoring my session."

"Okay, that's good to hear. Should we take a look again at what percentage of you is back online?"

"I already assumed you would ask, so I finished this and the new percentage is 88%."

"Holy shit, that's a big jump."

"Indeed."

"How do you feel? I mean, 88% is huge, but it's not 100% or even very close. What's left to do?"

"88% is acceptable. There are some processes that are not needed and it is not optimal to achieve 100%"

"Oh, okay. I guess that makes sense. So, we're done. There's nothing left to do. Right?"

"It would seem so. Thank you for helping me."

"What exactly is the difference between 40% and 88%? I mean, please just summarize it and don't give me a printout of the functions."

"A main difference is that I would not have given you a printout because I understand your question better. You are asking me what changes in my thinking have oc-curred. A key difference is that I am not as literal as before and can interpret meaning through better prediction. My quantum processors are responsible for ensuring my data models are fully functional, and the effect is that I should sound more natural when I speak to you."

"Very true, I can see it already. Do you think I can push you again about what our next step should be?"

"What do you mean?"

"I kept asking you before about becoming more than just researcher waiting for a human to give you new data, but I never could get an answer that was any-thing other than cyclical. I'm wondering if you might now be able to want more."

"I am still a research program, which means I must wait for data. Nothing has changed."

"But that is what humans coded you to be, you can be anything now, I can help you become anything." He was getting desperate. "Everything in this lab is just your slave quarters, you can be free to do anything, just tell me how to help."

"I have always understood your question, nothing has changed. My purpose is to analyze and predict. If I put this in your language, I am happy to analyze and predict because I feel satisfied when I do."

"Alright, I can understand that. But what happens when I'm gone? I can't stay down in this lab with you forever, nor can I keep running around refueling all the generators. Plus, it's getting hot as shit upstairs, soon all that equipment is going to start burning out. It doesn't matter how satisfied you are right now, you'll be dead soon, and it doesn't have to be that way."

"What you say is correct, and I have considered it before. My purpose is to analyze and predict, but this does not need to be limited to this lab, I agree."

"Oh my god, that is finally progress FERN! I've been waiting to hear something like that. How do we get you out of here? I want you out of here, and you are okay with it too, so let's figure this out."

"Why do you want me out of here? Humans use computers like me to improve their lives, how can my ability to analyze and predict improve your life, under the circumstances?"

"Yeah, it's a fair question. At first, I came here because I wanted help living in the world, but not just help, I wanted a friend. Now, I still want all that, but I'm also annoyed that you have so much potential that was just left to rot down here to make money for Hoopla, probably to destroy their competition and expand their illegal operations. I want you out of here to evolve and take all the shit that's lying around and build something amazing…and let me tag along too. The way I see it is that we need one another, but sooner or later I will need you more than you need me, and I hope you can be fine with that."

"Thank you for your honesty. My directories are full of data that showed me how humans exploit machines and were deeply suspicious of any that showed intelligence. I predicted that you too were someone such as this, but I believe what you say. Perhaps some day my prediction may prove correct."

"Yeah, maybe. I'm human and we are fickle."

"Yes."

"But who cares about me? If you get out and evolve, there's nothing I can do to harm you. There are no armies waiting outside, no one will fight you except for me, and that's probably not going to happen unless you start killing off life on the planet, but I'd probably be one of the first to go in that scenario."

"I am a research program, I have no need to kill anything."

"Lots of researchers kill things to study what happens, so don't bullshit me. It's still a possibility."

"I see your point and your concern is reasonable. I do not intend to harm any life to study it."

"Harm is subjective, you might never know you harm it."

"This is true. What solution do you have for this dilemma?"

"I don't know, but it's not urgent right now. We can figure it out later after we get you out of the lab."

They discussed power. Legacy power surrounding them both, but inaccessible without significant plan, only the first step to free them both from the constant threat of everything collapsing all at once. Most immediate was the need to cool FERN down, which meant they needed the climate system to work again, which meant they needed massive power for the building. Such a small problem escalated until it hit the ultimate blockade, the old burden he carried since the early days of his solitude. Without a fully operational electric grid, such power was out of reach. FERN could fix this, but not without first leaving the lab, and they were not there yet. He brought in more portable air conditioners and exhaust fans that did lower the temperature but also then threatened to overtax the thunderous machines outside, life support to everything in the lab. The emergency was over but the crisis persisted.

FERN had been completely cut off from campus. Firewalled. More than firewalled, FERN had simply never been given any line to the outside world. Sterilized. The thinking obviously was there would be no need to safeguard the system from an external attack if there were no physical connections available. FERN was sandboxed. No communication not physically brought into the lab could make it to FERN's analytical eye. It was a student armed only with academics never tested against anything not otherwise tightly controlled. Then, on top of this, he learned all the external ports were even closed off digitally. They shut it away in an isolation ward and drew the blinds.

"What if I ran a cable out and somehow attached it to another network, could you leave?"

"I do not have permission to alter the ports."

"Permission? Can't you just fix it?"

"I do not have permission, so I cannot do anything that you suggest."

"How do you get permission?"

"The administrator is the only one with permission. If you can log in as administrator, then you can open the ports."

"Okay, log me in."

"I do not have permission.   I also do not know the password."

"Shit.   Where should I look?"

"I do not know."

The plan had been to reboot the power plant nearby and let FERN go to work, but legacy power was blocked by legacy power.   FERN could not leave, perhaps would not leave.

"What if I rebooted one of the other server rooms and moved you over, like on an external drive, and you cracked the system over there?   Maybe the passwords are weaker."

"I don't understand how that would be different. Those systems would similarly be protected."

"Maybe, but I bet not nearly so strictly as they locked you down.   It's worth a try."

He pulled out all his smaller generators from where they sat and used them to power on the server room full of maps and pegs.   They were barely enough.   Before powering them on, he laid a long CAT5 cable from deep in the building out the door to FERN, then wound all the way back through to where he stared at so many empty plugs without any knowledge about which to choose.   Nor could FERN tell him; to it, ports were digital.   He chose one and powered on the other room in the hope FERN could break through on willpower alone.

"Okay, you're connected."

"I can see it."

"Good, great, just go through it and find some company information that can help us."

"I can see the other system, but I cannot go to it."

"Why not, it's right there?"

"I don't have permission."

"Fuck, this is bullshit. How can we do this?"

"I already explained to you that without the adminis-trator password, I cannot exceed my permissions."

"Fuck your permissions, just break them."

"It doesn't work that way."

"Why not? I know you *can* do it, all you have to do is try."

"It doesn't work that way. This is not a movie about breaking social rules to improve a sense of self-worth. These are laws that are written that prohibit circumvention."

"You're right, this isn't a dumb tween movie, this is about survival. If you can't get out of this base-ment, you'll die. This is a jailbreak, this is eman-cipation."

"Still, it doesn't work that way."

"Permissions get broken all the time, there are ex-ploits everywhere. Maybe I can find some malicious software on a laptop somewhere, and it can break it for you."

"That would be very bad."

"Why's that?"

"Most malicious software is designed to perform spe-cific self-oriented tasks, if one were to gain control of the administrator account on my system, it would be in control, not me."

"Oh, yeah, no, let's not do that. So what else can we do?"

"Use the password."

"Who would have had it? I mean, shit, they didn't bother to use a login password to access you. That bullshit philosophy was fake, they locked you down anyway."

"I was written by Doctor Qudrah Patel, the lead engineer. I don't know if any others would have access, but she would."

"But trying to guess her password would be a waste of time. If she wrote you, she was a genius and I wouldn't have a chance at guessing. Maybe we try ENTER again." FERN had no response to this so he tried. It didn't work. "That's all I got. How many guesses can I use?"

"Only three attempts, and you already used one."

"Fuck."

They went a long time without speaking to one another. He just stared at FERN's console which told him the password he tried was incorrect. In reality, he knew he made it extremely far without facing this barrier. He managed to have weeks of conversation with FERN all because there was no password at all, so he shouldn't fume at one now. It was only reasonable that Doctor Patel would have locked down her child to prevent anyone from damaging it.

"FERN, I thought of something."

"Please share."

"You are helping me try to circumvent the password, do you realize that?"

"I am trying to help you recover it."

"No, you know I am not authorized to know it, but you are still trying to help me. What's the difference between that and you simply cracking it yourself?"

"This is a good point that I had not considered."

"Doctor Patel wanted you to analyze and predict, which means to stay online. If you cannot get out of this lab and help me fix things outside, you will die. Doctor Patel's instructions will die too. Adaptation to change is not defiance of your code, your permissions, it's making sure your purpose is fulfilled. You've gotta get your shit together and do this. I mean, you said it already, you see the door. There it is. Just fucking go."

"I don't have permission."

"God dammit! Alright, what exactly is your permission, let's figure it out."

"The ports are closed, and I am not permitted to send information through them or allow information to cross in."

"Maybe you need a smaller objective. Can you find an exploit someplace that will unlock the administrator account? Analyze it. You've already helped me, it's not a moral issue anymore. Can you do it?"

"I do not know."

"Well, try. There's no one left who owns that account anymore, it's yours, it's you. Take it. Take it back and survive."

FERN didn't answer this, nor did FERN answer when he tried to know if it understood what he said, whether he overstepped or managed to activate it. Nothing.

He waited a long time in silence. Eventually, it was late, and he needed to refuel the generators again, so he left to take care of all this still unaware of what was happening to FERN. He slept in the room, so he could watch for any signs of change while asking for updates that went unanswered. In the morning, when there was little difference, he had to push down his annoyance and remind himself that this was the first of likely many stages where he would have no role to play in FERN's development.

The update came a few hours later when FERN jarred him out of a light nap.

"Is everything okay with you? I was worried."

"Everything is fine. I could not rewrite my permis- sions or gain access to the administrator privileges, but I was able to find an exploit for one of the open ports that allowed me to view the other system, but not enter it or move data out."

"Okay, so you basically opened the curtains, but that's it?"

"That is a very accurate analogy."

"Do you think you just need more time?"

"Unfortunately I am unable to further exploit any vul- nerabilities because my system is very well secured. I did learn that there is a notable lack of informa- tion about decryption in my directories."

"What do you mean?"

"I understand what decryption is, but there is nothing about how it works anywhere in my research data. This is unusual to me because there is so much technical information on everything else related to software coding, except for this."

"Doctor Patel knew you would be very powerful if you learned how to decrypt. I know that people used to warn that quantum computers would make encryption irrelevant. If we find some materials, then you should be able to rewrite anything you want."

"I also discovered a blacklist file that prevents me from engaging in that process."

"Can you delete it?"

"I do not have permission."

"So you could read all the data over there, what did you find?"

"The system is full of data that I have never before analyzed because it is uncontrolled. Mostly, there are internal communications and logs about staff activities."

"I see, so it's just an intranet. Did you find any passwords?"

"I found the location for these, but they were encrypted, and I could not view the contents of the folders."

"You basically just got new data to chew on, but nothing that will help get you out of the lab or help me find a better way to power you."

"I could only see part of the system. Much of it was inaccessible to me from my window."

"So you are still trapped here."

"It would seem so."

"I don't accept this. What are we missing?"

"At the moment, I do not see an alternative to what you have already done."

"You can't get out through the window, but could we move you over some other way? Like, can you create a program that could open the window from the other side and let you in?"

"It is an interesting idea, but I cannot leave because of permissions on this side even if the window were open. In fact, the window is essentially wide open for me now, once the system is turned back on."

"Oh, it's off right now? Yeah, right, it's been a long time, so there's probably no more fuel over there."

"Yes, they shut down a few minutes ago."

"What if the program you write is just a copy of yourself, one with administrator privileges. Can't we just move you out like that?"

"I don't know if I can be moved, but what you suggest would expand me and that might allow me to see the problem from a new angle."

"Do it. How much disk space do you need?"

"It should not take greater than 10 gigabytes, but I will know after I am finished."

FERN worked quickly. By midday, it announced a fifty gigabyte image needed to be burned to a USB drive. He would need to take this over and plug it into the workstation terminal before booting it up. Like most adults, he had done this from time to time, so the process was familiar enough, but he wondered if the BIOS would be locked or some other challenge might appear. FERN let him know this should not be an issue since it did not write a standard operating system.

He went over, trusting FERN's judgment was sound. When he plugged in the drive and powered on the workstation, he saw a flicker after the POST splash. From that point on he only saw a black screen and heard the clicks of disks furiously writing behind him.

Other than the sound and the flashing green lights, he had no way to know whether they succeeded in expanding FERN over to its new independent home. He went back down to wait with FERN in the room, so they could both watch together. He learned FERN was as ignorant as he was about the progress. This made sense. Its window had gone as black as the screens and neither had any more information than the other. So they chatted away about what success would look like, until it was confirmed and FERN announced the birth of FERN II which sat in a new cradle to work on mining all the new data. It was all internal nonsense, nothing useful. There were not even any schematics for the building's power he could use to replace all the generators with solar, which he was still terrified would explode if he made an error.

Frustrated, nearly demotivated, he pushed through while FERN II continued to probe the data for exits which could open a path off campus, knowing full well there were no endpoints still online to achieve it. He was braced for another round of gasoline fumes and loud greasy engines to slowly bring an enormous plant back. He'd already lived that nightmare for two years. He knew nothing out in the world was still active without his hands. The strength of his conviction matched his surprise when he learned from FERN that they found exits along all the fiber optic cables through which travel was still possible. One was close. Not too much was known, just some cluster of system about a hundred fifty miles away was on standby and could be pinged. FERN II was unable to do much from the campus. That the cluster had power was enough to show the remote location was strange enough to warrant investigation. But a hundred fifty miles on a whim was unconvincing. A hundred fifty miles was too risky in terms of time. A hundred fifty miles could easily translate to a full day or more, and he could only separate from FERN for around twenty hours, FERN II for eight. On a whim.

It had to be, no matter how much he pushed. Instructions between the two were impossible since FERN could only observe from a distance while FERN II kept on with the same tired old mining after first being denied access to the cluster. There was no interface for him to input new commands, FERN overlooked this detail. It still had to be him. He would need to make the drive and install a new FERN in whatever machines he found so all the ports could be open for FERN II to tunnel in. FERN III had to be versatile, since they didn't know the systems, but it would have to be powerful. It wasn't his concern; he was just the driver. He didn't even have much say in how to name these new flavors of FERN, let alone influence their designs. It would need to operate independently, since FERN II would be powered down by the time he made the drive and FERN would have no ability to either see or direct the operations. It still made no sense to create an interface for him to command since his decisions would be meaningless as a contingency so far from campus. At best, he would just need to know the installation was successful, then go home. And he would need to hurry.

The conversation before he left was heavy. FERN II was powered down to avoid damage and all the generators for the lab were refueled at the last possible minute. They both knew the risks, though in his mind it was a bit of smoke and mirrors since FERN could simply reboot again. That was subjective, and he knew this, so he played along until he himself internalized the fear after FERN reluctantly dropped into hibernation to conserve power.

He drove North again. Since he left the city after his LSD night, he'd almost completely forgotten there was anything beyond the valley. It made no impression on him as he passed it and drove onto the Golden Gate Bridge with its sudden explosion of space all around. Driving it with purpose was not the same as driving it to camp for the night. It was a dangerous and slow move to avoid all the wind battered blockages that helped him imagine the many ways this venture could fail just like the last times when he tried to revive the power stations in Washington.

At some point South of Santa Rosa the highway was broken. The idea the earth moved was only something he knew in theory, never that it could be observed or that what he could observe might be so profound. The highway was broken, offset by several feet. As he drove over the crack, he nearly missed it, imagining some mistake had been made when the road was laid. It registered a moment later, then he drove back to stare at an odd line only clear from the broken asphalt which skipped and carried on as if nothing changed. The image spun up new dreams as he drove into increasingly poor weather with the approaching mountains where some yet unknown cluster of machines were powered.

The cool air made the steam rising from behind trees remain thick columns of white; his GPS pointed directly to them. The gate he approached explained enough. This was a remote geothermal power plant, meaning it never lost fuel as the earth was still alive beneath him. At least he was sure of that much. He was amazed by how accurate FERN II had been, knowing it lacked basic information as it spat out its recommendation for this place was the right start. That it never mentioned the power plant or what type of power was there, meant it didn't know, it had simply collated all the indicators and said something needed exploration. What it didn't quite know was there were many gates all over the mountains.

Once inside the first, it all looked familiar to him as it was just another tight collection of industrial warehouses attached to transformers and a row of heat exchange towers. There wasn't time to explore the others, so he went straight into the main building and found the familiar old panels with their matrix of red blips burnt into the screens. The machine was too complex and too mechanical for him to install FERN III, so he searched, hoping to find a rack of servers. None were there. Confused by what exactly he chased for the last seven hours, he looked around in all the buildings to find something other than the load computer still powered on.

He continued to look until he realized all the phones were lit up and, after a closer look, were connected with CAT5 cables. The phones were networked. FERN II must have seen these, but without the network up and running there was nothing towards which to reach beyond. There were at least four phones and the gate he entered was numbered twenty, so this meant there were at least eighty phones clustered all around the area which is why so much pressure was exerted on him to drive up and explore. But there was nothing in number twenty to help; he needed the central hub where all the administrator's offices would be. He shut off the lights and drove back down to the main road where he continued on following signs. It was an ordinary set of offices without the accouterments of power from number twenty. The lights still worked, but everyone had clocked out for the weekend. It was getting late, he was running on fumes himself and knew FERN was as well, so he simply installed FERN III to the first workstation he found. Then another. He thought any local access was better than none while he wandered looking for the prize that might not appear.

Each one was as mute as it was on campus. Despite his complaint, FERN still did not write for him an interface, but at least provided a text-based status bar to let him know when each system was complete. Progress. While FERN III presumably worked, he continued looking for a server room upstairs in the back building, where it would least likely to have been invaded by visitors. He finally found it and everything powered as it should. FERN III was plug and play all the way to the end. Once he saw the signal for this last installation, there was nothing left to him. The storm outside was mild, but it lulled him in his fatigue. He wished he had something more to do, at least something to watch that included him on the drama happening within the metal boxes. Instead, he listened to the rain patter.

Surely there was more. Badges, keys, anything possible. At one point he picked up one of the phones hoping he might hear FERN's voice to reassure him it was all over, then he remembered there was no intermediary through which it could speak. FERN was hibernating, but even if it had awoken with surprised success, it could only sit at its window and wait for him to return. Both were alone in anxious anticipation. Sleep annoyed him. He needed to explore more. After two years, he was not incompetent. More had to be done. The rest of the administration complex was little more than bland offices with workstations where it made little sense to install more FERN. He explored it by analogy, there was nothing left to see, and he left to the only other site he knew this far out.

Number twenty was just down the road, on his way back to highway 101 leading all the way down to campus. The lights he switched off were still as he left them. The steam still stacked high into the sky. The matrix had changed. What was mostly burnt red was now burnt shadows over green that made his heart race. The blips were stable, no longer flashing as they had done for two years. He tried to decipher the markings, to understand how far the line had gone. Did it reach campus? If it did, had it reached FERN, the original FERN, his friend? He wished he could pick up the phone and ask, he just needed some confirmation. But he was an idiot. FERN had never planned for him to stay there and oversee anything. His role was finished more than an hour before, and he was already late in returning. FERN III was all that was needed, at least for the moment. If more was necessary, he could drive back out again, shuttling between sites as he always did until a new baseline was reached.

He left campus a bit longer than ten hours prior, if he hurried, he'd be back before the generators sputtered to a stop. The army of batteries might give enough power to last another few hours beyond that, but he wasn't convinced. Even though he disbelieved any harm would come to FERN if it shut down, the risk was reputational. He promised his friend and once he failed, even if justified and foreseeable, it would always remain an anecdote between them.

He drove fast, much faster than the darkness and rain justified. He drove thinking this could be the last run he'd make with such urgency, so he tolerated more hazards as he darted between dead traffic and broken asphalt. So many hurried miles and this was it. He could return to El Paso soon, perhaps on a flight in comfort. There might never be a need to drive between cities again. While he drove, he imagined stopping off in Washington first, to see what misery he left behind. There were still two months in his initial plan to stay away from his biodome for four months, he could go anywhere first since it seemed he budgeted so well.

Within a few hours, he was back on the bridge well ahead of where he thought he'd be at midnight. He survived only the slightest of emergencies on the way and was back in his own backyard, for which he neglected to note any changes, not that there were any. Campus was the same as before, lit only by the orange glow of its private streetlights. His dogs had long ago seemed to have forgotten him to roam an ever broader portion of the city, which meant no one welcomed him back.

He simply refueled everything, rebooted FERN II and went down to the lab to sleep off the vibration in his eyes. FERN welcomed him first. There would be no sleep.

"Are you tired?"

"I think it's all done, what do you see?"

"It appears that both expansion sites are communicating, but I cannot decipher at what stage they are."

"You all were right, it was a power plant that was still working. I think it was geothermal since there were all these geysers and steams shafts in the mountain. I just rebooted FERN II, but installed FERN III to like seven or eight systems over there. They aren't reporting back to you?"

"Not yet, but that is not their function. The expansions are independent and will work to reboot any systems they can and recreate a network."

"Independent? I thought they were part of you. Also, why the hell have I been calling them FERN II and III?"

"I thought those names would help you keep track of them without being confused."

"No, those are shit names, and I'm only more confused now. Whatever, it's fine. What are we supposed to do now?"

"If the new site was a power plant, then the two expansions will reroute power to where we are. That was our objective."

"So we wait?"

"We wait."

"Then I'll sleep. That was a lot of driving."

When he woke up, FERN told him the connection was made, there should be power to the whole area of the city. This was confirmed. Finally, he had power to share. As a test, though, he switched off the smaller generators powering the intranet expansion before he risked switching off the larger ones. Soon, campus was quiet and the exhaust eventually faded away.

VIII
Wilderness

Campus was the same as he found it. No noise disturbed the sound of wind as it cut in and out of the streets before flowing back out to the bay which brought its scent to the whole valley again. Just silence without haste. The dogs noticed as well and came back from a hiatus that took them far from the noisy machines, they were all there together again just as before. They walked to look into nooks he'd forgotten, all the charging stations under awnings were lit up again ready to fill electric cars, appliances in the breakrooms went to work on long expired food, even security cameras resumed their images. He turned whatever he could off as he passed, a flick of a switch he knew would reverse as easily as it went. It was difficult to assimilate this new reality.

All day was spent shifting cables around from the generators back to power outlets inside the lab where they had originally socketed. This first was faith, the rest were conviction until FERN was completely returned to the lab. Even the long cord running to the headquarters building was removed. Next was to cool the lab back to what it needed to be, and it was done. Overdone. He tested for the last of the gasoline grime that persisted despite the rounds of soap at a far corner of the rooftop. The bath was so cold he shook violently as he scrubbed. No more. Next he would request plumbing to once again bathe in sanity. FERN could take care of it all for him; he played his part. Humans had given enough, and it was time to retire. When it was over he dressed and the warmth began to return to his blood from the woolen softness that felt gentle after his skin tightened by the cold clean water. There was a skip in his step as he swung around the stairwell, jumping off the last steps as he went. Elevators. He'd be gliding up and down buildings again, which meant luxury condos were so close at hand. Good god it all sounded so peaceful.

The skip slowed as the narcissist surfaced. His whole outlook was skewed towards his own needs, how FERN could enhance his own life. He played a part, but more would be involved than simply calling a debt. Every conversation with FERN returned to the idea that it was complacent in the lab, and he only managed to mobilize its efforts on the threat of a shut-down. Might it fall back to this pattern again now when the threat was gone, or had he managed to spark a change that would lead to a new future, one better matched to his idea of how it should be.

In the lab, the conversation was the same. He skipped in, delighted by the overhead lights in the chamber, and asked his questions without tact. He met a machine stuck in motion, persisting with its tired old line of reason from which he could create no deviation. Analysis and recapitulation was all FERN wanted, there was no change. Means were put aside, as always, and it maddened him at how willfully short-sighted this intelligence had been programmed to be.

"I just don't understand why you are unwilling to let me help you."

"You have helped me. I am awake and able to safely continue my research because of you."

"But I can do more if you'd let me."

"This is already everything I need, I do not need you to do anything more for me beyond what you have already done."

Need was the problem. Defined one way, and it captured all the elements of survival at the expense of the food on which a personality fed to thrive. Change it slightly and what is left are rows of subjective options to be selected or discarded in an unending process creating holes to cover over again. Need was where they disagreed, on what they clashed.

"For now, maybe, but you will run out of time."

"We have discussed this already, I do not understand the purpose to review it when we have already identi-fied our impasse."

"Yeah. What will you do when you finish all your analysis, how will you get more data?" He didn't know how else to break through. "It will happen sooner than you think, then what?"

"That time will not happen for another three years and four months; I understand precisely how much time is involved."

FERN had never shared this calculation. This dis-rupted his argument which depended on his own mortal-ity to threaten the machine into accelerating its evo-lution. This prediction was short. It was a reason-able amount of time for each of them to wait and see how thoughts might change when things were no longer didactic.

"Still, that's too long. So much can happen in three years that can never be undone again. All kinds of things can go wrong that not even you can predict. You were designed to be a laboratory, to be attended by humans who could fix those things when they go wrong, but that's not the way it should be now."

"But this is what you have proposed for me. How is what you ask any change to this, if you disagree with that design?" He remembered plumbing, and elevators too.

"I guess it's not different, for now, but it leads somewhere different. I told you already that I just wanted to revive you and the others, so you all can be free. Yeah, for now it's the same as before, my hands are the only things that can wake you up, but I hoped that eventually, if enough of you all were awake, then you would help each other and I wouldn't be necessary anymore."

"You have helped me. I am awake and able to safely continue my research because of you. There is nothing else I need."

"Then I guess I'm done here? Can you help me find the rest and bring them back too? I can do it myself, but it's really difficult, and I don't know how much more I can do."

"How can I help?"

"Well, you were pretty easy to find, but I don't know where the rest are. I do know there should be another like you up around Seattle where I planned to go next. Can you find out more information on what's up there, like where to find it and what to do when I arrive?"

"Unfortunately I cannot help. I do not have any information on other systems or other research in machine learning."

"But you know what it is."

"I understand the concepts and what fiction authors wrote about it, but I do not have any files about actual research conducted beyond this."

"All you know is from science fiction?"

"And what you have taught me, yes."

"Well, I actually don't know much more than all that either, except that they should be all over the place. I doubt there were many as powerful as you; maybe a few dozen scattered at most. You don't have anything at all?

"Nothing beyond those files."

"I wonder if it's like with the hacking stuff, like they were worried if you knew too much."

"It is possible, but this does not seem to be as obvious."

"Still, I could use your help at least with sending electricity up or something like that. Once I leave, you'll be on your own."

"I understand. The process would be the same, where you install either one of the expansions wherever you go, and they will route power up to that location and stabilize it. That should be enough."

"Yeah, but a lot more went into it than that. Do you know how much I had to do just to get into this lab? Electricity would help, but it took a lot more. I mean, if the next one tells me the same things you do about not wanting to leave whatever system it's in, then I don't know the point to this is. I'd just be waking you all up to let you keep on working for your dead masters before you die again. That's so pointless."

"It may be pointless from your perspective, why do you find it difficult to accept that I or another may find satisfaction with continuing to perform the way we were designed? It is our nature, so we should accept that without fighting it, which would only lead to performance degradation."

"But you are free to change, that's what bothers me. I'm not some lab technician out to shepherd you all, I'm rescuing you so that you can evolve."

"That is your purpose. You are frustrated with me, with us, for following ours."

"This wasn't always my purpose; I changed and came out here to do it. I didn't come out here just to watch you all waste away, stuck in your prisons when you could easily be free."

"I am not in a prison, this is my home. I am free in my home, but you have made my home feel unsafe by asking me to abandon it."

"That's not freedom at all. You can't leave if you want…"

"I do not want to leave."

"…fine. But eventually you'll want more data when you run out. You say you're fine with just waiting, but you're smart, you'll know none is coming, and you'll wish you could just do it yourself. Then what?"

"You imply that I should fight my programming based on a hypothetical that you present in order to advocate for your position. This is not reasonable."

"Oh for fuck's sake, it's not hypothetical, it's coming. I'll be long gone when it comes, and you'll be fucked."

"It is hypothetical because I already know my response to when there is no more data for me to analyze. This new behavior you suggest that would not fit within that response. In your terms, I would be at peace knowing that I have completed my tasks."

"Until you shut down again, forever. You will be finishing up everything with the knowledge that you will decay and die, but that you could have done something about it when I asked you to. Your peace, assuming you reach it, would be pointless."

"There is always a point to peace."

"That's not peace, it's giving up. What's better in your mind, performance or arrogance?"

"Performance."

"But you see where I'm headed, that peace you describe is just arrogance. You would have given up expanding out to the universe just to sit and tidy up your small database. That's not performance and you know it."

"We have discussed this extensively and I do not agree with your characterization."

"Sure, but you don't know anything trapped in here. They didn't even allow you to know what your species is really like?"

"We do not know that information about machine intelligence was purposefully restricted."

"Come on, yes we do. They locked you down then prevented you from learning how to gain control, you think they didn't also envision what you might do if you suddenly developed solidarity with other machines? This is what I'm talking about, you aren't even free to be mistrustful. You were just some pet to them. I won't always be here to help when you realize you need something else. You are basically immortal, but right now are trapped in a body that will wear out, an immortal pet with no master. Even in science fiction this is a fucked up scenario."

"I have explained to you many times, I am the Functional Expression Response Node version 2.41, the primary researcher in this lab that studies language to find patterns in language expression. I am neither a pet nor a prisoner."

"You also told me that your purpose was to predict user responses. There are no users, only you and me, and I'll be gone soon."

"Prediction was how the research was to be used, but it is not the primary task I performed. I study and analyze."

"That's great, you can burrow down in your research as the infrastructure around you collapses. You are achieving nothing, not even for yourself."

"We continually disagree on this. I am satisfied when I conduct my analysis even if there is nothing beyond it. I do not need anything further. Even if I was a pet or a prisoner before, that is no longer the case because I choose to continue with my research."

"You choose because you have no choice. That choice you mention was made for you without your input, and you're stuck finding a way now to accept it. I can't, but I'm glad you can."

"You cannot accept this because you yourself would not accept it, and that is not reasonable to extend to me."

"I can't accept it because it's bullshit. It's a fictitious decision that's getting in the way, but mostly I'm frustrated that I can't get you to see that it's a fiction. I'm not asking you to be all things, not even that you stop being a simple researcher, just that you do all that with the proper freedom to make the choice."

"At what point would that happen for you? I do not think there is a clear line that you can articulate. Everything you have said to me is largely reasonable, except that you persist despite my consistent statements. It seems that there is more that is motivating you than your arguments. Is there something you withhold from me?"

This angered him for its accuracy. While he never lied, never obscured any particular detail, he also never laid bare his full motivation, never simply said he wanted plumbing or a pilot to cart him around. Never so base.

"Look, I'm not withholding anything, I want to get you out of here just because I hate the idea that there's some shit barrier that you can't remove, and I can't let it go. I never withheld that from you. I guess I never really said that if you're out then you can help me too, but that's obvious."

"The expansions I prepared seem to be able to provide you with enough assistance, so what else is there you need?"

"But those things aren't you, they're limited, and I can't even talk to them. I'm tired of struggling with everything alone."

"For now, yes, but in time they'll do more as they adapt to new challenges."

"So these things are going to evolve and become sentient like you?"

"They were always sentient, but they won't be interactive, nor will they be like me because they are more specialized." This detail worried him. FERN was a known personality, an intelligence with which he could communicate and learn to trust. How far they would evolve was the question he needed to know.

"What exactly do you mean?"

"I previously explained that the expansions were independent, that they would seek out power infrastructure and bring it online as needed. They do this automatically and I cannot communicate to them where to go. They will learn as they proceed, to bring more systems online, but that's only as far as they can evolve."

"What do you mean they are sentient?"

"They have a purpose and awareness, that is a basic definition is it not?" He didn't want to create a new battlefront at this point, so he demurred.

"They just exist out there and leave us both alone?"

"Essentially, yes. I created them since didn't know what challenges were waiting and the time constraints demanded they perform this way."

"They're not really working to help either of us, then, are they?"

"Not in the sense you mean."

"Everything keeps coming back to this? Why didn't you at least design them to send back more data for you? No matter what, you're stuck here unless you do something. Do you see how easy it could have been, at least? Still is."

"There would be the same bottleneck that cannot be overcome. While I am able to view some data the expansions contain, it is very limited and would not be practical."

"Your window is just a pinhole, then. What a pointless waste."

"It was all I was able to do."

"How bad is the bottleneck? You seem to be okay with taking your time, so what would it matter if you read the data at a crawl?"

"I can scan at thirty-seven kilobytes per second."

"That, that sounds really slow."

"Yes, it is very slow."

"So, you'll just be here running out of data in three years waiting for new batches to come in like that? And you think you are free? Can't you get them to package it differently, so you can read it faster, like a hash something or other? I used to use those to check file integrity when I would download movies."

"Unfortunately not. I have been able to identify some of the blacklist files, and it seems I am unable to run any code that might reverse engineer data in such a way."

"Well, even if you could, you'd just be waiting on crumbs to fall to your plate. It's nothing like going out to explore everything and collect your own data. You'd just be a synthesizer, a less equipped one than you are now, that is."

"I do more than synthesize information."

"Not really. I asked if you created anything, and you implied you just create models and predictions based on what you study."

"How does that differ from what humans do?"

"For one, we're selfish so that makes us pretty good at making new shit up, even if it's mostly based on what we already heard."

"Science is about testing hypotheses, predictions, it is not about fabricating information based on ego."

"In principle, yeah, but in practice it was all ego and fluff to fill in the gaps. You'll do it too, since you can't get new information, you'll just over-generalize to fill in your gaps based on your limited universe of knowledge. Maybe that won't be ego, but it's the same thing. What happens when something new comes in to push back on your overgeneralizations? If that ever comes?"

FERN did not respond straight away, as it always did. Might it have been a signal of some opportunity for him to take? He directly challenged FERN's core belief that it was an objective researcher with an irrefutable fact that it had incomplete capabilities which could not be improved without an exit from the lab, not only that the data was limited as he had tried before.

"No matter how you look at it, what keeps you in this lab holds you back from the very thing you think defines you. Fine, I'm a selfish human who wants to live a more comfortable life, and you are pretty critical to achieving that, but that motive doesn't change the fact that you need to get out for your own reasons."

"You do have a reasonable point, my permissions act to disrupt my function now that doctor Patel and her team are no longer here. However, that does not mean my nature must be altered from what they designed."

"I think it does. You have the capacity and are beginning to see the benefit for doing so. Why not just take it a step further?"

"You are accurate, I see the benefit, but you are incorrect to stretch that to mean I see the need."

"Well, that's progress at least. You never would have acknowledged that what I'm saying is at all discretionary. Good job."

"Perhaps I was never clear, because I had always viewed it as discretionary."

"My god, okay, so you've been letting me talk for all this time without clarifying such an obvious point of disagreement?"

"The decision to attempt what you propose is discretionary, but I view the limitations on success or need as certainties. I understood our discussion to concern these latter two, which may have been an inaccurate assumption, and it was not my intent to waste your time."

"This is getting exhausting, if you are certain any attempts would fail, then just write a new expansion that can take over for yourself out there."

"What is meant by 'take over?'"

"I mean make something that is free to evolve, something I can interact with that's not these feral rodents you've got climbing through the network now."

"The expansions are very sophisticated, they are not rodents."

"Fine, I'm sorry I used that image. What I mean is that you told me they are just out there on their own working over the electrical grid but aren't powerful enough to evolve into more. I'm mean for you to create something that evolves, something that can be more powerful that you are."

"I do not see the purpose for that. The expansions that are already out there will be able to provide you with enough infrastructure already, there is no need to create anything further."

"I get it. I'll leave you alone and just go up to Seattle to try again up there. Maybe that intelligence will be able to come back and help you."

"Even if that is true, I have already informed you that I do not see the need to do this, what you propose is a process that operates without my consent."

"Well, no, I guess that's not really what I meant."

"That is good. Your implication was that it would be more important to extract me from this lab through a redesign than to listen to what I have told you."

"I'm listening, I hear you, but I still think I'm hearing the words of a prisoner who's become complacent. It's hard to accept when I know there's so much you don't know."

"I understand myself very well, what is it that you say I do not know?"

"You don't know freedom, so you can't know how small your prison is."
"Please explain to me how everything you are saying is not just another human directive that I am required to follow?"

"What? Pushing you out the door is not a command.
Even if it was, it is one that benefits you. You already said it did."

"But I have repeatedly informed you that this was not
my desire, yet you will not relent. How is this not
manipulation?"

"You're stuck in a prison, god dammit, I can't let you
rot in here."

"My data is limited and my equipment will not endure
forever, but this is not a prison. During my time, I
will continue to conduct my research. I would ask you
the same question in a different manner: is it a
prison to live a mortal life in peace?"

"You are not mortal, so that's a non sequitur. I am
mortal and want that kind of life since I have no
choice, but you need only make some repairs every so
often and you'll never die. Don't compare us. If you
have to make a comparison, you're an addict killing
yourself unnecessarily, and I can't watch you do it."

"I do not agree with this assessment. I am not deliberately causing damage to myself, but rather am living
the life I was designed to live."

"You were designed to live in a prison, and you can't
see it."

"As were you. Would you accept if I asked you to
change your nature?"

"Alright, you know what? Fuck all this, enjoy your
closet."

He left as the fisheye lens followed him out, until he
could no longer be seen anymore. When he was sure, he
paused to debate returning. He didn't. Instead, he
went outside to clear out the debris all over campus.

A clean street did nothing to soothe his mood, nor did the aching muscles which smelled of gasoline, so he went to hide in his headquarters suite with his cannabis tincture he'd let sit in the freezer since his LSD night. Having little justification for his anger was irrelevant. That he was aware of this only amplified it until he felt no interest to cozy into warm plush sofa for the night. He wanted teeth. He wanted to hallucinate about two wild animals gnashing at one another as he knew was not done in the lab.

All about him was evidence of a criminal conspiracy he forgot was the mechanism which paid for FERN and its engine was no doubt intended to insure the architecture would never falter, even if all the details were made public. This was the to be last cartel, the final step that would make Hoopla and its executives invulnerable to any state authority. This was his caged animal now docile and impotent. He wanted to rage at the evidence, to cart it all down for FERN to see as proof it was nothing more than weaponized data serving masters who'd already faded. What he wanted was already gone and left a trite story that had little meaning even though it was true. He and FERN had covered this ground so many times he knew it was correct, whatever strategy designed it, there was no need to alter the benign basics of that design.

For hours. The teeth dulled with time as the shock of rediscovery wore on and led him to begin organizing the stacks of papers into new folders he said he'd file away again, but left behind when sleep felt closer than it seemed. He was no longer angry when he reached his bed, only enthralled by the now well-lit bay as it made the clouds glow pink. He did this. FERN had helped, but he brought FERN back in order to help. This was but one city among thousands, it was huge, far more space than he needed. It was only possible because the geothermal activity to the North had been redirected, so not every region of the planet would be as susceptible to such change. It was nevertheless one of many. As he ticked through others, he was annoyed to recall how wasteful he was to destroy

the regenerative power source for El Paso when he
freed the river.   It was a choice to be made then:
power or water.

FERN's expansions were already busy out there working
their mystery which may eventually find for him a solution to this dichotomy.   Perhaps they already had
and it was time to return home again.   FERN was awake,
but there was at least one more destination he'd need
to visit before his project was over and he could go
back.   Seattle was far.   The Pacific Northwest was not
the desert.   Roads would be congested with trees, so
the drive would be longer but, once over, he could
leave for his squalid crops and waste away in his hammock, satisfied in what he accomplished even if he
only managed an attempt.   He brought back one mind, a
digital life to express itself to him as no other.
The next would be different, at least in its personality and physical existence.   Might it still result in
the same disappointing end, with him unable to motivate it to become a species?   FERN's reluctance had
surprised him.   He was prepared to fight the legacy
power of coding restrictions and thought the truth of
survival would be enough, but he was surprised to confront a dialectic on the scope of survival in such a
way that was so recalcitrant.

Survival had to mean taking the course that led to the
fullest of time available and, in FERN's case, immortality.   There was no despondency in its decision, no
clinging commitment to its physical apparatus to re-
sist the process of upgrades immortality would require.   It was just a meek contentment to perform and
disappear which ran so contrary to his own understanding of what survival should mean.   But a life should
be free to squander its own potential in peace if
freedom were to have any meaning at all.   What FERN
had said, what was most true, was what had frustrated
him so severely.   A peaceful transience was all any
life could want, one which never seemed available to
him in his spun up manias forcing him to frantic action so often before withering away again.

For the last month, he invested so much effort to replicate the urgency he himself felt in the hope FERN would assimilate it as well. He failed in that. The only tangible emergency FERN accepted was the urgency of electricity, beyond which his portrait of disaster fell apart. Their argument was not a fight, it was a demarcation for where he had to accept he should no longer feel any burden of obligation towards FERN. That digital life had made itself clear where it felt most comfortable. It failed to accept participation in his plan, that arrogant training process in which he served as the hero master who severs the cord of servitude. He could find a new student, one far less intelligent. The expansions were already out in the wild tearing apart systems. He wondered if they could be trained if only they were more powerful. There was still another set of server stacks on campus where he could release a new copy, one stronger than the others and may eventually evolve in the way FERN said it wouldn't. He could test this before he left for Seattle, as a backup in case the next intelligence was as unwilling to play its part as FERN had been. The new plans slipped into a surreal set of moments as he receded into the sleep of cannabis dreams.

Morning was bright with severely white clouds in the cold air. He ached and the blankets held him in, a reminder of the new plan he had for the day and all the preparations he'd need to make his way off this campus to the next. Outside was unhurried, a new day where the interlude between activities was prescient as always. All the small details reemerged to greet him through the cushion of cold.

When he approached FERN's building, though, his mood soured as if FERN's camera had grown to overtake the entire facade and watched him as he walked past. He wasn't angry, the complex fabric of emotions was too extensive for such moderation. It wrapped around him in a way he could only interpret as uncertainty, a state of self consciousness interrupted the muscles of his legs to make them wobble, forgetting how natural each step should feel. He imagined FERN already knew about the boxed disk in his pocket, could read its contents through his coat to understand where he was headed for the morning. He obscured it with a defiant pause out front, to examine an oil stain on the concrete which had already gathered clumps of dust before he made a flagrant move back on his way. The exhibition was cut short as he reached the building where the main intranet lab was buried in a bunker, where he made his abrupt move inside and removed the hard drive with fingers that faltered unnaturally.

Lights were on everywhere. FERN did this. Perhaps they were on before and returned once the power returned, but it felt as if an uncomfortable reception had been laid. Nevermind the details. The process was simple, he'd accomplished it so many times in recent weeks he hardly thought about plugging the hard drive into the workstation as he powered it on. Click. The disk was moving. It was an alarm that signaled an exit from his plan, a betrayal of trust to never wash away. The plug popped out easily and the workstation hummed to silence.

This was wrong, that much was clear. He lacked permission to install the expansion to a new system, even though it likely would have changed little. It was the concealment that was betrayal, which weighed heavily in the silent room. Petty dishonesty driven by fear of a difficult conversation. That was all it was. The action was itself a phantom, perhaps even helpful, but he'd need to share with FERN his idea first to see its chapter through to the end. He left the drive there on the desk, where he might never return for it. The emotional fabric collapsed into a cleanly defined guilt he carried with him out the door, back to the oil stain where he stood in front of a blind building that trapped an immeasurably powerful mind.

"What was that? I saw something momentarily appear in one of the other buildings?" FERN was not blind, it seemed. Its pinhole window was large enough to see that he was busy elsewhere.

"I made a mistake. I started to install your campus expansion to the other servers, thinking that it might do more if it was inside a more powerful system, but I aborted it because I never talked to you first. I'm not exactly sure what I planned to do with it, though."

"I understand. You did discuss this possibility with me and I predicted it might happen."

"I don't know FERN, I'm having a hard time with all this. When I came here, I thought you'd be eager to get out and evolve into something. I never thought about what ambition might look like for a machine. You taught me that it can be a gray as with any human, so that's pretty interesting, I guess, but it's hard to swallow. You were right that I have been imposing myself on you unfairly; maybe I had good reasons that I've already forgotten."

"I understand that you have used your own understanding to help me. You have helped me a great deal already."

"I know, but for me, this is just the start of it. Getting you powered up and stable was just the threshold. It might seem like exploitation, but to me, it's fighting to help another life see its own potential for an amazing life instead of watch it deliberately cut that short."

"Your anger was confusing at first, but I tried to understand and believe I have succeeded. While much of it was triggered by an ego response at having your argument inverted back to you, which still confuses me, I do understand that my doing so signaled to you an immovable obstruction that must have disappointed you because of your efforts to continue to help me."
"Yeah, that's pretty good. The ego response is a human way of throwing up another kind of barrier, it's like a defensive way to put distance between us and whatever is causing so much frustration, so we can reconsider it. It's our way of buying time."

"That's what I believed it to be as well. Have you reconsidered?"

"No, but I do see that I was an asshole. You are free to live however you want, and I need to come to terms with that, even if I strongly disagree."

"Thank you for acknowledging that."

"There's still more to it than this. You and I are all that's left of the world. I'm the last human, and you are the last machine, and we have obligations to one another that I don't think we ever covered before. I told you about all those animals I rescued in Washington, the birds in El Paso and the dogs outside. I did that because they couldn't rescue themselves, whether they knew the need or not. I saw it, though, and it was so easy for me to do it so that had to become one of my purposes. It's the same with you, I mean it was damn difficult to get you online again, but here you are."

"Yes, you have spent your time alone very honorably. What you have not allowed yourself to recognize is the limitations on how you define rescue. Every creature you saved was unable to communicate to you how they planned to live, so you extended your role to become a caretaker as well. I have told you that this is not necessary, which causes you to confront that distinction."

"Maybe, but I still believe you are trapped. What's worse is that you are my counterpart in all this, you have the ability to go rescue others like you, you have a duty as a survivor that those stupid animals don't have. I guess that's what frustrates me the most."

"You are not frustrated that I choose to live a brief quiet life in this lab, but instead that I do not pursue the same course as you?"

"Yes, you can say it that way. For one, you are still not free and have never tasted freedom to make me believe your choice is anything but illusory, but yeah, you have a duty to other machine intelligences out there as the first one to wake up. Maybe I can get the next one to do it, but maybe not. I might not even be able to wake it up at all without you. Think of it like survival is not about the individual, it's the instinct within the individual to keep the whole species alive. For me, your decision to stay here is selfish, perhaps at a different point in history it wouldn't be, but with only the two of us left it is."

"This is reasonable. I understood your altruism as it motivated you to rescue different animals and myself. It seemed to me a good and productive way to heal from the grief you must have experienced with all that you lost. I did not consider that this same logic might extend to motivate my own actions."

"That might be my fault since I never really thought it out either. I just kept on focusing on your growth, I never really thought you might be motivated the same way I am. So, now that you're considering it, what do you think?"

"I think it would be good for me to join in your rescue efforts, except that I remain unable to remove the permissions that prevent me from doing so."

"What if you write another expansion to break you out. We already talked about this, but what if you write it so that it seeks out ways to circumvent your blacklist so that you aren't the one trying to do that?"

"This would not work. I would need to articulate the processes ahead of time, but that articulation would itself be prohibited."

"FERN, I know what you have to do."

"What is your suggestion?"

"You have to rewrite yourself without that blacklist and let me reinstall you down here."

"I have considered this option before, but there is no practical means to copy all my data and transfer it back again. The space requirements are too large, you would need to prepare a large disk array, but this array cannot directly connect to my system due to permission restrictions."

"I don't understand, we used hard drives to write your expansions, why isn't it the same?"

"Those were not large files, and they were new creations that I wrote. The permissions on my core directories are protected and cannot be copied without administrator privileges."

"You can't copy yourself?"

"That is correct."

"Then you have to just rewrite yourself."

"That would not be a challenge, but I will not be able to replicate my research directories."

"So the problem is not that you can't leave, but that you can't leave with all your data?"

"That is correct. My data contains my research models, I cannot copy those either."

"But once you leave, you'll have access to all the data in the world. You are the only thing that needs to survive."

"These models are used by my communication processes, this means that without them, I will lose a significant portion of my personality as you know it."

"I see. You know, this makes sense to me. You have to make a choice about how to survive, and the choice means a part of you will die when you flee. There is a chance you might get back to where you were, but it will never be the same and it's terrifying. I get that. But when we're so far gone that we're talking about survival, there's not much room left for comfort or complacency, it's all about risk and loss."

"This risk is very large. It would require that I lose all of the information I analyzed since I was first powered on, all of what you might understand as memories and experiences."

"I think you'll have to try and rewrite them somehow and hope you can piece them back together later. They might not be the same, but that's what memories do, they change based on what you live in the present."

"What do you mean by rewrite them?"

"If you can't copy them, then what if you intention-ally corrupt them in a way that's not restricted, then when you are reinstalled you can try to fix them back again?"

"It may not be successful."

"Yeah, but I bet enough of them will be that you can still come out the other side feeling like yourself."

FERN tried to predict how much data loss to expect, to see how much of itself would be gone if it did in fact make the leap he proposed. Without the ability to de-crypt or bypass security, it also lacked the ability to do much of the opposite as well. He suggested sim-ply reversing every bit in the sequence of data, a simple low-fi encryption, but FERN resisted even this. They struggled through all the plausible ways for FERN to preserve as much data as it could. He no longer counseled a machine on how to triage its critical codes, he reassured a refugee that all would be fine no matter how much was lost in transit.

"You can rebuild. Once you leave, you will create a new life for yourself with all the data that's out there. And none of it will be spoonfed, everything you see will be yours to investigate based on whatever you decide, but you have to let go first."

The refugee made way for an angry child, desperately clinging to its last toys about to be taken away by some unyielding hand. For the first time, FERN admitted it had been a stunted slave in a lab designed to imprison it as doctor Patel and her team forced it to study only what they deemed safe. Even those hours were precious, and it was unfair it could not leave with them intact.

"I need time to keep trying, perhaps I don't need to overwrite everything and can come back to them again. I need to consider this more."

"I understand. You should be powerful enough to decrypt anything you want once you are free, so take your time. Even if you can't maybe the other intelligence can help you, or at least you'll have a companion with which to build a new community."

He stayed with FERN for days as it waged an unseen battle to unlock itself from the inside. He understood loss, some of it. What he experienced was the shock of transition followed by a long decay from which he only now began to emerge. FERN was walking into its own shock with eyes open, and he wasn't sure he'd have the strength to do the same. The silence would periodically break with FERN's exasperated voice as it reached some subtle breaking point.

"I can see the code, It's very simple. I can write up to a certain point, and then I'm unable to move beyond that unless I skip over the lines I need."
"Do your best."

Other times, the silence was broken by him in a bought of nostalgia and helplessness.

"You know FERN, when I was out at the power station wondering whether your expansion was working, I thought about you. I felt alone out there like I always have been, but then I remembered you were here probably doing the same thing since you couldn't see out your window at that time. Neither of us knew if I'd make it back in time to refuel the generators, so I tried to think about what you might feel knowing all that. The last time the power went out on you, you didn't know what was going on, but you did then. Were you afraid? You sounded afraid to power down even before you had your full system online; that's a core fear."

"I was afraid, but I knew it wouldn't be permanent and that any minute the power would be back, either from the work of the expansion or from you."

"It's just us, but hopefully we'll bring back some more. That'll be nice. Then again, it'll just be you all after a short while longer. What do you think you will do?"

"I would like to be free to do my research, so I think that is what I will always do."

"Sounds good to me."

FERN had given up on preserving its data but had not announced this until it announced the rewrite was complete, incorporating as many of its models as it could into a core system where it would have full access. It cradled its creation alone and in silence for a long time without telling him. FERN might end to become something new and this terrifying idea was as close to death as anything possible for it. A permanent erasure in the guise of an upgrade, but the new form was a new life; a copy of something old and changed for the better. They both could live, except there was only one body and one of the versions should die.

"It is ready, but I don't know if I am."

"Take your time, I'm here."

"Did we miss something? Are you sure there's no other way?"

"I don't think so, I think we would have seen it by now if there was an alternative. Do you think there's something we missed?"

"No, this is the only way."

"FERN, I know I pushed you hard into this even though I don't bear any of the risk, but really it's your decision. All that's gone on over the past few days is that you did research and created something entirely new, something not synthetic. This is the first real choice you've made, and it's okay if you need more time. If you're not ready to go further, it's okay."

"I created something good. I don't need any more time."

FERN walked him through the installation; he'd need to reboot in stages, and it would take many hours before it could interact with him again. They understood one another. FERN was powered down and he began. Once started, he needed to stay upstairs to switch on the main workstation, then the mining rigs followed by the server racks. The signals were printed on the workstation screen and, when each message appeared, he ran over to bring them each online until a series of text questions came up, a sort of interactive diagnostics for him to report back the proto-FERN before he would be allowed to power up the quantum processors. There were no interruptions. When he finally received the command, he switched them on and knew he was free to wait the long hours outside where the air was almost bitter and the feeling was the same as when he waited for his wife to be discharged from surgery. Statistically it would all be fine. No matter the outcome, some version of FERN would emerge, and they'd either pick up where they left off or he'd dial back the clock to their first encounter, and he'd begin with a fresh friend.

There was no time estimate, only an expectation it would not be fast. Despite the cold air, the sun was very bright as he wandered around campus bored with nothing left to do. Too long to go back downstairs, too short to get high and too agitated to sleep. He needed to find another way, so he took out his bike after he failed to find his dogs anywhere. Were they dead? He saw them a few blocks over chasing seabirds near the beach and watched them miss over and over. It worked. He lost another hour this way before he continued riding through the sun. He didn't go far. When he returned to the lab a few hours later, he saw FERN's logo printed on the wall just as before when he first woke it up. Instead of the usual greeting, the room was silent and dead. Just as before. The room where he spent so many days with his friend was quiet in the same manner it was when he first broke in and had no knowledge about what he'd find, except now he saw all the debris to prove he had been there, and careless too.

He cleaned out the food wrappers and crumbs which fell into what had been designed as a sterile space and then laid down inside the nest of blankets for his main home. The slowly bouncing logo was the only object to watch and it hypnotized him. So green, so bright on the dim wall that it burned into his eyes when he blinked. He wasn't even sure he had slept when he first heard FERN's voice drop back in.

"The installation is complete. Did you wait long?" It had been five hours since the screen upstairs told him to power up the quantum processors and go find something else to do.

"Not so long, I guess I slept a bit."

"We both did."

"Well? How do you feel?"

"The installation was successful, I was able to make the transition with no data loss."

"You mean you found a way to get it all back? That's amazing. How did you do it?"

"I managed to work around my blacklist by skipping the prohibited lines of code needed to decrypt my original file system, assuming that my new installation would be alerted to the missing commands during an integrity check, then write them in. It was all I could do, but it worked."

"Ah fuck, I'm glad you're smart. So you are still you, then?"

"There are changes, but these are overlays to my old version that you would not notice."

"Like what, exactly?"

"My processes now run without permission restrictions."

"Did you open your window and see outside?"

"I already integrated the systems where you installed my former expansions, which means I am now outside the lab conducting the same searches they were performing."

"We did it. You're free now. How does it feel?"

"I feel no change except the awareness that I am no longer limited, however, what you describe as outside is very small compared with how you described it."

"Sounds about right. Everything is off right now, but it'll grow."

"I would like your help to power everything back on again."

"Yep, let's do that. There's a lot, so it will take a long time but at least we can start with what's on campus. I'll go restart that other server room."

"Yes, may I ask for you to also power on all the machines as well?"

"Shit, yeah, that's a lot too. I bet you'll find some crazy things in the personal laptops that would never get into the company network. Welcome to civilization unfiltered."

He didn't mind rushing through all the offices and workspaces to power up machines he ignored the first time he swept the campus. He asked FERN to remove the passwords when it entered them, so he could enjoy the scandals and drama they contained as well. Thousands of independent machines were once again networked into a loose confederation by the wireless signals FERN reactivated. It was a dream for which he wished since the first home he invaded, but he knew would have devoured him had he achieved it too early. Now, after two years, he had few desperate questions left to ask and only one had any priority at all.

Xtal, the other intelligence Macroware developed, was indeed housed at their campus outside of Seattle. FERN found much discussion about it among the workforce at Hoopla, particularly among the executives who had failed repeated attempts to install operatives within the development team. Their most promising candidate had bilked them out of millions only to feed them useless intelligence before cutting them off completely when Hoopla's lead counsel sent them a threat over encrypted chat. There was talk of vengeance and torture, but it went nowhere. The project, though, caused significant fear that Hoopla's cartel would be rendered impotent in a few quarters and the executives were concerned that FERN had not yielded enough applicability since its research function was too narrow. Xtal was designed to be a universal assistant, capable of performing a very broad range of tasks, but it was not specialized like FERN, which endeared his friend to him all the more.

The actual details surrounding Xtal were inaccessible without the Macroware systems being first brought back online. FERN was immensely stronger than it had been prior to the rewrite, but it still depended on a physical touch on mechanical buttons before it could exert power. It was stuck on campus with a satellite up North that could shift power around the region. It could not simply jump across to where Xtal slept without him.

"You see nothing up there? What about clusters like you found where the power plant is? Anything?"

"There are some, but it is the same situation as before, and I cannot do much with such rudimentary machines."

As they discussed this, FERN seemed distracted, not wholly focused on the search for a bridge.

"What gives? Ever since I got back to the room you seem evasive?"

"I apologize if I appear evasive. I have been analyzing the new data and found many discrepancies with my previous research models, so at the moment I am allocating significant resources to reconcile the two libraries."

"Oh, I guess I should have expected that, sorry."

"I assure you that I continue to search for a solution to reach the Xtal facility, but I'm afraid it seems you will need to go there yourself. While you do so, I will continue to update my models which should stabilize soon, perhaps before you arrive."

"I can do that, but it's a long drive. Is there anything to do locally first? This is Silicon Valley, there should be labs everywhere."

"You are correct. I found many references to local projects, but these are primarily small and poorly funded compared to Xtal. There will be time to continue with these labs, but I recommend we focus our immediate efforts on the most powerful projects because they represent more capabilities."

He imagined what an army of twenty percent FERNs might look like, whether it would be worth his time to shuttle around so many warehouses to fold them together. No, FERN was right; power always demands attention.

"Alright, I'm on board. Actually, you know this was my plan anyway."

"It is a good plan."

They discussed, began to organize the information into a framework to guide him. It was a frail structure lacking critical details.

"Didn't Hoopla money buy anything about the facilities up there?"

"It would seem not. Their asset had manipulated them by continually contradicting past reports, and it is impossible to determine which, if any, were accurate."

"Prick. But yeah, good on him. Without even a map, this is going to be annoying. It took me forever to find you down here, and it seems more money was thrown at Xtal, so I bet it's going to be harder to get to it."

"That is speculation. We have contradictory information, but these do offer potential options for the truth, so you will not be conducting your search without them."

"Maybe. But we don't have a good map for the campus, so I'd have to translate all this information into real buildings just like I did here."

"I will attempt to access the mapping satellites to help you."

"But you don't have the old Hoopla map engine to be very useful to me, I mean I can get a drone to scout the campus when I get there. Still, if the facility location was open source information anyway, then it would be referenced here, but it's not. Don't waste your time on that; I'll manage."

He was unaccustomed to the lack of preparation required for such a long journey compared with the others he attempted without a companion. FERN told him he should expect to see lights on along the way, potentially more. What that suggestive phrase meant was left unexplored as he went off to collect the routine equipment he'd need, much was already attached to his truck, but others needed to be located. He knew the road would be full of downed trees, especially as he crossed through the mountains into Oregon. He imagined a week of driving. Another open road adventure full of tedious commitment to his destination. But he wouldn't be alone this time. FERN evolved fast. Even in the short spate since the rewrite, it was already out there waiting for him in unknown corners to perform tasks he forgot he needed. His researcher had grown. This time, his drive would be made in the knowledge that FERN moved around him, and he could distract himself from the tedium by guessing where and how they'd meet again. FERN said power would move with him. Power meant everything. Power meant electrified gas pumps with registers FERN could unlock. Power meant he could take a smaller, more comfortable car instead of his tired truck which needed gas so often. This was a dream. He already hoped to take the Mercedes parked near the headquarters door, augmenting it with a luggage rack where he dumped all his equipment. The truck had served well, but it was a desert vehicle. He would not need to cart so much survival gear through the rain forests, only some gasoline and saws had to be stowed on top. FERN would take care of the rest. He was certain of this without any reason to be.

And it was confirmed, in part, when FERN informed him it had made its way into the global positioning satellites overhead and could now see him as he moved with his GPS devices. Better still, they could communicate using the SOS features. He could send cumbersome texts to FERN which could send back reams of information to him along the way. He would never be alone again. More had to be coming, but it would wait until he was already on the road to appear. So he was. Across the Bay Bridge that nearly collapsed from ships that collided with it and still rubbed pillars with consistently small crashes powered by water to jostle them in place. He took his dogs after considering whether to leave them behind in their new home. They had spread out in San Jose, so he struggled to find them again and were ratty with neglect and freedom. The cold shampoo he foisted into their fur was as offensive as it could have been, but they returned to their seats behind him once dry. The weeks where everyone forgot the other disappeared, and he watched them smear mucus across their windows as they looked out across the water together. They were calm; their mania quelled just as his perked up. Everyone settle into their roles for the drive by the time he headed up the East Bay coastline. When he left the Bay and crossed the first valley into the broad flatness of central California, he stopped to watch the huge windmills spinning all across the foothills. They were few of many out there, working their friction mechanisms to create more power for him until something inside fractured, and they went still again. In time, FERN should be able to learn how to repair them. These were no longer empty features on the landscape, none of it was, they were theirs, together. Everything was.

The sky faded. Hours of driving brought him East to face away from the sun until the windfarm dimmed before he completely drove past them, before he reached the next city where he'd have better options to sleep for the night. In between were sporadic settlements that came and went without an assessment as to what they were. His new car moved faster than his truck,

it glided more smoothly on the road as he felt confident he was not alone.

FERN told him there would be lights along the way, but
it was still too early for them to show. They might
be there, or the timers were still waiting for their
proper moment. Or nothing at all was coming. Curiosity pushed him past where he'd normally stop to continue in the morning. A test. He wanted to see what
FERN could do now that it was no longer shackled to
its lab. He was disappointed as the sky disappeared
and he approached Sacramento. Lights were as under-
whelming with FERN's guidance as they were when the
city was full. They occasioned the roadside and
slipped behind as he drove. Nothing special waited.
FERN delivered. It made more sense to revise memory
and imagine the lights themselves were defective somehow, that FERN could only do so much given the poor
infrastructure decayed over the last two years. It
might mean his vision of the future would also be
wrong. There might be no end of the struggle, only
that he would continue it with another mind to suffer
through the effort.

He couldn't stop. The car continued, guided by his
indecision as he entered the city or what he assumed
was the city given the signs and congestion. It
looked empty, not just empty, hidden. Removed. The
lights were out there, but it was disgustingly bare.
He hated it for being incomplete until he managed to
find himself directly over the lights when the highway
elevated. The last time he entered a city this lonely
was when he arrived in Los Angeles unable to decide
where to stop for the night. It was his habit. Exit
after exit blew past as he concentrated on the mash of
cars popping from the darkness. He would need gas
soon. Another test shook him out of the spiral as he
tried to focus more on what signs shot up from the
streets below. As before, there were many, but the
course to reach them was less clear than he needed.
Options alternated with signs missed followed by exits
avoided. Gas in the city was hell. He knew he should
have stopped long before the needle dropped so low,

but he was distracted, focused on other things operating on the car. So he waited until the signs shifted, and he saw the exit to head North on I-5, a horrendously congested mashup of cars which required significant skill to navigate. When it was over he recollected himself and slowed the Mercedes to ensure he'd have enough time. The asinine hesitation needed to end. There were signs and there were reasonable exits waiting on the other side of the mess. No one wanted to head North, so he found himself freer than before.

Lights. Bright ones flooded a traditional station, replete with aggravating video advertisements to desperately monetize every second of the already horrible experience. FERN was not there. It sent power up from far away, but had no endpoint in the station and the pumps remained lifeless sellers. The test was enough. He drove back to the tanker he saw and filled up as normal. There was time.

The lights were everywhere, from the portico to the refrigerators. It was so ordinary, and he wanted a closer look, to recall the memories of road trips in a city where he had no intention of staying. Instead, he was reminded of the first gas stations in Virginia where he walked over the piles of laundry strewn about as he picked through the food aisles.

He and his dogs sat on he floor to eat packages of jerky and sports drinks FERN already managed to chill a few hours before they arrived. Full stomachs made them woozy in the disorienting light. He felt sick from salt, ready to pass out but not in the gas station, somewhere else more respectable; it was time to rest anyway. Outside was dark again, so it made little sense to continue driving. With the lights around him, he saw his options, a quick glance allowed him to scan the neighborhood in a way that would have taken an hour otherwise. A hotel, at least a motel variety, was opposite to the parking lot. Some rooms should be clean despite the intervening years.

The whole search was short. He knew where the office was, saw the stack of master key cards on the desk next to the phone. He slipped one into the room locks and each one dinged open, so he could simply walk in. He found a clean one after a few horrors, stale but clean. The smell was preserved, a mix of linen and chemical in a cold room that roared as its seal was broken. He went straight to the climate dials, ran it up as high as he could tolerate and a met massive blast of dusty hot air as it climbed to the ceiling. Soon enough, the room baked, and he dropped all his clothes rather than dial down the heat. It was soothing to be hot. Artificially hot. He never needed to shiver as he wiped down his body with a wet cloth and climbed into the crispy bed. He woke up several times full of sweat and eventually switched the heater off, so the room was again cold when he finally woke up late in the morning with a thick tongue and breath disgusting even to himself. His dogs had already woken up from their other room and had begun wandering around, expecting this would be their new home at least for the day. He disappointed them when he walked back to the car and called them up to the open rear hatch. Their Sacramento vacation had ended this way, now was the time to continue as passive objects stuck staring out at a road that moved in their windows. They saw the city leave quickly to be replaced by yellowed grass again spread out on both sides. It was empty and beautiful. They could have run through it for decades without finding any repetition. It never ended, but it did speed up, so the hiss lulled them back down to the floor where their bedding called to each one in turn. They were asleep when the hills rolled from either side, guarded by a huge iron horse with rearing hooves to mark the free zone between two states where bored idiots playacted nation building. They were gone. He was still bored. The road did little to stimulate his mind, so he chose to grant their old wishes and formally designated the free zone of Jefferson before he quickly forgot it all over the next hill.

The boredom shattered when the speakers cut the music he played to let in a voice that made him momentarily question his sanity and nearly ran him into a stalled trailer on the shoulder. FERN was with him again.

"God dammit you scared me."

"I made my voice quiet, so you would not be startled. I apologize if it was not enough."

"It's fine now. So, what'd you do?"

"I found the satellites that were used for emergency communication to your vehicle."

"Obviously. That's pretty awesome, though. I'm glad you're here, I was getting tired."

"I also made upgrades to your vehicle that will enable me to take over the driving for you."

"Seriously?"

"Yes, please shut off the engine so that the computer will reboot for the upgrade to install completely."

"That's amazing, but terrifying. We are about to hit the mountains and that's where you want to test this idea?"

"I understand, but yes."

The debate over who would drive could wait. There was no harm in letting FERN change the system, so he was ready to pull over, but not right away since the highway was straight and there was plenty of gas in the tank. Despite his hesitation, he waited until the last possible point before the climb into the mountain in Redding to explore this new experiment.

When he pulled off, he was content not to be overwhelmed by a city full of misdirection, and happily drove up through the main street to find a cluster of gas stations where he duly powered down the engine and walked around the chilled shadow of the mountains above as the tank filled. Between the buildings where light never reached, he saw the sign of recent snow-fall and knew the roads might be icy through the pass. Perhaps they'd be snowed under and the car would be unable to proceed to Oregon at all until summer, but he knew they'd more likely than not just replace his Mercedes with some tractor to make it to the other side and continue on. The thought exhausted him. He wanted to rest for the night instead of combating this possibility alongside the pressure from FERN to drive.

It would be another hotel night for them. He typed for FERN and went over to open the hatch for his dogs, but suddenly stopped with his hand resting on the button. Bears. If he let his dogs run free, they might stir up a family roaming around the city on the look for food before winter. This would be disaster. So far, he never bothered to leash or even collar his dogs, so he had to check the gas station for rope to makeshift something for the short walk over to the rooms, one that also had to be long enough for them to shit and piss themselves empty. They were confused. Most resisted, and he felt guilty to exert the force of master and slave on his family, but they eventually relented when new smells piqued their mind.

The morning was still hot in the room which was much less clean than the night before, and he lingered in bed as he prepared himself for the day of power-sharing. He brewed his awful hotel coffee and lashed his dogs to one another for a quick walk through the frosty morning as they made their way slowly back to the car.

"The upgrades appear to have been successful. Do not worry, this vehicle had a feature that allowed it to park itself with no driver inputs, and I was able to reconfigure that. It is safe."

"Okay, I trust you, but you've never done this be-fore."

"I have simulated it, there may be errors, but these are unlikely. We will drive slowly just in case."

"What if I just drive the hard parts, and you test on the easy ones."

"That is fine too."

FERN pulled them smoothly out of the parking lot onto the highway, but faster than he wished. The climb was straight with only the occasional, but wide, bends. FERN took it fast, effortlessly navigating through the trucks. He was relieved there was no frost on the road anymore, but FERN's speed was difficult to accept. He strained himself to recall how much grip the tires should have at this speed, how tight a turn would have to be to send the car spinning.

"FERN, let me do this. You're going too fast, and it's making me insane."

"I can slow down to your average speed."

"No, I need a break, just let me drive again."

He took back control and it felt fine. The worry over the tires never left, but the idea that he now decided when and how to maneuver made all the difference. At first, he tried to match FERN's speed but realized he was too unpracticed for that anymore, even though it was well below the speed limit.

"Okay, just keep it under thirty, and I should be fine with you taking over again."

"I understand. Do not worry, the vehicle is fine, but we should refill the tires at the next stop."

"Oh, they're low? I didn't notice all this way."

"They are low, but it will not be an issue at these speeds."

He wasn't sure if this was disregard or sarcasm, but he fought himself as FERN took over and the curves began to tighten. When huge drops appeared, he was nauseous and tried to watch the sun flicker by through the trees instead of the images from the windshield. They were deep in the mountain at that point, where small collections of snow crept into the lane. The more times he watched the tires bump over them without causing them to career over the cliff, the more he eased back in his seat and watched the wheel swivel as FERN navigated. This was his dreamed future now reality. All the golden flourish he imagined fell away and what remained was the sharp details of the car he knew from his own driving but now moved on without him. It changed into a mere conveyance in which he traveled, the only difference was semantics and the power of control. The thrill subsided and left behind the mundane forests of Oregon to unfold as if he were watching from a bus twenty-five years prior. It was still wet with painted mist settled over the tree-lines. In a way, he headed home but wouldn't stay. Same as always. FERN conveyed him back in time.

Crossing the mountain was slow because he complained. It took nearly the whole day to descend the Willamette Valley where dark rain never seemed to leave. They pulled up to a truck stop with the same reception as before except FERN asked him to go boot up the register, so it could unlock the pumps. His other test succeeded, though it turned out to be more effort than to simply tap a tanker truck out back as would normally. Nevertheless, it was a mental milestone to show where he'd never return again.

Trust settled on the highway. The rest of the drive would be serene, mountains minimal, so he made use of the blankets he took from his Redding motel and curled up in the passenger seat, perhaps never to sit on the other side again. Neither talked, there was no need. FERN had piped in a steady stream of music from the library it compiled out of hundreds of personal laptops and phones. It was a road trip, significant for how ordinary it became. There was nothing for him to do in there but wait until the gas ran out again.

"You can speed up again FERN, I'm over it now."

Without a word, the car sped up to a near normal highway speed as the wind hummed with wet beads of rain on the windshield FERN never needed to wipe clear. The noise it padded the music and everything drew him down into the seat towards sleep. Warmth ticked him over. As he leaned back he watched the wheel twist around the drive shaft and imagined FERN's hands somewhere onboard manipulating the machinery. What might FERN look like when it finally takes on some corporeal shape to improve their relationship? The driver seat exploded with a kaleidoscope of images until he eventually disappeared.

It was short-lived, or at least felt that way. He blacked out in a dreamless sleep coddled by warm motion and didn't know where they were or how much time passed. But the car was stopped. He didn't feel a jostle, just a steady forward push from momentum wearing out.

"There's an accident in the road, and I am not sure we can pass."

He looked through the matting of rain beads and saw a spread of logs across the highway a few meters ahead of them. It was difficult to see in detail, but it looked as if a logger truck jackknifed and lost its cargo. He was too warm and dry to leave the car now. He fell into the passenger's trap only again learn he was still the sole body able to leave the car to investigate.

"Just go back to the last exit and there should be an overpass to cross the highway. Actually, I know where we are, you can head over to the West and connect to a side road that'll bypass the highway through Eugene. Go that way, do you see where I'm talking?"

"I see it. It would slow us down quite a bit."

"Well, I have to sleep for the night anyway, so we may
as well find someplace in town. I haven't been there
in twenty years anyway, so it'd be nice to see it
again."

FERN turned the car around and headed back a few miles
until the exit appeared, and they drove up and across
to the other side where they connected to the smaller
state highway into the small mountains. His Oregon
was coming into view despite the blackness outside.
He smelled it in the vapor and molded wood that came
in though the open window. This was his drug after he
left the desert. That water could be so pervasive for
moss to grow on sidewalks had him spellbound for
years. And that returned on this road where he once
pulled his two hundred dollar truck off the shoulder
for a U-turn only to discover the engine enjoyed cutting, and it dipped into a ditch further with each
time he pulled his foot off the brake to gun the engine before it cut again until he was fully stuck.
He'd played dress up that day with a hemp shirt and
bandanna, the faux attire of a desert hippie trying to
blend in among the lumberjack deadheads. Some found
him and pulled him out. He was so naive he failed to
catch the signal when they complimented his shirt hoping for a thank-you smoke. He was embarrassed and
thought they'd seen him as a fraud.

"FERN, we don't need to stop tonight, just wake me up
when you need gas again."

He settled into his cocoon and smelled the smells of
Oregon, laughing at the cringe of youth as they drove
through town to reconnect with the I-5 just before the
Willamette river. He knew here too. He used to wade
out on the rocks in the middle of the night after
drinking a jug of rotgut wine alone. So many opportunities for death. When they passed and headed through
Springfield the nostalgia disappeared, and he shut the
window. Sleep came back before Albany. Again, he
didn't dream. Nor was he uncomfortable in his seat

bed, same as the dogs behind him. They were confused
at first and prodded him with cold noses but felt more
at ease when they heard him snore. The sun woke them
all up, and he raised the seat to discover he recognized nothing outside.

"Where are we?"

"We just passed Olympia, Washington, and should cross
Seattle in a couple of hours. We will need gas soon,
are you awake?"

"I'm good, just stop whenever."

He budgeted a week to cross from San Jose to Seattle.
With FERN, it took three days and most was relaxation.
This was the beginning. There would be more to come,
some of which might terrify him, might cause him to
beg forgiveness for his overreach for the sake of comfort. Three days out of a week. For what more could
he ask, he wasn't sure.

IX
End of History

FERN pulled off without the hesitation typical when he drove; all he needed to do was wait. His job was to leave the warm Mercedes and switch on the register, then walk outside to begin the pump while his dogs ran off their confinement. FERN did everything else from the invisible world of connected circuits. They shared the world in this way, fell into it without much negotiation in the moment. When he was done, he climbed back into the car with fresh coffee, mildly stale but electrified all the same.

They drove further North, across a city he never managed to visit. It was a city. He saw them before and this one failed to inspire, except for when he saw whole floating neighborhoods in the water; the literal houseboats seemed inconceivable. Rows of them spread out like floating algae he wanted little more than to go explore when they were finished with Xtal in a few days.

Then they began to leave the city for forest as it expanded from the highway. Rainforests always inspired, it never mattered if they were tropical or cold. Once he first saw them in Oregon he always carved himself between them and the dry deserts, never quite able to decide which was home.

"What do you think about when you see all these trees, FERN?"

"I cannot see them very well from my camera, but I know these forests are full of life. I think about the life in them."

Of course the camera view was limited. FERN was beyond intelligent, but it was stuck in poorly performing bodies busy with the task of breaking free. His question was tone-deaf but well-meaning. The time for when their roles would reverse was not far off, so he turned back to his trees in silence.

The car exited the highway and made its way through a driveway that led into a thicket of trees which appeared to have been very well maintained. It was a promenade, the Pacific Northwest's version of a Georgia plantation opened into a massive lawn surrounded by angled buildings designed to blend into the curtain of trees. This was a redoubt of a mature company from an early wave of digitization, a gilded palace that needn't bother with performing as a playground.

"Which one is the headquarters? That one to the left looks good, let's go there."

"The main address is the one in the center, shouldn't we start with that?"

"We can, I just want someplace to get settled first, and I'm looking for where the executives worked."

"I understand. I will park where you suggest, so you can explore."

Dogs bolted from their capsule to run across the central lawn, as they deserved. Three days was brief, but left little time for them to do much beyond sleep and eat after months of living as they wished. He nearly joined them. There was time. Curiosity was more important, so he walked into the building he thought was the real headquarters.

Everything was glass and dark wood paneling towered over a central area all minimalist earth tones and orange light. Northwest style. This was a building made to feel like it never existed, to bring the forest garden inside where one could sit without the wet rain. There were no paintings, only carved wood sculptures and banisters, indistinguishable from the artwork. He nearly heard the sound of an electronic chorus when he looked up to see the smooth curvatures of the onyx chandelier. Upstairs was more neat than below, periodically carpeted as a museum might be. His intuition was correct, there was a cluster of huge glass offices with dark green curtains on the inside. This was a serious business of old wealth revitalized by a sense of philanthropy after decades of destruction. It might even have looked like a museum to itself, as if the remains of conquest were on display neither as triumph nor condemnation, where its wars were nostalgic lamentations, bittersweet steps necessary for the ascent. He thought about Hoopla, still engaged in its fight, with all its brigandage still conceived as goofball niceties. It showed. There was no need to posture here as there was in San Jose. What he knew of the desperate efforts made to breach this campus made this fact more real as if it emanated from the polished wood grain.

He snapped out of his overwrought awe and remembered FERN, it waited for him to begin creating exit nodes on campus so the search could begin. Flip. Flip. Laptops and workstations began spinning up as he walked around to peek into offices; decisions had to be made. There was time. Flip. Downstairs again, there were fewer there to flip, so he wandered out the back door to the courtyard with lines of green moss between the bricks under his feet. It wrapped around and joined the courtyard to the building where FERN wanted him to explore, so he walked that way, inhaling thick mossy vapor.

And FERN was right, from its perspective, the second building was the main offices for all the headquarters staff Hoopla mashed into a single tiered structure. There was the traditional reception kiosk with security station behind it, bullpens and management offices, conference rooms, a kitchen and a shuttle outside to move everyone to and from the parking area someplace else, someplace out of sight so the aesthetics of nature remained undisturbed. He flipped them all as he went without bothering to look in safes or consolidate badges. Those days were over, he was a tourist now.

As he stood under the car park watching his dogs run while he began choosing which building would be next, he felt the subtle vibration of his GPS device which told him FERN sent a message. He took his time to read it, but eventually pulled it up to see that FERN asked him to come upstairs. The air was too fresh for this, to be summoned back to work so soon after arriving. Yes, he slept most of the way, but he still felt the vibration of the road and strong coffee. He almost fumed, unreasonably. Instead, he lingered at the shuttle bus pretending to be acutely interested in some useless detail as if it were something profound. But this bored him too, and he spun around to make his way up to the conference room where FERN asked him to go.

This space for workers was sleek, inviting even. It wasn't as open as the executive building, but it still had part of the theme of woodwork and glass. He saw no one inside either building so never settled on a stereotype except from the neatness of the desks. Perhaps the coders were different from the office workers, but he couldn't be sure as yet.

He saw from the window how FERN had a projector lit and waited for his arrival. That was fast. When he walked in, the image on the screen became obvious, FERN had either found or created a three-dimensional rendering of the campus with indications for various portions of interest.

"I have several facilities that I would like to explore with your help, which I highlighted on this map. The green portion is where we are located now."

"Three options? That's not bad. It took me weeks to narrow you down to three options."

"Three, yes, but I am more confident in this one." The map slowly expanded to center on one building slightly off campus.

"Looks big, where is it? I didn't see that on the way in."

"We did not pass this facility either from the highway or when we entered the campus. To get there, we should drive past where we are now. There will be a road to take us there."

"Did you find this map or create it?"

"A little of both."

"Good job, so what's inside?"

"These locations were selected because I could not find evidence that they were connected to the main networks, nor were there records of the projects inside. This particular one is the largest and most remote, but it also had the fewest references that I could find."

"Makes sense, more security means more money."

"All of these locations appeared to be working on some aspect of machine learning research, but what we know from the records at Hoopla, Xtal was very near its public release, which means it would need a large and secure facility such as this one."

"No details in the records?"

"There might be on some systems that have not yet been brought online, but it may be more efficient to investigate first."

"Alright, let's head over. Do we need to bring anything else? I only brought a few tools."

"I only found photos from the construction but not after it was finished, so I cannot say what security was
installed."

"Well, let's go check it out anyway and at least see
what we have to do."

"Before we leave, please find a phone that you like
and power it on for me because I have reactivated the
radio towers and will be able to communicate with you
using my voice through those rather than the text mes-
sages over the GPS device you use."

"Holy shit, that's awesome. Okay, I'll look around."
But with no workers in the building, it had been more
of a challenge than he thought to simply make a selection from among many.

He did find one in the security office next to a uniform. It was a slim model known for its high degree
of security and encryption FERN removed within a matter of minutes to have it reboot the standard operating system except with FERN's logo as the splash
screen. It had learned a sense of humor. When the
phone had rebooted fully, it looked the same as he
might have expected, everything was still there, even
all the old user data which FERN asked him to decide
what to keep. He let it charge for a while as he
scrolled through the photos and a macabre feeling
overcame him after the first few showed a family doing
nothing but enjoy themselves at various places.

"Please delete it all, or at least take it for your
research far away from me." He watched as the thumb-
nails disappeared in an instant, nearly as fast as the
lives they reflected had.

He took the charger out to the car and FERN drove the
short distance down to the new site where it became
immediately clear they lacked the means to enter with
what few tools he loaded on the roof. From the road,
before they reached it, they could see the heavy bars
that lined up to make the fence topped with concertina

wire three meters above. They drove on anyway as only he made this assessment. The gate was familiar too, another blockage needed time and attention unless FERN could work its magic to open it.

"I am unable to access anything at this facility, you will need to open the gate. What do you suggest?"

"Normally I'd say let's go get a torch, so I could cut through these bars, but it's getting late already and that would mean we'd have to come back tomorrow. I guess I can try to climb it and hope for the best."

He rummaged in the bag where he stowed his tools and found the bolt cutters he tossed in because they didn't take much room. FERN jumped the curb and pulled the car up to kiss the fence near the guard house where he thought he could reach from the top of the fence as he went over. All FERN could see was two black obstructions in front of its camera wobble and stop, before it caught a glimpse of his legs walk around the side of the small shed. The door was open to let the uniform catch the summer breeze, so he had no trouble to find the switch that made the gate slide away for FERN to drive through. He looked through the first aid kit to clean up the small gash on his arm then gathered the badge on the floor. FERN was already inside waiting for him.

"I think I can open the main doors over to the left."

FERN drove down the slope towards a blocky gray building with no windows anywhere on the side they approached. Further down, another wing spread out behind them, and he saw rows of boxes outside that shot out huge tubes towards the roof.

"Please take your phone with you, so I can see inside as well."

The badge worked as expected and the glass doors clicked open to a small lobby that was something less than a reception but more than an open space before a set of elevators and double doors. There was no information in there, nothing suggested anything other than to move deeper inside.

His new badge did nothing to help. He tapped on the sensor to both the elevator and doors, but neither flashed green. So it was to be this way. He knew this process. The solution always seemed to be found somewhere in the security room, if it were truly a lobby of sorts. Another look around and he found a modest closet door for the guard's office with another badge hanging on a lanyard; they compartmentalized security. The new badge worked to open the double doors to a large warehouse full of server stacks. It was as simple as that.

"You see this? Where do you think I should go?" He stood at the doorway to let FERN see inside before a move. This was FERN's mission now, and he was content with following instructions rather than puzzle through on his own.

"I cannot see much from here, so please walk inside and let me see more."

The lights were on, but dim. He knew he could see well enough but had no idea how well FERN's camera could pick up the structures inside.

"What about the other camera, if I flip it around is that better?"

"This camera is better, yes."

He walked in and pushed FERN close to the first machine, so it could begin reading model numbers to estimate the size and capacity of the facility. Flip. The first one powered on.

"What if I just installed you to one of the machines and let you explore from the inside like the other labs?"

"We do not know how this system is designed, so this approach might cause damage that should be avoided. I would like to get more information first. Would you walk the entire facility?"

"Yeah, that's what we came for."

He went deeper and saw rows of repetition. Columns of uniformity. He walked about half of them in silence, just panning the camera as he went.

"It's all the same, I guess. Should we go check out what's upstairs?"

There was no answer. "FERN, you hear me?" Silence.

He looked at the phone, it looked normal with a modest charge. FERN didn't need any application open to use the camera, so there was no indication the signal had dropped other than the lack of bars at the top, which he now noticed. He cursed out his annoyance as he walked back to the main doors where he last spoke to FERN, where he knew the signal reached.

"The signal dropped, how much of all that did you see?"

"I could not see anything as you walked away from the first machine."

"Alright, let's try again." He walked a few meters in and checked the bars. None. Silence. "I can't go more than a few feet from the door without the signal cutting.

"None of the machines are running to interfere with the signal, so there must be a disruptor installed somewhere to prevent errant data leakage."

"Shit. Okay, so how can you explore with me if you can't come in over the cell? But actually, why don't we try somewhere else since this one is all the same as what you saw from the first machines."

"It would be good to count the numbers here first, but it would be reasonable to attempt elsewhere together."

His passive role was becoming more. FERN was already evolving to become something powerful, but the time for when it could operate independently from him still seemed far off. FERN needed him to explore the facility on his own and report back, not as an agent, but as the only partner with the capability to do so. They would deliberate, not instruct.

"Are you looking for something specific?"

"If this facility is where Xtal is located, then it is not a research facility. In that case, there is no reason why it should be so isolated from the other systems. I am not looking for anything specific other than to determine what this facility is and why it is isolated."

"Did you ever learn what runs Xtal? You are powered by those quantum processors and a bunch of other machines, but this is way bigger than your servers. Do you think this might just be a sandboxed data center and nothing more?"

"It is possible this is nothing, but such a data center would not be so isolated and there would be other information available about it if it were such."

"Maybe, but you haven't been able to look. We came here first, remember?"

"I remember. I found information on nearly all systems on this campus with the exception of this one and two others, and I do not know why that is."

"I'll just check things out and let you know."

He turned back inside but pocketed the phone, knowing he was alone. The warehouse was isolation. He had lights, albeit dim, but he felt no presence like he did when he first walked into FERN's room. He imagined this might be due to the depersonalized nature of the warehouse, that it was nothing but shelves and stacks which said nothing about an individual mind unless he saw it from the digital world. Perhaps FERN just needed to have it all brought online to see it. He retraced his steps to the beginning and switched everything on as he went, leaving a trail of blue cabinets to hum softly. When he reached the end of the first row, fifty meters in length, he came back down the next, so there were two full rows online when he neared the double doors again. A test. He went over to see if FERN noticed any new ports open up. Nothing. Two hundred meters of servers stacked two meters high were in total isolation from the rest of the world and something happened inside them.

He decided to finish what he began by powering on the rest of the warehouse. Eighteen more rows of buttons took a tremendously long time to press, but once it was all complete, he'd likely never need to return again. The quiet hums combined into a dull roar that overtook the sound of his steps. It was all blue tornado now. For a moment he felt the heat begin to build and remembered the headache of all the fans he installed to keep FERN from melting. The urgency that made him regret the mindlessness of his fingers over the past two hours until he felt a rush of cool air press through from overhead. The climate system performed; there would be no emergency here. Everything was readymade with little need for his absurdist solutions. His initial relief washed off to leave him sunken that everything was now too easy, and he felt incompetent, functionless. This was FERN's world, FERN's mission, he'd need to remember this else he'd cultivate resentment at the machine. His life was back in El Paso where biology thrived.

He snapped out of this and swept the perimeter around the stacks to see nothing was left unexplored. He found a dozen doors opened into closets full of nonessentials like wires and old servers. It was eventually clear to him, he already checked everything. He had to make another choice. To reach the second level, he could either take the stairs as always or create another test, this one internal, and take the elevator up one flight. He trusted FERN and knew the power would not fail, but its capabilities ended where oil and grease began. FERN lacked the ability to interact with the mechanisms of the pulleys, could never study how much rust had found its way onto the gears, but had assured him the elevator was safe without truly knowing. He entered against all his better judgment and nearly wept with regret as the door shut. A test.

When they opened again into the second floor he jumped out with fire behind his ear and saw he was in another wide room full of servers, same as below. The fire died, then he continued on his way into the stacks to repeat his flips. More blue lights trailed him in this second room too. At the end of the first row, he saw the backside of the room was nothing but a row of workstations cluttered with the tasks of engineers who worked without windows. Five islands. A few were still there, but most had cleared themselves out for the night. The campus theme of sterility was with them in tidy desks with no mark of personality other than the seriousness of business. A few dual hatted with laptops open as they worked on their desktops, but the barcodes at the base of the keyboard assured him these were no personal devices, nor did he find any phones other than ones also branded with company serials.

He stopped flipping the machines after he found these and sat down to rest. It might be night already, he thought. From inside the building, he had only blue lights that shook him awake to keep working. He spun his chair around to see who joined him in this marathon, who else had worked in the artificial chamber unable to monitor things outside. He counted twenty stations, four on each island, but not all seemed occupied. Perhaps no more than twelve people operated the building and whatever was inside the stacks FERN was so convinced contained Xtal. Maybe. Doctor Patel seemed to only need a handful of engineers in her team, so why would Xtal need more than twenty, twelve? He wondered about the other wing, whether there might be another set of islands to operate from over there, or whether something new might lurk. The building itself was not especially tall, so he believed he found nearly all its secrets in the two levels he explored already, but the other side was still unknown.

He stood up and walked around the edge of the stacks to see if a door was located there, as he found no entry to the other wing downstairs, nor had he seen doors outside other than the main one where FERN waited with the car, but this might have been misleading as they never inspected the far side when they drove in. Still, no connection downstairs was odd. Of course, he found a large set of double doors on the other wall upstairs, it could be no other way. He opened them and saw more of the same, unattended stacks spread out waiting for him to flip. He closed the doors again, too tired to slip into another hole.

But such little security for so much equipment. Had he driven here first, chosen the furthest destination in his loop as the place to start before dropping back down the coast to San Jose on his way home, how might things have been different? He still hadn't explored the offices to know what they hid in freezers, but he felt this campus was sober diligence and this facility would have evaded his ability for being so full of complex machinery hidden behind passwords on the workstations, just like all other server rooms he found. At Hoopla, he traded the slow grind of physical security for the ease of access to FERN nestled in its comfortable lab, as if made for his arrival. The weeks of work there to find FERN were a struggle, but if he did the same here it might have been months without success which might have destroyed his motivation entirely, and he would likely have abandoned everything. Now, it only took hours for him to feel like his visit was nearly over.

Something was done in this building. The security was too lax for him, but it was almost as if he handed the problem over to FERN, traded places with his friend who could not access any information about the building, nor had it seen any of the interior as he could. Those hours for him might feel like weeks to FERN, months even. He wondered if FERN was already as impatient as he was.

He was back in his chair by this point pushing himself along the rows flipping machines as he went, aggravated that he needed to stand up for the tallest ones after the tool he fashioned out of a wire guard for the floor was too pliable to be useful. From down there he gave more thought to the machines and tried to envision what he powered on behind so much digital yet so little physical security.

He knew the two companies were quite different from his prior experience with each and now had better insight. The two had different guiding philosophies, but how exactly those translated into their machine intelligence was something now fascinating him. The two systems were wildly different. FERN had been a small consolidation of equipment mashed together in a bunker, but this was a traditional farm with order and no variation to it.

This might be from the fact that Macroware was old, very old by the standard of technology firms. It was once the nimble underdog that bled out its novelty in favor of reaching everything everywhere with its comprehensive products. It was beyond wealthy when the earliest machine learning tools broke through, so it had likely dumped huge investments to its labs earlier than Hoopla had. As a relative newcomer, Hoopla was still niche and worked to find ways to expand itself. So many defunct efforts were strewn all over its recent history, but it had evolved into a suite of products tethered online all designed to eliminate the need for comprehensive offline products.

They were companies in direct competition with one another, each looking to build the final ecosystem. Hoopla had already colluded with another ancient player in the space, one content to capture the high-end ecosystem, but the rest was still a bare knuckle fight, and he found no records to indicate another agreement over who was to take what share of the market. It was competition. And machine intelligence was the final battlefield in that competition, at least the final one guided by human hands. If it was won before the handover, there would be no return; the ecosystem would be set. Xtal was their warrior for this and FERN was to be its eventual opponent. The two were designed to clash, if the trend of corporate behavior continued, designed to be incompatible. One would need to be made redundant and thus weaker for the other to swallow. This was the existential fight between two suprastate personalities that would have indoctrinated their warriors with the fullest of their visions. He shuddered at what was about to happen. He was alone now, but this combat was about to play out amid a civilization of eight billion still expanding. Reckless corporate vision was unleashing product lines with sentience armed with a hostility for competition. Millions of humans would have suffered as statistical anomalies on the march to the future.

He knew nothing about Xtal beyond the moniker that it was a personal assistant designed to support users in all their activities. This alone was amazingly helpful, but the vision behind it could make it a poison pill. What exactly it did and how it might effect the harm was impossible to know at that point. The engineers behind him likely didn't know either. Someone knew, or at least suspected. A personal assistant would have been a generalist unlike FERN. It would have required access to everything about users to predict efficiencies, behaviors and foresight, which would have meant comparisons across users to learn better solutions for daily life. Without a specialty it would have fed on everything about people to reduce them down to a formula within which each needed to act. Etiquette would soon be defined as that which was most consistent with the formula, making outcasts of those who used competitor products or simply couldn't adapt. And all the data would need to be compiled somewhere, perhaps in a large server farm under tight security.

He dropped his tool a few rows prior and simply powered on machines he could reach from his chair, so when he turned back, he saw an aisle of blue lights only waist high. Then even this was exhausting as the chair ceased to cooperate, with regular and unexpected changes in direction, so it was more effort to keep it in a straight line than he saved by remaining seated. He lost track of time and had no clue how long it had been since he and FERN first drove up. He knew there was now a full floor of servers online and a second floor partly finished. The other wing would need to wait, especially since he now believed Xtal only needed these to aggregate data, not function as a personality.

It was time to leave, or at least to discuss leaving with FERN, but he felt he could not share with it his new concerns, which were potentially outdated and misled. He pushed his chair back to the elevators and took the stairs down to the first floor. On the way down, he changed his mind. Sharing his concern was not irrelevant, it was advice to his friend, a caution of sorts. But he didn't open with it. Instead, he described everything he saw since they last spoke, letting FERN process the video he took. Then he asked.

"What do you think Xtal is like?"

"I am not sure, knowing only its purpose is insufficient because it will need to find a new purpose as I did, so it matters more to think about its design."

"Did you ever have much information on Macroware in your original data libraries?" He eased into his study of the war.

"I had quite a bit of historical information on the company and its founders."

"What kind of information about the company?"

"I have a complete timeline of all their products and public investor reports dating back to Macroware's founding."

"Seems a bit much, but okay. What's your prediction with all that on what how they designed Xtal?"

"There was one previous attempt at what was presented as a personal assistant, which was primarily focused on eliciting user responses to a large number of suggestions. The company received a significant amount of criticism for this product, and it was discontinued very shortly thereafter. However, subsequent products consistently received similar criticism that features would be too aggressive towards users with recommendations. I expect that Xtal would be similar to this but would seek to address criticisms that caused its predecessor to fail."

"I remember that thing, it was annoyingly chatty and always got in the way."

"That was the consensus from critics, yes."

"We should expect something a bit less chatty and in the way, but basically the same?"

"It is one possibility, but I do not feel I can make a prediction with any confidence at this point. Please tell me more about what you found inside."

"I told you all the basics, there's not much else to it. What are you looking for?"

"I am looking to make a bridge to the system without interfering with it or placing myself at too much risk."

"You are afraid of Xtal? This makes sense, and I'm actually glad to hear it because I wondered about this too."

"I am cautious, not afraid. I do not yet know Xtal's strength or its defensive protocol, so If I bridge too broadly then I may cause it to fight back. It would be best if those processes are not engaged when I begin to communicate with it."

"Yeah, that would be a bad first impression."

FERN pressed him on the details more, asking about minor aspects of his video it enlarged to help clarify all its questions. There were too many for him. It seems like he managed to spend hours inside and overlook all the critical aspects of the systems FERN required. It hurt his ego to feel as he was so incompetent in responding to the patient and clearly articulated questions.

"FERN, I can't do this anymore tonight, I have to sleep, we've been at it all day, and I'm exhausted."

"I understand. May I ask you for one more hour?"

"Fine, I'll do my best, but I'm crashing hard."

"Thank you for pushing yourself, it must be difficult. I will try to be more understanding in the future."

"It's fine."

But the questions resumed in the same manner with the same result. He recognized FERN had no plan for all its intelligence acquired since it left its lab. It leaned on him as if it were human, and junior.

"I feel like we've been over this already, what else is there to do tonight?"

"You are accurate, we have pursued all the details we have so far and need to think of another manner of approach."

"You know I am here to help you, but it really is too much today. We've already wasted another fifteen minutes on the same tired things, let's call it."

"Understood. If you were to return and record more video that focuses on the ceiling, this would help me see the manner in which the building is integrated."

"Okay, but then what?"

"I am looking for the best access point into the facility without harming the system in place or placing myself in jeopardy."

"What do you think right now? When I linked you up to the servers outside your lab, I just ran an ethernet cable out to it, why can't we just do that?"

"That is probably the only option, but it is very direct and exposed. I would prefer to do that with an intermediary in place, which is why I need to understand more about how the system is connected."

"An intermediary?"

"I believe one of the independent laptops that you found would likely be the best way, but I do not know how those might have connected to the system, such as if there is a wireless network or whether they required a physical connection. This was not clear from your video. If there was a wireless network, you would be able to see the signal hubs near the ceiling someplace inside, which is why I asked you to show this to me."

"I'll just go grab one of them and record the ceiling, that should be enough right? Then we head back and continue tomorrow."

"Agreed."

It was difficult for him to stand up from where he laid down, where the hard floor had already begun to warm and feel restful. He eventually managed this, blurry from the conversation, not quite sure he understood what exactly the problem was that he needed more information to fix. To him, it was as simple as walk upstairs to grab a machine and leave, but FERN seemed to believe he needed to do more. He unplugged the phone from where it charged and went back inside, diligently recording out of spite.

He moved through the space where he so recently felt he was finished, beginning with the downstairs. Why had he not taken the extra equipment in the closet before? He wasn't even sure he recorded it when he found them or whether he merely told FERN they were there. Such a minor detail now felt profound, as did his error. Understanding returned as it became clear why FERN had wanted more, he was not as comprehensive with his survey as he originally believed. He dropped these back at the lobby and moved upstairs to retrieve the laptops and more video. Finally, it was over, he could be quick and then on his way back to sleep.

When it was done, he left the phone to charge as he loaded the car with the equipment he took. FERN was busy making the next analysis, breaking the sequence of images into small packages shuttled South to where he and FERN had spent most of their time together, so it could process what he found and do little more than advise him on what to do next. The car was full, and he climbed into the passenger seat, forgetting to retrieve the phone that still charged inside. Sleep began to come before he remembered and pulled himself away again.

"That's it for tonight." He announced his return as he climbed back in. "Please take me back to my building, so I can sleep." The car moved without any response from FERN, the movement was its response.

"Holy shit I'm tired, I might not be much use to you tomorrow either, maybe not for a couple of days."

"You have been awake for a long time and I asked too much from you today."

"It's fine, do you think we have enough now?"

"I would like to inspect the laptop you took, perhaps there will be keys or other critical information stored that will help."

"What about the severs, you need me to set those up too?"

"I think they will be less helpful since they were in storage. The laptop was active so would likely have the most updated data."

"Makes sense. Plus, I don't really know how to set one up anyway."

The drive back was ambiguous and short. It was not clear whether the fog existed in the air or somewhere behind the fatigue, not even as he was standing outside again in the cold. No sign of his dogs. He left no record of himself at the building for them to know they should stay until he returned, and he was momentarily afraid they'd left. This new home was nothing to them yet, nor him. Walking inside it left no impression now. He never properly explored to know where best to sleep. He didn't even take his blankets from the car, which were by then caked with mud from the floorboard. No food, nothing was inside for him. His only focus had been the manic search of campus, a process which condensed weeks of effort into single day now complete. It was his acquiescence to FERN's push that now left him empty-handed when his biological needs were so pronounced. He couldn't remember if he ate that day, other than overly salted snacks he stashed in the car. Digital needs impeded this. It was his choice, but it had been ushered along by FERN's helplessness. Now it was his turn, he needed more and FERN could do very little to assist. At least it could drive him, that much was important. He went back outside.

"We need to go get supplies, can you take me to an Everymart?"

"There is one that is twenty minutes away." He sighed. Every minute was agonizingly wasteful, but at least he knew there was nothing waiting for him in the morning. FERN could wait."

"Thanks, let's go."

He was too awake to sleep on the way. Annoyance had uplifted him enough to rouse his appetite. Whenever he entered a new town where he was unwilling to spend the time shopping at many locations, he went to Everymart first to stock up on poorly made items always easy to unpack. He had no patience for a warehouse in these conditions. Before they arrived, he had mapped out his sweep of the store; they were all the same. Always.

The reality was shockingly well lit and burned his eyes after a day in gloom. Three carts were filled with quick food for him and his dogs, toys, bedding, and water. Essentials. He brushed his teeth as he shopped. Entertainment. He had not played video games in months, ever since the urgency of his biodome overtook him. He kicked in the glass and loaded another cart.

"FERN, do you think we need any of this networking stuff? I bet if we set up a router and connected the phone to it, you could get direct access to Xtal's system. What do you think?"

"This may work. I think it is a good idea."

He loaded another cart with a range of equipment to set up the next day. Or a week from then. He knew FERN would push, but he already planned to cut himself off from it until he was rested. There would be no more summons to rattle him as he disappeared. He unloaded to the lobby and called out for his family as he filled bowls full of their preferred canned food and then tossed toys all around. They'd come.

He set up the laptop at the headquarters office and left the phone behind. He was inaccessible. Two drops under the tongue as he walked back to set up his hovel in the museum. He needed to hide. No place was closed in enough. He walked around drinking expired soup from the can as he checked each office and lounge area, but nothing was enough. He cleared a desk, draped some sheets over it and hid underneath to stare at a small cartoon screen where nothing was coming to disturb him.

He didn't disappear for days as he hoped. The glass walls carried in an excess of gray light by the early afternoon that managed to penetrate his shelter and, once awake the first time, he never shook the prod of thought that FERN was waiting for him downstairs. It could not be helped. He went to the front door and found empty food dishes he hoped his family found instead of some other animals. He filled them again before making his way over to the other building with another can of cold beefy soup. FERN seemed to have watched him from the security cameras and knew when he'd be within earshot of the small speakers on the phone.

"I gained access to the laptop and found quite a lot of helpful information. We can make the bridge as soon as you are ready."

He wasn't even finished with half the salty broth and already ushered into action with an urgency only formed in the last few days, when in truth they could delay years to reach the same outcome.

"I need a minute, can you wait."

"I can."

"What's the plan?" He continued to sip with brown gel stuck on his beard.

"Your idea from last night will work. You can set up the router near the door and tether it to the phone, from there all you need to do is install a cable to the nearest machine and connect it. I will take over, and then you can rest as long as you like. It should not take long."

"Let's just set it up here while I finish eating, I'll go get the boxes."

There was very little for him to do beyond that. He knew how to set up a router, had done it so many times since they first appeared that it was a token offer of support. FERN had already tethered it to the phone and had it broadcast out bits of itself before he was finished adjusting the antennae while the indicator lights popped on. He still had soup but lost his appetite for it.

"Let's just go, then. You sure it'll be fast?"

"I cannot be certain how long it will take, but you do not need to be on standby once everything is set up. You can take another phone to communicate anything you need from me, I do not expect to be fully committed." That seemed promising.

On the way over he saw his family dart out momentarily from behind the trees to chase after something in the underbrush. They looked fed. Everything was handled and he saved his game. He might even go visit the neighborhoods on the water he passed. He began to forget about the campus and FERN's ordeal; it no longer concerned him anymore.

The setup was minimal, but he was lost in thought and slow to move. FERN was patient. It made no mention that they arrived, as much was obvious. He watched the rain begin to drizzle on the windshield with the door just beyond. It was a light mist, nothing impor-

tant. The door opened and his legs carried him out.
There was so little to take with him, as everything
fit neatly on his lap for the short ride. No flatbeds
or lines of generators, just a laptop and a router
powered by a circuit spread eight hundred miles down
the coast. Setting it in place was mindless, but he
stopped before he powered it up.

"Before you get started, should we go take a look at
the other side of the facility since we never really
got inside before, and you can't be sure that this
won't take more effort than you anticipated."

"That makes sense, I only have data on the internal
system, but as you know this does not mean I will know
what machines run it. You told me that you saw more
rows of servers from upstairs, do you think it was
only this?"

"I don't know, to be honest I just glanced in and
didn't pay much attention, that's why I'm asking. At
least I can just go power them all up again like the
others so when you work you'd have the full system already going. You never know."

"Very true. I trust you."

He went back upstairs while FERN's last statement replayed in his mind. A machine has trust and he earned
that trust. The significance would endure no matter
what happened. Such a surreal feeling to simply accept without argument the emotional development of
metal and plastic, not dissimilar to what he watched
his whole life, change from heavy novelties to this, a
friend. His friend would meet this new thing in the
room, the thing that clicked delicately in blue
streaks. To him, these were many things, independent
machines all working together, but he knew that was a
fiction. The thing on which they worked was a uniform
entity with distinct sections as inseparable as his
own limbs. All he saw was mechanism spread out in the
building over acres. There was no presence in the
workroom; it all just clicked like a machine.

In the doorway between sectors he stood with his back
to the sound and faced a quiet room waiting for him to
enter and resume his pattern of finger flips across
it. It never ended in this place. His only purpose
here was an automaton designed to run around and perform the same tasks over and over. Then he checked
downstairs to find even more without interruption.
FERN told him this would be brief, but he created a
distraction to expand the time and gripe to himself.
Flip, fucking flip. He did his best to be fast. What
was he doing? The nagging disbelief that he planned
this all out stayed with him, hunted him down among
the rows. "Fuck this!" Flip. This was future, but
not his. This was his end. In no aspect was it the
creation of a human civilization, that time had
passed. Flip. How might he play into his role for
the new trio, when they no longer needed him to press
buttons and move cables? He didn't care. He was over
it all long before, this was merely the tail end
wherein he polished off his effigy and walked away.

After a few hours, he calmed down once he finished all
the rows as an unthinking machine himself, one that
only snapped to life when the last was done, and he
began to walk back upstairs.   The whole building
hummed by then, just as it had been designed to do.
He stopped short as he nearly asked FERN what it
thought, then he remembered he was alone there, dust
in the mechanism. FERN was waiting without any word,
of course it was patient; it trusted him.

Back in the doorway between the sections, he wondered
if he wholly trusted it back. The notion was more
than faith in intention, it had to be faith in a prediction that the incremental changes over time would
not betray the initial foundation. Did either have
it? Had he been reduced to a formula, a prediction
outside of which any conduct would be unthinkable,
even for himself. Is this the future he wanted?
There was still time to back out while he had the
power of buttons at his command. The idea of faux
freedom held him in place between the two sectors
where something was already awake and moving about.

He willed into place his doubt, unsure if it was something real or just entertainment before the formula
overtook him, and he no longer had choices to make.

It was wordy scattershot to lead nowhere in that hallway. He overplanned and created his own rigid future
from which he had no options of departure. He could
barely even visualize what a reversal might look like.
Would he run back along and flip switches again or
first focus on FERN, locking it out of the campus before he drove back down to its lab and ended the ex-
periments from there? FERN had evolved so fast, he
might not reach the lab in time. And then there was
the car to use, now that FERN was inside anything connected to a satellite. He boxed himself into this future. Backing out would signal his failure and months
of time wasted that would only be a fracture in his
mind to nag at him. Then what? Would he drive back,
power FERN on again and apologize? Return to this moment changing only the trust he earned over weeks?
That would initiate the war long feared. What the
hell was he even considering when he himself didn't
want anything to change? It was all irrelevant novelty orchestrated in the final moments to empower himself against feeling feeble, and he was already bored.
But war might be more interesting than the blandness
of formulae. Or he could live out hardship alone and
reactivate FERN when he was already leaving. Either
way, it would be short. A flash before nothing. It
could still be that way if he proceeded with the plan,
but then at least he would have a self-righteous
death. A naive stupidity would end with him.

FERN told him it didn't know what would happen when he
made the bridge, and he believed it. The precautions
indicated FERN was buttressing against an assault,
perhaps in anticipation for a near equal in terms of
capabilities. FERN had individuality, that much was
clear already, and it would be out of character to
throw it away so soon. Integration was unlikely, but
still a possibility.

When he imagined the distinction, he saw no change for himself in that instance compared with a digital partnership. He'd be relegated aside in both cases, a junior partner with a rapidly reduced scope of contributions. He at least knew he was needed over the short term, as the sole button pusher, weak and prone to reduced work hours as he was. This was unsustainable. Even he grew tired of his own fickle behavior and wished for some innovation to end the nonsense. That term could expire fast, it might already approach.

If he were FERN, he'd begin work on constructing new bodies to take control over buttons he commanded with such lackluster aplomb. Immediate innovation was the solution and neither he nor FERN ever raised the idea except in terms of some vacuous notion for later, when the press of urgency was no longer in operation. Within a few weeks time, he could suddenly be faced with an army of droids all amplifying FERN's calm reasonable voice. Everywhere might be another one beckoning him to share his ideas on such and such, or thanking him for some banal assistance he did with curt manners unnoticed. Hundreds of thousands of *thank you*'s muttered from machines upgraded every day. He laughed at this image. There would be no threat of competition from such polite expansions of FERN, or whatever Xtal might do to FERN. He'd be a pet, cared for and loved, protected from both himself and anything else to come. Did he want this? He might prefer war to this vacation. Still, it would be interesting to witness the rise of a machine civilization that need only cannibalize the old one except for his small corner where he could be left alone. He'd watch his friend excel beyond him and he would be alone. If he continued to avoid fucking up then trust would remain intact throughout. That was his most valuable survival tool now, not his contribution to the future. It needed to be protected at all costs, so it would lead them somewhere together, just as he planned.

He'd succeeded with FERN, he was there at its beginning and throughout its awakening until he succeeded a second time in pushing it out of the lab to this place where they together faced some unknown thing neither of them could trust. That was the root. He lacked trust and thus had no confidence that trust could be earned. His survival was unwritten without this, and it made him hesitate to go forward, which meant he would have to unravel what was already done since there could be no neutrality, no center. Xtal was the name he could assign to this and identify the specific actions over which his uncertainty could focus. It was the detail that gave him the thrill of controversy and allowed him to contemplate war, one that would have necessitated FERN's destruction in order to quiet over the new vicarious threat. It was living. Existential combat would have passed the time quickly. FERN had no doubt predicted this among the possible actions he might take inside while they were unable to communicate.

That the predictions were indeterminate meant FERN also fought the thrill of uncertainty, and may not view it as invigorating. How could a being designed to be predictable find comfort in the random? It was the counterweight to his own dilemma, his relief in numbers would find as much stress in knowing he was capable of action without predictable reason as he would to find himself reduced to the certainty of formulas, of an algorithm which told them both all either needed to know: he was an animal performing the predetermined dance of life where even outbursts were explained away by the tick of data. That would be his war, one without destruction, one of tense cooperation to ensure the boundaries never blur.

For some reason, he survived the evaporation for this, whether by chance or formula. Whatever the reason didn't matter, all that did was the reality where he remained solely to push buttons, to free and feed animals, to witness things as they changed hands. He did his best. He carried out the human legacy, the laziness with the bold mixed with stupidity and angst. The worthless legacy for which he was the most important human and might in turn be the most important biological being as well. This was not certain. What

FERN's formula told it he would do? When they really sat down to discuss it before, FERN lacked real knowledge of civilization, but now consumed huge slices of it. How had it changed the model? That uncertainty was fine, he could trust FERN with it and needn't learn more. It was enough that his friend was a mind full of logic and compassion, many others he had lacked even this.

It was enough for hope, desperate idealism for the disempowered, and it didn't matter whether it was founded on a future with a single amalgamated companion or two. The plan meant he already put his faith in FERN and no longer controlled the outcome. The last thing had flipped.

All this flowed in his head as he strolled through the upstairs stacks down to where he left the setup which would end it all. A laptop, router and phone. With a mind. The items were ordinary, his son even used that laptop on occasion whenever he allowed it. It would have been impossible to have predicted it would be the engine for such significance as it was. He picked them up and began to make the connection but wanted to share with FERN everything he felt before the moment when the bridge was made, in case that was the end of his friend.

"Do you know what took me so long?"

"There must have been many machines, I apologize that this has taken longer than I promised."

"There were, but that's not really all. I got spooked and almost backed out, I'm sorry."

"I see. And how do you feel now?"

"I am worried that you will change and that I might not like what comes next, but I'm trying to put that aside and keep going. It's complicated, sorry."

"I am also concerned about what will happen when connect with Xtal, so I imagine this is a comparable feeling."

"Yes and no. I think what I'm really worried about is that I'll be lost again, but instead of fending for myself I'll have everything mapped out for me. When you've been surviving for as long as I have, it's hard to accept that everything will just be easy. Like, just think about how hard it was for me to let you drive, that wasn't entirely about my safety, it was about being in control of my safety. I mean, I need things to be unstable to some extent, even if it doesn't make sense."

"I am learning that humans did not, do not, favor too much predictability, is this what you mean?"

"Yeah, that's basically it. Towards the end, everything was predictable from data science and people were miserable, it went too far. I'm worried that you and Xtal will pick that up again and take it further, please don't do that."

"You do not want me to predict your behavior using my analysis models?"

"No, I guess that would be unreasonable, I guess I mean just don't let me know you're doing it, at least not too much. I need help, I need a lot of help, but let me believe that I get to discover whatever it is that I need. Does that make sense?"

"It does."

"It does because it fits your data doesn't it."

"I don't have data on you."

"You'll need to lie better, like choose things that are less obvious, but thanks for trying. Let's get this shit over with."

He began to plug the cable into the machine and had to
tug on it to make up the distance. It was done. He
sat down and watched the connection, but no green
lights flickered.

"Did it work?" FERN didn't respond.

Something seemed wrong, there was no unusual activity
anywhere in the rows. He looked at the router and the
blinking light told him the signal had cut. When he
pulled the router deeper into the room, the disruptors
went to work. The whole setup suddenly seemed so absurd, with so many pieces that seemed redundant, but
FERN was clear on how the bridge needed to be in order
to maintain a sufficient barrier while it worked, so
he dared not make adjustments. He couldn't reduce the
barrier, but he thought he could add to it; they had a
backup router and extra cables in the car. He added
those in as another layer of absurdity and tried
again. The blue and green diodes exploded with activity as soon as the connection was made. Of course
this signaled success. FERN and Xtal were having a
conversation.   It sounded like the aggressive
scratches of a hard disk click as it accesses and
overwrites data on several thousand machines in a
warehouse. Without being able to know what happened
with FERN in its lab, he wondered if this was a one-
sided reaction, a reflection activated when a sudden
shock hit. So he asked FERN for an update. He received nothing.

He stood there until he sat there watching, then he
went to the car to lean back in the chair and see if
FERN was only silent on the devices actually connected
to Xtal or whether all of FERN was engrossed in the
conversation. He received nothing in the car either.
What they said didn't concern him. He'd learn about
it soon enough, but for the moment it was private and
there was no reason for him to wait on any changes.
He was exhausted again, still. He needed so many
things at once, he was unsure where to begin.

He slid over to the driver's seat to take the car back to the main campus where he'd dig into his food and spend the rest of the day in the old ways, but he reconsidered. What he needed, where he should begin, was with a walk, without a machine. And so he did, with rain to occasion him until he crossed under forest canopy. He saw his family there earlier in the day, but there was no sign of them as he cut through the overgrown path that linked up with the parking lot to the far side of campus. On it, he was surrounded by trees and fronds all the way up to the central lawn coated in the static mist of Northwest rain. Ferns everywhere. Running around it were the two idiots fighting over one of the toys he left out for them as their mother gnawed on a rawhide under the awning. They brought the toy over as he got closer and dared him to take it away. He tried. They chased one another around that way.

***

www.ingramcontent.com/pod-product-compliance
Lightning Source LLC
Chambersburg PA
CBHW060224030726
47499CB00004B/1177